ROMANTIC SUSPENSE AT ITS BEST!
Praise for the novels of Cherry Adair

HOT ICE

"A relentless page-turner with plenty of enticing plot twists and turns."

—*Seattle Post-Intelligencer*

"[A] fast-paced and intricately plotted tale of danger, deception, and desire that is perfect for readers who like their romantic suspense adrenaline-rich and sizzlingly sexy."

—*Booklist*

"Adair has done it again! The chemistry between Hunt and Taylor is red-hot, and the suspense is top-notch."

—*Rendezvous*

"A very sexy adventure that offers non-stop, continent-hopping action from start to finish."

—*Library Journal*

"Get ready to drool, sigh, and simply melt. . . . Fascinating characters, danger, passion, intense emotions, and a rush like a roller-coaster ride."

—*Romance Reviews Today*

More . . .

ON THIN ICE

"A breathtaking ride . . . I couldn't turn the pages fast enough! No one does hot romance, ice-cold villains and nonstop adventure better."
—Mariah Stewart, author of *Dead Even*

IN TOO DEEP

"Sexy, funny, and wild! Hang on and enjoy the ride!"
—Andrea Kane,
author of *Scent of Danger*

HIDE AND SEEK

"A thrilling, mysterious, sexy read."
—Stella Cameron,
author of *Kiss Them Goodbye*

KISS AND TELL

"A sexy, snappy, roller-coaster ride!"
—Susan Andersen,
author of *Shadow Dance*

Undertow

CHERRY ADAIR

St. Martin's Paperbacks

PB ADAIR,
CHERRY

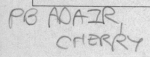

This is a work of fiction. All of the characters, organizations, and events portrayed in this novel are either products of the author's imagination or are used fictitiously.

UNDERTOW

Cover photograph of diver © Stephen Frink / Getty Images
Cover illustration by Dan O'Leary

For information address St. Martin's Press, 175 Fifth Avenue, New York, NY 10010.

ISBN: 978-0-312-37192-0

Printed in the United States of America

St. Martin's Paperbacks edition / January 2011

St. Martin's Paperbacks are published by St. Martin's Press, 175 Fifth Avenue, New York, NY 10010.

10 9 8 7 6 5 4 3 2 1

To the awesome, talented, and creative women of my Cherry's Lake Plotters: Carol, Christina, Ciara, Dragon, Heather, Julia, Kelli, Kristine, Laurie, Rebecca, and Shelli.

Thank you from the bottom of my heart for your friendship, and for letting me pick the fruit.

Acknowledgments

An enormous thanks goes to the following people for their help with all the research necessary to bring *Undertow* to life. Any inaccuracies, gaffes, oversights, or lapses in the details are mine, all mine.

Dr. Lubos Kordac lubos@shipwrecks-caribbean.com

Janelle Wolf Cryptologist Technician First Class, US Navy

Maria Drybread of RingPower.com

Daniel Randall Lieutenant Commander, US Navy CTR1 (SW/AW)

And last, but not least, to my extremely knowledgeable friend Tina Callais.

Chapter 1

Teal Williams looked like an unmade bed, and not one Zane Cutter wanted to sleep in. She'd been foisted off on him by her father, so he was pretty much stuck with her. But seeing her again made him realize she couldn't have been more tailor-made for his needs if she'd been special ordered.

Tall, skinny, and nondescript, Teal slouched, half hidden behind his brother Nick, at the other end of the long antique table. She chewed on her thumbnail as she glared at him from beneath shaggy, dark brown bangs.

He bit back a grin. Oh, man. Not only did she have the sex appeal of a mop, she didn't like him at all. A novelty he only appreciated today.

He wasn't attracted to her. *At all.* Not a spark. Not an ember of desire. Not a scintilla of interest. Nada.

A master marine mechanic *and* a woman he *wasn't* attracted to? Unprecedented. But *exactly* what he needed.

"No," she repeated, enunciating clearly, meeting him eyeball to eyeball without a blink. "I will *not* go with you."

"You *won't*?" Zane—known as Ace to the ladies—looked at the new Cutter Cay mechanic. It had been a long time since a woman had told him no. Probably before he hit puberty.

Her look said "Are you a deaf moron?" but she answered politely enough. "Would you like me to repeat that in another language? I know three."

Ah, pure Williams smart-ass, too. She was a real chip off the paternal block. Her short hair looked as though she'd cut it herself with a pair of blunt scissors, and it clearly hadn't seen a comb in a week. She'd obviously slept in the baggy, crumpled khaki pants and faded blue chambray man's shirt, and her nails were bitten to the quick. And if he wasn't mistaken—and Zane rarely was where women were concerned—she was wearing men's work boots on her size large feet, which were tucked out of sight under the table.

Her arms were folded in an "and that's final" gesture over her chest. A pair of double Ds could disappear under that voluminous shirt undetected, though her slim build suggested a more manageable size. Amused at her attitude and her complete lack of feminine wiles, Zane shot her his most charming, engaging smile, the one that had landed him in many a bed. It was met with stony indifference.

She was a fucking miracle! He wanted her on his payroll and refused to take no for an answer.

"How about a pay hike of ten percent to sweeten the pot?"

"*Ten?*"

He would've paid twice that. "Okay. Fifteen."

"No thanks." Her lips tightened. "I have all the money I need."

Her father, the Cutters' lifelong friend and resident mechanic, had recently been diagnosed with cancer. Sam and Logan had put their heads together and offered Teal the job so she could spend some time with Sam while he was still around. No good deed went unpunished, Zane thought, wondering why the hell she'd accepted their offer only to refuse the first assignment. "Do you have a reason?" he asked easily, intrigued, in spite of himself, by her belligerence.

Logan and Nick, the best brothers a guy could ask for, maintained their neutral expressions, but Zane felt their surprise at her refusal to go with him on his salvage. Diego Zamora, one of their captains, studied the ceiling fan while Brian Donahue, Cutter Salvage's head marine archeologist, stared out the window at the water rather than give away their entertainment at his impasse. Zane appreciated their efforts as he fought to capture his stubborn prize.

"I'm a master marine mechanic with over ten years' experience," Teal informed him in a flat, emotionless voice. "I've worked on every make, model, and size of engine. Diesel or gas. I can get a job—*on dry land*—anywhere in the world."

"Dry land? You're aware you accepted a job on an island, right?"

"I was told I'd have my own bungalow. I like my privacy. There's no privacy on a boat."

The building where they were meeting had seen its share of business deals, and this wouldn't be the last. Nicknamed the Counting House for obvious reasons the two-story wood structure looked as though the next tropical hurricane would blow it away. But like Zane's boat, its looks were deceiving.

Here they compared notes at the end of a salvage operation, drank beer, told tall tales, and this was where the fifty or so permanent island residents gathered for birthday parties, hurricanes, and funerals. The sturdy building had been constructed by his father to store his priceless treasure when he'd bought the private island thirty-some years before. The Counting House was where the Cutters and their other salvors brought multimillions of dollars' worth of salvaged treasure to be cleaned, cataloged, and sorted by Brian and his team of highly experienced marine archeologists. The building had to be, and was, as secure as Fort Knox.

No privacy on the *Decrepit* was one of the things Zane enjoyed most. He knew his crew better than he knew some of his friends. Come to think of it, other than his brothers, his team *were* his best friends.

"What did you think you were hired for?" Zane asked mildly. "Cutter *Salvage*? *Boats?*"

"To fill in for Sam while he's . . . out." The pause was infinitesimal. Her chin jutted out, daring him to knock that damned giant chip off her shoulder. "Here on the island."

His lips twitched. She was a real piece of work. "That's why I need you. To keep her going." Everyone said he was a lucky guy. He'd never struggled to fit in, he had a family he loved, good friends, and more money than he could spend in his lifetime. Women adored him. Hell, even little girls and old ladies gravitated toward him. He wore his good fortune slung around his shoulders like a magic cloak.

He took in the defiant jut of her jaw and the go-to-hell glint in her eyes. "I've got to have a top-notch mechanic," Zane told her cheerfully. She might not like him, but according to her father, she had a thing for sick engines. Perfect. "You were hired to be that mechanic. We leave in the morning." He looked at his oldest brother. "Didn't she sign a contract, Logan?"

Logan's eyes glinted with amusement, but his expression didn't change. "She did, Ace."

"You'll like the *Decrepit*," Zane assured her, his good mood rising exponentially the more tenacious and determined she became. God, he just loved a challenge. Got his blood pumping and put a fire in his belly. A great way to start a new salvage.

He felt alive. Invincible.

"The *Decrepit*." Teal glanced disdainfully out the window to the marina, and his beloved boat, showing her surprisingly delicate profile. Snooty little nose, pugnacious jaw, crazy hair. She turned back to give him an unfriendly look from beneath that mop of hair half obscuring her face. "Should be scrapped. Buy yourself a nice shiny *new* boat like your brothers. Then you wouldn't need a round-the-clock mechanic."

"Maybe I will." He followed her gaze to look beyond the large windows and prow-shaped, cantilevered deck, to the marina. A dozen sailboats and four large dive boats bobbed gently on aquamarine water. The rust-streaked hull of his *Decrepit* stood out like a sore thumb against the gleaming white of the other boats. He smiled.

He liked the well-worn look of her, including the battered yellow crane perched like a praying mantis on her bow. Oh yeah. Inside the *Decrepit* was a different story. It amused the hell out of him that his shitty-looking boat was a sore spot with his brothers. He enjoyed people underestimating him. He loved his boat, and had no intention of replacing her. Ever. Beauty was in the eye of the beholder. Zane loved every screw, nut, and rust spot.

Still smiling, he turned his gaze back to his problem, and added easily, "But not until after this season. Besides, you might be surprised. Looks can be deceiving."

She gave him the evil eye. "I've found that looks can be *confirming*. The answer is still no."

He wisely suppressed a smile. She was a hard nut, but he remained confident. She had all the skills he required and none of the distractions. Just a month of her working on the current engine. Sam had known how to keep the old girl running and had assured Zane that Teal could do the same.

He read the tension along Teal's tough jawline. Everybody wanted something. He just had to figure out what it was she wanted. "The pay is more than fair. What more do you want?"

"A Shetland pony."

Her unexpected, dry sense of humor, done with a perfectly straight face, was a bonus. "*Seriously.* What *do* you want?"

"Not to go with you."

Zane gritted his teeth. "Besides that."

She glared at Logan, who sat across from her. "Have someone take me to Tortola. I never agreed to work on that piece of floating crap out there. Keep me on the island or send me home."

"You haven't even seen your father yet," his middle brother Nick pointed out, trying to keep a straight face.

"I'll wave to him on my way out to the helipad."

Jesus. Insulting his precious boat was bad enough, but that was cold. Sam was terminally ill. Zane suspected Teal's father, a taciturn man, was looking forward to spending some quality time with his only child—not that Sam had said the words. The hop, skip, and jump distance to the wreck site would make their reunion possible. "Listen," he said reasonably. "It won't be a full month away. You can come and check on your dad whenever you like."

Zane remembered Teal as a child. Vaguely. He'd seen her around the island now and then when she'd come for her annual two-week school vacations. She'd been a shy little thing, always darting off when he went to see Sam. Skinny and plain even back then.

"I'm not going." She'd gotten over the *shy,* though. In spades.

"Chopper's already gone back to Tortola," Zane told her. "I'll be stopping by there tomorrow for supplies."

Teal tossed her bangs back and he got a good look at her large, dark eyes. Pretty. Too bad her hair covered everything but the angry glitter. "And you'll drop me off?"

"No. You'll be continuing on to St. Maarten with the rest of the team."

"Hasn't anyone ever told you no?" Teal scowled at him, then turned the scowl on his oldest brother. "You hired me as a mechanic for Cutter Cay; you didn't say anything about going out to sea. He can't force me to go with him."

"No, he can't," Logan assured her. "You can leave of your own free will; you're not an indentured servant. I'll tear up your contract right now if you really don't want the job. But I think your father deserves to know why you're changing your mind. He's the one who recommended you to fill his position."

Her shoulders tensed under the baggy shirt. "He di—" She gripped the edge of the table. "I want the *job*. Mechanic. *Here*. On Cutter Cay, where I can see Sam whenever he wants to be seen. I do not want to go to sea in a boat that will more than likely need salvaging before the season's over."

She was dead serious. Zane acknowledged a millisecond of panic. He'd spent four long, painstaking years searching for the Dutch frigate, *Vrijheid*. He'd finally found her. A hundred miles off the coast of St. Maarten. Right in his own backyard—right under his nose for God's sake! Would have found it sooner if it hadn't been hiding in some bizarre navigational dead zone, a stretch of sea where his navigational and detecting equipment tended to go on the fritz, if they worked at all.

Fortunately, Zane had decided to explore the area anyway, and it ended up being one of the best decisions of his life. Now he wanted no distractions for the duration of the salvage. There was a fortune in gold, silver, and emeralds a hundred feet under, and he was determined to return home with the *Decrepit* groaning under the weight of his treasures.

With *her*. Teal Williams. Mechanic. Certified diver. Undesirable female.

It was crucial to his focus that she didn't turn him on, although he usually *did* like them long and lean. Hell, he liked them short and round, and everything in between. He liked women. A lot. He liked the way they smelled. He liked the way they walked. He liked how their convoluted brains worked. He fell in love frequently, but never for longer than two weeks.

Now all he wanted from this particular woman was a month. One stinking damned month. Was that too much to ask? With the hurricane season fast approaching, and forecast to be a bad one, he couldn't afford to spend weeks searching for a different mechanic, not one with her level of experience and qualifications.

She was a woman. He'd dazzle her with wit and charm if necessary. "Can you cook?" That would be a bonus.

"No."

On second thought, that was probably a good thing. The way she was looking at him made Zane decide to make her sample everything before he ate it anyway. "I know you're a certified diver." Which was an enormous plus. "I just hope you can at least make decent coffee."

"Are you kid—"

He held up a hand. "I'll pay you a percentage of the profits from the *Vrijheid* salvage. It's got emeralds as big as this." He made a fist.

She stared at him for several beats. It seemed to Zane that everyone else at the table held their collective breath as they waited to see who blinked first. She chewed her lower lip, giving her thumbnail a break. "Over and above my salary?"

Which was more than generous already. "Sure." It was SOP to share the profits with one's crew.

She leaned forward, resting her forearms on the scarred table so she could see around Nick. The shirt swallowed her hands, and Zane was tempted to go over there and roll them up for her, but then he'd want to straighten her collar and hand her a damned comb. However, he suspected if he so much as came close, let alone touched her, he'd find himself with a broken hand.

Something mysterious flashed in her eyes before she asked, "How much of a percentage?"

Bingo. He bit back a smile. So, she did have a price, it was just a matter of negotiation. "We can draw up a new contract right after the meeting."

"No thanks."

She was just jerking his chain. He raised a brow. She was perfect—perfectly *annoying.* If they didn't kill each other before the salvage was through, it would be a miracle. If he killed her beforehand, there was the entire Caribbean ocean to dispose of the body. "You don't trust me?"

"Guilty until proven innocent." She gave him an unfriendly look that just piqued his curiosity. He'd interacted with her maybe four or five times over the years. He didn't remember her ever being this openly hostile before.

"Wow, you're cynical. Look," he said reasonably. "Cutter Salvage pays *damn* well. We had our pick of a hundred excellent mechanics—"

"There you go, then. Have at it."

"But it was *Sam* who asked us to hire you." Zane turned the screw. "If you're serious about not coming with me, your call. But you have to go explain to a dying man why you're throwing his good name back in his face."

"Zane—" Logan cautioned as Teal's cheeks drained of color.

"Wanna tell your father that you have better things to do?" It was a low blow and he felt like a shit for doing it. But Sam hadn't asked. He'd begged them to bring his daughter to the island. The plea had been unnecessary. She was good and she was experienced. And Sam had been an integral part of the Cutter brothers' lives for as long as Zane could remember. If her father wanted Teal nearby, then that's where she'd be. End of story.

She glared belligerently, her eyes so hot he was surprised his hair wasn't on fire. "Fine."

"Fine?"

"I'll go with you. Happy now?"

"Yeah, as a matter of fact," he said cheerfully. "I am."

Pleased to have gotten his way, he wondered what she'd do if he up and kissed her with gratitude. Probably bite. Then there'd be rabies shots . . .

"Great," Logan inserted. "You two stay after class and iron out the details so we can get to business before midnight. Brian has prelim info after checking out some of Nick's haul . . . Sorry, Diego." Logan's lips quirked. "We have an embarrassment of riches today, you'll have to wait your turn."

"*No hay problema,* amigo. I'm happy to sit here with the sun on my face, and a pretty girl by my side."

Brian rushed in, clearly eager to get to his report. "*Prelim* being the operative word. Two such enormous finds coming in at the same time—We've had less than twelve hours, but—"

Outnumbered by all the testosterone in the room, Teal quietly gave in to exhaustion. *Sam* had wanted her here? She couldn't even wrap her tired brain around the concept. She was physically, emotionally wrung dry. In no way had she been prepared to meet with Zane and the Cutter crew the moment she arrived.

Emeralds as big as her fist? That would cover Sam's medical costs, which were bound to be high, not that he'd discussed it with her. Nope, she'd had to pry the truth of his illness from him after Logan called to ask her if she wanted to fill in for Sam while he recuperated. Teal rubbed at her eyes.

This meeting with Zane hadn't been the cool, professional encounter she'd rehearsed in her mirror for the last few weeks. He pressed all her buttons and then some. He'd always been good at that.

Zane. Ace. Or better yet, *Casanova of the Caribbean.* She gave a mental snort. He'd probably given himself the nicknames. She wished she were in China right now. She'd made a huge freaking mistake coming here.

Brian waved a paper around as he talked, which took Zane's focus away from her and gave her some thinking time. Logan, damn him too, hadn't even given her a chance to take a shower and drag a brush through her hair before he'd brought her to the Counting House an hour ago. None of them was familiar with the word no.

Fighting the lure of sleep, she studied Brian Donahue. Skinny. About forty. He was the resident archeologist who cataloged and sorted the found treasure. He talked as if words were about to be rationed at any second. He had thinning red hair, thick black-rimmed glasses, and waved his hands excitedly to describe the haul they'd just brought in. She'd give anything for some of his energy.

To Teal's right sat a hot guy who looked like Antonio Banderas in his day. Diego Zamora apparently worked for, or was partner with, the brothers in their vast salvage operations around the world. She knew from various vacations on the island that the Cutters owned a dozen or more salvage boats.

This guy had apparently returned to the island the night before from a successful salvage near Greece. Same as Nick, who'd been gone for a year, Logan had told her. He'd just returned from a salvage in the waters off Vietnam, the *Scorpion,* his magnificent megayacht, loaded with a fortune in ceramics and china from a wreck in Ca Mau province.

Brian discussed Nick's treasure, his voice rising and

falling with enthusiasm. It was all "amazing examples of eighteenth-century china" and the "definitive ceramic find of the century."

"Saw it earlier," Zane told his brother as Brian paused to drink from his soda can. "It's great. And of course, Brian called the investors the second he got a look at what you brought in. Gave them just a taste, so they're already going ape-shit."

Zane had the kind of smile people responded to without realizing they were smiling back. A shark's smile. Teal bit her lower lip as Zane broke into one of his trademark lazy, cocky grins and caught her eye by accident as he was looking at Nick.

"*Spectacular* pottery and chinaware," he toasted his brother with his Coke, his smile slipping a bit when she gave him a blank look in return.

"Yeah. Stunning." Nick's smile was white and self-satisfied. But it didn't make her pulse skip like Zane's did. "Made at the kilns in Jiangxi and Guangdong provinces in China during the Qing dynasty, around 1723 to 1735." His blue eyes glittered with triumph. "Even after giving the Vietnam History Museum their share, our cut is estimated at—what did you guesstimate, Bri? Two point five mil?"

"Nice." Everyone around the table grinned in perfect unison.

Teal thought the brothers all looked as dark, swarthy, and uncivilized as their Spanish ancestors, which made their startling blue eyes that much more of a shock. Modern-day pirates. *I need a freaking nap.*

Golden sunlight inched into the room as the sun moved toward a spectacular sunset. A couple of dark wood paddle fans turned lazily, high on the beamed ceiling. Teal could tell by the way one of them wobbled that the capacitor had drifted out of value and needed replacing.

The surf lapping with a soft rhythmic shush at the piling

of the marina just a few yards from the building soothed her jagged emotions. She blinked her heavy lids. The men focused on Brian, and as she was practically hidden by Nick's broad shoulders, she slid a little lower in her seat, discreetly resting her head on the back of the chair. It was a struggle to keep her eyes open, but since no one was paying any attention to her, she let her lids stay closed to ease the dry burn of too many sleepless nights.

Brian's voice rose and fell. She jerked when she realized she couldn't keep track of what he was saying. Sitting up a bit, she rubbed a finger over one eye and tried to look engaged.

On her left, Nick slouched in his chair, twisting a pen between long, elegant fingers as he listened. He wore jeans and a wrinkled red T-shirt. His bare feet were crossed at the ankles and propped on the chair beside him so that Teal saw him in profile. He was a nice solid wall between Zane's line of sight and her own.

They called Nick "Spock" for some reason she didn't much care about. His dark hair hung well below his shoulders, and his handsome features were all but indistinguishable due to his thick black beard. The middle Cutter looked like a blue-eyed caveman. He'd given her a hug when she'd walked in and said he was happy to see her again. Teal doubted he remembered her at all, but it was a kind gesture.

Logan sat across the table. He'd called her out of the blue two weeks ago and hired her over the phone. He hadn't bothered to ask for references, said that Sam's referral was good enough for him. While the reasons for accepting the job sucked, Logan's timing couldn't have been better.

Unlike Nick, Logan was well groomed, his hair barbered, his face clean-shaven, his jeans and dark T-shirt immaculate. His brothers referred to him as Wolf. Controlled. Intent. He listened to Brian, holding up a hand now and then to ask questions, or jotting notes into a black notebook.

Which brought Teal's gaze back to the head of the table and Zane. Their eyes met in a shocking clash that caused her breath to snag in her lungs. A small smile played on his lips, but there was zero recognition in his eyes. Good. Excellent. Fantastic. If he thought that smile would charm her, he was sadly mistaken. She was charm-proof. Especially *Zane* charm-proof. She gave him a cool look back. This time she didn't turn away, just stared him down until he had to return his attention to Logan.

He wore jeans and his aqua blue T-shirt matched his eyes. A move, she was sure, calculated to enhance the color. Vain bastard. His deeply tanned, muscular forearms were stacked on the scarred wood table in front of him, a big-faced, multifunctional dive watch strapped to his strong wrist. His father had given him that watch for his sixteenth birthday. Teal had a faint scar on her inner arm where the band had scratched her.

She repressed a shiver looking at his large hands, which were surprisingly elegant for such an outdoorsy guy. The calluses at the base of his fingers had felt as abrasive as cat tongues on her skin when he'd shaken her hand earlier.

Everything about him irritated her. She resisted fidgeting. This would be over soon enough. Until then, she'd stick to her guns and try her damnedest not to leap down the length of table, grab him by his ears, and shout, "Remember me?"

If Nick's hair was too long, and Logan's too neat, Zane's dark hair was in between. Thick and glossy, the strands brushed his jaw and had a bit of a wave, which softened the hard planes of his face. In one ear, he wore a small gold hoop earring, just like a freaking pirate. Teal bet his women just loved the stupid earring. She'd once thought it the sexiest, most romantic thing she'd ever seen. His skin was very tanned, which made the shocking blue of his eyes that much more startling. As usual, he needed a shave.

And she needed to get a grip. The only positive thing to come out of this meeting was that she was over the crush she'd had on him for years. The only reason her heart was pounding so hard was pure aggravation.

Looking at the glittering sheet of water beyond the windows, she blanked out the drone of conversation as the archeologist rattled off facts and dates and superlatives.

She chewed the jagged edge off her thumbnail. *Sam* had asked them to hire her. Stunning. Zane Cutter was like a tap resetting the grooves to fit himself, then expecting everyone else to fall into line. She refused to allow him to deter her. She had her own agenda for accepting the job.

But, oh God. She did *not* want to go with him out to sea. First, she didn't want to be anywhere *near* him, day in and day out. That was just asking for trouble.

Second, she really, really didn't want to go on his piece of crap it's-a-miracle-it's-still-afloat boat. The thing looked like a moth-eaten junk heap and about a rust hole in the hull away from sinking.

Third, right up there with the number one and two reasons to avoid Zane Cutter at all costs, was the humiliating fact that being on the ocean waves made her horribly and embarrassingly seasick.

And while the mere thought of throwing up on Zane's shoes held some appeal, she'd then have to fling herself overboard with mortification. Clearly, his *Decrepit*—and wasn't *that* the perfect name for it—needed an engine whisperer. Zane spent so much time wining, dining, and sleeping with all the women who fell at his feet, she doubted he took proper care of his boat.

She was an excellent mechanic, but she didn't own a freaking magic wand, for God's sake.

Good-looking, charming men with Peter Pan complexes gave her hives on her hives. Her ex's good looks had hidden a multitude of sins, and now—unfortunately for any gorgeous, self-aware male—guilty until proven innocent was her new motto. She'd never do vulnerable again. Been there, done that.

Not that she was bitter or anything, Teal thought with a little mental snort of self-deprecation. Denny's lesson had really stuck, that was all. Like Zane, her ex came from family wealth and had a playboy reputation.

She'd naively thought she was woman enough to settle him down, that her love made the difference, but he'd taught her better. Live and learn.

It wasn't diplomatic or politically correct to have refused the first assignment the Cutters gave her. So much for holding her ground. She'd folded like a wet tissue. Strong-armed by Zane's gorgeous blue eyes and easy charm. There'd been the chance that instead of giving her the option of being close to Sam or going with Zane, he could've said, "Go on the *Decrepit* or don't bother unpacking your bag. Thanks for coming, good-bye."

Of course, if Logan had bothered to mention that she was required to go to sea, with *Zane*, she would have refused his generous offer in the first freaking place.

Then she remembered how Sam had sounded when he'd gotten on the phone after Logan had made his offer. He said, offhandedly, "Come if you want. There's room for two good mechanics on Cutter Cay." He hadn't asked *her*, but apparently he'd asked the Cutters. Sam had never asked her for anything. How could she refuse him this?

Pros: working on an engine that really needed her. She loved to dive. Being *in* the water was wonderful and didn't make her seasick. She'd be closer to Sam.

Cons: Zane. Being on board his rattletrap of a boat for weeks on end. Fighting the urge to hurl over each wave.

Logan was speaking now, but Teal's gaze kept accidentally slipping to Zane at the other end of the table. His hair fell over his forehead, and he raked it back with one large, tanned hand. The Cutters were all tall, well over six feet three or four inches. But Zane, so much larger than life, seemed to suck all the air out of the room with his presence. He always had.

She tried to concentrate on the actually very interesting questions everyone was asking Brian, but the heat of the setting sun streaming through the ceiling-to-floor windows, and the low drone of Logan's deep voice were soporific. She longed for a cold shower and a soft bed. Not necessarily in that order.

She tried to unkink her back without being obvious and swallowed a yawn. The flight from Alabama, the unexpected overnight layover in Miami while they searched for her luggage, the rapid turnaround in Tortola to catch the helicopter to Cutter Cay—all followed by walking into a meeting totally unprepared—had left Teal feeling drained when she most needed her wits about her.

Zane didn't remember her. She swallowed something bitter at the back of her throat. What if the enforced close proximity in a confined space triggered his memory? She chewed what was left of the top of her thumbnail. Remaining on the island presented a whole other set of complications and pitfalls. After this meeting, she'd have to go and see Sam. Another difficult man. While her father battled his illness, she'd pick up the slack for him. It provided her with a job, albeit temporary. And a safe place to stay. Temporarily. And some time with her only living relative—also temporary.

She turned her body to get more comfortable, the chair fabric scratchy on her left cheek, the sun warming her right. Nick was talking about the value of priceless blue-and-white china, and Diego chimed in about gold. They wouldn't even notice if she kept her eyes closed for just a few minutes.

She dreamed she was lying on a cool, white-sheet-draped bed as a tanned, naked man rained gold coins down on her nude body while he served her tea in a blue-and-white china cup.

Chapter 2

Logan glanced up from his notes. "You were pretty hard on her," he told Zane mildly.

Teal had conked out. Several million dollars' worth of treasure was being discussed, and Zane's mechanic/diver/soon-to-be-pain-in-the-ass was fast asleep. The sunlight streaming through the windows made her skin glow, giving her some much-needed color. She looked damned uncomfortable scrunched sideways in the chair like that.

"*Sam* wants her here," Zane pointed out, not needing his brother to remind him he'd been a dick. He already felt like a bully, and it wasn't a comfortable fit. "*I* want her here. She wasn't cracking. I did what was necessary."

Logan held his gaze. "He didn't want her to know he was the one who asked."

"Well then, he's an idiot," Zane told his brother without heat. "He needs to connect with her before it's too late."

"Not our call."

"I hear you." Zane didn't understand how two people who were related, communicated so little. Sam and Teal had such a fucking odd relationship. And he used the word loosely. They'd seemed like two strangers on the odd occasion he'd seen them together over the last—hell, what was it? Twenty years? And she hadn't been back to Cutter Cay in a long time. Seemed to Zane, now that he came to think of it, they danced around a relationship. He didn't get it. Why didn't they just sit down and have that conversation?

"I'll play it by ear," he told his oldest brother. "If she has a hard time being even that far from him, I'll send her back." Man, that would screw with his plans. But he wouldn't force a woman to be where she didn't want to be. No matter how much it suited him.

"Good enough. Okay, where were we?"

Back to business. Good. Zane glanced over at Teal. She snored. It was quite ladylike, but there was no doubt that the sound she made while she slept was a snore. He shared an amused glance with Nick. His brother mouthed the word "Cute."

Zane shook his head and muttered under his breath, "As a sea urchin."

"Okay, Ace—" Logan turned his attention from Diego to Zane, "you have the floor."

"Considering we've lost more than fifteen percent of our audience, I'll make it fast." Zane leaned back in his chair and smiled. "Four years and the *Vrijheid* was in our own backyard this whole time." His brothers had both had huge discoveries in the last year while Zane had searched in vain for his own. It was a matter of pride. Hell, it was a matter of the ten-thousand-dollar bet they made every year. Brother with the largest haul in twelve months would take over the CEO title and perks for the next year and cash in on a ten-grand wager. Logan had been CEO for five years. Time to dethrone him.

Competition was standard operating procedure in the Cutter clan. It was all good natured, but still fierce and a point of pride between them. There were two months left and the treasure he anticipated claiming from the virgin wreck, *Vrijheid,* was head and shoulders above anything they'd scored to date. He was a shoe-in to win, *if* he could get there before the storms shifted the sands, and *if* he could keep his engine firing on all cylinders until he ordered a new one.

"Sometimes what we're looking for is right under our noses." Logan rotated his head to ease the tension in his shoulder. The sun was sinking into the horizon, leaving the room in shadows. They'd been talking for a couple of hours. Zane loved his brothers and respected both Brian and Diego. But he'd rather be out there on the glassy, aubergine-colored water than sitting inside.

Nick got up to grab a beer out of the refrigerator in the corner, held up the Stella, and took orders. He returned with several chilled bottles and handed them out. "Who're you taking with you?" he asked.

"The Berlands." Maggie and Ben had dived with Zane dozens of times and were always his top pick. Maggie, a marine archeologist, was also a damn fine diver. Ben, a retired schoolteacher, had followed his wife's love of the sea to the islands thirty some years ago.

"Timing's good. We have a month or so before the weather turns to shit, and Catherine and Liz's baby is due next month. Maggie and Ben didn't want to be on the other side of the universe when their second granddaughter arrives."

"Still good with that?" Nick asked, lifting the bottle to his mouth and pausing before drinking.

"I just made the deposit," Zane reminded him easily, shooting a quick glance at his mechanic curled up awkwardly in the chair between Nick and Diego. None of her business. It wasn't his secret. The Berlands' daughter, Cat, and her partner Liz, already had a daughter via in vitro, using Zane's sperm. Now it was Liz's turn to have a baby. "You should go see them before you hare off again. Meet Jessie," Zane told Nick, who'd been gone before the couple's first daughter had been born. "She's a little princess. Damn cute kid."

"I can't imagine you having a daughter, let alone two."

"I don't. Cat and Liz do." His middle brother reminded him of the Wild Man of Borneo. Nick had a little sideline that probably accounted for his appearance. Zane quirked a brow. "No barbers in Nam?"

Nick looked fit and happy and deeply tanned from his voyage. "No time." Their eyes met briefly.

Yeah. Zane got it. Nick had been doing a little something else between dives. Still, once you were immersed in bringing treasure back to the surface, you didn't give a shit about minor details like haircuts and shaving. And if a man had a sideline—that also explained the unkempt look.

"Who else?" Logan asked, not looking up as he scribbled something in a notebook. He looked distracted, which was unusual for him.

"Unfortunately, Garth Sead broke his leg skydiving last week. So we're one short. She," Zane jerked his chin at Teal, "fits the bill."

"Excellent diver, too. You lucked out." Logan muttered. "Sam did us a favor there, I think. You picking up your usual suspects along the way?"

"Yeah." He'd already signed on a few more reliable divers. How could she sleep with her head like that? Zane wondered. She must be pretty damned exhausted to be twisted like a pretzel and still be zonked.

"So she's Dutch?" Diego asked, intrigued—probably because the majority of wrecks found in the Caribbean were Spanish. He was referring of course, to the *Vrijheid,* not Teal. As he spoke, he leaned over to move the point of her collar to keep it from sticking into her eye as she slept.

Zane frowned. There was no need to touch her. She wasn't even aware of them *talking,* let alone a piece of fabric brushing her cheek.

"VOC?" Diego referred to the Vereenigde Oost-Indische

Compagnie or Dutch United East India Company that used to ply Asia and the Pacific routes.

"Unofficially." Feeling oddly proprietary, Zane realized he didn't like Diego touching his mechanic. A lot. Weird. "The Berlands and I discovered her a month ago. There'll be gold and silver and," his heart tap-danced pleasantly in his chest, "the manifest listed emeralds. *Colombian* emeralds. *Muzo* and *Chivor* emeralds."

Nick whistled. Logan's avaricious eyes glittered; Zane had told him about the emeralds two weeks ago. "We're talking 'round about *one hundred and eighty carats*," Zane elaborated, his grin widening. "I do believe I'm going to take that ten-grand pot and make you buy me that new engine for *Decrepit,* gentlemen."

"Have to get it to the surface and home first." Nick pointed out, tossing his empty beer bottle across the room, where it hit the rough paneled wall and dropped into the trash.

Zane's smile widened. "Oh, ye of little faith. Watch me and learn, Spock, my man. Watch me and learn."

*   *   *

Only forty minutes? The trip between Cutter Cay and Tortola seemed like a freaking *lifetime* to Teal, and the *Decrepit* had barely cleared the dock. The gut-churning nausea had started the second she'd set foot on board, despite the sea being as smooth as aquamarine glass. Fingers white-knuckled on the stern railing, she lifted her face to the warm breeze and tried to sip the salty air to quell the roiling of her stomach.

As if anything short of a coma could do that. From experience she knew she'd get over the seasickness after a few days. Thank God. In the meantime she'd make sure Casanova didn't know about it.

A long trail of frothy white connected the *Decrepit* to

the island like a tenuous tether. The spray cooled her hot cheeks, but Teal couldn't look down at the swiftly moving wake. She could actually feel her eyeballs rolling around in her head like ball bearings.

She watched the water between the island and the *Decrepit* widen. *Please, God, just kill me now!* Would anyone notice if she jumped overboard? Probably not until that pathetic engine crapped out. The *Decrepit* looked worse up close and personal than it had from a distance.

She shuddered to think what her engine room looked like if the jerk couldn't even be bothered to paint his boat. Still, Sam must have at least done some servicing. How bad could the engines be? She'd look at the maintenance logs as soon as her eyeballs stayed focused. She bet she'd have to deal with crappy fuel, and God forbid the bearings were worn, she'd have to drop the whole damn bottom end and pull the mains and rods. The thought of the price tag for *that* almost made her smile.

She looked longingly back at the island, which was incredibly beautiful, even from this vantage point. An emerald in an exquisite sapphire setting. A small extinct volcano had pushed its way three hundred feet above the lush vegetation. Thousands of years of freshwater runoff from the peak had killed off a wide section of coral in only one section, which was surrounded by unmarked and dangerous coral heads just below the surface of the water. Deadly traps for even the smallest boats.

The pale swath of white sand under the water could only be seen from the air, making the canal an obstacle-dense, extremely dangerous, path to Cutter Cay harbor. Three sides of the seven-acre island were made up of sheer granite cliffs surrounded by a ring of almost impenetrable coral. That sandy path was the *only* way a boat could approach the island. And even if a person knew the canal was there, navigating the shards of coral would be as complicated as trying to fish a fallen screw out of a carburetor. In other words, one wrong move and you'd be FUBAR.

It was an excellent place to store treasure. The Counting House sat front and center, right near the dock and marina. The imposing building was a gateway to the homes and cabins on the hillside. Three large dive boats waited in the marina, as did half a dozen sailboats with primary colored sails. As a backdrop, the green hills rose to the flat-topped peak. Untidy rows of brightly colored cabins were strung up and down the hills like gaudy wooden beads. Some of them were occupied by local residents, and some were kept ready by the Cutters for visitors, like friends or investors. The large, ultra-modern house on the windward side was Zane's.

Teal rubbed her upper arms and scowled into the spray. She'd said no. She'd meant no. Yet here she was. Had Sam really wanted her here?

Whether that was fact or fiction, emeralds as big as Zane claimed they were would go a long way in paying her father's medical bills and setting her up in her own business. She'd never have to rely on anyone else again. Of course, the presence of emeralds the size that Zane had bragged about could be B.S. And they might not discover any treasure at all. A percentage of nothing would be a big fat zero.

She heard Zane laugh as he talked to the men, but didn't turn around. She hated feeling like a kid with her nose pressed to the toy store window. *Go over there,* she told herself. *You're part of the team, too.* But her feet stayed glued to the deck.

Out of the corner of her eye she watched the blond guy tell what was apparently a hilarious story that involved broad hand gestures and comical facial expressions. Even though she couldn't hear him, she smiled.

The smile froze as her gaze shifted to Zane—his bare

chest gleamed in the sun, and his earring winked as his
shoulders shook with laughter. He looked vital, and more
alive than any man she'd ever seen in her life. Zane Cutter
was a force of nature, and seeing him so carefree and gloriously, unabashedly *happy* made her chest ache, and her
mouth go dry.

She hadn't been the only one who'd gravitated to the
youngest Cutter when she'd first met him years ago. Everyone on the islands loved him. He was everyone's friend.
She envied him his capacity to have fun and his innate
ability to make and keep friends. He was everything she
wasn't. The chaos of her conflicting feelings for him infuriated her.

She watched him as he tossed back his head and roared
with laughter. Sunlight tangled in his dark hair and glinted
off the little gold pirate hoop in his ear. He punched his
friend Ryan on the shoulder, then started a story of his own
that made the men laugh harder.

She realized she was staring and snapped her head
around to gaze out at the water. What the hell was she doing waving good-bye to land ho and sailing the high seas
with a pirate? She'd lost what little was left of her mind.

In the distance, the shadowy forms of small neighbor-
ing islands seemed to float along the horizon. None of
them were close enough to swim to, either. She actually
loved being in the water, but because of the seasickness,
she hated, loathed, and detested being *on* it. Tough when
she was en route to more water. It was hard to reconcile
what her eyes were telling her—calm seas—with the roiling of her stomach.

"How're you doing?" Maggie Berland asked sympa-
thetically, strolling up to the railing to join Teal. Tanned,
fit, and friendly, Maggie was in her early fifties. They'd
met on the dock moments before sailing. She handed Teal
an icy bottle of water.

"Thanks. Couldn't be better," Teal told her cheerfully,

swallowing bile. Even the bright tropical sun wasn't getting rid of the cold, oily nausea persistently climbing the
back of her throat.

"Keep your eyes on the horizon and take small sips,
you'll get your sea legs in no time."

The horizon *moved,* and just the thought of swallowing when what she wanted to do more than anything right
then was throw up made Teal's stomach pitch ominously.
"I'd rather take cyanide."

"Think about something else," Maggie suggested, giving her a sympathetic smile. "Come and meet everyone."
The others had moved inside to pore over charts.

"Maybe later." The slight swells didn't seem to bother
Maggie. Teal's stomach did a double axel. She tightened
her sweaty grip on the railing. She knew she only had
minutes—maybe seconds—before she embarrassed herself, and practically launched herself away from the rail.
"Be right back."

Startled by Teal's abrupt departure, Maggie took a step
forward. "Wait, where are you—"

"Engine room." The only place that never made her
sick. Only the smell of diesel fuel would help.

"Confined space will make it wo—"

Teal fled, lurching like a drunken sailor, pushing
through a tight group of men in the main salon. "Excuse
me. Sorry. Thanks. Sorry." Her mouth filled with saliva.
Gripping the brass handrails on either side, she took the
spiral stairs three at a time.

Panicked, she scanned the small hallway at the bottom. Which door led to the engine room? The calming
pulse of twin, V12, four-stroke diesels under her feet was
the only thing holding her nausea at bay. All she prayed
for, other than a swift death, was that if she was close to
an engine the smell and vibration would kick the nausea.

Or it wouldn't and she'd be somewhere private when
she hurled. In three, two—.

"Hey, gorgeous, lost your way?"

Teal's eyes traveled up a clean, white T-shirt pulled taut over rock-hard abs, up his tanned throat, climbed to his darkly stubbled chin, over his straight nose, and landed, reluctantly, on a pair of piercing, annoyingly *amused,* blue eyes.

Zane freaking Cutter.

God, seriously? Kill me now.

Just as he came closer, the boat pitched, tilting her off balance. She staggered, but already unsteady, couldn't manage to right herself. It was grab at Zane to break her fall, or fall on her face. In a split second she opted for the latter. She did not want to touch—Ah, shit! She fell against his chest.

Hard. Hot. *No. No. No.*

"Whoa!" He grabbed her by her upper arms, hauling her upright as if she weighed no more than a bag of laundry, so that her breasts were inadvertently caressed by the hard plane of his chest. The contact was like an intense electrical shock that zoomed through Teal's body and fried her brain.

She blushed like an idiot. The physical contact was too much. She couldn't breathe, she couldn't think. She tasted his coffee-scented breath on her lips and felt the heat of his skin through his clothes as his fingers tightened on her arms. Rattled by the contact, all she could do was blink up at him for what felt like an eternity.

He frowned down at her. "Okay?"

Teal stood there for just a few more seconds inhaling the scent of his skin as her heart went ballistic and her brain cells scrambled to reconnect.

His worried frown morphed into a slow smile. Annoying. Confident. "Are you—"

Her nausea returned full force. Gritting her teeth she slapped her palm, hard, against his midriff, fingers splayed. "Out. Of. My. Way."

*   *   *

"They're up there watching us, aren't they?" Teal asked Maggie. When she'd finally emerged from the head, Zane was—mercifully—nowhere to be seen. But she knew he and some of the guys were up in the wheelhouse, masters of all they surveyed.

It was a little damn late in the day to discover that she'd made a colossal mistake coming to the Caribbean, Sam or no Sam. She'd rather have fallen and broken her nose earlier than have Zane touch her. Her arms still felt the brand of his touch like a particularly bad case of sunburn.

No. More. Touching. And how was she supposed to sail the freaking seven seas while her stomach heaved?

The other woman smiled. "Not us, you."

"Great." Teal resisted curling her shoulders and settled for looking straight ahead.

Maggie seemed nice enough. She had a lovely golden tan, gray eyes, and an infectious smile. She and her husband, Ben, were part of Zane's team. Teal hadn't met him. He'd already been on board with Zane when she'd *reluctantly* arrived.

Casting Teal a humorous glance from under a straw cowboy hat, the older woman gave her a once-over. "You're still a little green."

A little green *looking* was better than the antifreeze green Teal was *feeling*. "I'm fine." A pair of Cutter-blue eyes bored into the top of her head, sending a shiver down her spine. She glanced upward, then scowled. He and several guys were looking down. "Surely, it doesn't take three guys to steer this itty-bitty thing." Maybe she'd get lucky and the pile of rust would sink right here, a mile from Cutter Cay.

Maggie grinned. "A thirty-five-foot-wide, hundred-foot-long, three-hundred-ton boat is *bitty*?"

"Anything less than an entire continent is small to me

if it's floating on water." The idiot had called her *gorgeous*. She couldn't quite figure out why she was annoyed. Calling a woman gorgeous or darling was a smooth way to cover that he didn't remember her name.

Holding her hat, Maggie rested against the railing and asked with studied casualness, "So what do you think of the brothers?"

Teal's gaze stayed focused on the island as it got smaller and farther out of swimming distance. She didn't realize that she'd turned her face up to look at the wheelhouse again until Zane caught her eye. With a big, white grin, he raised his Coke can in salute.

How friendly of him, Teal thought sourly, redirecting her gaze to the woman beside her. "Zane thinks he's God's gift to women. He's too . . ." She'd responded a nanosecond too quickly to filter her answer. The tropical sun beating down on her shoulders and the top of her baseball cap had nothing to do with the annoyed heat in her face. *Shut up.* "How long have you known them, Maggie?" She changed the subject, anything to get her mind off piercing blue eyes.

Maggie leaned back, elbows on the metal rail. Dressed in white shorts and a navy tank top, sunny hair blowing in the wind, she looked about twenty. Great genes. Behind her, the sunlight danced like diamonds across stunningly peacock blue-green silk. Teal was tempted to take a dive into the warm water to prevent her imminent death by nausea.

"I've known the boys since they were quite small. The kids all went to school together in St. Maarten. Ben and I started working with Zane about ten years ago. He and our daughter Cat are very good friends, too. We adore him. He's one of the most honest, loyal, *joyful* people I know. We love him like a son."

Honest and loyal and joyful sounded like a golden retriever. It also sounded like a veiled stay-away-from-my-daughter's-guy. Teal could have assured Maggie that the hands-off warning was completely, utterly, absolutely, *unnecessary*. She wasn't his type, if his type *had* a type. She suspected that as far as Zane was concerned, pretty much any woman he encountered would be a case of instant attraction. Just add opportunity and a willing female. Maggie's daughter was more than welcome to the Casanova of the Caribbean.

"I hope we can be friends too, Teal."

It was hard for her to make friends. Being so painfully shy growing up had given Teal a sense of disconnect that was hard to shake. She frequently found herself feeling like the outsider looking in. The years with Denny had just enforced what her mother and Sam had started. "I'd like that," she said sincerely.

"Good." Maggie's voice was brisk and upbeat. "Come on, honey," she tugged on the brim of Teal's cap. "Let's take a walk. It'll do your tummy good."

Teal sincerely doubted it, but she fell into step with the older woman anyway. Taking off her baseball cap, she ran her fingers through her short, damp hair, then stuffed the cap in the back pocket of her cargo pants. The sun felt good on her skin. Better yet, she saw they were approaching Tortola. Land ho. Yay.

"Too what?" Maggie asked as they stepped into the shadow of the battered yellow crane perched on the prow. They both stopped to watch the approaching island.

So close and yet so far. Teal's stomach heaved alarmingly. She looked at land and sucked in a deep breath of salty air. The moment they landed, she was going to bolt off the boat and kiss the ground. She didn't care who was watching. She glanced over at Maggie and blinked at the non sequitur. "I'm sorry?"

The other woman smiled. "Zane is too . . . what?"

He was the very last person Teal wanted to discuss.

Especially with someone she not only didn't know, but a woman who was clearly considering him as a future son-in-law.

Watching Tortola get larger and larger, Teal rubbed the back of her neck, still hyper-aware of being observed from above. Hopefully, after a few days he wouldn't even notice she was on his boat. Nor remember the shy girl who'd spent two weeks a year on his island. Heck, she'd hardly seen any of the Cutter brothers much. More than half the time she'd visited Sam the boys had been off on a salvage with their father, and they'd barely acknowledged her when she'd been there for their father's funeral. That visit was indelibly etched on her mind, like the engine's VIN number, marking it as one of a kind.

Teal's heart thumped painfully, and she felt a prickly wash of hot and cold from head to toe. God . . . "Too good looking." She looked straight ahead. Stupid of her to have said anything at all, thereby drawing attention to a subject she was trying hard to avoid. "Too full of himself. Too rich. Too charming. Take your pick." Been there, done that. She didn't relish being around yet another guy who felt entitled just because he was rich and good looking, a guy who used his charm like a weapon.

"All true, but we see all those things as attributes, not faults." Maggie laughed, her eyes sparkling with female understanding. "Our Zane is a breath of fresh air. I must admit, I have a particular soft spot for him. He's so gregarious, charming, and naughty. And of course, delightfully charismatic."

"*And* he knows it too."

"Wow," Maggie murmured, looking a little puzzled. "All that and you haven't seen him in what? Six years?"

"I was here for the funeral." Eighteen months, twenty-two days, and fourteen hours ago. Not nearly long enough as far as she was concerned. She felt cold to her core in spite of the heat. Tortola got larger and larger as they approached, the water so clear she could see fish swimming on the pale sandy bottom.

"You have some pretty strong feelings about Zane." Maggie was like a dog with a bone. "How about Nick and Logan?"

Teal didn't really want to talk about *any* of them. Other than being on dry land, she really wanted to go down and inspect her engines. The sooner she evaluated their condition, the sooner she could go to work.

"I don't know them." This was going to be a hellishly long trip if she had to spend it avoiding Zane *and* redirecting Maggie's questions.

"Maybe not, but I'd hazard a guess that you have an opinion anyway."

Maggie didn't sound quite as friendly now. *Okay. Now I've pissed her off by not worshipping at the feet of her retriever.* Teal felt a pang of regret and wished she hadn't shared those truths with someone who could've been an ally on the trip. Navigating the shoals of a friendship was treacherous. Teal had already failed, and they weren't even an hour into the job.

"Logan's pretty reserved, I think." The oldest sibling's dark and brooding exterior seemed to match a dark and brooding personality. Sam had told her once he was called Wolf and wasn't very social. Well, neither was she, but she wouldn't want to bump into the oldest Cutter in a dark alley. He made her nervous, too, but in a different way than Zane did.

"He seems like a guy who wants to be left alone," she muttered diplomatically. And despite the lifesaving offer of a job thousands of miles away from Orange Beach, Alabama, and light-years away from San Francisco and Denny, she'd try to give him a wide berth.

"Logan values his family highly. He's a good man to have as a friend. A good guy to have at your back."

Teal suspected he'd make a powerful enemy if crossed.

"I'm grateful he offered me a chance to fill in for Sam." She felt the sting behind her lids. Fill in. As if the type of cancer her father had was curable—as if he might ever come back to a job he loved. She was lousy at interpersonal relationships. Give her a freaking knocking engine any day. Yeah, she got that from Sam, all right. Denny'd called her an antisocial misfit. Half an hour in her company and Maggie was already wishing she was somewhere else.

Engines were less complicated and a lot easier to talk to than people. There was a wrong way and a right way with engines. No middle ground. No guessing. It either worked or it didn't. If you gave it half an effort and fixed it, then it performed exactly the way it should. Not so with people. You could put in all the effort you wanted. You could try to fix the relationship and despite your best efforts it could all go sour.

"I'm guessing you don't care much for Nick either?" Maggie's tone was decidedly cool now.

Oh, hell. "It's not a case of *not* liking any of them. I don't know them well enough to honestly offer an informed opinion. Nick seems like a solid guy." Cold and emotionless was what she vaguely remembered from her vacations. Yeah, Spock fit him to a T. Although he *had* given her that brief hug yesterday when she'd walked into the Counting House with Logan, so maybe he wasn't as cold and standoffish as she remembered.

"Nick knows who he is and who he's not. Don't let his frosty exterior fool you. Like his brothers, he prizes family. He's another man to have as a friend." Maggie touched Teal's arm briefly. "They're good men, honey. Give them a chance. Give *yourself* a chance to see what a great guy Zane is." She rubbed her hand up and down Teal's arm. "I want to run in and see if Ben's taken his blood pressure meds. Want to come in with me? I'll introduce you to the others."

"Thanks." Teal's chest hurt with the pressure of not

breaking down. Too bad she couldn't have left herself behind in San Francisco with Denny. But no, wherever she went she had to take her socially inept self along like an anchor.

She was horrible at this. Awful and inadequate and interpersonally awkward. "I still feel a little pukey," she spoke evenly with effort. "I'd better stay out here for a while. Go ahead. I'll see you later. Thanks for the water."

"Put your cap back on," Maggie ordered after a moment of uncomfortable assessment, which made Teal extremely self-conscious and feel more miserably inept. "Your skin's so pale you'll fry." The older woman turned around and walked off, disappearing from view behind the rusted, ancient crane.

Teal would never know what her first look at Tortola would've been. Her eyes were filled with tears. She hated the Cutters for inviting her into paradise—a chance to fix what was wrong in her life. She hated herself for being weak enough to leap at their offer. Most of all, she hated being silly enough to think being here would change anything.

Chapter 3

They'd dropped anchor before dinner, and the salon was quiet except for the occasional rustle of paper. The windows were open to the hot night air, bringing with it the smell of salt and the remnants of the BLTs Zane had thrown together for dinner. Sandwiches and the occasional barbecue were the extent of his culinary skills. Fortunately, they'd all take turns cooking.

The ocean was as calm as a piece of glass, the blackness reflecting a million pinpoints of light from the stars and the lights on board.

The glow of several lamps bathed the room in a homey warmth. The main public space was comfortably furnished with several worn brown leather sofas, a card table, overflowing bookcases, and a huge flat screen TV. Practically every flat surface, including that of the breakfast bar separating the room from the galley, was currently covered with maps, papers, and books. Saul Redding, the magnetometer operator, was asleep with a book open on his chest. Everyone else was digging into every available source Zane had collected over the last four years.

"Seen Teal?" he asked the men, who were all engrossed

in their reading as he passed through from the wheel-house.

Ryan Beck glanced up from the copy of an old document he was reading with a large magnifying glass. "Not since dinner." Despite his sun-bleached blond hair and the peeling nose of a surfer, he was a smart guy, one of Zane's best divers, and a good friend.

"I think she went down to the engine room," Colson Clark, Maggie's assistant, offered as he turned around on his chair in front of one of the computers on the long, built-in desk area. The college student shoved his glasses up his nose.

"I'll start there." Of course she'd be in the engine room. It was ten o' clock at night. Where else would the woman be?

Zane shoved the engine room door open and stepped inside. The room was, as always, spotless. The engines were quiet and the generator hummed efficiently.

Teal sat on a blanket on the floor, her back against the bulkhead, her long legs stretched out, ankles crossed. She looked comfortable enough with several bed pillows stuffed behind her back as she read a book on local fish. Since she wore ear buds, she clearly hadn't heard him come in.

Zane did a double take. She wore a baggy, much washed T-shirt that read, GOT DIESEL? in faded black letters. And boxer shorts. Yeah, they were baggy—but still. *Shorts.* The room was hot, and the sheen of perspiration on her skin made it look—touchable. Williams had pale, creamy legs a mile long.

Not fair. *Big time,* not fucking fair. He was a leg man first and foremost and the shock of seeing that his mechanic's were prime, threw him for a momentary loop. Holy shit! Who could've thought she was hiding *those* under those god-awful baggy khakis?

Zane dragged his gaze up and up and up. She'd showered, and her short dark hair was slicked back, combed off her face. The day outdoors had given her face a rosy glow, which made him notice the freckles across her pert nose. She looked . . . girl next door sexy. The most insidious kind of sexy.

Oh, no you don't, Zane warned his libido as he felt an unwelcome, unexpected heat suffuse his body. Teal Williams, he reminded himself, unwillingly noticing the way the well-washed cotton of her baggy shirt molded over her small, plump breasts, was not here for his sexual pleasure. She was here—at his insistence—because he *wasn't* attracted to her.

Something to keep in mind when he saw her lick her lips as she read. God. What a mouth. It was meant for things a guy dreamed about in the dark hours of night. Hell . . . He walked up and tapped his foot against hers to get her attention. Her gaze shot up to meet his. Pretty eyes, even if she was looking at him like something she'd scraped off her shoe.

"You didn't stay for the meeting after dinner—"

Long, dark eyelashes swept up to highlight large, chocolate brown eyes. She frowned. "What?"

He gestured for her to remove the ear buds and when she did, said, "You have a perfectly good queen-sized bed, Williams, why are you camped out on the floor?"

Teal gave him a wide-eyed look. "Is it against your rules?"

"I don't have any rules."

"That's what I thought." She replaced her ear buds and picked up her book again, resting it on her pale knees.

Concentrate, damn it. No looking at her legs. He plucked the ear buds out with a little tug. "You don't need to babysit the engines. I promise you, they'll be here when you get up in the morning."

"Why aren't we moving?" she demanded, sounding cranky and out of sorts.

"Because we dropped anchor three hours ago."

She perked up. "We're back in port?"

"No, Teal, we're at B-seventeen."

She looked blank. "B-seventeen?"

"Code name for the first dive site. Which you'd know if you hadn't lit out of there before any of the rest of us had finished eating."

"Okay. And?"

"And?"

"What are you doing in here?"

"It's my boat."

"And these are, according to your royal decree, *my* engines for the duration."

"I don't expect you to work twenty-four seven."

"I'm not working." She held up her book. *Caribbean Marine Life.* "I'm reading."

Lord she was maddening. "Did you have a chance to visit Sam before we left?" A change of subject was in order. But when he saw the look on her face, he wished he'd chosen a better subject.

"No." She gripped the book so hard her knuckles turned white.

"You can go and see him any time you like. The speedboat will get you there in an hour."

She gave him a stony look. "Thanks."

"We all care about Sam and, by extension, you. He's a great guy, family. I know his illness must be really hard on you." Sam Williams had terminal bone cancer, and probably had only months left. Hard to tell since the stubborn bastard refused to go to the hospital, and hadn't seen his doctor in months.

Zane felt a serious twinge of conscience for strong-arming Teal into coming on this salvage. She should be back on Cutter Cay, spending time with her father.

He was just about to tell her he'd have someone take her back when she said flatly, "He refuses to have treatment, so I guess he's okay with dying." Teal gave him an emotionless, dismissive glance.

"He sent a message that he was too tired to see me before we left. He didn't ask if I was okay with him dying, and he doesn't seem to want my opinion." She swallowed. Zane watched the movement of her throat as she somehow kept her cool. "Fact is, I can't change what's going to happen. If he wants me to go see him, I'll see him. He's got the number here."

Her voice was cold, but her big, brown eyes were haunted. A look Zane would've missed if he hadn't been so intent on *not* looking at her braless breasts moving under her PJs.

Sam hadn't *asked* her to stay. Zane almost groaned. Jesus. The apple hadn't fallen far from the tree. Both Williamses were stubborn, antisocial, and fucking uncommunicative. He wondered if he should call Sam in the morning, feel him out. "What happened to your mother? Sam never talks about her."

The delicate skin around her eyes contracted. A tiny flinch? "Why would he? They were never married, and she died more than five years ago."

Teal would've been what? Twenty-two? Twenty-three? "You weren't close?"

Zane couldn't fathom how that could be the case. His mother had died a few months after his fifth birthday. He didn't remember much more than her soft, sweet smell and warmth. But he'd always known unequivocally that she'd loved him. He'd adored his father, and loved his brothers unconditionally, and they him.

Given Teal's strained relationship with her father, he'd hoped she and her mother, at least, had been close.

Teal tossed the book on the floor, then drew her knees up, wrapping her arms around them, and shrugged dismissively. "She had some problems and was gone a lot.

Don't get comfortable," she warned as he leaned against the bulkhead.

Zane stuck his fingers in the front pockets of his jeans. "What kind of problems?"

"What is this? Twenty questions?"

"Just curious."

She got up, her movements jerky as she gathered the blanket and pillows. "I'm going to bed, but in the future, if you want me to stick around and do my job, stay out of my engine room. I like my privacy."

Wow. The quills were bristling. "Just one more thing . . ." he said, just waiting for her reaction.

She spun and glared at him. "What?"

"You left your book," he said mildly.

"I'll get it tomorrow." She swept from the room, chin held high, the blanket dragging behind her like a royal train.

*   *   *

The second she was in her cabin, Teal slammed the door and sat on the edge of the bed in a tumble of blanket and pillows without turning on the light. This was *not* going to work. It wasn't going to work on so many levels it made her dizzy.

He couldn't just go barging into places he wasn't welcome. It was intrusive and really annoying. Everything about him annoyed the hell out of her. He was just too . . . cheerful. Too impervious to her rudeness. Too—Teal punched a pillow, then clutched it to her chest.

She didn't want chatty, or charming, or inquiring. She wanted to be left the hell alone in her engine room, which held the seasickness at bay and didn't ask stupid, intrusive damned questions. Zane Cutter brought out the mean in her. She didn't know which was worse: that he didn't remember what had happened between them the night of his father's funeral, or that she *did*.

She'd had a crush on him since she was six years old. That crush had developed over every summer until Zane freaking Cutter, Casanova of the Caribbean, was all she could think about, dream about. Dennis Ross had been the closest she thought a man could come without being the man himself.

Wrong. Wrong. And God. *Very* wrong.

Maybe she needed some sort of mind wipe. She'd probably be a better person for it, Teal thought angrily. Feeling used, and yeah, she admitted it, heartsick for someone who didn't even know she existed, had driven her into a relationship with Denny. She'd even married the bastard and look how well that had turned out.

Stupid. All the way around stupid. Denny had been a bad Zane clone—Zane, who eighteen months ago had made her believe she was beautiful. For one night, he'd made her hope that she could have a normal relationship. Then the next morning, he'd told her to "get the hell out" without bothering to open his eyes.

Oh, she'd tried to forget him. In fact, she hadn't returned to Cutter Cay since the funeral. But then Sam's cancer intervened. She'd come back out of duty, to check on her father, and found her heartache hadn't improved, it had just been on vacation.

Rolling off the bed, she switched on the nightstand lamp, which bathed the room in a warm glow. It was a nice room—*cabin*. Queen-sized bed. A small, comfortable easy chair, couple of lamps, a tiny bathroom all to herself. The hum of the generator down the hall was faint, and the hollow sound of the water lapping against the hull made her tummy roll.

A glance out the small porthole showed only the running lights competed with the reflection of starlight on the water. Everyone had gone to bed. She'd wait another half hour and take her blanket back to the engine room and sleep there. In the morning, she'd be the first one up. Nobody had to know how bad her seasickness was.

She dug in her duffel bag and took out her phone to start counting down the days until she was once again on terra firma. Zane had said they'd be out here in the freaking middle of nowhere for a month. She entered the date on her calendar. She'd hold him to it, too. And while she had the phone in her hand, she checked to see if Sam had called. He hadn't. What a twit she was to think that he would. A person didn't think about duty when he was dying. He'd passed along the message that he'd call if he needed her. He'd asked her to fill in. That was all he wanted. And she was the desperate-for-Daddy daughter that bought into his dying wish, despite heaving and heartache.

Really, Teal thought with wry amusement as she opened the door carefully and listened for movement from the other nearby cabins, she should get some balloons for her pity party.

She gave herself an attitude adjustment as she spread her blanket on the floor between the two Caterpillar D398 marine propulsion engines and fluffed her pillows. The humming power fed into her body like a current of soothing energy and her belly calmed.

Tomorrow she'd be sweet and nice to anyone she talked to.

Reaching up, she patted the metal sides of her engines. "Night, my babies."

She couldn't figure out why the hell tears were leaking into her ears.

*   *   *

"Teal—" She half turned to give Zane an inquiring look. She was sitting in the shade with her fish book. Probably trying to ID some of the fish she'd seen in her last dive.

She wore a baggy blue T-shirt and butt-ugly shorts, re-vealing her long, pale legs once again. "I hate to bring up a sore subject, but you haven't asked about your father," Zane said gently, dragging his gaze away from her sur-prisingly sexy feet. "I talked to him this morning."

Sticking a finger inside the book to hold her page, she tilted up her face to look at him. Hope leaped like a flame in her curly-lashed brown eyes. "He called you? How is he?"

Zane leaned against the base of the crane, careful not to get too close to another prickly Williams. "You know he's refused to go to radiation treatments or chemo since he was diagnosed last year."

"I only found out that he was even sick when Logan called about the job a couple of weeks ago. Sam never said a word until he got on the phone that day. It was . . . It was quite a surprise." Her soft lips tightened. "He's stubborn and intractable."

Zane's lips twitched. "Like someone else I know."

"Is that why he called you?" *Instead of me,* hung in the air between them. "Is he worse?" If Zane hadn't been so attuned to her, he wouldn't have noticed the way her shoul-ders tensed as if she were waiting for the delivery of bad news.

He shook his head. "No. He called to tell me he went to the doctor in Tortola today."

"Really?" Her body tensed as she added cautiously, "That's amazing."

Amazing, Zane knew, that Sam had been even closer geographically and yet, still hadn't seen his daughter. He could tell that Teal's outer indifference shielded deep feel-ings. What kind of messed-up relationship did they have that Sam's own daughter felt like she had to hide her love for her father?

He said as gently as he knew how, "You know that it's

too late for any treatment to make a difference, don't you? He has less than a year. I'm sorry, Teal."

She turned away for a brief second. "Me too."

"He loves you," he told her quietly. "Brags about you all the time. Told us we couldn't get anyone better to take his place."

"He asked me to 'fill in.'" She stared down at her short, jagged nails.

Zane's heart twisted in his chest. No wonder she'd come along. She had integrity, and if she'd agreed for Sam's sake, no loss of personal freedom "on land" would stop her from doing as she'd promised. "It's just hard for him to show emotion. You probably get that better than anyone."

"Yes, I do." Teal shifted her feet. "If he has any warm and fuzzy feelings for me, he's kept them smothered for twenty-something years." She shrugged. "He's a decent man who takes his responsibilities seriously. I was a duty he acknowledged when he didn't have to. Not like my mom was going to take him to court. I've always been grateful for his generosity in paying my way out to the island for all those years. It meant a lot."

Zane ached for her. Damn Sam. No matter how fucking sick he was, did the man have no idea how much his daughter craved his love and attention? Apparently not. The thought made Zane angry. He liked Sam, always had. But this was ridiculous. Especially since the man had a finite time to make amends with his only child. "But he's your dad. He should have done those things. Maybe more."

"We're basically strangers." Clearly uncomfortable at this personal revelation she moved restlessly, shrugging as she brought her eyes back to his. "It's not a crime. Nobody's fault, that's just how it is."

Zane's gut clenched. "Were you close to your mother?"

"I already told you no. She had a pretty bad drug problem and OD'd on my twenty-second birthday."

"Jesus, Teal."

She picked up the can of soda on the deck beside her and took a swig. Her throat worked for a moment as she swallowed. Zane had an insane urge to press his lips to the damp hollow. To grab her and hold her. Shit. If ever there was a woman who needed a hug, it was Teal. He shoved his hands in his pockets and stayed right where he was. She might need physical contact, but she sure as hell wouldn't welcome it.

"I can only imagine Sam's shock when she sent him a picture of his surprise kid. I look like him," Teal gave a crooked smile, "so he agreed to a child support plan. Mom snorted the money or shot up before she paid the rent."

"Did Sam know?"

She shrugged. "He never wanted to talk about her, and to tell the truth, it was nice to have two weeks a year when I didn't have to deal with her drama. Don't get me wrong, I loved my mother in spite of her habit. I went to Al-Anon. I knew I was enabling her by living at home and taking care of her. I hardly had any friends all through high school, because I didn't have time and I really didn't want to bring anyone home."

All Zane wanted to do was scoop her up and hold her. He settled for holding her attention instead. "So you were already shy, which isolated you to a certain extent, but your mother's addiction made that even worse."

"My years watching Sam paid off. I got into vocational school and worked while I took classes. Sam's money went to drugs, mine paid the rent and put food on the table." She paused. "Thanks for telling me Sam decided to try treatment. I hope . . ." she trailed off. "I hope it isn't too little, too late."

Yeah, he got it. She hoped her father somehow managed to make it. She hoped there'd be time. What else did she hope for? Zane watched her as she joined the others.

It was interesting that even though he'd made sure she sat in the middle of the group, she always seemed to be, not a part, but apart from what was going on.

She seemed to like the others and they her, but Zane had noticed that she preferred keeping to herself more than socializing. The exact opposite of the way he did things, which was both confusing and intriguing.

The more time he spent in her company, the more little details he remembered from her visits with Sam over the years. Her hair had been a soft brown then, and long, not as black as a starless sky and chin length. But she'd had the same big brown eyes and gentle mouth. Maybe it was the shyness that had seemed to plague her as a kid that kept her separate from the others. But shouldn't she have outgrown that by now?

Hell, he didn't know. All he knew was he kept feeling the ridiculous urge to wrap his arms around her and pull her into the center of the group with him. Of course, there were several other more base things he'd like to do with her, but those options weren't on the table.

Maybe he was just horny? That would explain his U-turn from unattractive and perfect, to attractive and . . . Available? Shit. Not going to happen. He'd make damn sure it didn't.

And wasn't that a fucking switch-a-roo? When the hell had he developed a conscience? When had he not at least tried to charm, cajole, or seduce a woman into his bed? If the woman was willing, all bets were off and he used the full arsenal at his disposal to seduce their panties off. And as much as he was starting to feel some physical response to her, he liked her. The thought startled him.

Damn. He *liked* her. A lot. She was sassy and snarky, and funny in her own quiet way.

Ah, man. *Don't go there, Ace!*

He fell in love on the spin of a dime. He loved being in

love. Hell, he'd been in love a couple of dozen times in the last few years alone. And in lust more times than he could count. But *like*?

That was a fucking undertow he'd managed to avoid. So far.

*   *   *

It was going to be a perfect day, Zane thought with satisfaction as he leaned against the rail. No matter how many beautiful days he'd experienced in the Caribbean, it never got old. This morning the sun hovered shyly a few inches over the water, not quite ready to share its heat. Soft pink, tangerine, and lavender smudged the horizon with promise.

Standing on the starboard deck of the *Decrepit,* he breathed deeply of the early morning air tinged with the robust fragrance of freshly brewed coffee and the bacon and eggs he'd just inhaled for breakfast. Now wasn't that a surprise from a woman who claimed she couldn't boil water?

His heart pounded in anticipation of the upcoming unveiling of his four-year quest. A hundred feet below lay the bones and secrets of the *Vrijheid.* Soon the sea would give her up, sharing her treasure and century-old stories.

Anxious as he was to get started, he'd stick to his original plan of moving several times before they started the salvage operation. Another week to throw off the competition and they'd be back, filling their hands with gold, silver, and emeralds.

No matter how eager he was to get started, Zane knew from experience that taking time to put the competition off his scent was the smart move. So, while there'd be no "official" salvaging today, he thought with regret, they could certainly spend a few hours down there reconnoitering and taking a few more pictures for the grid they'd set up later.

He leaned both elbows on the railing, cradling the warm, oversized, bright yellow mug between his palms and tried to ignore the siren song of the challenge that was Teal Williams.

"Keep your eye on the prize, pal," he muttered softly to himself. The *Vrijheid* was all the challenge he needed right now. He saw the frigate in his mind's eye and practically salivated to begin work. God it was good to be here at last. The cool would heat up soon enough, but for now, the breeze felt silky against his face and tasted salty/sweet on his tongue.

The deck shifted gently beneath his bare feet as he sipped from a steaming mug of Williams's excellent French Roast. The susurrus of wavelets lapped musically against the hull, and faceted, pale gold light danced and shimmered across the surface of the water. They were almost a hundred nautical miles east off the coast of St. Maarten. Out of the path of cruise boats and day-trippers. The tiny green smudges on the horizon were the small islands of Anguilla, Saba, St. Barts, and St. Eustatius, but for miles in every direction was nothing but smooth, clear turquoise except for the telltale lacy white froth as the surf crashed against the coral reef just beneath the smooth surface of the water.

The same reefs that the *Vrijheid* had crashed on back in 1622.

The thought of showing his prize to Teal was just as enticing as seeing it again himself. Unobserved, he watched her chatting with his friend. She wore creased black cargo pants, scuffed sneakers without socks, and an oversized yellow-and-blue striped man's soccer shirt. Efficiently covered, once again, from top to toe. Her moppy hair hid most of her face.

He'd never met a woman with so little regard for her appearance. She dressed like she'd grabbed the first thing to hand. Zane wished to hell he didn't have a mental image of a bed while watching her move efficiently around the small galley. Those butt-ugly shorts last night were starting to have a starring role in his fantasies.

He conjured, instead, an enticing image of treasure chests spilling with emeralds the size of dinner plates. He thought about swimming through cool turquoise water, he thought of her naked swimming beside him . . . damn it! Wrong image. Wrong woman. Wrong time. Wrong place. And yet . . .

He'd pigeonholed her and didn't want to have his mind changed. Not now. Not when being *un*-attracted was the whole point of her presence. If there'd been a guy to hire with her qualifications, Zane wouldn't be thinking about his mechanic in shorts. Logan had done the research, and she had the experience as well as a sterling reputation. She knew her stuff. That's all he required.

It wasn't only her surprisingly gorgeous long legs and sassy mouth but what lay behind those big, serious brown eyes and bad attitude that intrigued him.

Nobody was that defensive and adversarial without a root cause. He was a nice guy. Women liked him, for God's sake! None of them had ever treated him as if he were the devil incarnate.

She rubbed the back of her neck, and he bet she felt him watching her, but she didn't look at him. She had an intriguing face. Not quite plain, but not exactly pretty. The combination of large eyes, generous mouth, straight nose, and a scattering of golden freckles was surprisingly striking. Her chin-length dark hair was slicked back off her face, still damp from the shower she'd taken after breakfast while he and Ben had cleaned up the galley. She looked a little on the pale side. Zane hoped to hell she wasn't getting sick. He needed her expertise with the engines as much as he needed a fourth diver.

There was absolutely no artifice with her. No makeup and no bullshit. It appeared that Miss Williams was also flirt proof. Zane grinned inwardly. He'd see about that. His middle name was "I'll take that bet."

Carrying his coffee mug, he casually strolled over to join her and Ben. "Thanks for fixing breakfast."

"Don't expect that every morning," she warned waspishly. "I'm here to work on the engines and to dive. That's *it*."

Zane was charmed by her in spite of himself. Jesus, she was an odd, prickly little duck. "Yes, ma'am." He took a sip from his mug, then paused to flash her a mock scowl. "This isn't poisoned, is it?"

"Quick-acting."

"I've already had two cups."

She shrugged. "Must've used the slow-acting potion today."

Ben laughed. "Anyone for a refill?" he asked, eyes twinkling as his gaze went from Zane to Teal and back again as if he were watching a tennis match. Zane shook his head and with another chuckle the older man went inside.

This required perfect timing, Zane thought. Wait too long and she'd bolt, go in too early and . . . he bit back a smile—she'd bolt. "When was the last time you were on top of something amazing?" he asked, keeping his tone light.

"Excuse me?"

"The *Vrijheid* is directly below us. Want to go down and take a look at my sweetheart?" He set down his mug on a nearby ledge.

Antagonism forgotten—or at least on hold—Teal turned luminous eyes on him. "Already? I'd love to."

Zane heard that slight breathless quality to her voice. God. He wanted her to look at him *exactly* like that. He wanted that luminosity for himself. He wanted her to look that thrilled. Excited. He wanted her in his bed. Under him. Around him. *Ah, shit!* What the hell had happened to not attractive? It was like waving a red flag at a bull. Every hunting instinct inside him rose up and howled.

He had to ignore the prey-drive. Ratchet back, buddy. "I've already checked the tanks."

"And I'll check mine again, but thanks."

"Good girl," Ben came outside in time to give her a high five. "A good diver always checks their own equipment."

What had made her so self-reliant? No—he'd met self-reliant women before. This was different. Teal was adamantly self-reliant, which meant that someone, somewhere had let her down. Who besides her mom and Sam? Someone else she'd cared about? Sam wouldn't win a father-of-the-year award, but this seemed to go even deeper.

Maggie came outside wearing a green swimsuit and her ubiquitous cowboy hat. "Colson's doing some research for me, and Saul's giving him a hand. What are we waiting for?"

"Ryan's going to join us in a minute." Zane gestured to the ocean. "Let's suit up. I'll take you all on a mini tour to whet your appetite."

"I don't have a wet suit," Teal said regretfully, her yearning gaze going to the water.

"I have extras." Maggie came to her rescue. She sized Teal with her eyes. "You're taller, but we can't be that much different in size. Come on, let's go to my cabin and see what we can find for you."

Ryan stepped aside to let the women through the doorway. He took a moment to admire the view from behind before joining Zane and Ben on deck. Zane made a mental note to give him a hands-off warning when they were alone.

"Not the first time you've brought a woman with us," Ben mused. "But Teal's different."

"Yeah. Contrary and with an attitude," Zane said dryly. "Williams isn't a girlfriend," he pointed out in case the guys got the wrong message. "She's the mechanic Logan hired to take over from Sam."

"Yeah. Maggie mentioned that." Ben drank his coffee. "She's got that quiet sort of beauty that takes a man by surprise."

"Haven't noticed," Zane muttered. "She's just a member of the crew." Like hell.

Ben gave him an innocent look. "Like Ryan here, or Maggie?"

"No." Zane glanced at his watch. "She's less experienced."

"Doesn't look like either Ryan or my Maggie in that swimsuit."

Turning around to look was knee-jerk. Big mistake.

Every pale, silky inch of Teal was revealed in a modest, black one-piece swimsuit as she carried Maggie's borrowed wet suit out on deck. She had long *gorgeous* legs, a slender body, and small, high breasts. All lovingly displayed in a thin layer of nylon. Zane just about swallowed his tongue. He instantly felt himself go hard as stone, his erection so swift and painful he had to turn to the rail and shift his weight to ease the discomfort of it.

That didn't stop him from looking, and taking his fill, however.

Her clothes had been a pretty damned effective camouflage for a spectacular, athletic body. It took a second for him to notice that she wasn't at all comfortable being so exposed.

Unfortunately, for him, now that he'd seen what she'd hidden beneath baggy clothes and a bad haircut, he wasn't sure he'd ever be able to see her other than as revealed as she was now.

Seeing his stare, Teal lifted her chin and gave him a "fuck off" look that should've singed his eyebrows. Zane grinned and gave her a thumbs-up. She looked away.

Good. He couldn't think about seeing her in little more than one thin layer of stretchy fabric. Instead, he concentrated on getting geared up. He pulled the stretchy neoprene suit over his shoulders and zipped it as Teal and the others did the same. They checked the O rings on the tanks, slid the regulators over the top and tested the mouthpieces for airflow, then strapped their tanks onto their buoyancy compensators, or BCs.

Zane turned, standing his tank toward him, then reached down, slipping his arms through the BC, and slung the whole contraption smoothly up and over his head to land on his back.

The wet suit did interesting things to her tall slender body. Zane's heart did a pleasant little tap dance in his chest as he secured his weight belt and seated his diver's knife on his thigh. There were three other divers waiting to go in the water, but the only one he saw was Teal. "Ready?"

"God, yes."

They adjusted their masks in unison, put their regulators in their mouths, and stepped off the dive platform, holding their masks in place.

Chapter 4

Sometimes, Zane thought, being under the water was almost better than sex. Almost.

Teal stayed beside him as they descended into a silent world of stunningly clear turquoise water, dappled by the filtered gold rays of the waking morning. Fingers of shifting light speared like honey to highlight the tips of the two clearly visible ribs of the *Vrijheid* as she came into view. Zane and the Berlands had already noted the last time they were here that the scatter pattern of the wreck site was erratic. The frigate had split into half a dozen pieces against the reef, her contents spilled across the sand for what seemed like miles.

They'd done a rough grid, but now Saul would lay it all out on a software program for more accurate readings—fortunately, that particular program still worked fine. The ship's navigation and detection equipment tended to go on the fritz when they hit these waters, but he'd manage to map the area in spite of a few technical bugs. First, they'd drop buoys and bring in sophisticated metal detectors. Then they'd see just how far the scatter pattern really was. All part of the discovery process. Zane loved it all. His chest swelled with contentment as Teal touched his arm to indicate a small school of blue tang darting like swiftly moving blue confetti between *Vrijheid*'s ribs.

Mostly buried by sand and time, the almost four-hundred-year-old bones of the *Vrijheid* lay broken and scattered in a pale, sandy depression dappled with filtered sunlight.

Seeing her again was almost a religious experience for Zane. He hung in the water, just above her, letting the BC hold him neutral like a fish, swaying with the surge of the current. Eighty people had died here. Men with families, men who'd loved and been loved. Families had mourned their passing. As thrilling as the discovery of a new wreck was, he never forgot that the site was also a graveyard.

Teal reached out and touched his arm, her eyes saucer-like behind her mask as she stretched out her arms to indicate the size of the wreck. Her hair, stick straight in the water, fanned around her head like a black halo. She gave him a double thumbs-up.

Zane winked. Sliding his hand down her arm, he laced his fingers through hers and tugged her along with him as they glided through the water together closer to the wreckage.

Trenches would have to be dug, sand blown out of the way. There were hours and hours of backbreaking work both under the sea and on board. The cleaning, cataloging, the removal of *Vrijheid*'s treasures—but there wasn't an aspect of salvaging that Zane didn't relish.

Just anticipating the hard work that would soon be involved with exposing all of her secrets filled him with intense pleasure. Christ, she was magnificent. Her glory was in no way diminished by the hazy blue of deep water. Decorated in the gaudy colors of coral and the moving ornamentation of small, brightly colored fish, she was like a partially unwrapped present just waiting for Christmas morning.

The *Vrijheid* had been alone when she'd been hit by the hurricane. A small piece of flotsam in a vast ocean. She hadn't stood a chance against Mother Nature. Her manifest boasted of the gold and silver, of a king's ransom in emeralds, but the personal wealth of both the passengers, and the seamen who'd assisted in the loading of the loot, would have been kept secret.

All secrets untouched until now.

He took Teal on a slow circuit around the fallen frigate, pointing out the square piles of conglomerate, the hard material formed by centuries of chemical reaction. The shape indicated that the redwood boxes, used to transport the contents, had been eaten away by teredos— shipworms—hundreds of years before. He saw a glint of gold on the sand and tugged her along as he swept it up in his hand. He peeled open her fingers and pressed the gold coin into her palm. It was as bright and shiny as if it had been freshly minted. Teal's eyes glittered behind her mask, and she twisted the coin between her fingers in awe.

Scattered unnoticed at her feet were piles of charcoal gray lumps that looked like small loaves of bread. Silt had covered them the last time he'd been down. The hair on the back of Zane's neck rose with excitement.

Silver bars.

Dozens and dozens of silver bars.

He couldn't wait to come back. It took everything in him not to start fanning the sand for more right that second.

Patience, he reminded himself. Everything would still be there at the end of the week when they come back.

The huge timbers of the *Vrijheid* had broken apart over the centuries, but if one had a good imagination, one could see the shape and size of her. Most of the timbers had been eroded away by time and teredo worms, and shifted out of whack by hurricanes and storms over the centuries. To Zane, she was absolutely beautiful.

He pointed out a forty-pound cannon and two twenty-pounders. Teal didn't look too excited by the conglomerate-covered cannon. It was impossible to identify them, disguised as they were by the hard material formed by centuries of chemical reaction with the metal. But he'd save that revelation for when they came back.

He indicated they go all the way around the wreck, and she immediately swam by his side. The chirps and swishing sounds of fish mingled with the sound of their aerators into a kind of white noise, heightening Zane's sense of sight. The colors of the fish and coral were intensified underwater. He never tired of it. He touched Teal's arm to indicate the slow passage of a parrot fish as big as his hand, with a bright blue tail and matching side streaks as it glided by.

He pointed down and took her to see more of the cubed items once held by crates. His hands itched to see what those boxes contained. He estimated what he'd need to bring down with him next time so that he could retrieve them intact if possible.

The contents could be anything. Emeralds? Artifacts? Gold? Silver. Nothing? The anticipation alone was sweet.

God. He wanted to start *today*. Now. This very second. He glanced at his digital air gauge. The tanks weren't even down by half yet, but if the *Decrepit* stayed at anchor here much longer there might be a feeding frenzy. Other salvage operators would be down here scooping up his find, his treasure. He wanted to blur the trail a little, lead his many followers on a little chase. Play a little bait and switch game to amuse himself while he was at it.

Reluctantly he pointed up.

*   *   *

It was after eleven, and the stars were out in full force. Zane stood at the propane barbecue grill on the aft deck, doing a quick post-dinner cleanup. Tiny lights, strung around the railings, swagged through the cleats, twinkled, but they were no match for the bright stars glittering overhead. Music drifted out of the salon, and the water lapped against the hull. Calm seas, good friends, and the intoxicating anticipation of a successful dive. The good life. His magic cloak was fitting just fine, thank you very much. He inhaled deeply and felt an intense contentment permeate his entire body. Life was fucking *superb*.

He heard a soft intake of breath and turned his head to see Teal standing in the doorway of the salon. "Oh, I didn't see you there . . ." she trailed off, half inside and half out.

"Come and join me," he told her softly. "Nights like this are so perfect they just beg to be shared."

Stunningly, he couldn't think of anyone else he'd rather be sharing it with right then.

She hesitated, then padded over to join him at the rail. She stared out at the twinkle of the stars dancing on the dark water and let out a little breath. "Beautiful."

She was beautiful. Zane's heartbeat stuttered as he took in the curve of her cheek, and the dark fringe of her lashes as she looked at blackness beyond the deck where they stood. She was a good six feet away, but he smelled the fresh scent of soap on her skin, a combo of floral and musk that made him think of hot nights and cool sheets.

She wore a pink tank top that showed the tantalizing slope of her breasts, and plaid shorts that accentuated her long pale legs. Ready for bed. He bet she hadn't expected to see him when she stepped outside.

Zane leaned over to rest his forearms on the rail and turned his head away from what he wanted to reach for. He was shocked at how aware of her he was as she stood there in his peripheral vision. Teal was blissfully unaware that the sight of her unfettered breasts, the length of her sexy legs, was giving him an erection that she could hardly miss if she cared to glance at his shorts.

"Thanks for taking me down today," she said quietly. "That was amazing. It's different at night, isn't it? Beautiful from up here, but scary. I imagine there are sharks hunting at night."

There was a shark right here who wanted to nibble on her tender bits. But of course he didn't say it. "The ocean can be a dangerous place. But everything she has to offer makes that danger worthwhile."

"And you thrive on it, don't you?"

"Danger? Nah, not so much. High adventure? Thrills? The challenge? Hell yeah." He grinned. "Never gets old. I've waited a long time for something like the *Vrijheid*, and I do believe she's going to reward me for my patience."

Teal's laugh sounded a little rusty. "You've never been patient or waited for anything a second in your life."

"You'd be surprised," he told her dryly.

"How does one go about *finding* a wreck?" she asked, her gaze focused on the pinpoints of light shimmering in the water. "And then, when you *do* find it, how to you know that there'll be treasure on board?"

He glanced beyond Teal through the window of the salon. Maggie smiled and gave him a quick thumbs-up. So she'd sent Teal out. Zane made a mental note to buy her flowers the next time he was in port. "Went to the archives in Spain four years ago, looking for a likely virgin wreck for a salvage." It was impossible not to look at her and he stopped pretending. Her eyes looked very dark in the moonlight. What was she thinking when she looked at him that way? A little wary? A little intrigued?

"Spent weeks scouring information at the Seville Archivo de las Indias," he told her. "Local archives, newspaper articles, books, testimonies, monasteries, and churches—they all had their own chronicles and reports, and there was usually at least one priest on board the

Spanish boats to write it all down. The only reason I know about the *Vrijheid* being in this area at all was from a few small and very annoyed notations in Spanish log books. She was *Dutch* and shouldn't have been anywhere near the Caribbean. The fact that she'd been a thorn in Spain's side, intrigued me."

"Of course it did." Teal's voice was dry. "But why?"

"She was a pirate ship."

Her wide eyes picked up the light. "Really?"

Warming to his story, Zane wanted to hold on to her rapt attention. "And she was *fast.* That girl could give the Spaniards a real run for their money. She was like a gnat on the nose of a pit bull. And yeah, her admiral, van Wassenaer, was an honest-to-God pirate. And a good one with an excellent track record. He was returning to Rotterdam and retirement. But this time, he didn't want to go back with the usual haul of spices or tobacco or hides from Cape Horn. He wanted a *much* more valuable treasure on his last voyage."

Teal leaned forward, totally enthralled, and out of habit when a woman showed any interest, Zane leaned in too. Inside, he did a double fist pump "yes!" at finally having her attention, without the attitude, and kept the story going. "So on his final voyage, van Wassenaer boldly crossed to the West Indies and got the haul of a lifetime—only to lose it in a hurricane. And that's where we come in."

Teal's eyes lit up. "Emeralds as big as your fist, huh?"

He shifted his bare feet, moving closer to her. "All sorts of gemstones." He had no idea how big they were, or even if the stories were true, but he loved seeing her bit by the treasure bug. "And plenty of them, just waiting almost four hundred years for us to pick them up off the ocean floor. Also an estimated in the multiple millions of dollars, in today's market, in gold and silver."

"Why aren't we down there right now?" she demanded.

"We'll goof around for a while to throw some of the

competition off the scent. Although they'll track us soon enough."

"Competition? I haven't seen anyone else out here since we left port."

"Oh, they'll be here eventually. Hopefully later rather than sooner. There are the usual suspects. The *Sea Witch* for one. She can smell a good salvage from the other side of the ocean it seems. This time, I'm taking great pains to keep her, and any other bottom-feeders, off my ass. All my salvages are important, but I don't want anyone getting their hands on any part of the *Vrijheid*."

"Is it dangerous? There could be a fortune down there. People have been killed for less." She turned to fully face him, leaning her back against the rail. The sparkling lights on the wavelets behind her seemed to dance around her head. "How do you stop other salvors from just diving down and helping themselves?"

Only two feet separated them now. Teal didn't seem to notice, but Zane's entire focus was consumed with touching her cool, translucent skin and kissing her sassy mouth. "There are laws governing salvage." He watched her chew a corner of her lower lip, and damn—he wanted in on the action. "I've gotten all the necessary paperwork filed. I'm the custodian and exclusive salvor for the *Vrijheid* until—" He made air quotes. "—'The salvage operations are completed.' There's a prohibited zone a mile in diameter from the wreck. And if, and when, anyone shows up, we'll give them a copy of the federal arrest warrant that outlines what will happen if they violate my custody. It's all good."

"If whoever shows up is a law-abiding citizen and/or they can read." Teal said dryly.

Zane grinned. "That too."

"I'd better—"

"Do you—"

They talked over one another. He didn't want her to go inside. Not yet. "Stay," he murmured softly.

"I—"

He reached out to cup her warm cheek—had he ever met another woman who blushed? He found it sweet, and charming, and sexy as hell. He slid his fingers under her hair to cradle her nape. Curving his other hand around her waist, he held her gaze as he stroked his thumb over the soft, warm skin beside her ear. She sucked in a startled breath and shuddered. He gave a gentle tug, then dipped his head.

For a moment she stiffened in resistance. He stopped, merely holding her, praying her opposition would pass. After a few erratic heartbeats, her body softened to allow him access to her mouth. He pressed his closed mouth against hers. Her lips were cool. Smooth. Delicious. Not exactly eager, but not reluctant as he nibbled and tasted. He was 90 percent there, all he needed was for her to meet him the remaining 10 percent.

For him the reason for the kiss was the reason for the kiss. This wasn't a prelude to anything else. Knowing there'd be no sex, no intimate touching, heightened his senses and heated his skin. He kept his hands where they were. Nonthreatening. But he wanted to kiss her more than he wanted his next breath. He made a soft humming sound against her upper lip, then nipped her lower lip until her eyes fluttered closed. He parted her lips with his tongue. She tasted sublime. Teal mixed with coffee and a faint hint of the cinnamon in Maggie's after-dinner apple pie.

Zane forced his tongue to behave. Small, soft nips of his teeth to her lower lip, a thumb stroked with maddening slowness across the curve of her ear, gentle pressure around her waist to draw her ever closer. He coaxed her using his considerable skill and more restraint than he'd ever used in his life.

He traced her upper lip with the tip of his tongue, and wonder of wonders—hers came out to greet him. His heart leapt. He danced his tongue with the very tip of hers, holding back the punishing kiss his entire body craved. A kiss he knew, with absolute certainly, would drive her away.

He slid his hand up the small of her back, feeling the tension along her spine under his splayed fingers. With his other hand he combed through the hair near her temple, feeling the heat of her scalp and the silky coolness of the strands spill over his fingers like silk.

Her tongue glided against his, hot and sensual. His body responded, but he tamped it down. This was all about Teal. All about just one glorious, sensual kiss.

Her shaky sigh rasped his nerve endings, but he didn't exert any more pressure, didn't delve any deeper, not until Teal pressed closer, tilting her head back and opening her mouth to him. He felt the rapid, manic beat of her heart against his chest as she kissed him back, her palm on his chest.

His fingers tightened around her back, tangled in her hair as he swept his tongue inside the hot cavern of her mouth.

Zane couldn't remember ever getting such a high just kissing a woman. He wanted to devour her right there on the deck outside the salon where anyone could see them. He deepened the kiss, reading her desire by her equally avid responses. He wanted—

She jerked her head away, stepping back. In the sparkling fairy lights he saw the rapid pulse at the base of her throat and noticed that her breathing was uneven as she stood there paused for flight.

"Nice to be of use," she said, gasping for breath. "I'd hate to see you lose any of your considerable skills just because your choice of partners on board is limited. No point getting out of practice. I see where you get your nickname," she said coolly, patting his chest as if he were a well-behaved dog. "You're good. Very good. Night, Ace."

She turned around and strolled inside, leaving Zane shaken and very much stirred by her response.

Heart pounding, his body wired, he sagged against the rail. "Holy shit!"

* * *

Teal was having a wet dream. Not the good old hot-and-bothered sexual kind, but one where she was soaked to the skin while fully clothed and the boat was sinking. Zane didn't feature in it, but she just knew he was involved.

She rolled over, hugging her pillow. It squelched.

Her eyes sprang open as the cold permeating her shorts and tank top pierced the dream. It wasn't only the feel of water lapping at her toes that got her attention, but the pulsing blast of the general alarm.

Ten short bleats. Silence. Ten short—

The ship was taking on water. Fast.

Hot and cold prickles of adrenaline-laced fear shot through her body as her heartbeat picked up the rapid pulse of the emergency alarm. She went from prone to standing on her bedroll in seconds. The dim amber glow of the LED light near the door glinted on the rippling sheet of dark water surrounding the island of her bedroll. "Shit!"

Seawater pipe leakage? Probable. Rust was a given on any vessel as old as the *Decrepit*. An overboard valve rupture? That was a strong possibility as well. Water inched higher. Even once she found the source, it wasn't like she could pull a plug and let the water out. It was illegal to discharge any liquid that had oil particles suspended in it out to the open sea, and she could see the iridescent sheen on the surface of her new indoor swimming pool.

"Think, damn it!"

The rising level of the bilges would damage the shaft generator, and if she didn't do something right that damn *second,* the pumps in the bottom platform would stop functioning. She couldn't wait for help. Knowing the alarm would alert the others, Teal stepped off her bedroll, which was already covered in inches of dark water. The cold water hit her mid shin. Right now pumping out the bilges *immediately* was her only thought. She plunged her hands into the dark liquid, her fingers questing for the valve handle, her mind spinning furiously. The injection valve could bypass the main sea chest in case of emergency. If she could just get it set so that instead of the sea, water would be drawn from within the ship itself, it'd help. She'd checked the valves—all the valves—just that morning. Thank God.

She quickly and efficiently connected the emergency bilge injection valve as the cold water crept up her shins to lick at her calves. "Can't you people hear the freaking alarm?!" she yelled over the cacophony. Her wet fingers lost purchase of the valve spindle, and she almost sliced off a finger.

"Someone? Anyone? Get your ass in here!"

The connectors clicked into place, and finally, she had some good news: The pump immediately started sucking seawater from the lowest points in the engine room. The bad news was that water was coming in as fast as it was being sucked up.

She was woman enough to know when she needed help, and this problem required all hands on deck. Wading through the cold, rapidly rising water, Teal yanked open the watertight door. A mini waterfall spilled over the raised threshold and started spreading down the dimly lit passageway. Her feet slipped and slid in several inches of water and she slapped her hand against the wall to keep from falling flat on her ass.

She looked up to see Zane was running toward her. Okay. Not *her*. Toward the engine room. But she was so damn happy to see him, she'd take it. A triangle of tanned, hair roughed skin showed in the open V of his unbuttoned shorts while he finished tugging down his dark T-shirt.

As soon as he reached her, he grabbed her upper arms. "What the hell?"

His grip wasn't nearly as gentle, subversive, or insidious as it had been a few hours ago when he'd been trying to seduce her. But this was an emotion she was equipped to handle. The answer to his question was pretty obvious, but she answered anyway. "Engine room's flooding." She had to yell over the sound of the alarm.

Maggie, Ben, Saul, Colson, and Ryan crowded behind him. Nobody looked sleepy, although it was three A.M. A foot of water on the lower deck was an instant wake-up call.

Zane's fingers were warm on her bare skin. She remembered his kiss and shivered, but she didn't step back, and he didn't let go.

"Damaged pipe?" His mouth was a grim line while his eyes glinted with worry in the dim overhead lights.

"Maybe." There were dozens of ways the boat could be leaking. That was just one. "Could be a leak in the propeller shaft or corrosion in the hull. I have the pumps going, but I'll have to check them all." The whole freaking boat was a pile of rust.

"Ryan, with me," Zane said with admirable calm. Teal's heart was beating so fast it almost blocked out the strident screech of the alarm. "Maggie, coordinate everything from topside," he instructed. "Saul, Ben, and Colson help Teal."

She shivered as his thumb did a sneaky caress across her chilled skin. The man played touchy-feely even in an emergency. Unbelievable. Then his fingers tightened around her upper arm. His eyes seemed exceptionally blue as he held her gaze for several painful heartbeats. "Don't do anything stupid, Williams."

Too late. She'd kissed him back earlier tonight hadn't she? Teal tugged free. "Ditto."

*   *   *

Zane's heartbeat thudded in his ears as he tipped backward over the edge of the dive platform and slipped into the pitch-black water. He forced himself to keep his breathing slow and rhythmic even though his mind raced. Unless he found the source of that leak, he was screwed. They were all screwed. No more treasure. No more boat.

He and Ryan stayed together, their lights slicing through the darkness in long narrow beams. They stayed close to the hull as they swam down to the propeller shaft.

Damn it to hell. He started to second-guess himself. Perhaps he should've waited to salvage the *Vrijheid* until after he'd taken *Decrepit* in to dry dock for that overhaul. The ship had seemed sound enough. Maybe he'd just let himself believe it was. His eagerness to squeeze the last few weeks out of the season could well be putting everyone on board in danger. If nothing else, he might be responsible for sinking his own ship to lie beside the Dutch frigate for all time. His damn luck was taking a fucking vacation at the wrong time.

Ryan tapped his arm and jerked his head toward the hull as if to urge him forward. Normally he loved night diving, but there was a different vibe to the infinite liquid darkness when other people's lives and his entire operation was at stake.

Zane shook his head, trying to stay positive. If the leak did involve one of the shafts, it was repairable. Maybe it wouldn't even require putting in to port and taking a time-out in dry dock.

Before anything else could be done, he had to find the leak. It was a bad idea attempting to fix both the seal in the engine room and the problem down here at the same time, since that would let in more water from both simultaneously. Teal and the others had to be sweating bullets as they waited.

He shone his light on the rudder post. Yeah, that was where it was leaking all ri—What the fuck?

Frowning, Zane directed his flashlight beam directly on the flange. Everything surrounding it was corroded, dirty, or covered with verdigris. The scrapes and gouges made by a tool shone bright and obscene in the light.

Shit. This was no accident. Someone had gone to a lot of trouble to remove and then replace the nut.

Some scurvy son of a bitch had tried to sabotage his boat.

Chapter 5

"What are you doing here?" Zane asked Nick as his brother stepped into the *Decrepit*'s salon the next morning. Everyone was getting a late start due to being up half the damned night repairing the damage to the rudder. Zane was talking to Ben about the ramifications of sabotage when his brother strolled in.

"You asked me to drop this off on my way out." He set several large, heavy boxes—Zane's requested wine—on the counter. "Consider it dropped." He glanced around. "Why does everyone look like shit on a shingle? Up late partying last night? Not a wise move when you have to dive today, Ace."

Zane led his brother outside. "Someone removed a nut from the propeller shaft and took the flax out of the packing rings," he told Nick grimly as they walked out on deck. "We took on a couple of feet of water before we got it taken care of and repacked, but it was a bitch of a job. Especially in the fucking dark."

"You haven't left her for more than an hour that I know of in the last month or more. Leak like that would've been noticed before."

"Someone went to a hell of a lot of trouble to make sure it happened slowly, and when we were way the hell away from land. It could have happened anywhere and anytime in the last week."

"You've got to be kidding." Nick gave him a startled look. *"Sabotage?"*

Zane didn't doubt it for a second. "Tool marks all over the flange and bolt."

"Damn. I don't like the sounds of this, Ace. You're a lover, not a fighter; who could you possibly have pissed off enough to do something like that?"

Zane shrugged. "Nobody I know of." It had taken a couple of hours, but they'd all pulled together and managed to repair the damage and pump the water from the engine room. Still pissed off, Zane leaned against the rail. "Whoever the hell did this knew that removing the flax packing in the shaft wouldn't be noticed until it was too late."

"You can't be a hundred percent sure it was intentional," his brother pointed out reasonably. "The boat is older than dirt. Fittings come loose, the packing could've—"

"Fallen out? Not a chance in hell. That flange was removed, the packing pulled out, and the bolt put back. Those bastards knew it would be a slow steady leak."

"I hate to suggest this, but it's obviously someone on board who did this."

"Jesus, Nick. There's no one on board *Decrepit* who'd sabotage me. I've worked with these people for years, you know that. They all want this just as badly as I do."

Everybody except Teal, that was . . . Zane thought about that for a nanosecond and then dismissed her as a culprit. She was many things, but sneaky and underhanded, she was not. Teal would stare him in the eye as she drove a jackhammer through the hull, but she'd never do it behind his back.

"There's a lot of money at stake, Ace. Money is a great

motivator. People have sold each other out for far less than what's down there."

Zane shoved his hands into his pockets. "Someone sabotaged my ship, but it's not one of mine. Trust me. This isn't over by a long shot. And yeah—before you hit me over the head with it for the umpteenth fucking time—I'll outfit her with that security system you and Logan have been bitching about me getting for years. But in the meantime, it's a stellar day, we didn't sink beneath the waves, and good things are out there just waiting to be scooped up in all their glory." He smiled at his brother, not quite as sanguine as he was pretending to be. Something was rotten in Denmark, but until he figured it out there was no point flogging the problem to death. Time to change the subject. "You read my notes?"

"You'll watch your back, right?" Nick cautioned, then accepted that for now the subject was closed. "Yeah. Pretty damned exciting."

Zane leaned back against the rail. "I'm going to win the bet, you know."

"I hate to say this—but I think you just might."

"Want in on the action?"

Nick shook his head. God, it was weird seeing his brother with all that facial hair. He looked like someone else. "You do know you look like a deranged primate with all that fur on your ugly face, don't you?"

Nick laughed. "I'm not deranged."

"Matter of opinion."

"You can pay me back for hauling my ass out to play errand boy. I need Teal to take a look at an engine problem."

"Where's Mario?"

"Not here." Nick shot him an inquiring look. "Got a problem with your mechanic coming over to take a look, Ace?"

Zane thought of their kiss last night, then he thought of

Teal climbing aboard his brother's boat. Man, he didn't like the idea one bit. "Of course not."

As if she'd read their minds, she came up the ladder and walked on deck. Then peeled out of her wet suit. Even though he knew it wasn't intentional, watching Teal do the slow striptease out of the tight wet suit gave him an unwelcome erection. Which was starting to be a permanent condition.

Underneath, she wore a perfectly respectable, plain black maillot that looked as if it had been painted on. He frowned.

Nick waved a hand in front of his eyes to get his attention, which was when Zane realized he'd been staring like a randy schoolboy. Crapshitdamn.

"Hey, Teal!" Nick yelled. She was standing near the crane with Colson, who was showing her a sleek purple shell the size of his face. "Grab your sunglasses and get ready to see what a *real* ship looks like."

Zane narrowed his eyes as Teal smiled at his brother. The smile was wide and easy. She liked Nick, that was obvious. Hell, he liked his brother, too. Most of the time. But he didn't appreciate him waltzing in to swoop one of his team members off the ship. "How long are you keeping her?"

"Depends on how long I need her."

"In case you failed to notice, we're in the middle of a dive." They'd moved to a new site the day before.

"I thought the real dive didn't start until next week? This is just a decoy dive, right?" Teal glanced from Nick to Zane, and Nick smiled.

"Teal, my engine needs your expert eye. Can I kidnap you for a while?"

"Sure. Let me get a cover-up—"

Nick slung an arm around her shoulders. "Nah. Why bother?"

Why bother? Because as modest as her one-piece

swimsuit was, Teal was *naked* underneath it. Nick might appear cool, calm, and reasonable on the surface, but underneath ran a boiling inner nature that was lethal to women. His sex appeal was subversive. Stealthy. Unsuspecting females never saw it coming. Then *bam*! Teal might not know it but Nick was every bit as masterful with the ladies as Zane could be. On his worst day, of course.

Not happy with the turn of events, Zane pulled his T-shirt over his head. She wore armor when he was around and Lycra with Nick? One thin damn layer of nothing? Not acceptable.

"Here. Put this on." He glared at his brother, who hadn't said a word. Teal stood there mutely holding his shirt.

"She hasn't built up a tan yet," he muttered to no one in particular. "She'll fry." He cocked a brow at her. She was looking at him as if he'd lost his mind.

Hell. Maybe he had. "Don't hold it like you're about to swab the deck with it," he snapped. "Put it on, woman."

*   *   *

Teal admired the *Scorpion*'s sleek clean lines as Nick brought the launch alongside the dive platform to tie up. The megayacht was a little smaller than Zane's boat, but the contrast between *Scorpion*'s crisp white paint, miles of gleaming bright work, and immaculate teak decking, and Zane's *Decrepit* was like night and day. Nick's boat boasted a hot tub and a helicopter pad as well. She couldn't imagine anyone less likely to frolic in a hot tub than Nick Cutter. Now *Zane* was another story.

"She's a beauty, Nick." Zane's T-shirt enveloped her from shoulder to knee, and smelled like him. It was enough to make her even dizzier than the short, fast trip between the two boats had done.

"My home away from home. Engine room's this way." He led the way down several sets of stairs and through various companionways before opening the door into the bindingly white engine room.

Teal's heart actually skipped a beat with the sheer magnificence surrounding her. "God, this is *beautiful*." Stepping inside, she took a deep breath and let the calming perfume of diesel fuel fill her lungs. Fortunately, the nausea wasn't as bad as it had been at the start of the trip. Maybe after almost going down with the ship she'd found her sea legs.

Nick leaned against the open door. "I'm picking up my engineer, Mario, on the way to my site, but that won't be for a week. We're experiencing some sort of valve issue. Would you mind taking a look?"

"Mostly with the intake valves?" she asked, heading over to the pristine engines. "Dropped and excessive valve recession?"

"Something like that," he said dryly behind her.

Teal forgot he was there as she checked the intake air for proper filtration. "Hmm. I'm not sure about the quality of the metal in the seats and valves . . ." She checked the fuel air ratio control next, then straightened, wiping her hands on the clean rag Nick handed her. "I'd give Caterpillar a call and have them do more tests, then they can provide the results in writing for your engineer. I know they're making a lot more intake valve lash adjustments when they perform adjustments for older—" She looked up at him. "You don't care, do you?"

Nick smiled. "Not as much as you do. Will the problem hold until Mario gets here?"

"Sure." Which she bet her last dollar Nick knew perfectly well. "Sorry I couldn't be more help."

"Knowing it's not a serious problem helps enormously. Come on. I'll feed you lunch before I take you back. It's the least I can do for dragging you over here to work."

"Are you kidding? I could happily spend a month down here."

He firmly took her arm, and escorted her out of the ER. "Instead we'll be topside enjoying seafood fettuccini."

He showed her to a luxurious head on the main deck so she could wash up, and told her to meet him in the galley.

He was prepping lunch by the time she got there. He poured her a soda and instructed she sit on one of the sleek black leather bar stools at the counter. The *Scorpion* was high tech and deluxe, but Teal was surprised at how attached she'd grown to the *Decrepit,* and wouldn't trade Nick's amenities for those on the Zane's boat. Well, except for his engines.

"What are you up to, Nick?" She sipped the Coke at the black granite counter in his expansive galley while Nick expertly prepared the shrimp and scallops in a large frying pan. A big pot of water boiled on a back burner. The fragrance of the buttery garlic mixed with the seafood perfumed the room and made her stomach grumble pleasantly.

"Up to?" He shot her a puzzled look through the steam. "Maybe I'm flirting with a pretty woman on a beautiful day?"

"And maybe you're not," Teal told him dryly. "I'm sure if you put your mind to it, you'd be irresistible, but since flirting isn't on your agenda, what's going on?"

Ice tinkled in her glass as she shifted on the bar stool, sending him a mildly suspicious look. Really, all three of the Cutters had lethal charm in varying degrees. And God help *any* woman when they turned it on, as Nick had been doing in his cool, subtle way for the last fifteen minutes. Just because she didn't play the romance game didn't mean she was stupid.

"An enjoyable lunch with charming company." He smiled. "Do you like fresh parmesan?"

"Sure." Nick was high-octane energy set on idle. Teal suspected that with him, what he felt was hidden just below the surface. He wanted something—and it wasn't her.

"I appreciate the lunch, but we both know that you didn't need me in that engine room today," she said as he tossed fresh pasta into the boiling water. "And I should point out that if you *are* trying to seduce me, charm me, or whatever me, I'm Cutter-proof, so why don't you just get to the point?"

He laughed, a deep relaxed rumble. "Hell, I must be losing my touch if a woman has to ask what I'm up to."

Teal smiled ruefully. Even with that pirate-like thick beard, Nick was good looking. The fact that he had Zane's electric blue eyes was disconcerting, however. "I'm sure you haven't," she told him, swirling her glass in the moist ring on the counter. "But I'm pretty much immune. And since I'm sure you didn't sail all the way out into the middle of the ocean to see *me,* I suspect it was to jerk your brother's chain for some reason. Mind telling me what that reason is, or is that a deep, dark, Cutter secret?"

"I just dropped off some stuff Zane wanted from Cutter Cay. Then he mentioned the leak." He paused to look at her. "The situation concerns me, Teal. A lot. Yeah, the *Decrepit* lives up to its name, but my brother keeps his boat well maintained nonetheless. This was no accident." Nick grated a wedge of fresh parmesan cheese, whisking it into a cream mixture. "You know Zane. He's never met anyone he didn't like. I suggested an accident, which we all know is highly unlikely. A member of his crew? 'Course he adamantly denied it. Ace's a straight shooter. What you see is what you get," his brother told her unnecessarily. "Unfortunately, Zane assumes everyone else is the same way. He's too damned trusting. This stinks of sabotage, and I'm concerned the danger is all too real." Nick poured out the water, returned the large pot to the stove, and added the seafood in the frying pan to the noodles.

"I'd like to hear your opinion on the missing flax and tampered-with screw."

"You could ask Ben, or Ryan."

"I value your opinion."

She flushed with pleasure. It had been awhile since anyone had wanted her opinion on anything other than an engine. "I also think it was sabotage," she admitted. "But then, despite how casual Zane acts about what happened, I think he knows that, too." She took a sip of her soda. "Your brother's a smart guy. He knows his boat from stem to stern. And he's not in any way naive. He doesn't trust everyone, Nick." He'd told her to get the hell out of his bed that fateful night, hadn't he?

"You're a levelheaded woman, Teal." Nick ladled the fettuccini into two enormous, shallow, Italian-looking bowls and added another dash of grated cheese. "I'm asking that you keep an eye out as well. You're the new kid on the block, so the crew will have their guard down around you. Maybe you'll see something strange, or someone will say something that doesn't sound right. If that happens, let Zane know ASAP. If someone's willing to punch a hole in the bottom of my brother's boat with all hands on board, then they'll stop at nothing to get whatever it is they want."

Teal rubbed a chill from her upper arms. "What would they gain by sinking his boat?"

"Putting Zane's *Decrepit* permanently out of the running would certainly give another salvor a clear field to arguably the largest treasure since the *Atocha*."

The chill turned into a shudder of foreboding. Teal put her iced drink down, and wiped her damp hands on the hem of Zane's T-shirt. "The treasure he described would be worth killing for if it truly exists." Which Zane believed one hundred percent, and she'd seen some with her own two eyes.

"If my brother's done his homework, then it exists." Nick nudged her plate closer. "Pigheaded idiot. I'd hate to see him in danger because of a silly bet."

Teal rolled her eyes. "Jeez. Another bet?" She remembered the boys used to bet on anything and everything, even when they'd been kids. Zane had, in fact, bet *her* her first bet at six, the day he and his father had brought Sam to Tortola to pick her up from the airport. She'd been violently, embarrassingly sick on her first boat ride back to Cutter Cay. Zane had bet her she couldn't stop puking before they hit dry land. She'd managed. Barely. The thought made her smile. She'd even won a prize. A prize she'd treasured for over twenty years.

"I *do* remember *several* bets you guys made. Particularly that summer you bet Zane he wouldn't eat a live crab. Whole." She laughed. "He did it too. You do know he threw up for hours after that?"

"He swore it walked up his throat."

"I'm sure it did. Encouraged by his finger."

"Ah, to be twelve again." Nick's stern mouth twitched. "The current bet is that whoever brings in the most valuable treasure wins ten grand *and* becomes CEO for the next year."

Teal shook her head and smiled. Had Nick lost his mind? "First, if Zane finds what he believes is down there, it will be worth a million times that. And second, he'd hate being CEO. I've never met a guy more determined to feel the wind in his hair and a boat rocking beneath his feet. All the paperwork involved would drive him nuts. So I sincerely doubt ten thousand dollars and a suit will appeal to him at all."

Nick lifted a brow. "You know him pretty well. The point isn't the prize. It's winning. Zane takes this betting shit seriously. I hope to hell he doesn't let it cloud his good judgment, that's all."

"He's very much aware of what's going on around him, Nick. Zane won't do anything that would put his boat or his crew in jeopardy." Except that he was a daredevil and thrived on a challenge. Teal heaved an inward sigh. "I'll keep my eyes open."

After a moment, Nick nodded. Then indicated her plate. "Eat."

Teal forked a bite of fettuccini into her mouth. The rich, savory taste of seafood, garlic, and cream burst over her tongue. "God, this is amazing."

"My culinary talents notwithstanding, the engine and Zane's problem weren't the only reasons I asked you to lunch," Nick told her. "I wanted to check that you're doing okay. I know you didn't want to join his crew. I felt bad, taking part in strong-arming you into joining Zane's team."

Her eyes widened. "You came to check up on me?" The very concept stunned her.

Nick gave a one-shoulder shrug. "You're family."

Her mouth went dry, and her heart actually, *physically* hurt at the very idea. Nobody had ever championed her. Ever worried about her. It was a strange and uncomfortable fit. "You don't even know me."

"We've known Sam all our lives. We consider your *father* family, and by association, you as well." Nick reached out and covered her hand with his. "I don't know what happened back in San Francisco. Logan said you took the job pretty fast—you didn't even know Sam was sick before you said yes. But I have a feeling whatever it was, was bad. I just want you to know I'm here for you, Teal, no matter what you need. So are Logan and Zane."

She rubbed her upper arm with her free hand. The sun still shone, but a familiar chill seeped into her bones. They didn't know anything. No one knew what her marriage had been like, because no one knew she'd even been married. And she intended to keep it that way.

"Nothing *happened* in San Francisco, Nick," she said uncomfortably, sliding her hand from beneath his and resuming eating a meal she suddenly didn't want. "Thanks for your concern. Really."

Something must've shown on her face, because he suddenly asked, "What about Dennis Ross?"

His question caught her completely unaware and her

jaw dropped. "D—How do you kn—Who told you about Denny?"

"Let's put it this way. I know things. Sam mentioned you moved from there to Orange Beach in a hurry round about the time my dad died. He expressed concern. I looked into it."

She'd tried to make her voice less hysterical on the phone when Sam had called her as she raced to the airport, to tell her Zane's dad had died, and the funeral was the following week. "Does anyone else . . . *Know* things?" she demanded, appalled.

"Not unless you choose to tell them."

Her bare toes curled. "I don't."

"Fine."

"It was a fairly amicable divorce." God, how to explain she'd been an idiot? If one considered fleeing in the middle of the night, shearing off waist-length hair and dying it black in a seedy hotel room, hiding in a multitude of small and large towns, and peeing her pants every time she'd heard a knock on the door *amicable*.

"I don't want to pry. Just making sure you're okay."

A lightbulb went on. "You think *Denny* is responsible for the leak in the *Decrepit*?"

Nick shrugged. "Not out of the realm of possibility. Especially if he's paying you a large chunk of change in alimony."

"He's not even paying me a *small* chunk of change in alimony. Not a red cent. And I'm fine with that. I didn't want any paper trail. He doesn't know where I am, Nick, and I'd like to keep it that way." Nick's eyes, so much like Zane's, were like powerful blue lasers.

"He knows where *Sam* is, however. Would you mind if I discreetly checked to see where Ross is and what he's up to?"

A cold chill prickled across her skin. "I don't want his

cage rattled, Nick. He's not a nice guy, to put it mildly, and I don't want him coming back at me if you—"

"I know people who are discreet," he assured her. "He won't know. I promise."

How did Nick know "people" in San Francisco? "I think it's a waste of time, but if it'll make you feel better knowing he has nothing to do with this, then go ahead." And now she'd be looking over her shoulder waiting for Denny to show up. Teal sucked in a sigh. Just when she'd thought it was safe to get back in the water . . . Cue ominous freaking music. The *Jaws* analogy fit perfectly.

"And talking about Sam," she said to change the subject. "Did you see him before you left? How is he?" she asked casually. Zane had spoken to him, but Sam was a master of understatement and reticence. Seeing how he was would give Teal a truer picture, if only he'd let her close.

She'd flown all the way from Alabama to Cutter Cay, and he hadn't even worked up the interest to see her before she left with Zane.

Instead, he'd called *Zane* to tell him he'd changed his mind and was going in for treatment. Not his daughter. That stung.

The time she should have spent on Cutter Cay was supposed to have given her time to connect with him. Now she was a hundred miles away, and he was communicating with everyone but herself.

"He's doing as okay as can be expected." Nick told her. And obviously hadn't sent a message for Nick to pass along either. What the hell had she expected? That he'd welcome her with open arms? He hadn't before. Now that he was so sick, his daughter was obviously the last thing on his mind. She got it. It hurt a bit, but she got it. "Good. He's a strong guy, he might surprise us all."

"I didn't have a great relationship with my father." Nick said casually, leaving off the word "either," though it hung unspoken in the air between them. "We were just too dissimilar. He was like quicksilver. Zane's a lot like him."

She crossed her arms over her belly, not really sure she wanted to talk about fathers. Or Zane. Both were uncomfortable subjects that she'd tried over the years to analyze, and ended up with more pain than answers. She was better off leaving both men out of her thoughts.

"The only time I've ever seen Zane blind drunk was at Dad's funeral," Nick told her. "Of the three of us, he was hardest hit by his death. They were so damn alike—outgoing daredevils, always the life of the party, the center of attention. But they're different too. Zane had a hard time seeing Dad's faults, although God only knows they were in flashing Technicolor. Logan and I, maybe because we're older, saw the other side of him that wasn't so pretty. Women were a way of keeping score. A passing fancy easily obtained, and just as easily disposed of."

"I think Zane saw exactly who your father was and has tried to emulate him since he was in diapers," Teal told him, feeling pissy. She didn't need to be warned off. She got it.

Nick drank from his glass and gave her a considering look. "I think Zane fools a lot of people with his personality. But there's more to him than being the life of the party."

Right. He had a well of hidden depth just waiting for the right woman to plumb. If she was beautiful enough, if she was amusing enough, if she was—whatever. Hell. If she had a freaking *pulse*. *That* was Zane's kind of woman.

Teal turned to stare over the calm, crystal blue water at the *Decrepit*. Zane and Colson stood near the crane, talking to Maggie.

The sun gleamed off his shoulders and hair, and a glint of light sparked off his earring. A pang of intense longing pressed deep inside her chest. Yesterday's kiss seemed a lifetime ago. She didn't want him to know how much that kiss had affected her. Kissing Zane, she thought, wishing . . . Her breath snagged in her throat. Kissing Zane was as insubstantial as holding glitter in her fist. He'd kissed her because he could. She'd kissed him back because she couldn't—*not*.

But it couldn't happen again. Wouldn't happen again. No matter how wonderful, no matter *how* freaking tempting. She was done with being meaningless.

As if he felt her eyes on him, Zane suddenly looked up, glanced over at the *Scorpion*, and waved. Cocky devil.

After a nanosecond, Teal casually waved back, then turned back to Nick, intentionally leaning in just a bit closer to him. "Everyone has faults."

"Yeah. But Dad liked his alcohol, drank too damn much. Other than that one night for Zane, none of us do. We saw Dad passed out enough times to know we didn't want to go down that slippery slope. It was no secret that he was a womanizer, and his behavior hurt my mother intensely."

That she knew. Gossip on the island was that Mrs. Cutter had taken the boys away. "You all went to Oregon?"

"She knew about his affairs, but what could she do? She was stuck with three boys to raise while Dad went off on the next grand adventure. He usually took a woman with him. And he cheated on them as well the moment he reached port. When Mom finally had enough, she took us to her mother in Portland. I don't know what precipitated it, if it was just the last straw on the camel's back, or something else, but she filed for a divorce."

"But your father got custody?"

"By default. We were in Portland less than a month. Dad was a very wealthy man. He wasn't going to tolerate anyone, even our mother, taking us away from him. He hauled us back to Cutter Cay and brought in the expensive lawyers and fought her for custody with everything he had."

Teal sat up straight. "But he drank. He cheated."

"Yeah. Chances were, he wouldn't have won. But it didn't matter—Mom was hit by a drunk driver a few months later. He didn't let us go to the funeral." Nick shrugged like it was ancient history, but Teal felt his pain.

"So we adapted to life without her, kids are resilient. We had a great life on the island. There were always women around. Long leggy blondes, short curvy brunettes, sleek redheads—"

"I get it." Nick was flogging a dead horse. She so freaking got it.

"We liked most of Dad's lady friends—he'd bring them home for a month or two if he was between trips, and when we were old enough, we'd go with him."

"What does this have to do with me?" She shouldn't bring it up, the night Zane got so drunk he didn't remember her, but it was like touching a bruise to see if it still hurt. It did. "I'm not sure why you're telling me this."

"I guess I'm trying to explain where Zane's coming from. We had a hard-drinking, womanizing father, and no mother. He—"

"Zane's a womanizer. Not that it matters. His lifestyle doesn't affect me at all. And let me point out that you and Logan didn't pick up those habits from your father. Zane is exactly who he *wants* to be."

"Teal . . ."

She uncurled her legs and rose, emotional blast shields firmly back in place. "I'll take care of these dishes, then I really should go back to see what Maggie and Saul found. This is a decoy site. We didn't expect to uncover anything."

He rubbed the bridge of his nose. "I have people to do dishes. Just take a break. I guarantee they won't go anywhere without you on that hunk of junk."

Teal raised her brow in defense of the *Decrepit,* surprised that she felt a sense of ownership. "She's well maintained, don't let her looks fool you."

"You *like* that rust bucket?"

"Well, let's not get too effusive about it, but yeah. She's growing on me. Warts and all."

He studied her face with obvious interest. "You and Zane are the only ones that feel that way."

Chapter 6

Nick ferried Teal back several hours later. Zane had kept a watchful eye on the *Scorpion*. If Nick was in a seducing frame of mind, she wouldn't stand a chance. Had he? Had they?

He waited while his brother handed her on board the *Decrepit*. Her hair was windblown, her nose and cheeks a little pink, and he loved what she did for his T-shirt. He wanted to take it off of her. Slowly. "We found a wreck that hadn't been completely cleaned out. Nothing big, just some coins. Go take a turn cleaning so Maggie can take a break," Zane told her.

"Of course." She flashed him a narrow-eyed look, then smiled at his brother. "Thanks for a fun lunch, Nick." She strolled off, all long legs and attitude. He admired those luscious legs and imagined pressing his mouth to the tender spot just behind her knee, right in the sensitive bend . . .

He turned on Nick. "Lunch? *That's* why you needed my mechanic? To help you eat *lunch*?"

Nick ignored him, his eyes fixed on Teal as she headed inside. "She's had some . . . issues."

"Yeah. Having a *friend* putting the moves on her. What

the hell were you *thinking,* Spock? You have no right to mess with her. She's not like the women we know. Under that cranky, sassy exterior she's . . . I don't know. Kinda fragile, I think. She's not up to your speed. Seriously."

"Or yours." Nick seemed to choose his words carefully as he said, "Practice what you preach, Ace. I think she was abused."

Zane's body went icy cold, then blazed with heat. Oh, no. Oh, fucking no. He didn't want to hear this. But it *fit,* God damn it. Not Sam—unless it was neglect. "Abusive boyfriend?"

Christ—The thought made him sick, but the emotional disconnect, the bits and pieces he'd observed. Ah, hell. Anyone who hurt someone smaller and weaker than himself needed to be castrated and hung up to dry. That anyone would hurt *Teal* was unacceptable on every level.

Thinking, Nick stuck his hands in his pant pockets and stared at the spot where Teal had stood moments before. He turned back to Zane as if a decision had been made. "Husband. She was married."

Zane stared at his brother. "*Married?* Teal? Are you sure? She hasn't mentioned it, and Sam's never said a word."

"She didn't want anyone to know. I'm breaking a confidence here, Ace."

"Why would she keep a husband a secret from her own father? Wait a minute. How do *you* know?" Zane pointed his finger at Nick's chest. "Did she tell you?" And why was she confiding in his brother?

"She let it slip over lunch that she didn't want her ex to know where she is. Think I'll do some digging."

"Jesus, Nick. No fucking digging. That's a gross invasion of privacy." Zane clenched his hands into fists.

"Your boat was fucking *sabotaged,* Ace. I think you need to cover all your bases, don't you?"

"You think the *ex-husband*'s responsible?"

"Got any other likely perps? Her employer—us—has

a right to question any suspicious people in her background."

"First of all, I'm her employer at the moment. Not you. And the fact that she was married and divorced has no bearing on her job performance."

"True. But she's *family*. I think that warrants a little more than the usual reference check. I'll be discreet. If the guy pans out, you can cross one more suspect off your list."

Family? Zane imagined kids with Teal's choppy bangs and fuck-you attitude, then wondered if he'd had too much sun. "Since I didn't know about the asshole, he was never on my list. But yeah." His conscience warred over the right thing to do, then he waffled. "Go ahead. Let me know what turns up. I won't mention you told me about this guy. But if there's a need to deal with him, I'll take care of it myself. After that, butt out, Spock. I mean it."

Nick gave him an odd look at his vehemence. "There's a story there."

"Fine. But it's not your story to discover. Drop it."

"Dropped. As long as I can look into his background and confirm where he's been in the last week. Fair enough?" Nick gave him a hard look. "And let me return that warning. Don't *you* mess with her, Zane. I'm serious. If she's not up to my fighting weight, she's sure as shit not anywhere close to yours, Mr. Love-'em-and-leave-'em. Women like Teal don't do *temporary*. Just sayin'."

"Don't you have your own boat?"

Nick went back to the *Scorpion* and Zane went up to the wheelhouse to talk to Teal about his plans for the dive.

Why would a woman keep her marriage a secret? Why would *Teal* keep her marriage a secret?

Since there were a dozen answers, all of them shitty, Zane decided to do a little digging of his own.

The fact that Nick was ballsy enough to give him a warning fucking pissed Zane off. He wasn't *doing* anything, God damn it!

*   *   *

"Do we have a squatter?" Zane asked, looking around the engine room as he stepped through the door. It was the creak of daybreak the morning after her lunch with Nick. *Well, hell.* She hadn't heard the door open. He was as stealthy as a panther.

He was wearing black board shorts. *Just* shorts and that gold hoop gleaming in his ear. No damn shirt or shoes. He was tanned, his muscles covered by taut, satin smooth skin. An arrow of crisp, black hair matted his chest and disappeared beneath the waistband. His ripped abs looked as though he did five hundred crunches a day. In between other calisthenics she didn't want to think about.

Teal's mouth went as dry as a seized engine. Her stomach muscles clenched. *Damn it.* Five minutes earlier, and he'd have caught her sleeping on the floor, hugging her pillow. Thank God she'd tucked her bedroll out of sight moments before.

Unfortunately, the easy chair and lamp she'd dragged out of her cabin yesterday were right there for all but a blind man to see. Her clothes from last night, as well as the damp towel from her pre-dinner shower, were slung over one arm of the chair. Her book on Caribbean sea life rode the other arm.

"What are you doing here?" she demanded suspiciously, trying to appear taller. She was unnerved by his close proximity, and annoyed that she felt that way.

He shot her a stern look. "Wednesday morning surprise engine room inspection. Didn't you get the memo?"

"It's Thursday. And you should've started inspecting these engines before now," she said, humoring him. "You have crappy fuel," she told him crossly as she pretended she was in full body armor instead of just a couple of layers of soft cotton. "It's cloudy and it stinks. The fuel jets are probably clogged with gunk, but I won't know for sure until I can crack it apart when we get back." Actually, she'd been surprised at how clean and well maintained everything in the engine room was. Sam, of course. The engines were old, but in pretty good shape. But she wasn't about to tell him that.

They hadn't been alone together since the night they'd kissed, a kiss he'd clearly forgotten, but one that was insidiously, indelibly stamped on her memory no matter how hard she tried to jettison it.

He was standing too close. A predator about to strike. He was so blasted big and took up too much space. Tall, and beautifully proportioned, his body was athletic, his muscles developed from hard physical labor. He smelled of soap and fresh air. He needed a shave, which was par for his course, but his hair was still wet and slicked back off his face, exposing his cheekbones and piercing blue eyes. He looked like a fallen angel, or a sexy underwear model, Teal thought sourly. Really. He should wear a warning sign around his neck. A big, red, stop-sign-sized warning sign.

His startling eyes, clear, sharp, and intrusive, inspected her bare legs before slowly returning to her face. She felt that sweep of his eyes as if he was touching her skin. Lightly. She shivered, and his lips twitched.

Flirting was Zane's stock in trade. His weapon of choice. It wasn't personal, he was just in constant training. God help the woman whom he considered the main event. She tried not to be charmed by him and lost the battle.

She took a step back. She'd entirely lost the thread of conversation and had to mentally scramble to connect the dots. "You *really* should wear long sleeves and pants in here. There are all sorts of dangers in an engine room." Zane freaking Cutter being one of them.

He looked at her tank top and plaid shorts. "Yes, Pot. By the way. I want my T-shirt back. It's my favorite."

She'd slept with it covering her pillow. Thank God she

hadn't slept *in* it. The shirt was tucked in her bedroll. "Sorry. I had to use it for cleanup when I got grease on my hands. It went in the incinerator." Teal leaned her hip on the small built-in table as far away from him as she could get.

"It wasn't a gift," he said, absently prowling around her engine room like a hungry panther. "It was a loan. You can buy me a new one next time we're in port."

He strolled farther into the room, which wasn't nearly big enough for two of them. He looked around. There wasn't that much floor space; two engines and two people, plus all the other stuff, like the generator and spare batteries. A chair and a lamp. And her bedroll, which he pulled out from behind the chair. He dumped it on the seat cushion, and raised a brow. "Don't sweat the small stuff."

"Somebody has to." Damn him, he was invading her personal space. Did the freaking man have no boundaries? The smell of soap on his skin made her dizzy, but she wasn't going to back up. She lifted her chin and gave him a bland look. "If you've ordered the new engine, you'd better get a bigger generator while you're at it. I'm not going to be part of you trying to weasel through inspection to have this one re-rated."

He grinned, the insult bouncing off his broad shoulders. The way Zane was looking at her heated her skin and made her—Nothing. It made her *nothing*.

"Why are you sacked out in here? You have a perfectly good cabin, and I think we discussed this before—a very comfortable queen-sized bed."

"How do you know how comfortable the bed is? Did you sleep there with one of your too-numerous-to-count girlfriends?" More than likely, she thought. She was *ecstatic* she wasn't sleeping on that skanky mattress.

"I bought the mattress. The only bouncing I did on it was at the store."

"I prefer sleeping on the floor. I like to listen to my engines at night when it's quiet. Consider my sleeping arrangements a diagnostic tool. I won't even charge you overtime."

"Good of you."

"I fixed the electronic sensor that someone,"—she gave him a pointed look—"no names mentioned, jerry-rigged."

She, better than anyone, knew that what one saw wasn't always what was hidden underneath. The *Decrepit* looked like a piece of crap. But, while the engines were past their prime, they'd been kept in tip-top condition.

"I'm not asking for a report. I know how hard you work. You're doing a fantastic job. No complaints from me."

"Then what *are* you doing here?"

There was a dangerous gleam in his eyes as he reached out and casually tucked her hair behind one ear. The shiver *that* elicited went from her ear all the way to her toes, and paused to tingle at several strategic points in between. He was good at the subtle touches, and little flirtations that lulled a woman into letting down her guard.

"To ask you to be my partner on the first official *Vrijheid* dive." He gave her one of his devastatingly effective, boyish grins that instinctively made her smile back.

"I don't want to wait until next week. People will eventually follow us anyway. Might as well officially start the show. We're going to do it, Williams. See what bounty she's willing to relinquish to us after all these years. I want you there with me."

Already disoriented by the light brush of his fingers against her cheek, the comment stopped Teal in her tracks. Her heart did a little tap dance in her chest. She blinked him into focus. "You're asking me to partner you on the first official dive?" His happiness was contagious.

His teeth flashed white. "Yeah."

She had no idea how he'd gotten so close. She smelled toothpaste on his breath. She wanted to place her hand on his face, to feel the soft prickle of his unshaven jaw under her fingertips. She had the crazy need to run her hands down his strong throat until she got to his chest . . . She felt the insane urge to lean into him. Her heartbeat thudded in her chest and in all her pulse points. She wanted to lean into him, just to feel the heat of his body against hers.

Kiss me. Get the hell out of my space. Kiss me.

His blue, blue eyes moved over her, a slow hot lick that stripped her bare. "Teal—"

Her skin hummed. A vibration that had started between her legs and spread outward from the epicenter. She put out her arm to keep him away, but somehow her palm flattened on his chest and she ended up with her fingers splayed over his heart. Lightning zinged up her arm from the contact, sparking a darker need that she had to . . . put . . . a . . . stop . . . to . . .

His heart beat with an unsteady rhythm exactly like her own. The blasted man had his own gravitation field and it just pulled her right in, willy-nilly.

Time to put a stop to this. She sucked a breath into constricted lungs and had to wet her lips with her tongue to push the words out. "Do *not* think you can just stroll in here whenever you like, and kiss m—"

"Haven't kissed you." His voice was low and velvety, his eyes seemed to glow demonically in the dim light. "Yet." He cupped her face between his palms and pulled her mouth up to meet his. This kiss wasn't suggestive, or insidious. He went from zero to a hundred in point zero seconds.

Heat scalded her body as he plundered her mouth in a ravishing kiss that curled her toes and set her entire body on fire.

She yielded with a small whimper, wrapping her arms around his neck and standing on her toes to give him better access. He was fully aroused, but, God, so was she. His tongue swept against hers and she was nothing more than pure sensation—

"Zane? Hey buddy, you in here?"

Zane reluctantly released Teal, hyperaware of her beside him as Ryan swung his body into the engine room at warp speed. "*Sea Witch* just arrived," he said, out of breath and annoyed. His sun-bleached hair stood on end, and he still held a flipper in one hand.

It took Zane a minute to come out of the sensual haze brought on by Teal's kiss. "You've got to be shitting me." He ran a hand through his hair "How close?" The last time, *Sea Witch* had dropped anchor a hundred feet off the *Decrepit,* crossing anchor lines in the process. If that was again the case, then Zane and the redhead were about to have words. Again.

"The required mile," Ryan answered. "She seems to be staying put. For now."

Tolerable. "We'll keep an eye on her." The captain of the *Sea Witch* always seemed to know where the Cutter brothers were. Her boat had been bobbing a mile away at the last three of Zane's salvages, and he knew she'd followed both Nick and Logan on several occasions over the last few years. She was a royal pain in the ass. Worse, she'd stolen thousands of dollars' worth of treasure from right under their noses.

He thought of the damaged rudder. Was she trying to up the ante with the attempted sabotage? He wouldn't put it past her to try and get him out of the way long enough to harvest even more of his loot.

Or, hell. What if Teal's ex *had* decided to come pee in his pond as Nick had suggested?

Teal crossed to the laptop computer on the small table

near the engines. Once again all business, she'd opened the Cat ET, Caterpillar's Electronic Technician diagnostic tool.

Trying to pretend that kiss hadn't happened? Nice try sweetheart, Zane thought, seeing the flush riding her cheeks. Jesus, she had a pretty mouth, and if Ryan hadn't blasted in like the hounds of hell were on his ass, Zane would be finished kissing his mechanic within an inch of her life right about now. He pulled his gaze back to Ryan.

"The *Sea Witch* is one of the vultures we've been trying to throw off with our decoy sites. She's a major thorn in our side," Ryan expained to Teal. Then he turned back to Zane. "I've told you before, that freaking woman has it in for you, buddy. Mark my words. She's a bottom-feeder. I wouldn't put it past her to have messed with the rudder herself. We'd all be smart to keep our eyes on her flaunty little ass. If we turn our backs, she's going to be in our wreck, helping herself again."

Teal turned to Zane. "Can she do that?"

"Impossible to find a wreck and *not* to have some friendly competition. So yeah. To a point. And whatever she retrieves, she has to cough up our percentage. *If* we know about it."

"Isn't there anything you can do?"

"Not unless she does something illegal, which she hasn't so far." Unless he could prove it. If she *had* messed with his boat, her ass was going to be toast. "But Ryan's right, she's like a damned pilot fish, feeding off our ecto-parasites and leftovers."

"I'm guessing she isn't old and homely?" Teal addressed Ryan.

"Late twenty-something, stacked, redhead."

"Ahh. Some girlfriend whose name you inconveniently forgot?" Teal asked Zane sweetly, folding the towel she'd flung on the chair. It left a damp mark on the upholstery. "Did you try honey, or sweetheart?"

"I don't know her personally, nor do I want to. She's nothing more than a modern-day pirate." He turned to Ryan. "Let's increase security and take all precautions. And just to be on the safe side, get a couple of guys in from St. Maarten to beef up security for the duration."

"Aye, aye, Captain." Ryan gave him a mock salute. "I'll take care of that right away." He glanced from Zane to Teal and back again, hummed, "Hmm." And walked out.

"This woman sounds dangerous."

"Up to now she's been a pain in the ass, but dangerous? Nah. Doesn't mean she couldn't be. Once she knows the value of the treasure, and if she's as smart as I believe she is, all bets might be off. Money, the kind of money I know is down there, can make people greedy."

"But she doesn't know what the *Vrijheid* carried or the value, does she?

"She doesn't give a rat's ass. She's ripped off artifacts from us valued at a couple of dollars, and shit worth several thousand dollars. No rhyme or reason, she just wants it, so she *takes* it. She's made it her business to know where all Cutter Salvage boats are at any given time. Just my bad luck that I'm her target this week. As to the how: Anyone with a computer can find out simply enough where a ship is at any moment," he told her grimly.

"What do we do now?"

"We're going to drop anchor and start hauling ass."

*   *   *

Teal hoped this was what heaven was like when she died. Peaceful. Tranquil. Solitary. And as clear a blue as Zane's eyes. The water felt like warm silk against her exposed skin. The BC strapped around her chest had nothing to do with how buoyant she felt. She and Zane swam side by side. Close enough to touch, but not. Their limbs were in perfect sync as they seemed to fly in slow-mo through the crystalline water in a lazy descent. They carried metal detectors and each had a goody basket.

Above them, the shadow of the *Decrepit*'s keel cut a dark footprint out of the early morning sunlight filtering through the water. Schools of brightly colored fish moved as one, their tiny bodies neon red as they darted and twisted in perfectly choreographed unison.

Zane put a hand on her shoulder and pointed at the blacktip shark passing them in the fast lane. Teal held her breath as the streamlined body swam within ten feet of them. Zane shook his head, indicating that she inhale. Exhale. Holding one's breath on a dive was dangerous. She knew better.

He glanced at her to make sure she was breathing normally, observing the little bubbles streaming from her regulator. After she gave him the OK signal, he went back to keeping an eye on the shark. He'd drawn his diving knife from the scabbard on his thigh before he'd stopped her. A precaution. The shark didn't look interested in them. Brown on top and a dirty white below, with a white racing stripe down its side, the shark was almost as long as Teal was tall.

They hung suspended, hands and flippers barely moving as it turned to look at them. Beady blinkless eyes seemed to calculate their body weight and caloric value before it swam off. Noted and ignored.

Teal raised her brows behind the mask and pantomimed eating. Zane pointed at her, then to the retreating shark. She shook her head. She didn't want to eat *it*. He grinned around his regulator and rocked his hand back and forth, then pointed down.

Below, in bits and pieces, and buried under white sand and lumps of coral, lay the *Vrijheid*. The sand rippled with currents like a veil. In her mind's eye, Teal saw the broken frigate whole and glorious as she sailed halfway around the world to plunder priceless treasures from well-armed galleons, and thumb her nose at the Spanish.

There was very little to identify her now. Just a few indistinguishable lumps and bumps on the ocean floor. Any one of those lumps and bumps and intriguing shapes could be disguising a cache of pirate gold or a trunk-full of jewelry fit for a queen.

Even though she'd seen the *Vrijheid* in her final resting place the week before, seeing the frigate again made Teal's heart dance and her pulse race.

Zane pointed to his watch. She checked her own. Gave him a thumbs-up. She was so ready to get started. Zane wiggled his arm, warning her to keep her eyes out for any hiding moray eels. She shot him an impatient look, too happy, having too much fun to be annoyed with him today. He'd given her a ten-minute lecture on the whats, whens, and whys before he'd announced her ready to dive.

He yelled what was probably *yahoo,* then spread his arms wide, giving her the entire wreck. Bubbles rose and danced in a column over his head, growing larger as they neared the surface. Teal bowed at the waist and, twisting her body, swam off to explore.

She could've stayed there all day, but aware of the time limit, started dusting the sand. Zane did the same, working about twelve feet away. She saw a dull gleam, mostly hidden beneath the grains. A piece of yellow plastic? How disappointing. She went to pull it free so she could dispose of it topside.

Not plastic she realized, giving it a gentle tug, *gold.* How freaking cool would it be to discover an entire cache of gold coins? It lay just under the edge of a clump of what looked like dark gray coral. Zane had given her the very first gold coin retrieved from his wreck the other day. Was this another? More than one? The thought made her giddy.

The coin he'd generously, but oh so casually, given to

her the week before was tucked away inside the little silver box he'd given her when she was a child. Her winnings for the bet not to puke anymore. The thought made her smile.

That little container he'd prized her with had been fresh from the sea, blackened and covered with conglomerate. She'd treasured it, because it had come from her hero, even when she had no idea it was anything more valuable than a chunk of gray coral. It wasn't until years later that Teal had it professionally cleaned and discovered it was an oval, silver, lady's powder compact. She carried it everywhere with her.

Like her one night with him, Teal doubted Zane remembered giving a shy little girl such a priceless gift.

Two, if she counted the gold coin.

She fanned the sand and gently tugged her treasure free. Her heart did a hop, skip, and jump as a heavy chain emerged from the sand link by link. Carefully, cautiously, she started easing it out of hiding. She desperately wanted to call Zane over, but refused to let the chain go in case she couldn't find it again.

Forty inches if it was an inch, she decided, holding it against her throat to calculate how long it was against her arm. She held it out to admire, awed by the beauty of the piece. The links were heavy, embossed with a relief pattern of intricate . . . leaves possibly? Hard to tell with the ebb and flow of the tide, which caused shadows and drifts of light to dance over her hands and the gold chain. It looked as shiny and new as if it had just come from a jewelry store. Amazing. Stunning. Magical. She looked up to hail Zane, but he had his back to her.

Teal tucked the chain carefully in the basket. Then looked back to see if there was anything else nearby. Her breath snagged as she picked up what looked like a man's ring. Big and heavy with a large clear stone. A diamond?

Into her goody basket. Carefully dusting the sand with a methodical sweep of her hands, she found a large gold medallion with a rough cut, dark green-ish, possibly black stone in the middle.

She kept going, her excitement building. She completely forgot she could've alerted Zane by knocking on her tank. Her basket was half full when she bumped her knee on the clump of coral where she'd discovered the chain. Damn that hurt. She glanced down at the offending rock-hard protuberance.

Hang on . . . A brush of her hand showed it had a square edge, not found in nature. *Holy carburetor!* A box of some sort?

It was too big to pry out of the sand and lift by herself, although she tried her damnedest. This called for reinforcements. Excited, she remembered to take out her dive knife and rap the handle of it against her tank. The ringing sound echoed in the water.

Zane swiveled in her direction at the noise and swam toward her. His basket was already filled with interesting artifacts that they'd take up for Maggie and Colson to clean and catalog. Beside herself, Teal showed him what she'd found, then hovered impatiently beside him as he inspected it from every angle.

Together, they pried a box, about the size of an overnight suitcase, out of the sand using their hands and finally their knives. They wouldn't attempt opening it until they had it on the *Decrepit* and Maggie got a look at it. But Teal's heart raced with anticipation. It *looked* big and important. Zane indicated they leave it there to take to the surface later. She was disappointed, but there was so much else to look at, she contained her excitement and impatience for the time being.

They found a ring with small red stones and a brooch the size of Teal's palm, shaped like a dragonfly, with what looked like sapphire eyes and emerald markings. Another ring, large, with an emerald the size of Zane's fingernail. They stared at each other over their treasures, and grinned around their regulators like crazy fools.

Chapter 7

The money was going to be great, Zane thought, standing up in the pilothouse, looking down at his team on the deck. He liked money just fine. Liked spending it even more. But the adrenaline rush of being the first to salvage a treasure frigate site, a frigate that only a few people, if any, had ever bothered to pursue as a viable wreck, that's what made his blood pump and his heart pound. Yeah. The money was always sweet, but it was just a way to keep score. The dive was everything.

Maggie and Colson were telling Teal about some of the artifacts they'd found that day. Much as Zane enjoyed being the teacher, he figured he'd be better served staying away from Teal for a couple of hours.

Diving with her, here, now, had felt . . . *right* somehow. He didn't want to overanalyze that. He just knew when emotions were running so high he might say or do something a little *too* impulsive. So in an atypical move, he stayed in the wheelhouse alone. Savoring the taste of victory and watching a long-legged brunette with go-to-hell eyes laugh at something his friend Ryan was telling her.

Even she, for a brief moment, forgot that she was antisocial and shy.

Maggie was eager to get into the heavy box they'd found and wanted it brought on board as soon as Zane could retrieve it, especially now that they had visitors. A dozen or so boats of various sizes had been dropping anchor all afternoon. Safety in numbers? Perhaps. But Zane would be lying to himself if he didn't admit that it unnerved him to have so many potential troublemakers so close to his site. But odds were, they had no idea what kind of treasure they were sitting on. It would be a challenge to keep it that way, but he lived for a challenge.

He thought of the box Teal had discovered. It could contain anything, from nothing to gold bars. Zane decided to hold off on hauling it up until early the next morning. Their competitors were less likely to notice them bringing it up if they moved it at first light. The downside was that he would have to wait to find out what was inside.

He leaned back in his chair, watching the activity on the deck. He smiled as he cupped the back of his head with both hands, his lungs filling with anticipation. "This, *this* is the start of something *big*."

*   *   *

The box was gone when Zane and Ryan went down the next morning to retrieve it. "Did you go back for it when you went down with Ben yesterday evening?" Zane asked Teal after the two men surfaced later that day.

She was helping Maggie clean and bag gold coins in the shade of the crane. "No." She tilted her head to see him from under the brim of her ball cap. "Shit. It's gone? I didn't even notice it was missing, we fanned a different area this morning."

"Damn it," Zane told the two women, his voice grim. "Someone helped themselves to our prize."

Teal felt proprietary about "her" box. "Coupling this with the sabotage to the drive shaft and hull and the *Sea Witch*'s appearance pisses me off."

Maggie pressed a hand to her midriff. "It gives me a squirmy feeling in the pit of my stomach."

"I hear you."

"Let's go over to *Sea Witch* and see what she has to say for herself." Teal was freaking ready to rumble.

Zane shook his head. "The two of us together couldn't lug it onboard, and she's over there alone. Unless she had help, not possible."

"Maybe she has someone on board with her?"

"I've been watching. Not that I've observed."

"Fine. Then we'd better figure this out sooner than later, because *someone*'s responsible." Teal got to her feet and glared out over the sparkling water. "*Look* at them. Any freaking one of them could be our guy."

The area was filled with possible culprits. Sailboats, other dive boats, and cruisers kept to the one-mile rule, but there were dozens and dozens of people on board. Teal considered them all guilty until proven innocent. She'd start keeping track—names of the boats and a list of who she saw on board, with descriptions and random observations.

On one of the cruisers, three elderly ladies had brought their knitting out on deck and settled into lawn chairs to watch the proceedings, which Teal thought bizarre.

"They're observing the one-mile rule," Zane pointed out, leaning against the base of the crane.

"Aren't you pissed off?" Teal demanded turning back to him.

"Yeah. Big time. But until I figure out who's responsible, there isn't anything I can do about it. I'll laminate a copy of the federal arrest warrant and tack it up on the tallest timber of the *Vrijheid*."

Teal's eyeballs throbbed. "You think a piece of freaking *paper* is going to stop whoever is doing this?"

"It's a start. Don't freak out. I'm working on it, Williams. Just do your job, chill, but keep an eye out for anything odd."

"I'm looking at something odd right now," she said with asperity, making Maggie snort behind her. "If you were any more laid-back, Cutter, you'd be in a coma."

He smiled, no teeth, no sparkle in his eyes. "Don't let my sangfroid fool you. Make no mistake, Williams, I'll catch whoever's doing this."

"How? When?"

"I called in the authorities to make a casual inspection of the surrounding boats. They'll go 'round and say hey, what'cha doing, how's it going? And hand out a copy of the federal arrest warrant so they know what they're up against if they poach."

"That's it?" Teal wanted to personally go to every boat armed to the teeth, accompanied by a phalanx of Navy SEALs, and demand their treasure back, right this freaking second.

"For now," Zane told her flatly. "People are curious, they just want to watch how a salvage operation works. They have no idea what's down there, and I intend to keep it that way. Eventually, they'll get bored and leave. Observing is boring as hell, especially from a distance."

He clearly wasn't going to fire warning shots across the bad guys' bow. She sucked in a sigh of frustration. "Will the *Sea Witch* bug off, too?"

"Doubt it. She usually hangs around a couple of weeks before she disappears like a bad smell. This is a big fucking deal. Like I said, I don't think they know the extent of what's down there," Zane told her. "For all they know, there's a minor wreck we're excavating, and the *Sea Witch* is simply keeping tabs on us to see what we've found. If we keep the excavation quiet, chances are she'll give up and go elsewhere."

"What worries me is how quickly they all showed up," Teal said, crossing her arms and staring out at the "enemy" boats. "In spite of the fact that we've been staging decoy sites all week. And in spite of the fact that this particular area is notoriously hard to navigate. The way they swarmed in the minute we dropped anchor . . . it's almost like some-one tipped them off about the site." She turned and faced him, her arms still crossed defiantly. "What if it's some-one on board?"

"Despite what Nick told you—because I know my brother, and I know that he's the one who put a bug in your ear—my crew is sound. Anyone can go online and see ex-actly where we are. It's not a secret. And people in the know keep an eye peeled on all things Cutter, in the hope that they can get in on the action. But they don't know what we have, or what we hope to find. *That's* a secret. I'd like to keep it that way as long as possible." Staring out at the an-chored vessels, Teal wished she could go to each boat and check them from stem to stern for stolen artifacts, then rip the lips off the thief.

Zane had spent years searching for this site, and Teal couldn't stand the thought of some bottom-feeder swoop-ing in and snatching his hard-earned prize, only to sell it on the black market and lose a piece of history forever.

"So that's our plan then?" Teal asked. "To haul as much treasure up as fast and as quietly as we can and hope they don't realize what we're doing?"

"Exactly, and the first phase of the plan is to throw them off the scent. And that's why we're inviting every-one on the surrounding boats over for a big-ass party."

"A . . . *party*?! Are you freaking nuts?"

*   *   *

Zane made sure he didn't dive every dive with Teal, although he enjoyed going down with her. Her eagerness and pleasure in discovering even the smallest thing gave him a buzz that lasted all day.

Every day brought with it more incredible finds, and more and more people closing in on the site. Zane still hoped to keep the discovery quiet, which meant keeping up the appearance that they were excavating a minor wreck. So he decided to host a party, because that's exactly what he would have done had the *Vrijheid* been a minor wreck.

The one positive thing about having people and the press around was that they'd help keep the artifacts safe. The local authorities as well as the Dutch government were also keeping an eagle eye on what was being retrieved. Stealing from Zane was money out of their own pockets.

He'd invite everyone to the party. Meet the host of suspects up close and personal, and look them in the eye. Better the devil he knew than the devil he didn't. Besides, he was ready for a crowd. He liked dancing, liked noise, liked laughing.

And it would pull his addled brain away from his mechanic.

He kept a weather eye on the storm front closing in, pretty typical for this time of year. Despite the waves, none of the surrounding boats quit and went home—everyone seemed prepared to wait the bad weather out. One morning several days later, he passed Teal in the narrow passageway going to the head, a towel and toothbrush in her hand. She looked as sleepy and disheveled as a baby owl and didn't notice him until he neatly blocked her way so she had to stop and talk to him. Zane felt ridiculously like he was in junior high. Except in junior high he'd been the jock, and the girls had been all over him.

Being around Teal made him realize how little thought he'd ever given to his popularity. He'd never been vain about it, hell, he'd never given it a nanosecond of thought. Until a woman *wasn't* charmed by him. He should leave it at that. But it rankled more than it should have. He liked her just fine. *More* than fine. Why didn't she like him?

"How's the new mattress?" he asked, leaning against the bulkhead. Her hair was all spikes and cowlicks and flat on one side, and he thought she looked ridiculously cute for a sea urchin.

Teal's sleepy brown eyes rose slowly, and she blinked as if seeing all six three of him, standing in the companionway on his own boat, was a big shock.

"It's . . . firm."

The interesting thing about her not liking him was that she was wearing the T-shirt he'd lent her for her lunch with Nick last week. The shirt she'd claimed she'd incinerated. His shirt was so long and big on her it came halfway down her thighs. Was she wearing anything under it? He wanted to slide his hands up her thighs to find out.

"Comfy?" He plucked the sleeve, which came down to her elbow. No sliding up thighs. Unfortunately. He should be up for sainthood.

She swatted his hand away. "It's too early."

"For what?"

"To spar with you. I have to pee, Zane. Can I please get by?"

He flattened himself against the bulkhead. "Be my guest. Why don't you use mine instead of the one the guys are using?" Which he'd offered several times and been refused several times. But she couldn't fault him for offering. "It'll give you more privacy, especially now that we have all the security guys on board."

The thought of her naked in his shower gave Zane his first woody of the day.

"There's a lock on the door."

"Your choice."

"A good thing for you to keep in mind." Giving him

the evil eye, she managed to slide by without touching any part of him, even the part sticking out.

*   *   *

The *Sea Witch* rode anchor just beyond three other boats. Teal didn't see a redhead, but she saw every other color hair as women hung over the railings of the other boats, practically falling out of their bikini tops. Several scantily clad people talked to Zane, Ben, and Ryan, who fielded their questions and downplayed the value of what they'd been bringing up all day. Maggie and Colson were belowdecks having multiple orgasms as they photographed and cleaned what everyone had brought to the surface all day.

When they were done, everything would be packed in sea water and hidden in the *Decrepit*'s secret compartments.

They weren't taking any chances. What they uncovered every day was immediately brought to the surface and cataloged. Zane and his team packed the most valuable pieces carefully, then put everything in garbage bags, which Brian and his guys took on their boat as if it was *Decrepit*'s garbage. The bags were piled on the deck for several days while the men "visited." When they left, they took several million dollars' worth of gold and emeralds with them.

When it became obvious that the operation was yielding more treasure than could be transported discreetly, Zane brought in security specialists who made a big deal of their arrival, especially the weapons they all carried. Since with their arrival it was impossible to hide the scope and value of the artifacts, Zane decreed that no one came on board without his express invitation, and a dozen armed men enforced the rule. Every afternoon at six, a nondescript motorboat came in to remove the most valuable pieces and return them to Cutter Cay, where more high-powered security people made sure no unauthorized people came ashore. The island was almost as secure as Fort Knox.

Ironically, it wasn't the dollar value of the treasure that made Zane's heart race. Money was just for spending. It was the rich color of the emeralds and the amazing patina of the gold coins they'd found that gave him the zing. Every day was a revelation. He split his dive time between Ryan, Ben, and Teal. Once in a while, Maggie wanted to see things firsthand, but she was too busy and too excited to want to leave the *Decrepit*, even for an hour.

Between dives and security arrangements, Zane had sent Colson to each boat to invite everyone over later. The man was certifiably insane, and she didn't hold back when she told him so.

Zane laughed off her protests.

She mentioned that anyone on the surrounding ships might be pirates, for God's sake. Any one of the smiling, airhead-looking people could've sabotaged the *Decrepit* or stolen her box, which she'd convinced herself had been filled with fist-sized emeralds. That for all *he* knew they were the bad guys, lying in wait until the *Decrepit* crew did all the work, then they'd waltz in and help themselves.

Zane had soberly told her that was an unlikely possibility.

Still, Teal just hoped she wasn't on board when the bad guys did their hostile takeover. Next time the *Decrepit* might sink while they were all fast asleep. He'd better give that some thought.

* * *

Teal shifted her chair out of the setting sun and, coincidentally/on purpose, used the wall of the salon to partially block herself from the gathering. She was sweaty and cranky. Her khaki pants were too hot, her long-sleeved shirt clung to her skin like a shroud, and her sneaker-shod feet protested their confinement. She was not about to get back into her swimsuit with all these other people on board. Let Zane be the exhibitionist. He was so damn good at it.

This stupid freaking party was wrong on so many levels it made her head spin. She absolutely did not see Zane's logic on this. At all. How did inviting all these people help him solve the puzzle? How did he think he was going to ID whoever had tried to sink his freaking boat?

This party was illogical. Impractical. Intrusive and downright freaking annoying!

She lifted her soda can to her mouth, feeling a little sick watching him. He wasn't wearing much more than his guests were. His low slung, white linen, drawstring pants showed off the darkly tanned expanse of his muscles and his washboard stomach. The man wasn't fond of clothing, she'd learned on this trip. She bet if she and Maggie weren't around he'd walk around bare-assed naked all the time. And wouldn't that be a sight to behold?

A heat rash spread across her chest.

Two greased, mostly naked females had draped themselves on either side of him. One toyed with the string holding up his pants with long red nails and a sly, glossy smile. Zane, chatting to the blonde on his left, put his hand down and removed the skank's fingers without even glancing at her. Now *that* was too practiced, Teal thought, feeling pissy and not proud of it. It was his boat. He could invite anyone he damn well pleased. He could be fondled by anyone he pleased. Didn't mean she wanted to sit here like a third wheel and watch strange women smearing oil slicks all over him.

The good news was, the women looked too stupid to be pirates and their escorts too lazy. Still, she'd keep an eye on all of them just in case their looks were deceiving.

The crowd had cranked up the music, and everyone was talking at once, so nobody even noticed her sitting there feeling . . . *annoyed*. The booze was flowing, the music was loud, and she'd tried, twice, to go down to her engines to seek solace.

Zane had told her to "lighten up." She'd like to take those matches on the table beside the unlit candles and set his pants on fire.

Childish. Stupid. Warranted. She slouched in her chair and ran the cold can over her forehead. A bald man with bushy, untrimmed, gray eyebrows like Andy Rooney on *60 Minutes* came over to talk to her. He was in his mid sixties, about Ben's age, without Ben's taste. He'd come on board with the quarter-his-age blond nymphet who practically had her hand down Zane's pants. "Hi babe, wanna dance?"

She'd already bet herself he'd be a *babe* caller by counting the gold chains around his neck. "No."

He stood way too damn close. Teal crossed her legs and accidently kicked his shin. He took a cautious step back, but held out his hand and wiggled ring-bedecked sausage fingers. "That song's got our names on it."

"I'm sorry," Teal opened her eyes wide. "I'm a paraplegic. My dancing days are over."

"Come on! You just kicked me."

"Awful isn't it? It comes and goes when I least expect it. I don't really mind not being able to walk." She lowered her voice so that he, and his manly five gallons of cologne, had to lean in closer. "It's, well, it's the diapers I have to wear for this damned incontinence." She touched the corner of her mouth. "And of course, there's the embarrassing problem of drooling . . . It's not a *lot,* really, but it does bother some men. But if you really want to carry me around the deck . . ." She gave him a hopeful look.

He fled.

"That was naughty," Maggie laughed, coming for a

soda from the cooler. She looked young and pretty in a tangerine-colored, halter-neck summer dress, her feet bare.

"Hey, it saved his life. If I'd been forced to shuffle around the deck with him, I'd have been tempted to push him overboard just to wash off some of that cologne . . ." She trailed off.

Zane had a large-breasted brunette, in the tiniest red string bikini Teal had ever seen, plastered against him. Their feet barely moved. The woman's hands were on his ass, his fingers were spread on the small of her back. Dancing? Teal swallowed a rude snort that somehow got tangled in the back of her throat and hurt.

She leaned over and took a beer out of the cooler. If ever there was a time to have a beer, it was now. "That oil she's covered in is going to be hell to get out of linen."

"I haven't had a chance to talk to you. How have you been?"

"Fantastic." Teal watched Zane's long fingers move to the string tie of the woman's top barely noticing Maggie as she wandered off. "Great. Perfect." He wasn't going to undo it here in front of her boyfriend and everyone else was he? Even for Mr. Freaking Casanova of the Caribbean that would be outrageous. He wouldn't dare . . .

Now his back was to her, but Teal could see the girl's face over the side of Zane's bare arm. Her bright red mouth looked sticky, her expensive veneers scary white as she nibbled on Zane's bicep. "Rabies alert!" she muttered under her breath, then drained her beer because her throat ached.

Zane was like an alien life force. And as hard as she tried, she couldn't rip her gaze away from him. The man loved to laugh, and dance, and be half naked. It's a wonder the blasted guy didn't purr with so many females stroking and petting him and sticking their tongues down his throat.

She pressed her fingers into her eyelids and tried to

figure out what the hell her problem with him was. Every time she was around him she was like a cat with her fur rubbed the wrong way.

Even after kissing her—*twice*—he still didn't remember that night. Fair enough, she had to admit, if only to herself. He'd been destroyed by his father's unexpected death; he'd been drunker than a skunk; and he hadn't expected her to show up at his door. As a rational grown-up, she had to accept at least half the blame. He hadn't done anything with her she hadn't been more than willing to do. He was Zane Cutter, Casanova of the Caribbean. She'd known that when she walked into his darkened bedroom that night and willingly let him take off her clothes. Okay, take off was mild. *Rip* off would be more apt.

Teal realized she was sitting there, on the sidelines, and she was shaking. *Stop it! Right now. Get a freaking grip.* A surge of hot and cold prickles suffused her entire body, and she thought she might faint.

The truth hit her with a blinding flash and wave of nausea. She was so in love with him, *still,* that she was sick with it. She was pissy and defensive because the opposite was to beg him for something he was incapable of giving. And while she'd learned to handle the lack of love from Sam, she'd known deep in her secret heart that being rejected by Zane would kill her spirit worse than anything Denny had ever done. She'd been in love with Zane for years before she walked, willingly, with full knowledge of what she was offering, into his room that night. The truth was devastatingly simple, and now that she finally acknowledged it, it was going to be a thousand times worse being on board with him.

She was trapped on the unrequited love boat, with no way out.

Nothing has to change, she told herself firmly. Nothing. No one knows about what happened or how I feel. It'll stay that way until it's time to say good-bye. She'd reconciled herself to pretending to ignore Zane for years. She could handle two more weeks.

Sitting in her favorite chair beside the wall of the salon, she sipped a second beer she didn't want, and watched Zane, who had switched partners and was now dancing with an attractive redhead whose lime-green dental floss excuse for a swimsuit didn't cover a damned thing.

Leaning back, Teal scanned the crowd and tried to estimate the yardage of the clothing, the carat weight of their jewelry, and the age spread of the guests. Minimal, immense, wide. Was one of Zane's guests the thief? Because in spite of security on board, and intermittent inspections of the surrounding boats, stuff was still being lifted right under their noses. And that was just things they noticed.

They had no idea *what* they were missing from their find because not everything had been photographed and documented yet.

Nick was right. Zane was just too freaking trusting. Zane's little plan to throw them off the scent was merely an invitation to rob him blind.

Zane was being passed around like a damn pull toy. Clearly he liked it. His smile was wide, and he moved with lithe grace as he fast danced with a tall bare-breasted chick with dreadlocks who wore nothing more than a short red sarong and a come-hither smile. He looked up, caught Teal's eye, and broke away from his clearly disappointed partner.

Oh hell, Teal thought, a little panicked as Zane wove across the crowded deck, heading her way, doing the samba as he made his circuitous route between the dancers gyrating to the compelling beat of Lady Gaga's "Samba Rock."

Now what? She was here, wasn't she?

There was a gaggle of gorgeous women on board. A veritable feast for a guy like Zane Cutter. He'd danced nonstop all night. Trying to cull one from the herd? Teal wondered sourly.

"Hey," he said quietly, reaching for her bottle of beer and taking a swig. He handed it back. "How you doing, Williams?" Sweat gleamed on his chest and trickled down his throat. His damp hair curled like licks of black flames around his neck. She had an insane urge to jump him, wind her legs around his waist, and lick his throat. To hell with decorum or all these people. Fortunately she hadn't lost her mind. Yet.

"Now what?" she asked, waving him aside as if she wanted a better view of the dancers. He stayed right where he was, foursquare in front of her so that she was eye level with his inny and rock-hard, gleaming six-pack. *No fair.*

She went completely deaf as her gaze, reluctantly, tracked up his chest to his face. She managed the feat without once taking a breath. Her lungs felt constricted, and her heart was manic. With annoyance, guilt, and self-loathing, she assured herself.

She gave him a fierce, don't-mess-with-me look. "Whatever you want, my work day is over. I do *not* want you to make me do another command performance and stay up until the cows come home again. I've already lodged a complaint with the labor board and my congressman about the crazy hours you insist I keep. I'm exhausted. I'm going down to my cabin now."

"No, you're not. You sleep in the engine room like the Mad Hatter."

Breathe, lungs. Do not respond to that humorous glitter in his eyes. Do not be charmed by him. Charm, she reminded herself, was this guy's default setting. "That was the Mad Hatter, and it was in a teapot, not an engine room."

He gave her a stern look. "I think that wall knows how to stand all by itself now." He knocked on it twice. "Nice and solid." He held out his hand. "Come dance with me," he ordered, a hint of laughter in his deep voice as he wiggled his fingers.

Said the spider to the fly. No way. She did not want to be in his arms. She could smell his subtle and expensive soap and the clean, male sweat was an aphrodisiac. And not only for her. She was fine right where she was, thank you very much.

Teal slouched down in the chair and crossed her arms over her chest. She was acting like a five-year-old because she was as scared as one. "I don't want a pity dance, thank you, I'm perfectly happy sitting here minding my own business and communing with nature."

Still blocking her view, he spread his feet like the freaking King of Siam and laughed. "There's not much about any of them that's natural, do you think? I bet they have their plastic surgeons on speed dial."

"Are you their second number?" she asked sweetly, but without any heat. She'd been deluding herself to think that she could maintain the equanimity with which she'd been treating him for the past two weeks. Her love for this . . . *charmer* . . . was fathoms deep. But it was also mixed with a healthy dose of reality and resentment. How could she have returned to the scene of the crime and *not* resent Zane for what he'd done to her eighteen months ago? He didn't *remember* her. But her stupid heart didn't give a damn, because she'd never fallen *out* of love with him. Even as a shy, unwanted, six-year-old kid, she'd seen something in him that had captured her heart. She'd fallen helplessly, hopelessly in unrequited love with him then. And even given his lapse in memory, she loved him now. Teal was so mad at herself she wanted to jump overboard and swim to Florida. She gave him a stony stare.

"Come on, Williams. I dare you. One dance won't kill you."

Little do you know! "I don't dance."

Zane grabbed her hand, brushing her breast as he

wrangled her fingers from their death grip on her upper arm. Electrical sparks flooded her body. There was a couple of seconds of tug of war as she tried to clench her fist against her tightly folded arms. But he won by brute force, and the freaking twinkle in his demonic eyes. It was almost impossible not to give in to his good-humored persistence. He tugged her off her chair until she stood in front of him.

"Can you shuffle your feet?"

Keeping her gaze averted from the amusement and challenge in his, she planted her sneakers, imagining they were spot-welded to the deck. "Let me rephrase that." She forced herself to meet his blue, blue, wickedly blue eyes. "I. Do. Not. *Want*. To. Dance."

He wrapped his arms around her waist, crossed his wrists in the small of her back, and drew her against his body. His bare chest touched her breasts. Teal had to lock her knees to remain upright.

"You can't sit there all night glowering at people."

"Of course I can." Being this close, it was impossible to look up without getting a crick in her neck, so she addressed the curve of his shoulder. She was tempted to stick out her tongue and take a little lick to see if his skin tasted the same as it had that night. She refrained by biting her tongue until she tasted blood. That worked.

"If they don't like it, they can go to their own boats."

"That's not very neighborly."

"Neighbors borrow a cup of sugar, then go home and bake a pie or something. One of these people could very well be the one who tried to sink us, and swiped my box of treasure and those amazing candlesticks you were so pissed off about losing yesterday." She felt weak with longing and resentment. Easy for him to stroke her back like he was doing. To him all cats were gray in the dark. Her every nerve ending was attuned to him like little antennae.

"If that's the case, they'll be brought to justice. But no tonight. Why are you so cranky?" he chided softly, resting his chin on top of her head. Teal felt his warm breath through her hair while he swayed to the music, moving her with him, whether she wanted to sway or not. She felt feverish and itchy on the inside. Zane had that effect on a lot of women.

"I'm *hungry*." She tried to use her elbows to put a millimeter of space between them. "Let me go so I can go in and make a sandwich." *And sneak down to the engine room.* The music was giving her a headache. Seeing Zane with all these gorgeous women was giving her a . . . heartache. And being in his arms again was heaven *and* hell *Oh, damn. Damn. Damn.*

Heat emanated from his all-but-naked body as he started moving his feet. "There's enough food here to feed Haiti."

"Nobody we know prepared that food," she told him tightly. "There could be anything in it!"

"Like what? Glass? Drugs? Oregano? Come on, sweetheart. Lighten up and have some fun."

The "sweetheart" infuriated her. The "lighten up" would keep her up all night plotting ways to light his fuse. "Fine. Eat whatever you want. I don't give a damn if you get ptomaine from eating any of that crap, or . . . or *rabies* from kissing so many strangers. Let me go, Zane. Seriously."

Really. It wasn't as though he had her held fast with a vise. His strong arms surrounded her loosely. But that casual hold was a prison without locks or screws.

She wanted so badly to pull away, to offer up another snarky remark, to stomp on his foot and run back to the safety of her engine room. But as she stood there swaying with Zane, she was utterly intoxicated. The smell of skin, the heat of his hard, muscled body, the rasp of his whiskers as he leaned in and whispered in her ear.

"I know I scare you." His breath tickled her cheek as he whispered softly into her ear. "But, know what, Williams? You scare me a little bit, too."

"You don't scare me in the slightest," she assured him, lying through her teeth as she inhaled the heady fragrance of his bare skin, which was right beneath her nose.

Damn it. She'd been here before, in this exact same spot. Let herself get lost in the moment and gave herself to Zane, only to have her heart smashed into a million tiny pieces. No. No. No. Been there, done that. She had to do better this time.

She tried to pull away. "I can't do this. I've got to go."

"Teal—"

"Let me go, Zane. Seriously."

She shoved at his chest with both hands. His skin felt—Warm. Alive. Familiar. Oh, God, oh God. She was in way over her head. "Please?" she begged a little desperately.

After a few erratic heartbeats, he let her go. "Damn it, Williams. I don't understand—"

She didn't stick around to hear it. She turned around and walked away, as fast as her aching heart would allow.

Chapter 8

She'd worked just as hard as everyone else and she de
served a day off, Teal decided the next afternoon as she
sat on the deck with Maggie after a fruitful dive. They
were bagging and tagging coins and other small artifacts
mid deck, to the accompanying loud noise of the com
pressor the dive team was using to move sand on the
ocean floor.

The weather was overcast and oppressive. She sipped a
soda and tried to keep her mind blank. Hard to do since a
herd of squirrels were racing around on a wheel in her
brain. Zane. The way things ended between them last
night. The saboteur. Her dying father.

She'd called and left several messages for him, but he
had yet to return them. She supposed he simply couldn'
handle talking to her more than every couple of months
But she knew this would be her last visit to see him or
Cutter Cay. A woman could only handle so much rejection
She might be a slow learner, but it eventually sunk in. Ap
parently, the fact that he was dying didn't give him any
sense of urgency to see or say good-bye to his only child
So be it.

She wasn't even disappointed. Much. It was what she'd expected when she'd accepted the invitation to fill in for Sam. The Cutters should have hired a full-time, permanent mechanic and left her the hell alone. She'd started making a good life for herself in Orange Beach.

Maybe this time she'd try . . . Denver. She'd buy a fabulous condo with a spectacular view of the mountains. She was pretty much done with wide expanses of exceptionally blue water. In fact, when she decorated, she'd be sure to exclude any and every shade of blue. Being here just reminded her of what she'd tried for years to forget. Sam didn't care one way or the other if she were bobbing on the Caribbean or dumpster diving in Kalamazoo.

Oh, boo hoo, didn't she feel sorry for herself? *Get over it,* Teal told herself firmly. *When I walk away, I'll be a very wealthy woman. I can start my own business. I'll go anywhere, do anything I damn well please. Hell. I can buy myself a sexy boyfriend if I want to.*

Speaking of buying things, Teal needed to go shopping. She hated shopping, but her two pairs of pants and a handful of shirts and T-shirts weren't cutting it. Maggie wore shorts or sundresses with her cowboy hat. She looked cute and cool. Two things Teal wasn't in her khaki pants and chambray shirt. Both of which she now hated. She'd started feeling that her wardrobe was inadequate right after the party, but she didn't want to read too much into it.

"I need to go St. Maarten to buy to some things," she told Maggie. There were only a couple of boats hanging about today, and several people were in the water swimming, and talking loudly.

"Oh?"

"I'd love to get a nice fat roll of duct tape and cover their mouths," she muttered as a woman's maniacal scream pierced her eardrums, making her wince. She shot Maggie a humorous glance. "Think that would be seen as antisocial behavior?" she said, only half joking.

"I'll hand you the tape." Maggie laughed.

Teal had to raise her voice a little. "Would you like to come with me?"

Maggie didn't look up from her notebook where she was writing. "*Love* to. Shopping is my second favorite thing to do. Okay," she glanced up with a smile. "*Third*. Even though I hate to stop there for even a second, I'd love to go and visit my daughter, and see our grand-daughter, Jessie, even if it's only for a few hours—" she paused to flip to the back of her notebook where several pictures of a baby were stuck under plastic. She handed the folded book to Teal. "This is my baby's baby. Jessica. You may tell me how exquisite she is for as long as you like."

Teal smiled as she accepted the book for a closer look. She knew absolutely nothing about babies. You fed one end and cleaned up the other. That was the extent of her knowledge, but she was willing to be wowed. "She's adorab-le . . ." her voice faltered.

The child—about two-ish, Teal guessed—had curly black hair and a sweet face. And Cutter blue eyes. *Zane*'s eyes. The DNA evidence staring her in the face was too strong to disprove. Teal was frozen in place. She presumed her heart must still be beating because she was still sitting upright. So this was why Maggie had a "soft spot" for Zane. He was the father of her grandchild.

Maggie took the notebook out of Teal's unresisting fingers and jotted down a notation. "When do you want to go?" she asked, still writing.

"Now?" Teal suggested a little too eagerly. Zane was diving with Ryan. The timing was perfect. "I'm sure Zane wouldn't mind if we took the launch." The baby *could* be Nick's. Or Logan's . . .

"He won't mind at all. But how about going tomorrow instead, honey? It's pretty late. If there's anything you need, I'd be happy to share whatever I have with you."

"I've already got dibs on your wet suit," Teal told her dryly, stretching out her legs on the warm wood of the deck. Her mouth was so dry she could barely push the words out. It was none of her business if Zane fathered a dozen children. None. *Oh, yeah?* Her heart twisted painfully, and her chest hurt. None of her business, but God it hurt on a level she didn't even want to analyze.

She didn't *want* to sit here in the glorious sun, wondering how and why Zane Cutter unwittingly had the power to elicit these emotions in her. And the worst part was that it wasn't just simple jealousy that hurt so much. It was the fact that she'd been right about Zane all along. She's been right to run away from him last night. There was no hope of changing the man. This child was just further confirmation that Zane was a lost cause.

She breathed deeply, observed that her heart was beating just fine, and her lungs were fully operational. He wasn't doing anything to intentionally hurt her or make her unhappy. She was doing a fine and dandy job of that all by herself.

Stop it! Count blessings instead of emotional voids.

Ummm—Her tan was coming along nicely even though she'd made no effort and used sunscreen religiously. And other than her feelings for Zane, she felt fit and healthy and strangely at peace for the first time in a long, long time.

Baby Jessie was just another Zane-ism she had to deal with all on her own.

Teal leaned her head against the wall at her back and watched two men on another boat do perfectly synchronized dives into the water to the accompanying shrieks of their girlfriends, who were already in the water. *Are you the thieving bastards stealing our stuff?* In the distance, the *Sea Witch* sat like a bird of prey. *Or is it you?*

"I really hate shopping. I think I'm missing the girly gene," she admitted, forcing the tension to leak out of her body a bit at a time. "But the necessity has become critical."

Denny had loved to shop for her. His taste was questionable, but she'd always had plenty of things to wear. She'd left every thong, merry widow, and lace bra behind in San Francisco when she'd walked out. She didn't care what she wore as long as she was comfortable. Denny's choices had been anything but.

"How about if I lend you a pretty sundress to wear tonight? Let's have a girl's afternoon, we'll give each other a facial, do our nails, fix our hair . . ."

"Who are you, and what have you done with Maggie?" Teal tried to joke. It fell a little flat.

"I've seen the way you look at Zane." Maggie said gently. "Glaring at him all night isn't going to stop him flirting with all those silly women. And dressing out of the laundry hamper isn't going to get you what you want. Sorry. Rude, I know. But what are friends for? Don't you want Zane to see you as a desirable woman?"

Teal didn't know where to begin decoding that piece of dialogue. She felt sucker punched. "I have to look at him to talk to him." She was embarrassed to hear how sulky she sounded.

Maggie reached over and laid a hand on Teal's knee. "You're in love with him, honey. Let's do something about that."

"That's not why I want to go shopping," Teal said defensively, not acknowledging the statement. "I like my clothes just fine. I don't want to dress as someone I'm not."

"A hot and sexy woman?" Maggie smiled. "You have beautiful eyes, which no one can see properly because you hide behind your hair. And a pretty mouth if you'd just smile more often. Let me—"

Teal's chest hurt, and she tried to hide the feelings of betrayal behind a cough. Maybe if she explained? But if

Maggie was really her friend, she should already be good enough.

"I was with a man who spent every waking moment of the three years we were married doing his best to change everything about me. None of me was up to his elevated standards of perfection." She scrambled to her feet, eyes brimming. "I hated it, but I wore long red nails, dyed my hair, and had extensions—which itched like hell, by the way. I'm never going to be stupid enough again to believe that changing my outsides for a man will make him love me."

The fact that Maggie claimed friendship in the same breath as she suggested a makeover told Teal everything she needed to know. No wonder she loved her engines so much. They couldn't break your heart.

Maggie stood up and reached out her hand, but Teal stepped out of reach. "Honey, *no*. Lord, no. I don't want you to change—Oh blast it! I'm sorry. I don't—"

Blinded by tears, Teal turned and crashed straight into Zane's chest. He still wore his wet suit and was carrying a lump of blackish . . . something in his hand. He frowned as he scanned her face. "What's going on?"

Teal shoved his chest, and he fell back a step. "Get the hell out of my way!"

Zane turned to watch her run across the deck, then swiveled round to Maggie. "What did I miss?"

"The part about her husband trying to change her?" Maggie asked worriedly as Teal disappeared inside.

"No," Zane said grimly, "I got that part."

"She wanted to go to St. Maarten to do a little shopping. I suggested a girl's afternoon with facials and maybe a makeover instead. Darn it. I hurt her feelings, which was the last thing I wanted to do. I'll go down and talk to her."

Zane touched his friend's arm. "No. Let me go." This conversation was long overdue.

*   *   *

Zane checked his watch. Again. He'd given her fifteen minutes to be alone. She liked alone. He didn't. Time for a little compromise.

Carrying two cans of soda, either as a peace offering or for self-defense, Zane walked into the engine room. Teal sat at the small, built-in desk, staring at the closed laptop. She'd changed from the swimsuit into coveralls, the sleeves wrapped around her waist, and a little white tank top that showed off her lightly muscled arms and the small globes of her breasts.

He'd have to be a blind man not to see her nipples, the palest of pink, poking through the thin material. And damn it, he wasn't blind. She was braless. The woman had weapons she didn't bother using.

He closed the door behind him with a firm click. "Maggie's sorry she hurt your feelings."

"She didn't." Jaw set, Teal opened the computer and turned it on. "I need to check the strainers on the cooling system . . . So if there's nothing else?"

Zane set the colas on the desk, then reached over and closed the computer, ignoring her indignant, *"Hey!"*

"You know what it was like to have my brothers return home with shitloads of treasure while I was searching like a lunatic for the *Vrijheid* in all the wrong places for four *years*?" He stepped back, letting her absorb him in her space.

He noticed that she'd commandeered the coffeepot he kept in the wheelhouse for late-night trips, and a red-and-white striped canvas cushion he'd last seen on a lounger on the forward deck. He could feel her bristling with un-named emotion.

"Frustrating," he told the back of her head. "Annoying as hell."

He picked up her ugly blue chambray shirt off the

chair, and brought it to his nose. Attar of irritation, he thought, half amused and half baffled by this woman who attracted him like no other. He buried his smile in the scent of her for a moment since she wasn't paying attention.

Teal was an original. An acquired taste, and God help him, his taste buds were changing. "It's not about the money," he tossed her shirt back on the chair and resumed prowling the spotless room. "Although it's a damn fine bonus. No, it's all about the win. The race to the finish. The bet the three of us made and who comes in first place."

"Fascinating." Teal sounded anything but. "However, this isn't new information." She flipped open the computer again. "So if there's nothing else, I have work to do."

"Teal—"

"Why do you care anyway? I have no idea what the deal is with you and Maggie, but it all seems incredibly twisted to me. She must be some kind of free love proponent to be pushing you off on every woman she knows and enabling your philandering ways."

"Enabling my—what? What are you talking about?"

"Never mind. Forget it. Not important."

He stared at her for a moment, clearly perplexed, then shook his head. "Teal, all I know is that if two members of my team are at odds, it taints the work we're doing here. Do you get *that*?"

The computer hummed to life, and he heard her grind her back teeth. "I'd be happy to leave. I didn't want to come in the first place." Her straight spine was too stiff to bend.

Zane ran all ten fingers through his hair in frustration. "People here care about you. *Maggie* cares about you. Can't you at least try to be friendly?"

"You're confusing caring with the temporary bond forged among coworkers." Her detached voice gave him chills. How hurt had she been in her life to slip so quickly behind emotional walls? She tapped at the keyboard, her posture ramrod straight. "I found an emerald the size of a teacup the other day. I can cook without burning the galley down, fix the engines, and I clean up after myself. I'm practically employee of the week." Asperity and disillusionment laced every syllable as Teal logged in to the computer, then paused and looked at him over her shoulder. She chewed her lip as if weighing her words.

"It's not like that. We're family."

With a quick negating shake of her head she said, "I—I don't get close to people easily." She shrugged, still facing her computer screen rather than him. "I just don't. I'm sorry if Maggie was offended that I didn't want to play dress up, but I'm fine the way I am."

Yeah. He could read how "fine" she was by the way the air bristled around her. "You are better than fine. You are strong, independent. Smart. Dangerously amusing. And—" He paused to savor the truth of his words. "—beautiful." She quickly blinked a couple of times and glanced up at the ceiling before glaring at him. In any other woman, Zane would have suspected she was holding back tears. But Teal didn't look like she'd tolerate tears. Especially from herself.

"Right. Thanks for the pep talk, Captain."

Her glacial expression showed how little she thought of his compliments and he mentally retreated. "We're all just people, Teal. Be nice and most folks will be nice right back."

"Maybe in your world. Me? I like engines. I understand how they work and how to fix them when they don't. But people . . ." Her hand fluttered, then dropped back to the table.

"People aren't that complicated, sweetheart." He reached out with one hand. "Everyone wants to be understood and loved by the people they care about."

"Don't call me that." She gave a small shake of her head and turned back to the computer, freezing Zane with icy silence. What kind of asshole was her ex? What had the guy done to her? For the first time in his life, Zane was floundering when he wanted to be his most compelling. He wasn't even sure what he wanted from her. But he wanted it bad.

She'd turned over one of the plastic buckets Maggie used for preserving artifacts to use as a side table. He quietly picked up a small, antique, silver box. Something inside rattled as he ran his thumb over the smooth worn surface.

He weighed his words. "My point is, I've worked my ass off for this. It's proved to be more than I ever dreamed about. We could feasibly spend five years right here."

She choked on a quick breath, then exhaled. Her fingers hovered over the keys, but they didn't move. "Kudos. You beat your brothers. I'll look for you and the crew on the Discovery channel. I agreed to a month. I have two weeks left, unless you want to send me home early for bad behavior." The quick look she tossed over her shoulder was filled with desperate hope.

"Forget it. I just want everyone to get along. Dissent leads to accidents."

"Who are you, Rodney King? Listen, if it will get you out of my engine room, I'll go apologize to Maggie so that she's not upset. But if you're truly worried about accidents, you might want to hit the sack early every once in a while, and avoid getting drunk at parties and sticking your tongue down the throats of thousands of strange women—"

Too far. He crossed the room in three floor-eating strides and lifted her by the shoulders so that she'd have to deliver her stinging insults straight to his face. He hung on to his temper by a thread. "Jealousy doesn't become you, Williams. And it's clearly clouded your judgment. My father was an alcoholic, not me. I had one beer at that party. One beer. And as for sticking my tongue down the throats of strange women, I've been a damned saint on this trip."

Her brown eyes looked as soft as melting chocolate. Zane's libido rose as he detected the telltale hint of desire in the dilated pupils. He swallowed. "Not," he said roughly, giving her a little shake. "Not that I haven't *wanted* to stick my tongue in all manner of interesting places lately. God only knows why."

She glared up at him, her face pale. "What stopped you? All those woman were stripping you with their eyes. When they were over here using up *my* power, draining *my* generator, drinking your booze, and scarfing down our supplies. Any of them would have gone to bed with you in a heartbeat. All you had to do was crook your little finger and smile."

"That party really got you bent out of shape. Funny, I never pegged you for the jealous type," he taunted, just to see her eyes spit fire. Which they did.

"Oh please. I've never liked warmed-up leftovers."

Zane's expression went from amused to serious, and a moment later he looked downright grim. Tightening his grip on her shoulders, Zane gently drew her up until they were nose to nose.

"Tell me something. Did your husband beat you?" he asked. "Abuse you physically in any way?"

She scowled. *"No."*

"Is that true?"

"Yes!" She deflated, shame evident in the twin circles of red on her cheeks. "It was mental . . . verbal. Nothing I couldn't handle."

Yeah. Explained the lethal dry wit of her tongue. Self-defense. "Just because he didn't beat you with his fists doesn't mean you weren't abused. He's an asshole." He moved in a little closer, felt the soft puffs of her breath against his lips. "And you were smart to get away from him before his words turned into something worse." She shuddered and his temper flared. "I'd kill anyone who put their hands on you."

Her body bumped his and stayed there, her soft breasts pressed to the hard plane of his chest as she said thickly, "You have your hands on me."

"I'll probably kill myself for this later," he murmured, his eyes playing over her now flushed face. Teal gave a choked half laugh, half snort. It was all the permission Zane needed. Gliding his palms across her shoulders, up her arched throat, he tunneled his fingers through her silky hair, holding her head exactly where he wanted it.

"In the meantime," he murmured, watching her eyes for signs of fright or flight. He saw, thank God, neither. "There's something I forgot to give you last night when we were dancing. So for once in your life, Williams, could you please shut the hell up and cooperate?"

"N—"

His mouth closed on hers. The woman was just full of nos. For one second, Zane thought he'd pushed too far. Her lips were compressed into a tight line, and he felt the tension of her opposing urges pulsing through her body. But he also felt her erect nipples pressed against his chest, and her hips against his as she strained higher on her toes.

Reading her body language, he went in for the kill. Third time lucky. Fight it all she wanted, she was starting to feel some of the same sexual pull. Hell, nothing he liked more than a challenge, Zane thought as he angled his head, softened his lips. Just as she opened her mouth to say . . . something.

Her lips were open when his landed. She tensed when their mouths connected. A long shudder traveled down her body, and her fingers tightened on his back.

She tasted of hot cocoa, and smelled of redemption. Sensation shot through his body as she touched her tongue to his. Zane explored her pliant mouth as he felt the frantic pounding of her heartbeat in her temples, like a small bird beneath the fingers he had wound in her hair.

He used every technique in his not inconsiderable

arsenal. Tongue, teeth, hands. Good, nonverbal communication that she seemed to understand better than words. Teal's entire body participated in the kiss, and she slid her arms around his waist, her fingers gripping the back of his T-shirt as he plundered the warm recesses of her mouth.

In an annoying moment of sanity, Zane realized if he didn't put a stop to this right now, he'd have her flat on her back on the floor. Anyone could walk in. And frankly, this wasn't where he wanted to make love to Teal for the first time.

He eased away slowly. Her lips seemed to cling, and he went back for a brief, juicy kiss that left his body hard as a rock, and his pulses pounding. "The door isn't locked," he murmured, unable to resist nuzzling his nose across her hot cheek.

She shoved him away with the flat of both hands. "You are really amazing, you know that?" She wiped the kiss off her mouth with the back of her hand, eyes hot. "Is there nothing between zero and one-twenty?"

"Plenty." Zane realized that while he was shaken, she was rock steady. Or was she? Her eyes were luminous in her pale face as she chewed a nail, shooting him a hot, considering look. Then she strode across the room, untied the overall from her waist, and jammed her arms into the sleeves, then yanked the zipper of the coverall to her throat.

"Well, test-drive someone willing."

He spread his feet and crammed his fists into the pockets of his shorts to hide the bulge. "That was quite a response for a woman who was unwilling."

"And *you're* delusional. I have no intention of being a notch on *Ace* Cutter's headboard."

Taking his hands from his pockets, Zane, his breathing back under control, sauntered across the short distance separating them. "No notches. No headboard." He swiftly ducked his head and brushed a kiss on her mouth. "Anytime you're not willing to kiss me again, you know where to find me."

Something heavy slammed into the door as he closed it behind him. He grinned. "My point, I believe."

*   *   *

I should have slapped him, Teal thought for the ninety-seventh time. Instead, she'd hidden in the engine room all night, trying to make sense of her reaction to Zane's habit of kissing her whenever and wherever he felt like it.

This morning she'd acted like nothing had happened—something she was very good at. She'd exchanged professional words with him, because to avoid him would give that freaking kiss too much importance. She'd made a point of talking to Maggie, but they hadn't touched on what happened. No time.

Flat, calm weather had produced visibility of over a hundred feet. The helicopter had done its six P.M. pickup, taking with it the day's haul. Minus, mysteriously, a row of what Zane believed to be silver bars that had disappeared while they'd all been having lunch. It was as though the thief or thieves were invisible ninjas who slipped in when their backs were turned and just freaking swam away without anyone seeing them.

Lifting the hair from her nape, Teal searched the clear sky for storm clouds. The late afternoon air felt heavy and oppressive, matching her mood. Her stomach grumbled, the tuna sandwich she'd had for lunch a delicious memory. They'd all worked so hard that maybe a few dozen cookies would lift everyone's spirits. Zane had been right about dissension between crew members affecting everyone on board.

My fault, Teal thought, feeling crappy about altering everyone's happy mood because of her own shitty attitude, however well earned it was. As she checked to make sure she had all the necessary ingredients, she vowed to do better. Be better.

Baking soothed her, giving her time to think. It had the added benefit of keeping her off the deck while the others waited for the hordes to arrive for the evening. Maggie walked into the galley as she slid the first baking sheet into the oven. Teal's body tensed in preparation for a possible confrontation. But the older woman slipped onto a stool and propped her elbows on the counter.

She'd dived earlier, and her wet hair left a dark stain in the neck of the purple T-shirt she wore over her swimsuit. The older woman tugged at the brim of her straw cowboy hat. "I've got daughters, honey. And one of them liked to wear makeup and get a mani/pedi with me to lift her spirits. The other one would rather stick a nail file in her eye."

Teal smiled slightly, her heart warming as she accepted the idea that maybe Maggie didn't hate her. "I was being too sensitive."

Maggie removed her hat and settled it beside her, then ruffled her wet hair. "With reason. I tend to barge my way into the lives of people I care about, thinking I can make everything easier with unsolicited advice."

Teal stilled, biting her lower lip as she clarified the woman's statement. "You care about Zane. I get it."

"True. God, those cookies smell delicious. I care about you, too." She hopped from the stool and reached around the counter for a mug and the coffeepot, definitely in Teal's space. "I forgot that you were an only child."

Teal felt an insane urge to cry as she scooped spoonfuls of chocolate chip batter into neat rows on the second baking sheet. Was Zane right, and her fellow shipmates considered her more than just a coworker? Not sure what to say or how to deal with the surge of emotion, Teal uttered a low laugh. "If you think I'm antisocial now, you should've seen me as a kid."

"Tell me."

"Painfully shy was an understatement." The hurtful memories made Teal's chest ache. "I didn't know how to talk to the other kids, you know? They thought I was a snot, so they left me alone," she added softly, making sure every cookie was exactly the same as the last and the rows were evenly spaced.

"Oh, honey," Maggie murmured. "That must've been so lonely for you."

Teal swallowed and tossed her head so the bangs would get out of her way. "I read a lot, tinkered with stuff. Sam taught me how to listen to the hum of a well-run machine. I already knew how to listen, but this took it to the next level."

"You're a genius. As good as, if not better than, Sam. All the guys say so."

The compliment helped settle some of the tension in Teal's belly. She glanced at Maggie and flashed a wry smile. "You'll probably find this hard to believe, but my teachers equated my shyness with being rude."

Maggie laughed as Teal had hoped she would. "We went to a school counselor, but since Mom had issues, we couldn't exactly tell the truth, which was that she was a drug addict. I was 'documented' as secretive and uncooperative." She kept her tone cool and even, hating the memory. "Secretive because my mom didn't *look* like a druggie. She'd show up for those school meetings looking the picture of maternal concern."

"Teal," Maggie said in a voice filled with angry empathy. "How could you expose your mother? Of course you protected her. At a high cost to yourself. You had nobody else."

Staring at the oven buzzer, begging it to beep so that she didn't have to feel, Teal brought her thumbnail to her mouth, then shoved her hand into her pocket instead. "I don't like to talk about it."

"I think hashing out bad memories puts them to rest, but I'll try harder to mind my own business from now on. We can talk about something else, if you'd like. I'm sure there's all sorts of things I don't know about you. Last night, for instance, you surprised me when you mentioned that you were married. I had no idea"

Another fun subject. Maggie had a nose for uncovering secrets. "And divorced. Three years of lying in the bed I'd chosen before I realized I didn't have to stay there."

"Thank God you did. A lot of women don't ever leave. You're one strong, amazing woman, honey."

The buzzer dinged, allowing Teal to take out the cookies and put the other tray in the oven. She started moving the hot cookies to the cooling racks, giving her time to get her shit together. "I was young. Stupid. Dennis was my first real boyfriend, and I thought he was the answer to all of my prayers. Handsome, outgoing. He loved being the center of attention, and he made me believe that I belonged there, too. But only once he made me into Super Teal."

"Super Teal with the extensions?"

"Yeah. Dennis promised fun and excitement." She offered a hot, fragrant cookie to Maggie. "The parties weren't all I thought they'd be, and the after parties were ten times worse. That's when I'd get critiqued on my performance for the evening." Her gut clenched at the humiliating memories. Not busty enough, not pretty enough, not flirty enough.

Maggie set the cookie on the counter before sliding off the stool. "I'm hugging you," she warned, daring Teal to say no as she wrapped both arms tightly and maternally around her.

Teal's throat clogged and her eyes stung as she inhaled Maggie's scent of coconut suntan oil, clean ocean, and coffee. She wanted this hug more than she'd ever wanted a hug, but she stood there surrounded by Maggie, unable to return the gesture without completely falling apart. She patted Maggie's shoulder awkwardly, and Maggie hugged her tighter.

"Oh, honey, I'm so sorry. I get it now. I get *you* now." The other woman pulled back, her eyes filled with empathy as she scanned Teal's face. "Screw that bastard ex and anyone else who didn't' get you—you're perfect. Just the way you are." She brushed Teal's bangs out of her eyes. "And someday you're going to find a man who appreciates who you are."

Eyes stinging, and feeling a little uncomfortable with all the touchy-feely stuff, Teal moved away and sat down at the counter. Maggie was making an effort to be friends; the least she could do was make the same effort. "Someday you're going to have to tell me your secret for a happy marriage. You and Ben obviously have the real deal."

Maggie leaned against the counter and picked up her warm cookie. "Everything in a long-term marriage isn't all hearts and flowers. Believe me, we still have our rough patches." She took a bite. "Oh, yum, Teal. This is delish—" After chewing and swallowing, Maggie said quietly. "Ben and I have had some very—*heated* discussions over the last thirty years."

"I can't imagine you two fighting."

"You'd be surprised. Back in the day, Ben was a gambler. Cards. Horses. You name it, he'd throw money at it. It wasn't a hobby, or a fun way to pass a weekend. He had a gambling addiction, and we fought about it all the time. We had a family to take care of, and he made some horrific, stupid decisions. Finally we lost our house, and I'd had enough. I gave him a choice. His family or gambling." Maggie smiled. "Luckily for him, he chose wisely. We moved to St. Maarten, and never looked back."

"Good for you." Teal picked up a cookie she wasn't going to eat. God. What if Ben was still gambling on the sly? With an Internet connection, he could be secretly gambling even while he was on board the *Decrepit*. Was

Ben responsible for the sabotage and for the thefts? If so, where was he hiding what he'd stolen? Teal couldn't help but wonder if his old addiction had caused him to sell out his oldest and dearest friend.

"Can we change the subject for a minute?" Not really a change of subject, Teal thought uncomfortably, but she was trying for subtle here. Zane would be devastated if Ben was responsible for what was going on. "Do you think someone on board is responsible . . ." For trying to sink the *Decrepit*, pilfering treasure from the site, calling in the *Sea Witch*.

"Do I think for a moment that it's *Ben,* you mean?"

Oh, shit. "No—Maybe. I'm sorry, Maggie. But we're all trying to figure out who would want to hurt Zane, and or this salvage—"

"I'm not offended. Your suspicions are valid, given Ben's gambling history. However, I promise you. He hasn't gambled in over twenty years."

"I believe you." Teal chose her next words more carefully. "So who do *you* think is responsible?" Ryan? Saul? Colson? None of them made sense either. But what did she know about *any* of them? "Don't you think it's a little freaking strange that Zane spent weeks setting up decoy dive sites, yet the minute we reach the wreck, a host of other ships swoop in, including Zane's worst competitor?"

"Anyone who knows about the Automatic Identification System can track where we are, honey. It's not a secret. It's public knowledge. I keep telling Zane not to be quite so . . . exuberant with his finds. But you know him. Everyone is his buddy, and he loves to share."

"Show off, you mean." Teal thought of the lavish party where Zane had acted out his Casanova fantasies.

Maggie smiled. "A little, maybe. But he *does* love to share his knowledge and love of salvaging with anyone interested enough to ask. And people are fascinated and eager to see what he's discovered. It's not uncommon to have a dozen boats around just watching to see what's brought to the surface. And in Zane's defense, I think he's done a remarkable job of downplaying what's down there."

"Not from everyone." Teal thought of the missing pieces. "If it's not someone on board." Teal wasn't completely convinced that was the case. "Then it must've been one of Zane's many adoring salvage stalkers."

"Possibly . . ." Distracted by whatever she was thinking, Maggie trailed off. "But there's something . . ."

The hair on the back of Teal's neck prickled at the other woman's tight expression. Shit. Now what?

Chapter 9

Teal found Zane on the deck talking on his phone. While he looked to the world like he was enjoying a breezy chat, she knew he was making tactical plans to secretly move another load of treasure off the ship and on to Cutter Cay. She wished he'd done it with a shirt on. His broad shoulders looked smooth enough to stroke. She stuck her hands in her pockets and stared out at the water as she waited for him to finish his conversation.

As soon as he stuck the phone in his shorts pocket, she turned back to him. "I'm glad to catch you alone. There's something I need to tell you."

"That you can't resist me any longer and you want me to take you right here, right now? Okay, but let's go back to my cabin. We'll be more comfortable there." He grabbed her hand, but she swatted him away.

"I'm serious."

"*Too* serious." Zane grinned as he shifted closer. "Would it kill you to crack a smile, Williams?"

When she straightened, she found he'd moved back into position. They were only a few inches apart. Teal's mouth went dry at his closeness, but she didn't move. "I smile."

He touched her bottom lip with one finger, and said huskily, "Show me."

His eyes were impossibly blue, the naughty gleam dancing in them, compelling. Teal bit her lip as she tried not to smile, but she was so discombobulated with his nearness she couldn't pull it off even if she wanted to. "Stay away, Zane," she told him; her voice hoarse, but without heat. "We've already had this conversation."

His face got closer as he held her gaze. "Yeah?"

"Yeah." Not a word, merely a breath.

His hands rose, and he tucked her hair behind both ears, then cupped her face in his palms. "Close your eyes," he murmured.

Her lips felt stiff. "Why?"

Zane huffed out a laugh. "I want to give you something."

Against her better judgment, she closed her eyes, and he brushed his mouth over hers with a kiss as soft and non-threatening as a butterfly's wing.

When he pulled back, she opened her eyes. Her lips were buzzing and her brain had turned to mush. And body parts that had no business participating were lit up like the Fourth of July.

"Now, what were you saying?" He gave her a cocky grin that made her pulses pound and her good sense falter.

"You really have to stop doing that."

"Why?"

Her body echoed his question. Teal shook off her mental haze and pinned him in place with a scowl. "Listen up, Ace. This is important. About the pieces that have been stolen—"

"I'm listening. What's the problem?"

"Maggie's sure stuff is being stolen *after* we bring it on board. A few pieces she remembers seeing that hadn't been processed yet."

Zane just stood there, his expressive eyes hidden behind

sunglasses. When he didn't respond, she grabbed his arm.
His skin was hot, his forearm rock hard. She gave him a
little shake. "Don't you get it? The thief's gotten way too
confident. Not only is he ripping off treasure *underwater*.
Now he's waiting until we bring it up and then ripping it
off *on board. And that means it's someone—or ones—
close by."*

"If Maggie's concerned about possible missing pieces,
why hasn't she brought it up to me?"

"She thinks maybe she's misremembering things, or that
she simply couldn't find the items listed among all the other
pieces we've been hauling up. She wants to be one hundred
percent sure of her facts before she raises the alarm. And in
the interest of full disclosure—"

His lips twitched. "Yes?"

"I've searched everyone's cabin. Nothing major. Just a
quick look around to see if anything jumped out at me."

His left brow winged up over the rim of his sunglasses.
"Find anything?"

Her face felt hot, but damn it, her actions were justified.
These thefts affected everyone involved. Not just Zane.
"No, but I think that as captain of the ship, you should do
a more thorough investigation."

"Unnecessary, because it isn't anyone on board the
Decrepit."

Just because she hadn't found the stolen loot didn't
mean that at all, but Teal kept her mouth shut on that one.
He could probably have her tossed in the brig or something for invading people's privacy. "Then it's one of your
friends out there. Or they've gotten on board somehow."

"Who? One of those airheaded women with
pneumatically-enhanced boobs and small brains? Those
cute little old ladies"—he waved and they waved back—
"or the old guys with their chains and pinkie rings? Not."
He tucked her hair behind her ear, and the shiver went all
the way through her body like the vibration of a tuning fork.

"Sweetheart, Maggie's a great diver—and she has a host of other strengths. Among them, being the heart and soul of this ship. But she *does* have a bad memory, and she's miscataloged things before. Not to mention the sheer volume of what we bring to the surface. We sent sixteen tubs back home last night. Who's to say if what she thinks is missing went in one of them? *Sea Witch* has been pilfering shit from us for years. She's a nuisance, and she's probably the one picking over the site. But getting on board the *Decrepit*? Not possible, and besides, *I'd* know if anything major went missing."

Clearly he was blinded by the redhead's . . . assets. Honest to God. Laid-back was one thing, but was his eye on the ball here or not? "How about a zillion-dollar emerald, or a priceless . . . diamond-encrusted something or other?" she demanded with asperity.

He grinned. "I'd know if we found either of those, and I'd sure as hell notice if they were missing."

Teal suppressed the urge to growl. Nick was right. The man was entirely too trusting. Too trusting and too pigheaded. A veritable flotilla of boats, large and small, surrounded the *Decrepit*. Possible suspects on every freaking one of them, including his own team.

In an interesting optical illusion, *Sea Witch* hovered over Zane's shoulder like a bird of prey. Teal squinted at the boat. She'd kept a good distance away, so Teal couldn't see much.

"My bet's on her," she muttered. "Hang on, I'll be right back." She went inside, found the binoculars, then joined Zane at the rail.

He stepped up behind her as she adjusted the focus on the binocs, neatly trapping her body between his and the railing. "What are you looking at?" He bent down to speak quietly against her ear, his breath warm against her cheek. She swatted him away like a pesky fly, then used both hands to bring the binocs up to her eyes again.

"The Sea Bitch. I'm looking at *her,* and she's over there looking right back! What is she . . . ? She just held up her hand for me to *wait.*"

She jabbed him in his hard belly with her elbow. He wasn't a butterfly now, he was a hundred-and-eighty-pound gorilla at her back. "Would you mind stepping back? You're giving me claustrophobia."

The woman staring back at her was simply stunning. Her hair, the color of fire, hung down her back in a dead straight fall held back by an orange face mask. She had a dynamite body, nicely showcased in an orange-and-turquoise wet suit.

She was so Zane's type that Teal felt a recurrence of her seasickness; worse, recurrence of all her insecurities. Had he intentionally left out pertinent details about their history together?

He braced both hands on the rail on either side of her body, making a cage of his arms. "Don't engage her, for God's sake. She's just baiting y—"

"Oh, the sneaky thieving *bitch*! She's holding up something she stole! A gold . . . Damn it, what *is* that? It's some sort of medallion! I'm going over there to kick her ass!"

Zane huffed out a laugh and settled his hands on her shoulders. Probably to restrain her from diving over the side of the *Decrepit* and swimming over there. "Take a breath and let it go. We can't prove anything, and we'd never catch—"

"*Ohh!* The sneaky thief just gave me the freaking finger!"

Zane plucked the binocs out of her hands. "Don't take it personally," he told her dryly. "That finger was probably meant for me."

Teal turned around. A tactical error, since Zane had practically been standing right on top of her, and now his broad chest was pressed dangerously close to hers. "What did you do to her? Why does she hate you so much?"

"Nothing," he told her coolly, but his eyes were hot as he searched her face. "I don't even know her name."

You didn't know mine either, Ace, but you still had sex with me. "Did you sleep with her?" Teal could've slapped herself. She held up her hand. "Never mind—none of my business, I don't want to know."

"Well I'll tell you anyway. I can tell you in all honesty that I've never slept with the *Sea Witch*'s captain."

"That could just mean you stayed awake all night."

Zane broke into that easy laugh of his that made her feel hot and cold and itchy all over. "It could, but I've never even met the woman." He put one hand over his black octagonal heart. "Swear."

"How can you be so—so *relaxed* about all of this. Doesn't it piss you off that someone is stealing your stuff?"

"Of course it does. And I'm working on it. But it doesn't help to get freaked out about it. When I have more of an idea of who might be responsible, I'll take action. Until then I watch and wait."

"What's to stop the Sea Bitch from stealing even more while we wait? How will you stop her?"

"We won't, but the law will."

"Oh, like she gives a rat's ass that the law says don't steal! Give me a break, Cutter."

"Williams, she's followed Cutter Salvage for a couple of years. She's nothing more than a pain in our ass nuisance."

"So far."

"So far," he agreed. "And if and when that changes, I promise you, I'll deal with it."

Teal slipped sideways between him and the railing. She half believed him that he hadn't slept with the redhead. But the other half of her wasn't so sure. And she didn't believe for a moment that the Sea Bitch was as innocuous and unthreatening as Zane thought. The redhead had traitorous bitch written all over her.

"If I were you, *Ace,* I'd send flowers. Lots and lots of flowers. Maybe even chocolate. Or better yet, stick her sorry, thieving ass in jail and throw away the key."

*   *   *

All the women in this new batch had names like Barbie or Bambi or Bitsy. They'd come over at Zane's invitation and had draped themselves like skanky, sparkly tree ornaments all over the deck and railings. Six bikinis didn't have so much as a quarter of a yard's worth of fabric between them.

The guys they were with had a lot of chest hair, not much head hair, and wore plenty of gold chains and pinky rings.

Another freaking party. How the hell Zane expected everyone to push off and leave them the hell alone, Teal had no idea. She was once again cranky and out of sorts.

One thing she knew with absolute certainty: If Zane had even an inkling about how she felt about him, he'd be relentless. Relentless for two weeks. Because that was all the time he'd have to toy with her. If that. There were prettier, *nicer* women everywhere he looked. He had the attention span of a water newt as far as women were concerned. She, of all people, knew that truth firsthand.

He was a teeny, tiny bit intrigued because she was a challenge, but that minimal interest would wane the second she gave in or someone more interesting came along. All she had to do was ramp up her verbal defenses so he'd never suspect how she really felt. It was exhausting.

The minute her tour of duty was over, she was so out of here. She'd take her cut and be gone so fast his head would spin.

He'd come to the engine room earlier this evening and told her about the party. Then he told her, in no uncertain terms, that she'd better get her ass topside, or he'd come in and carry her out bodily. Teal slouched down on the fringes of the party, hot in her khaki pants and blue shirt because she still hadn't taken the time to go to St. Maarten to shop.

Earlier, Maggie had left a stunning red dress folded neatly on her bedroll in the engine room. Clearly still walking on eggshells after their little tiff, Maggie had included a gentle note. It simply said that Teal would look wonderful in red, and Maggie looked forward to seeing her in the dress someday. There was no mention of the party, though she knew that was Maggie's real intention for leaving it for her.

For a moment, Teal even considered wearing it. Then she thought better of it. She still didn't feel ready for that kind of attention—especially not from Zane.

She hated knowing that her marriage to Denny had colored every aspect of her life. He wasn't worth awarding that kind of power. But try as she might to be a better, stronger, more proactive version of her former self, she saw her ex in the Cutter brothers. And particularly Zane. It was hard not to. All three were ridiculously handsome, all were tall, dark, and dangerous looking, and they all had charm and a natural charisma that was hard to resist.

Denny was all that.

And he'd almost destroyed her. Belittling her with digging comments that had shredded her already thin self-esteem.

Resisting that brand of male sensuality was imperative to Teal's continued emotional growth. Hell. To her freaking sanity. Denny had sucked the backbone and self-worth right out of her. It had been so slow and so insidious that she hadn't even realized it was happening until it had been almost too late and she'd lost herself altogether.

He'd separated her from her friends, interfered with her job by trash-talking her to her boss enough times that the poor guy had apologized profusely as he'd fired her. Denny had wanted to keep her all to himself.

Teal didn't need counseling to tell her that it was a toxic relationship, one of verbal and mental abuse. She'd been a slow learner—but she *had* learned. Part of the reason she'd been so attracted to Denny in the first place was because he'd been so much like Zane. At least on the surface. She'd learned too late that underneath there was nothing honorable about him.

Regardless of that difference, the similarities between the two men shoved the bullshit meter way over into the red danger zone with Zane.

Crazy. Intellectually, she was perfectly aware that he'd never crossed any of her numerous lines in the sand. He hadn't pushed her to do anything she hadn't practically leapt at the opportunity to do. A kiss. A brush of hands. But he was a shoe waiting to drop. It wasn't logical. It wasn't adult. It wasn't even fair. It was just the way life had hardwired her. From her absent father to her mother's druggie boyfriends, she'd kept the male species at arm's length. Denny had tricked her into believing she was worth loving. Her childhood crush on Zane Cutter had made Denny the perfect man to slip past her defenses.

The reality was, Zane Cutter wasn't *ever* going to love her. If she offered herself to him—again—she wasn't even certain he'd accept. That just made her a poor, pathetic fool. Screw me once, shame on me; screw me twice, shame on me double, to paraphrase.

So when Zane cut through the crowd, she put on her toughest armor.

"Would you do me a favor?"

"No."

Zane laughed. "You don't even know what it is."

"Does it have anything to do with my engines?"

"No."

"Diving?"

"Sort of."

"The answer is still no."

"Have mercy, sweetheart. That boat over there is filled with—"

"Skimpily dressed, sex-starved, beautiful women? Yes, hard to miss. What do you want me to do? Pick out one each for breakfast, lunch, and dinner?"

"Pretend to be my girlfriend. I need to work. They won't bug me if they think we're an item."

"You're delusional. Both in the fact that you think you're God's gift to women, and that those surgically enhanced specimens would believe—for a second—that *I'm* your *girlfriend*."

"Come on. Please, Williams? I'll get a new engine for *Decrepit* if you put your heart and soul into it. Keep them off my back and don't let them distract me. Consider yourself my handler."

"That's like trying to wrangle a tomcat."

She was here. In her chair. Minding her own freaking business because she had no interest in minding anyone else's. She wasn't going to pretend to be Zane's girlfriend. She wasn't that good an actress, and as stupid as these women looked, no one was stupid enough to believe a man like him would look twice at a woman like her.

"I said no! What do you not understand about that? I told you I didn't want to come on this dive, I didn't want to kiss you, I didn't want to come to this stupid party, and I certainly don't want to pretend to be your frigging girlfriend! I'm warning you. Back off, Cutter."

Teal left him standing alone before she made a scene.

*   *   *

Contrary woman, Zane thought. He veered north, and she indicated she was going west as they dived together the next afternoon. Why was he so amused by prickly independence?

They kept each other in line of sight. Visibility was

good, about two hundred feet, which was awesome, but that wouldn't last with the impending storm.

The seabed was relatively flat sand, with an occasional coral reef outcropping. He and Ryan had run the airlift yesterday and cleared an area of about thirty feet in diameter, exposing the hard mall bottom six feet beneath the sand and sediment.

When the sand had settled, they had a nice big hole, and the exercise had exposed two bronze cannon. Ten-foot sakers with slender barrels that were well preserved, because like gold, bronze wasn't prone to conglomerate. Even though the *Decrepit* carried a crane, there was no reason to bring the cannon to the surface.

Zane opted to leave the "six-pounders" where they were. He expected to find more cannon, different sizes, different materials. He'd log them and leave them too.

The hole they'd made had several things of interest that he and Ryan had brought to the *Decrepit* yesterday. A dozen Mexican silver coins dated between 1550 and 1575, an ivory elephant tusk, and a few wormy timbers. Ben and Teal had taken a turn and returned with one gold coin between them.

Despite the king's ransom in treasure they'd already found, Zane's gut told him they'd only scratched the surface of what the *Vrijheid* had in store for them. He ran his gaze across the area they'd cleared yesterday. Nothing appeared to be missing. But if anyone had come down after they'd closed shop, how the hell would he know what *could* be missing?

He glanced in Teal's direction. She was like a terrier with a bone since she'd made the first big find and had stuck to that location all week. Spanning all her dives, she'd found several more gold chains, and a few gold and silver coins, some personal artifacts, probably carried by passengers, but she hadn't found any more emeralds. She was bound and determined to do so.

Brian's estimate of the beauty she'd found the week before was around the one-point-five mil mark. Not shabby for her first official dive. He spotted something; another box, similar to the one Teal had uncovered? Smaller though. Zane swam over to investigate. A small pile of sand had drifted over the area he and Ryan had dusted and he fanned it to see what he'd found.

While discovering an amazing and valuable artifact was extra sweet, he enjoyed coming across a four-hundred-year-old nail or a piece of worm-eaten timber almost as much. All were intriguing pieces of a greater puzzle.

That he'd already won the bet with his brothers was a given. Maggie and Colson, as well as Brian and his extensive team, hadn't cleaned or priced a quarter of what they had, and their heads were spinning like that kid's in *The Exorcist*.

Zane grinned around his regulator as he started systematically fanning the section of sand he was interested in. He exposed a man-sized length of worm-eaten timber and prolonged the anticipation of finding another box by swimming down the length of the chunk of wood.

Even while curiosity ate at him, he took his time trying to figure out what part of his virgin wreck this timber could be. Hard to tell. Several yellow-flecked French Angelfish accompanied his exploration, following him like puppies, weaving between chunks of gray coral and the worn wood as Zane moved slowly down its length.

A grouper darted out of hiding inches in front of his mask as he reached the jagged, broken-off end of his timber. Possibly a piece of the hull.

Now.

He put on more speed as he swam back to where he'd seen that intriguing square corner. Dusting the surface, he saw it was a smallish box about the size of a loaf of bread. His heart raced as he picked it up. Hard to guess weight in the water, but it felt heavy enough to be interesting.

The first box Teal had found had been sealed shut by conglomerate. The bastard who stole it had probably pried the thing open with a can opener to discover the contents. It chapped Zane's hide, and he knew Teal was still pissed as hell that someone had swiped it right from under her nose.

But this little oblong gem, with a little help from his diver's knife, opened easily. Inside lay a nest of finely wrought gold chains. He didn't remove them, just sifted through the delicate links with his finger. Looked like a woman's jewelry box. He found three bracelets with good-sized, square-cut emeralds on them, and a gold ring with a slightly bigger emerald in the center. Zane tucked the ring into the sleeve of his wetsuit for safekeeping since it was so small, and once open, the box wouldn't close again. Maggie was going to have his ass for prying it open with his knife instead of the usual procedure. Finders, keepers. He placed it in his basket to take back to the surface.

Glints of gold caught his eye, dots in the pale sand that had shifted with his movement. He picked one up. A gold coin. And another, and yet another. He didn't need to run the metal detector across the sand. The doubloons were as plentiful as pebbles on a beach. He filled his basket until there was no more room. Pumped, he went in search of what he'd seen an hour before. Christ, what could be better than hands full of coin?

Gold bars! His heart pounded hard as he reached out and picked up a worn bar from the pile. Hot damn. He wasn't called Ace for nothing. The soft metal had been worn away by the sandpaper effect of the shifting sand over hundreds of years, but the protection of the reef, and the sediment that had covered it well, preserved it for him to find. The gold bar on his palm caught the sunlight filtering through the clear water.

He rapped on his tank to alert Teal. She glanced over his way, then started swimming toward him, agile as a seal in her dense black wet suit, her short hair fanning around her head.

As his own elevated heartbeat throbbed in his ears, Zane had an insane urge to peel her out of her wet suit. He wanted to see her pale, sleek body here, where he was going to make his name in the salvage world. He had a crazy thought that he wanted to stake his claim on Teal, just as he was doing on the *Vrijheid*. Take her right there, a hundred feet under the water.

Here. Now.

He held up a finger. Wait. He scooped a double handful of coins out of the basket. When he turned around, he raised his arms and dropped them over her head. Golden confetti. Bubbles rose from her regulator as she spun in slow motion, hands extended to catch the falling coins. Her face said it all.

He motioned for her to wait again and grinned when she scowled and shook her head no. He motioned for her to close her eyes, and when she did so, took her hand and laid a gold bar across her palm. He tapped her on the shoulder and she opened her eyes. Inside her mask her gaze went wide.

Hellya! They'd hit the mother lode.

Chapter 10

Zane reclined on a padded lounge chair in the dark on the foredeck, listening to the faint sound of a piano and watching the tiny pinpoints of lights from the other boats reflect in the dark water. He breathed in the heavy air. *Storm coming.*

Mixed with the faint wisp of ozone was the fragrance of the barbecued chicken Ben and Ryan had taken turns burning for the current crowd. Logan would've hated all those people talking and laughing. He claimed crowds exhausted him. So did Teal. The only person Zane knew who wanted to be left the hell alone more than his oldest brother did was Teal.

Nick had called a few minutes ago to tell him he had people on the trail of Dennis Ross, who was currently somewhere in Europe. Zane found the vague hints about his older brother's "people" fascinating. But Nick always laughed it off as friends he made through his "hobby." Zane would love to know what that hobby was, but Nick usually told him he'd have to kill him if he told him.

Zane grinned, appreciating the theatrics of Nick's secret. Still his brother's "friends" had gathered quite a bit of information about Teal's ex in a few short days. Ross sounded like an arrogant prick. He was old money and part of San Francisco's society. He and Teal had been the golden couple for the three years they'd been married, then Teal had stopped attending parties with her husband.

Eventually Ross had announced their quiet divorce. Nick had told him, "In the press, his friends claim the split was due to Teal being so far beneath him on the social register. She never fit in. But the reality, *off* the record, was that he was a bully and a womanizer and tried to control every aspect of her life. Teal wasn't shitting me when she said he wasn't a nice guy. He's a self-entitled asshole."

"She told me some of this already. I should kick his ass."

"From what I hear, he doesn't sound like the kind of guy who'd go *mano a mano* with a man. His kind likes to control women. Still, I'd keep a lookout for the guy. He's definitely a possible contender for your saboteur, and if he's still got a thing for Teal, he might come after her."

"He'll have to fucking come through me first," Zane had told Nick grimly.

He stared up at the clouds.

So her husband hadn't hurt her physically. Zane was damned relieved. But verbal and emotional abuse were just as bad, if not worse. Harder to recover from, Zane suspected. He stacked his hands under his head because Teal had commandeered the lounger's pillow for the engine room. He wasn't quite sure what to do about his tangled feelings for her. He wasn't used to putting much thought into any of his relationships.

Other than with his siblings, pretty much all of his relationships were carefree and uncomplicated. He cared about his friends and showed it. He didn't associate with people he didn't like, rare as those were, because life was just too damned short.

But Teal—Teal required *thought*.

Thinking needed . . . thought. Zane grinned up at the

scudding clouds. On the plus side, she was a captive audience. On the negative side, she clearly didn't see him in a positive light. His reputation as a womanizer was only twenty-five percent . . . Okay—*thirty-five* percent true.

At twenty, he'd thought his nickname as Casanova of the Caribbean was a rite of passage. It had belonged to his father before Zane was ever born. People had tried to stick it on Logan in his late teens first. Which was pretty damned amusing. Mr. Fuck *you,* not Mr. Fuck *me.* Then they'd tried anointing Nick with the title. Mr. Cold Shoulder, not Mr. Hot to Trot. Finally, Zane had been the last heir to ascend—hell, maybe it was *descend*—to his father's throne. It was a pretty good fit, if he did say so himself. Even though the king was still firmly seated at the time, his father had thought Zane following in his footsteps was most excellent.

Over the years, somewhere in the back of Zane's mind was the niggling thought that his *mother* would have been pretty fucking disappointed in him. Much as he'd adored his father, Zane was the first to acknowledge the man had put Casanova himself to shame. Zane was attributed with a hell of a lot more conquests than had actually taken place. The numbers were grossly overestimated. But once that ball had started rolling, it was hard to stop it. And if he were being truly honest, he'd kicked the thing downhill a time or two just to see if the rumors would roll faster.

So here he was. Interested in a woman who could mean something. Who was practically part of the family already as far as his brothers were concerned. And his reputation was screwing him before he even made the first move. Ruined by his, *and* his father's, own reputation. Well, fuck.

Across the water, the lights on the *Sea Witch* winked off, so that the sleek little boat hid in plain sight in the dark. *Had* the redhead upped her game of cat and mouse? If so, she'd changed her MO from incredibly annoying to dangerous. She usually sailed alone. Zane hadn't seen anyone else on her boat as long as she'd been hovering out there. Could she have carried Teal's heavy box, as well as a six-foot-long chunk of conglomerate conjoined silver bars, onto her boat by herself?

Maybe she'd hired partners? Could be any one of the dozens of people hanging around.

Shit.

He scanned the dark water. A couple of fancy yachts still hung around, but Zane was done with people tonight. A dozen partiers were still on board the *Decrepit,* happy to entertain themselves while their host went off to enjoy a rare moment of solitude.

Okay, screw it, call it what it was.

Zane admitted he was fucking brooding. He probed his first brood like a sore tooth, and discovered a twinge of jealousy and a stab of annoyance hiding there. He'd never been jealous of anyone—ever. Yeah, he joked with his brothers and they bet on anything and everything. But he'd never been jealous of their success, or they of his.

But Teal—

Jealousy. *Well, hell.* He was proud of his path through his newfound emotional, mental masturbation. Holy shit! He felt quite . . . evolved. He let the mellow music and muted party noises lull him as he stared at the clouds. Too bad he didn't feel lulled, or mellow. *Enough of this shit.* Time to talk to the maddening woman.

*   *   *

Zane knocked on the door of his own engine room. After a minute-long conversation with the door, he let himself in. Neat as a pin and empty. He tried her cabin next, giving three swift knocks.

"Maggie?" Teal's voice was muffled.

"No, it's me. Are you decent?" He opened the door and walked in. "I hope no—"

She wasn't naked, but the sight of her was enough to make his breath snag.

"Get out!" She reached for her khakis, slapping the bunched up fabric to her chest.

"I knocked." God, he could hardly breathe. She'd put her hair up in a messy, sexy as hell female tumble that bared the sweet vulnerable curve of nape. And she must have borrowed that dress from Maggie.

A *red* dress. A *strapless* red dress. Which meant she wore no bra, just precarious elastic holding the scrap of material over the soft globes of her breasts. The whole thing could be whipped down in less time than it took to blink. The thought sent a jolt of heat straight to his groin.

"God, do you always just walk into people's rooms when they're getting dressed? Typical . . ."

"Sorry." His voice was hoarse. He caught a glimpse of her lovely back in the mirror behind her, her pert derrière looking round and luscious under the thin fabric. He managed to get his breathing under control with difficulty. "Coming back to the party?"

She made a rude noise. "As if. Thanks for stopping by. See you in the morning."

"Were you going somewhere?" *Meeting someone?* "Why are you all dressed up?"

"This isn't dressed up. It's a simple sundress. And it's none of your business what I do alone in my cabin. I'm dressed up for myself. Is it a crime to want to feel like a girl once in a while? God, it's like you've never seen a woman in a dress before."

He searched his brain for something funny to say, but for once in his life, Zane's mind went blank and his quick wit deserted him.

He reached for her hand, and removed the bunched up fabric she'd slapped over her chest. He tossed her pants onto the bunk behind her, then held her arm away from her body. "You're beautiful."

Her eyes narrowed, and she tilted her chin. "No, I'm not."

He reeled her in until they were inches apart. "I'm a connoisseur, trust me." His voice was husky. "You're absolutely gorgeous." He wanted to touch her skin. He wanted to ease down the top of her dress and fill his hands with the tantalizing weight of her breasts. He wanted to feast his eyes and mouth on her, and then he wanted to fill her liquid heat until he couldn't think.

"The dress . . ."

"Pretty, yeah. But it's not what you're wearing, trust me, Williams. You'd be just as beautiful out of it." More so, he thought when her eyes narrowed even further.

"Why are you here, Zane?"

Ah, Jesus. The million-dollar question. He knew the answer to that one. He wanted her flat on her back. Her belly, or knees—hell, any way he could get her. He touched two fingers to her flushed cheek, searched her big brown eyes for consent. She was hard to read, his prickly sea urchin. "The party's almost over," he told her easily when he encountered no encouragement. "Come for a walk on the deck with me?"

She looked unsure. Which beat a "fuck off."

"A walk?"

"Dare you," he taunted softly.

"No kissing."

"Not unless you ask for it."

"I won't."

Yeah. She would. But he could wait.

"Excellent, see?" Zane pointed out as they emerged on the empty deck a few minutes later. "Everyone's gone home."

The *Decrepit* looked better in the dark. The partial moonlight filtering now through the clouds filled in the rusty gaps and assorted scars, scabs, and wounds of time. In the dark, she was quite pretty. The tiny white

lights swayed in a gentle breeze, reflecting in the choppy
water.

Zane wanted to put his arm around Teal's bare shoulders, but he kept his hands in his pockets. He'd gotten her
to come, but there was a risk of spooking her by pushing
too far.

"How did your mother feel about you coming to see
Sam every summer when you were a kid?" He didn't
much care about her mother one way or the other, but he
was starting to care about Teal. Everything and everyone
who'd made her who she was today interested him.

"She—" Teal shot him a quick glance. "She met Sam in
a bar—picked him up, I suspect. Whatever. It was a one-
night stand. He split. She—for reasons I never could figure
out—had me. When I was six, she apparently read about
your father and Sam in the paper."

"Dad had discovered the *Santa Teresa*. It was big news
because of the value and amount of gold coins salvaged.
That was the first time you came out to Cutter Cay." Zane
smiled. She'd been a nervous little kid. Shy. Quiet. "I went
with them to pick you up in Tortola. If I remember right,
you were terrified and puked a lot." And he'd been pretty
annoyed that some strange girl had shown up to steal
some of his limelight from his father.

"Oh, yeah. Major motion sickness." She smiled without
looking at him. Which gave him a chance to look at her.
Her skin had picked up a light tan, but was still very fair.
And smooth. And very touchable. He refrained. Priding
himself on his self-control.

"You were what?" she asked. "Twelve? You barely noticed me, and Sam . . . Poor man. He had no idea *what* to
do with a little *girl*. He hadn't known about me, of course.
I came as quite a shock. My mother . . . Well, let's put it
this way, she used me as a bargaining chip for child support."

Zane wished he could wipe the bad shit away with a sweep of his hand.

"What she never understood was, Sam's a decent man. As soon as he knew of my existence, he would've paid her. To give him his due, he always tried to connect, but, face it, I wasn't an easy child. But I—God, I *lived* for those two weeks every summer."

"How so? It was brave of you to leave everything familiar to go someplace you'd never been."

"For two glorious weeks I could be a kid. And no matter how undemonstrative Sam was, I was never afraid of him."

Ah shit. "You were afraid of your mother?"

She gave him a wry look. "She was an addict. Coke. Meth." Teal swept her bangs back from her forehead. "She was . . . erratic. Angry and emotionally unavailable. Not to mention, I was always worried about money. Rent. Food." She shrugged. "Stuff like that. I didn't have to worry about any of that when I was with Sam. The food was simple, but all I could eat."

"Which probably wasn't much." He remembered her as being all arms and legs and hair. "Sam's a fixture on Cutter Cay," Zane said easily, his heart swelling with empathy. Her childhood had *everything* to do with who she was today. He could only imagine the inner strength she had to have to cope with being the adult in that situation when she'd been no more than a shy, frightened child herself. "I was shocked when he told us he had cancer."

"Yeah. So was I." Teal chewed her nail. "I had to practically beg him to tell me anything more than the diagnosis. And even then he downplayed how dire things really were. Logan filled me in." A slight breeze fluttered her hair around her face, and she paused to rub her bare arms. "Sam's always been so proud of the work he did for your father. I think the death took the oomph out of him. He doesn't even sound like the same guy he was a couple of years ago.

"They were best friends."

"I know. I wish—"

"What?"

"That he and I were . . . closer." She smiled slightly and pushed her hair out of her eyes. "But he taught me life lessons through engine repair." Her voice lowered and she mimicked her father. "Clean each piece until it shines. Dirty engine's a sign of a black heart." She shook her head. "If I'd checked Dennis's BMW engine, I could've saved myself some trouble."

Zane smiled. "Dad and Sam built practically everything on the island from the ground up. Dad discovered the virgin wreck *Conde de Santa Clara* the year before he bought the island."

He shrugged. "Money to burn after that. A private island was just the thing. A wife was next. He met my mother in Miami, married her, and brought her to Cutter Cay after he'd built a house. Small then. But that grew with the family."

"Sam told me about your mom. He said she was the kindest, sweetest woman he knew. I think he was a little bit in love with her."

"Yeah, she was amazing. Everyone loved her. She died when I was a kid. Car accident. Drunk driver." Years later, when he'd found out *why* she'd left the island with himself and his brothers, he'd never understood how she'd lasted so long with his father. His father had actually bragged about how many women he'd had during his marriage. He'd never been faithful. It was one thing womanizing when a guy was single . . .

Teal blew her bangs back to see him better. "I'm sorry."

"Me too. She'd taken us to her mother in Portland. Dad came to get us. The fights were horrendous. Dad already had the three of us back on Cutter Cay while she went through legal channels. Money would've won, but she was killed before the divorce was final." Zane rubbed a hand across his jaw. This conversation wasn't exactly going to breed seduction.

He reminded himself of the old adage, "Be careful what you wish for." He'd *wanted* to know more. But he was the one spilling his guts. "Your dad was his mechanic, chief cook, and bottle washer. They were together longer than most marriages—almost forty years before my father's heart attack."

He glanced at her profile in the moonlight. Zane didn't give a damn what they were doing. As long as he was close to her and she wasn't snapping at him, he was making progress.

"I know you and your dad were close. You were with him when it happened, right?"

It still felt like yesterday. A big, invisible hand grabbed him by the throat, squeezing hard. "Yeah. Almost two years ago. We were standing right here in the galley. The *Decrepit* was his before he started raking in the loot." Zane tried to ignore the sensation, to banish it by focusing on Teal's face. But his eyes still burned and his chest ached. He didn't want to remember the terror he'd felt, alone in the middle of the ocean with a dying man, hours from help. It hadn't mattered. He'd realized after the fact that while he'd been crazed doing CPR, his father was already dead. But he'd felt guilty all the same.

Sure, he shared his grief with his brothers, but they hadn't been as deeply affected. He'd been the one most like his father. He'd been the one there watching through an unstoppable sheen of tears as his dad's lips turned purplish, then blue, his tan leaching away as he grew colder by the minute. It was Zane's fucking fault, and he regretted it every day.

"I'd spent years looking for the *Vrijheid* and had written off this site. I never got a hit on any of the sensors—which

I now realize is because equipment tends to go on the fritz in this particular corner of the ocean. Still, I never considered that it might be the wreck site. I was down here on a pleasure dive when I found a cannon. The minute I saw it, I was a hundred percent sure it belonged to the *Vrijheid*. I wanted to talk my father into coming after her with me. It would've been sweet to share this with him. He was excited—hadn't seen him that way in a long time . . . then he died."

Her eyes were like melted chocolate as she gave him an empathetic look that wrenched his heart. "He was always kind to me, and I know he was crazy about you and your brothers. You were just about all he talked about. You must've been scared. *Horribly* scared out here so far from help. But I bet it was the way he'd have wanted to go. Being with you, out here, doing something he loved . . . Better fast than slow. But still horrible."

Zane rubbed his chest. Sudden wasn't better. Sudden sucked. Sudden made you realize all the things you'd never get to do. All the things you'd never say. *Sudden* took everything and gave you nothing in return but a big, gaping hole that never seemed to fill no matter how much pleasure you took in life. "You still have a chance to connect with Sam. It's not too late."

"What?" Her shoulders hiked.

Too close. Her emotional barrier had been breached. He curled his arm like Popeye to show a muscle, and teased, "Until my father died, I'd always felt immortal."

"You're still immortal." Teal looked out over the water, a few stray wisps of hair dancing around her face in the breeze. "*And* very lucky."

"She's pretty amazing, isn't she?" he said, referring to the *Vrijheid*. Teal got it and mirrored his smile. The ache started to ease. Getting her to smile was like watching the sun come out after a hurricane. Not only was it glorious, it made a guy realize that no matter what had happened, the worst was over.

"That's why you're called Ace, right? The sea and pretty girls give you everything you want," she teased, brown eyes dancing in the moonlight.

"Not all of them," Zane told her, seriously, holding her gaze. He leaned forward and brushed her hair out of her eyes. She froze, but when he dropped his hand and leaned back, she relaxed. He braced his hands on the railing behind him, and said smoothly, "Some pretty girls still manage to resist me. It's baffling and quite mysterious when I'm such a nice guy." He wanted to kiss her again in the worst way. He wanted to strip that beautiful dress off her and see her bare breasts. He wanted . . . to take it fast. He had to take this s-l-o-w.

Maggie had cautioned him, "Ask the girl to dance, listen to her answer. Do *not* rush her onto the dance floor just because your foot is tapping."

He slid his arms around her waist, pulling her gently so that her back was to his chest. He nuzzled his nose against the soft, fragrant skin of her neck, just below her ear. He knew he was playing with fire, but she didn't stop him, and he couldn't find it in him to stop himself.

She tilted her head to give him better access. Feeling like he'd just won the Nobel Peace Prize, Zane nuzzled the delicate nerves behind her ear with his nose, then ran the tip of his tongue around the shell. Her shoulder came up as she shivered, but she didn't pull away.

She tilted her head a little, so her silky hair brushed his nose. "Not . . ."

The smell of her skin enveloping him was at once hauntingly familiar, and excitingly new.

Wanting her, he turned her to face him. He couldn't begin to define the sensation he felt, holding her willing body gently against his. The soft brush of her breasts against the hard plane of his chest was shockingly erotic when he knew it probably wouldn't go much further than a kiss. He couldn't think straight. His entire being was fully engaged in the anticipation of a mere kiss.

His body was a furnace, his temperature spiking as his heart galloped pleasantly and he lowered his mouth to hers.

Just as he was about to dive in, she stiffened and turned her head. "What *is* that?" she whispered, pointing at the dark waves.

For a moment he thought she was referring to his erection. Gritting his teeth, Zane adjusted his shorts over his rock-hard dick, and reluctantly turned to see what she was looking at.

Ah, hell. The unmistakable play of halogen lights underwater. "Someone's down there helping themselves again."

"The Sea Bitch?"

This was getting fucking annoying as hell. "Maybe." He had to nip the redhead in the bud sooner than later. He waited a few minutes until one of the security guys did this leg of his circuit, and instructed that two of them track the lights to the source. "My first suspect is the woman on the *Sea Witch*. Start there," he instructed.

The guy went off to get his partner, and a few minutes later the Sea Ray left a white wake behind it as it crossed the water.

"What if it's *not* her?" Teal watched the wake dissipate behind the small boat. "Nick said he'd check to see where Denny was . . ."

"He did. It's not Ross. Your ex is currently sitting in a very nasty jail cell in Turkey for bringing pot into the country. He's off the hook. For the thefts anyway," Zane told her dryly. "Has to be Sea Witch. She's the only one not sleeping off their drunk after our party. Everyone else was here tonight."

Teal chewed her lip. He wanted to chew it for her. "Not the three grannies."

He smiled. "I can't see those three little old ladies taking a midnight dive any more than I could see them partying down with the bimbos. Can you?"

"Well, it was either the Sea Bitch or whoever's on that Hatteras Power Cruiser. I didn't see anyone from the *Good Fortune* crew at the party, did you?"

Something niggled at the back of Zane's mind. Niggled again. Harder. "The *Good Fortune*?"

"Yes, that's the name of the grannies' boat. The Hatteras Cruiser? I noticed the name when we were out diving yesterday."

"The *Good Fortune*? Are you sure? That was the name of an eighteenth-century pirate ship."

*   *   *

The next morning, Teal was cleaning her dive equipment when a stunning blonde in a sleek little cruiser pulled up at the *Decrepit*'s dive platform as Teal was checking her tank. Unfortunately, she was the only one around.

"Hi," the blonde shouted, "You must be Teal. I'm—"

Whoever the hell she was, was obscured by the sound of the blowers Maggie and Colson were using on their dive. Teal indicated she'd come down and jumped onto the platform to help the blonde tie up. Her boat was a sweet, twenty-four-foot Bayliner Cruiser, not new, but well maintained. As was the blonde. Mid thirties, tanned, buff, with about a mile of sunny blond hair, loose of course. She looked like a sexy mermaid in turquoise shorts and a little tank top that showed off her tan, her belly button bling, and size C boobs. Teal hated her on sight.

They tied up the boat, and Teal indicated she go on ahead to the salon. Zane was with Ben in the wheelhouse. Teal climbed up to the wheelhouse and said, as graciously as she could manage while a green-eyed monster ate her heart, "You have a visitor."

Zane glanced up, his eyes softening when he saw her. Teal told her skipping heart to stop being ridiculous. Zane probably thought she'd come up to tell them lunch was ready.

"Who is she?"

"Didn't give me her name. Long blond hair, light eyes—" Which probably described ninety percent of Zane's women. "Bayliner Cruiser?"

"Cat!" Zane looked pleased.

Great. "I'll leave you to your reunion, Ryan's waiting for our dive."

After joining Ryan and suiting up, Teal was just in time to see the blonde fling herself into Zane's arms and give him a big kiss. They were practically welded together.

Ryan, standing beside her, saw her line of sight. About to jump into the water, he stopped her with a hand on her shoulder as she was spitting into her mask.

"She's Cat Berland," he offered, although Teal would've bitten off her tongue before she asked. "Maggie and Ben's daughter? The three of us went to school together, she's a good friend, but she and Zane have always been close. Especially since Jessie was born."

The sun was shining, but Teal's blood turned icy cold. Mask in hand, she turned fully to face Ryan and enunciated carefully, "They have a child together." Not a question.

Well, there she had it. The precious, black-haired, Cutter-blue-eyed toddler in Maggie's Grandma book? Confirmed as Zane's daughter. Ryan looked as though he knew he shouldn't have said anything. Teal could tell. Well, too bad. Secrets like that didn't stay secret long. Especially when the Cutter DNA was so strong.

"Not officially," Ryan quickly added. As if the child not being "official" meant Zane didn't have to take responsibility.

Teal arched her brow.

"Look, I wouldn't worry about it okay? It's—Shit. I shouldn't have sai—It just slipped out. Ask Zane to fill you in, okay?"

Not officially? And the Berlands still *talked* to him? Teal put on her mask and nodded. Right. She'd ask Zane can't-keep-it-in-his-pants-Cutter when hell froze over.

*   *   *

Cat Berland might have shown up unannounced, but everyone was so happy to see her, it became a party. Maggie and Ben were clearly delighted their daughter had come out from her home in St. Maarten to see them. Cat looked a lot like Maggie, with a pert nose, generous mouth, miles of wavy blond hair, and light blue eyes. She laughed a lot, touched Zane a *lot,* and was very friendly. It was obvious she and Zane were old friends, and in between all the stuff he had to take care of, he took care of Cat. He'd sling his arm around her shoulder, or tug her hair, or bring her a Coke before she was thirsty.

Acknowledging to herself that she was jealous, both of Zane's friendship with the stunning blonde, but also at the closeness of mother and daughter, Teal tried to be gracious. Own it and move on, she told herself. She tried hard to be her sweetest, the nicest she could be.

It was hard to dislike someone she actually liked. Which made her feel worse. Things would go back to normal. Cat was leaving the next morning. Teal didn't ask where she was sleeping, and no one mentioned it.

It was one of the longest days of Teal's life. Unfortunately her brain refused to switch off. She tried reading, she played with the CAD on the computer, she fiddled with the generator. Nothing helped. What she needed was a long walk around the deck and some fresh air.

The companionway was narrow, the lights dim.

Everyone had had a long day and sacked out early. Even
the adrenaline high of the past few weeks was no match
for exhaustion. And a tired diver was at risk of making
stupid mistakes. Other than the guys whose job it was to
stay awake and alert and guard the *Decrepit,* everyone
had gone to bed hours ago.

She'd worked her ass off all day. She'd dived three
times, filled in log reports, and taken photographs of the
treasure for Maggie. She'd also scouted around to get a
sense of what the mystery divers had taken the night before. Unfortunately, the security team hadn't turned up
any new information. The Sea Witch appeared to be on
her boat, though it could have easily been a well-planned
ruse. And by the time the security team suited up and
scoped out the site, the thieves were long gone.

As Teal surveyed the scene, it became clear that a cen-
tral portion of the dive site had been tampered with, and
a large urn was missing. It was unclear what else they'd
gotten away with.

There was one thing about the thieves that Teal was
grateful for, however. After she hotfooted it away from
Zane, she made the rounds and checked up on the crew,
making sure everyone was accounted for.

They were all on board, including Ben. He was in the
galley drinking port with Maggie, the two of them giggling
like teenagers.

Teal had felt terribly guilty just then for being so suspicious of him. And though she'd never admit it to Zane,
she wondered if maybe she could learn a thing or two
about trust from him. Maybe, just maybe, she could be a
little easier with people, let her guard down, trust a little
more.

Then Zane's baby mama had shown up and ruined everything.

Chapter 11

It was very still, barely a breath of a breeze on a very warm night. She headed for her favorite spot in the bow, under the crane. It was graceless and never used, but she had a soft spot for it.

She was used to the noises the *Decrepit* made. The creak of wood, the chimes of metal brushing metal, and the soothing lap of the wavelets against the hull. Now that she had her sea legs, and didn't have to do the one-minute mile to find her little yellow bucket, she was starting to enjoy the novelty of being at sea.

There was a moon, but it was playing coy with the clouds. God, had she ever heard quiet like this? Never. The *Sea Witch* was still off the port bow, although she was dark and hard to see. Teal stopped as she heard a soft, light female voice. Sound carried over water, and there were the other boats nearby. Maggie? Or, her heart thudded unpleasantly, Ben and Maggie's stunning daughter Cat?

All she saw was a double silhouette at the rail. The exact same place on deck where just hours ago Zane had fondled her boobs. The dog!

Cat's long hair was unmistakable, and Teal would recognize Zane from a mile away. The two were in a clinch, murmuring softly to one another. For a moment Teal thought her seasickness had returned. Then she realized her stomach was reacting to the scene in front of her. Having Zane flirt and tease and joke around with the skanks who'd come on board before was bad enough. But finding him with a woman who'd borne his child, and in a secluded place, on a dark deck . . .

Teal carefully backed up, then turned and quickly went inside. She took the stairs three at a time.

By the time she arrived in the companionway where the cabins were, she was running. Stupid, stupid, stupid.

A hard hand grabbed her upper arm and spun her around.

"It's not what it looked like," Zane said quietly, his fingers like a manacle on her arm.

Teal wanted to cry. Exhaustion and frustration made her vision blur. She wanted to hurt him. She wanted his heart to break. "With you, everything is *exactly* what it looks like. Subtlety isn't in your makeup. You want, you take. Tough shit for everyone else." God, where were the words coming from? She wanted to take them back, but her chest hurt so bad she could barely breathe. "You're *just* like your father, Zane Cutter."

It was the worst insult she could think of right then. She tried to jerk her arm out of his grasp, but he was mad and he wasn't letting go.

"*What* did you say?" Zane asked in a soft, dangerous voice that should have had Teal running for her life. Still, Maggie and Ben's cabin was only a few doors away. The security guys were just a few doors down. One yell and they'd come running.

She should have kept her mouth shut. She was way overtired, and her emotions were already all over the freaking place. But seeing Zane with that woman had made her head spin and her heart hurt.

"I said," Teal whispered. "You'd screw anything that wasn't nailed down. You're *exactly* like your father."

He crowded her against the bulkhead. "Take it back."

"What? Are you *ten*? It's the truth. And aren't you the guy that tells it like it is?"

"I'm nothing like my father."

"Tell that to all the women who've loved you and seen your back as you scurried off into the sunset."

"Don't knock it 'til you've tried it."

"Oh, plea—" Suddenly he crushed his mouth on hers, cutting off every rational thought. Hot. Wet. Hard. He tasted of coffee, and brimstone. He tasted like temptation and unfulfilled fantasies. He tasted—like heaven. As his tongue swept between her parted lips, his hands slid down her arms, then pulled her hands up either side of her head and held her there, imprisoned by his hard body and the punishing kiss in the middle of the companionway.

Her breath rasped through her constricted lungs as he feasted on her mouth. She felt every luscious sweep of his tongue throughout her body. Her skin burned from the inside as if she had a high fever. Sound came distantly, as if she were underwater. She couldn't see. All she could do was feel.

She should do . . . *something,* but the thought drifted out of her lust-addled brain like fog. She wanted her hands free, but Zane held them firmly in place.

She managed to draw away just enough to give her leverage to nip his bottom lip with her teeth. His eyes flared and he closed the gap. This time, the kiss was slightly less violent as he teased her tongue out of hiding and challenged it to a duel. Teal rose to that challenge and, at the same time, twined one leg around his calf.

His erection pressed against the juncture of her thighs,

and she felt the rapid pounding of his heart against her breasts. She twisted her hands in the manacle of his fingers.

He lifted his head slightly. "Gonna hit me?"

"Let me go and see."

He kissed the side of her throat, his mouth hot and hungry as he trailed his lips to her collarbone. Teal wrapped her freed arms around his neck, sliding both hands up into his thick, silky, too-long hair.

Her nipples were so hard they hurt, and she guided his head to her breast and stood on her tiptoes to give him better access. He groaned low in his throat and closed his teeth gently on the distended nub through two layers of fabric, making her moan. The pleasure was sharp and sweet. With her leg, she drew him more tightly where she needed him.

"You're playing with fire, Williams."

"Talk's cheap, Cutter." She barely managed to get the words out through tingling lips and constricted lungs. Even the effort of whispering was out of the question; she'd never been more turned on in her life.

"Willing to see my back?"

"Thanks for the consideration, but that's assuming *you* walk away first."

His laugh was hoarse. "Put your legs around me." He slid his hands under her arms and lifted her. Teal wrapped her legs around his waist. Somehow they maneuvered from the companionway to his cabin. A small lamp illuminated the wide berth with rumpled white cotton sheets and pummeled pillows. He lowered her onto the cool surface and came down into the cradle of her thighs. Her legs fell free, but she kept her arms around his neck. She ran her tongue across his shoulder to taste him. Salty male. An aphrodisiac and dangerously addictive, she knew.

Her hands roamed the crisp mat of hair on his broad chest. It was softer than she remembered. His smooth skin stretched taut across iron-hard muscles. She ran her tongue along his collarbone as he efficiently unbuttoned her shirt, brushing the sensitized tips of her breasts as he one-handedly shoved buttons through buttonholes.

She wore a plain, white cotton bra. No frills or lace. Not what he was used to, she bet. "You're good at this."

"Years of practice with a bra and a pillow."

Laughter bubbled up in her chest. God. She felt euphoric, giddy. Even her eyeballs throbbed with lust as he spread the fabric aside and leaned back, his eyes navy blue and filled with a kind of wonder that must be a trick of the light. He frowned. "You're . . ."

Too skinny. Flat-chested. Lousy in bed. Too fast. Too slow. She could take her pick of insults. Damn it. She'd forgotten and hadn't braced herself for his expert appraisal. And why hadn't she? Zane Cutter was literally God's gift to women. He could have any woman he'd ever wanted, and had. Alternating waves of heat and ice flooded her already oversensitized body as Teal struggled to cover herself. But at the same time as she was fumbling for two sides of her shirt to draw them back over her chest, Zane was tugging the fabric free.

Heat scorched her skin and tears of fury and embarrassment burned behind her lids. "Let m-me up." Somehow this was going to affect her far worse than anything Denny had ever said. She felt small and stupid and waited for the righteous anger to well up and protect her. Like a trapped animal, Teal froze.

She felt the hard, erratic thumping of his heart against her breast. She was excruciatingly aware of the hardness of his eager penis nestled in the moist heat between her legs. Like a pinned butterfly, she couldn't get away. Struggling, as she knew, was always useless. She stayed deathly still, heart manic. Waiting . . . "I have to—"

"Perfect," he murmured hoarsely at the same time, talking over her.

Teal blinked him into focus with a confused frown. "W-what?"

He was staring reverently at her breasts, then stroked his finger along the shallow hills and valley, tracing the edge of her bra. Back and forth, back and forth. Her entire body—*yearned*.

"Your breasts are beautiful. Small and heavy and perfectly fit my hand. See?" He slid the fabric aside to bare one plump mound, then cupped it in his warm palm and ran his thumb across the tip in a maddening caress that had her shifting beneath him. His hand looked shockingly dark against the milky pale skin of her breast.

He bent his head, and his cool, shaggy hair trailed an erotic path across her sensitized breasts. This time, there was nothing between the hot cavern of his mouth and the painfully hard peak. As his teeth closed over her left nipple, Teal's body arched off the mattress. He used his tongue as well as his teeth to drive her insane. Then skimmed her plain cotton panties off and away without her even realizing that he'd shifted off and then back on top of her. His swim trunks were gone too. The shock of feeling hot skin, too hot skin, made her heart manic.

Her pelvis jerked in response as he came back into the cradle of her legs. "I want you so bad, love. . . ."

It took a moment . . . for . . . the . . . penny . . . to drop.

Teal used both hands to shove at his unyielding chest. Hard. "Get off me, you—you—Get *off*!"

The second Zane levered himself up on his arms to look down at her with lust-filled eyes, and a bewildered expression, Teal wedged her leg between them. He was too heavy to move unless he chose to do so. She pushed at his shoulders again using both hands and a knee, putting some muscle into it. Angry tears smarting behind her eyes.

The feverish surge of blood heating her skin from nose to toes infuriated her. She was hot all over for a completely different reason. "I changed my mind," she punched his shoulder, and when he remained still, punched it harder. And again. "Let me up."

Rolling off her, Zane held both hands up in surrender. Like hers, his breathing was harsh and uneven. Strands of dark hair clung to the sheen of sweat on his face. "It's your prerogative to change your mind, but sweetheart, what—"

Love. Sweetheart. What'shername. Same. Same. The freaking *same* as a freaking cat in the freaking dark. "And I'm exercising that right." Jaw aching from clenching her teeth so hard, Teal scrambled off the bed. Where the hell was her shirt? "And don't call me sweetheart. Or love. *Ever.*" Damn. Zane was sitting on it.

"What happened, Ace? Did your baby's mama tell you she changed her mind and wants you back? Is that why you two were so freaking touchy-feely all damned day?" Teal snatched his T-shirt off the floor and pulled it over her head, inside out. It smelled like him, clean sweat, salty air, and Zane's own brand of sex appeal.

"What . . . ?"

"Here's a news flash, *Ace*. Just because you have an itch to scratch, and I'm here, doesn't mean I'm yours for the taking."

"Of course n—"

"I work for you. That's *it*. If you have an itch—scratch it somewhere else."

"Okay. I get it, but—"

"If you touch me again, I'll—" What? Tell her father? Laughable. Tell Logan or Nick? Ridiculous, they'd care even less than Sam would. "Make you sorry." As threats went it was weak, but tears were building up behind the dam of her eyelids. If she didn't get to her engine room, she was going to compound her mistake and bawl like a baby.

He slipped off the end of the bed, gloriously, unashamedly naked. Magnificently naked, Teal thought bitterly.

The man didn't have a modest bone in his body. He took a cautious step forward.

She held up a hand. "Don't touch me."

He stopped in his tracks, his expression softening. "I'm sorry if I hurt you, Teal. I thought what we were sharing was mutual. Was I too rough? I wanted you so badly, I went a little crazy."

"You didn't hurt me. I made an error in judgment. You didn't want *me* so badly, Zane. You just *wanted* to get laid. And the next time I'm with someone, I don't just want to be anyone. I want to be *the* one."

He frowned. "I didn't—"

Teal slammed the door behind her and ran like the hounds of hell were on her heels to the engine room.

"Enough of this bullshit," Zane snapped, shoving open the door a nanosecond after she stormed in. She discovered watertight doors didn't slam well. And this one didn't lock.

With her rigid back to the open door, arms crossed, she said around the thickness in her throat, "Get out." Her beautiful yellow engines wavered in her vision. Her chest hurt. She felt like an idiot. She had no excuse for her own behavior, and she had no one to blame but herself. These were all lessons she'd already learned. Yet she'd gone and done it again. Fallen victim to his lethal charm. Again. She *knew* better. A leopard never changed his spots.

He walked like a cat on his big bare feet. And because she didn't hear him sneak up behind her, he manacled her wrist and tugged before she could react. "Come with me." The words were an unsympathetic snarl.

This was Zane unleashed. The charm gloves were off. She dug in her bare heels. "Go to hell."

He didn't wrench, but he wasn't letting go either. "I am *not* talking to you in here," he said savagely. "Come willingly, or I swear to God, Williams, I'm going to throw you over my shoulder and *carry* you out."

He'd taken the time to yank on his shorts, thank God. She'd never heard him angry before. His anger fueled her own. Her heart was going ballistic, and hot and cold prickles flooded her body. "*You* don't have a right to be pissed off, Zane Cutter." She struggled to free her wrist from the handcuff of his fingers. He wasn't hurting her, but she couldn't break free.

"I do when you insist on slandering me."

That got her attention. She swiped at her cheek with her free hand before turning her head to look at him. "*Slander?*"

"A false statement that injures a person's—that would be my—reputation."

"Give me a break! Injure *your* reputation?" Teal's laugh was mocking. "You thrive on everyone knowing you're a bad boy." She used her free hand to try and pry at least one of his fingers off her wrist. But his hand was like a ring clamp firmly locked around a hose. It wasn't going to budge without tools.

"No, Williams," he whispered as he started down the companionway, tugging her behind him like a pull toy. "I do *not*."

They passed the Berlands' cabin. "Maggie—"

"Sleeping," he snarled. "Wanna wake her up so she can witness this display of obstinacy?"

She made sure her voice was as low as his. "Wouldn't bother me. *I'm* not the one—"

He swung her into the open doorway of his cabin and shut the door with a heavy and final snap, pausing only long enough to lock it.

*   *   *

The Captain's cabin was big. Big bed, big built-in desk. It shrank as he dragged her over to the bed and put his hands on her shoulders. He didn't even have to exert that much pressure. Her knees turned to jelly as he forced her to sit on the end of the mattress. Rumpled sheets and all. Teal crossed her arms and glared at him. "Yay. Back to the freaking scene of the crime. Fine. I'm here. Let me—"

"Sit there, and shut the hell up until I'm finished." His voice was at a normal level, but his skin was pulled taut over his cheekbones, and his Cutter blues glittered dangerously. "When *I'm* done, I'll be happy to listen to what *you* have to say."

She had nothing to say. Her gaze swept the room dismissively and hooked for a second on the crumple of white on the carpet a few inches from his right foot. Her panties. She brought her attention back to him, leaning back on her hands. "You have the floor. And when you're done, I'm going to use you to wipe it. Talk away. *Ace.*"

He speared his fingers through his hair and took a deep breath. "Cat Berland has been a good friend since I was in high school—I'm not done yet," he snapped when she started to rise. Teal flopped her butt back on the corner of his bed.

"I love her. *Like a sister.* Cat is über intelligent, beautiful, and happens to be gay. I gifted my sperm to her and her partner, Liz. Jessie is their child. *Not* mine. Liz is now pregnant. Also my gift. That child will be their second daughter. *Not* mine." He fired each word like a bullet.

"Oh," she said, not sure what to do with the information that was so far from what she'd thought to be the truth. It left her feeling small and petty. Of course, if he'd bothered to mention, however casually, what their relationship was . . . And why would he? Clearly, he figured it was none of her freaking business. She brought her thumbnail to her lip, then dropped it to fold her hands in her lap.

"Yeah. *Oh.* She came to see her mother because she's worried about Liz. Maggie and I both reassured her that Liz's hormones are out of whack . . . Shit. Never mind that. She was upset. I gave my friend a hug."

Teal got to her feet, wishing she could disappear. Determined to take her humiliation and run. "I'm sorry I jumped to conclusions." She automatically tried to shove her hands in her pockets. Not only did she have no freaking pockets, she had no pants or panties on. Under Zane's too-large T-shirt, she wore nothing but an unfastened bra and a bleeding heart. "*Really* sorry. I had no right to—"

Zane took the two steps to confront her up close and personal. Since his bunk was behind her knees, there was nowhere to go. He glowered at her, his mouth taut, his expression thunderous. Yet, when he threaded his fingers through her hair and held her head in his palms, his touch was incredibly tender. One snap and he could break her neck. Or her heart.

He lowered her onto the crumpled sheets. She'd expect black silk. But no. Crisp, white cotton. Smelling of sunshine, not sex. He was very heavy as he kneed her legs apart and settled into the cradle of her thighs, his fingers still holding her head. Heat emanated from his body as his erection pulsed against her delta through the thin fabric of his swim shorts, turning her girl parts to liquid fire.

"At the party, I flirted with all those big-boobed, no-brain women to make you *jealous*. You saw what I wanted you to see, but you're too damned contrary to get that I was trying to manipulate an emotion from you that came straight out of junior high." His forehead touched hers, and she felt the warm rush of his breath as he sighed against her mouth. "It was a stupid thing to do. I get that. But, sweetheart, you can't hold stupidity against a guy who is doing everything in his power to make the girl he likes like him back."

The tension in her chest ratcheted a little tighter. "I'm a woman. Not a girl," she said, but there was zero heat behind it. His words kick-started her heart as if he'd used a jumper cable.

"Jesus, give me a break here, would you please?" One

hand moved from her hair down her shoulder, fingers trailing down the sensitive skin on her arm then slipped under the edge of her T-shirt—*his* T-shirt—to the bare skin of her midriff.

"Thank God for small mercies," he laughed unsteadily. "Stop thinking so hard for once. Lower your drawbridge, sweetheart. Let me love you."

If only. Goose bumps rose on her skin at the cat's tongue rough glide of his callused palm on her sensitized skin. Teal's nipples pulled into hard tight peaks against the unyielding muscles of his chest. They were breathing the same inch of air.

"I like you," she said a little unsteadily. "Most of the time."

He huffed out a laugh. "That's a start." His hand glided up her ribcage too close around her breast, and her eyes fluttered shut.

"Am I too heavy?"

"No," she lied. She could barely breathe, but she didn't want him anywhere else. That night almost two years ago rushed into her addled brain. The darkness, the feverish coupling. This was nothing like that. It was exactly the same, but completely different. Not quick and desperate, but gentle. As if they had all the time in the world to explore, and taste, and relearn each other.

He shifted his hips slightly, taking some of his weight on his elbow, and nibbled her lower lip, making her body ache. Deep inside her, a pulse throbbed unevenly. Her hips shifted to accommodate him. Sliding his hand to her nape, Zane whispered against her mouth, "Kiss me like you mean it."

I mean it. I've always meant it. Slowly, she opened her mouth, inviting him in. Her tongue explored the inner softness of his mouth as she wrapped her arms around his shoulders. *Don't go. Don't go.*

Zane allowed her to take the lead. The novelty went to her head like fine wine. He tasted wonderful. A combination of after dinner coffee and something indefinably Zane.

While she used her tongue and teeth on his mouth, he caressed her breast, his fingers tugging at the engorged nipple until her back arched and she had to pull her mouth from under his to suck in a life-sustaining gasp of air.

The bedside lamp shone into her eyes, and she closed them as she wrapped her legs around his waist and pulled him hard against where she wanted him.

"You're so soft here." His fingers cupped and stroked across her breast. His other hand tightened against the base of her skull. "And so fucking hard here. You are, Teal Williams, absolutely perfect."

"The prospect of sex is making you delusional," she whispered unsteadily against his damp mouth. She couldn't get enough of kissing him and went back for more. She didn't think any further than her body's prime directive.

It was minutes or hours later when Zane managed to speak. His breath was gratifyingly ragged. "The prospect of sex with *you* is making me irrational and so horny I can't think straight. You're . . . damn. I can't explain this; you're like coming home."

Her heart went into overdrive, and she was about to strip her gears with pure, unadulterated lust. Her body was on fire from the inside out. "More," she demanded in a voice she didn't recognize.

His mouth came down on hers in a punishing kiss that shot her already manic heartbeat into overdrive. The man knew how to kiss and Teal drowned in the sensation. Her nervous system was on overload with his hand on her breast, his erection at the juncture of her thighs, and his tongue sweeping hers. Who needed to breathe? She felt her way down his side to the waistband of his trunks.

He sucked in a ragged breath as she touched his penis through the cotton. He was huge, thick, and hot to the touch. Teal circled the hardness with her fingers. Still kissing her, he groaned, his hips pushing against her grip.

She let go, flattening her hand to slide it inside the waistband. It restricted her wrist, but she was able to touch his bare, silky, hot flesh. Touching him so intimately sent little shockwaves up her fingertips. Using her finger, she spread the bead of liquid across the head. With a full body shudder, Zane wrenched his mouth away from hers. His hand leapt from her breast to the button on his shorts, and instead of feeding the button through the hole, he just ripped at the fabric with a feral growl that made the hair on Teal's nape tingle. Then there was nothing between them but intent.

He shifted over her, his skin burning hot. The rough hair on his chest abraded her sensitive breasts, and she realized that somehow, sometime, he'd stripped her T-shirt off without her even noticing.

Holding her hips, he slid down her body, his mouth soft, his skin rough as he loved every inch of her until she couldn't remain still. He licked one nipple, then rolled it gently between his teeth as he laved the hard nub with the rough slickness of his tongue and the cool hardness of his teeth. He moved across one breast to the other, feathering his tongue lightly across the distended bud until she was pure, pulsing sensation.

Teal speared her fingers through his hair to hold his head against her breasts, but Zane had other ideas and broke her hold as he kissed his way across her rib cage, kissing and licking a hot, damp trail as he went. His shoulders spread her thighs even wider, and he slid his hands under her to hold her steady, his fingers gripping the firm globes of her ass. Head thrashing as the shock of pure sensation raced like wildfire through her veins, she brought her knees up instinctively. "Zane—"

He buried his tongue between her wet folds, licking her like an ice-cream cone until her head pressed deeply into the mattress, and her hips strained up to meet his hungry mouth. She gripped bunches of his hair in both hands. Holding him there, yet so sensitive that she could barely tolerate the persistent stroke of his tongue on her most intimate flesh. She came while his mouth was on her. Her hips bucked in the vise of his hands, and his fingers tightened on her ass, his face buried between her legs.

While her body caved in on itself, while she shook and her everything gathered and strained, he slid up, his body heavy as he flexed his hips and then plunged inside her to the hilt. She cried out at the sweet, sharp, achingly familiar sensation of him inside her. Her body spasmed in an orgasm so powerful it made her deaf and blind.

Zane wrapped her in his arms as her entire body shuddered, and her internal muscles milked him dry. He was spent, exhausted, and exhilarated at the same time. He had an insane urge to stake his claim in some caveman way that would mark her as his. He didn't remember ever feeling this way about a woman, no matter how spectacular the sex had been.

She lifted her face against his shoulder, and he kissed her softly, sweetly, drawing the arm supporting her head up so she rolled further against him. He tangled his fingers in her silky hair, his chest full, and his mind filled with a kaleidoscope of images of her.

No. I won't. Arms akimbo, chin out.

Narrow-eyed as she demanded, *What is this? Twenty questions?*

The prospect of sex is making you delusional.

You have no idea how much I love you, Zane Cutter—

No. She hadn't said that. Wishful thinking, Zane knew, combing his fingers through her hair. He had an unfamiliar flash—just a second—of her lying under him, her eyes filled with love, long blond hair tangled across her breasts as he pumped his anguish into her body. Then the image was gone as he let his eyes take in *Teal*'s flushed cheeks, and the way her short, choppy, black hair curved around her stubborn jaw.

She stroked a hand across his chest, then curved her arm over his body as if to hold him there.

God. He wasn't going anywhere.

She slid one leg over his flank, positioning herself over him, and straddled his hips. He loved that cat-got-the-cream, sultry smile, and the naughty gleam in her still slumberous brown eyes.

He lifted his hands to cup her breasts. Watched the puckered response, saw how dark and large his hands looked on her as he slid his fingers to rest on her slender rib cage. "For such a fierce warrior, you're made like a sylph. Delicate and strong at the same time." Forged by fire and as elusive as a magical mermaid, hiding shyly among the seaweed.

He steadied her hips with his hands, helping her find her rhythm. Frantic to get even closer, a sheen of sweat on her pale skin, Teal flung her head back, her nails digging into his chest.

Zane gritted his teeth, the tendons in his neck straining as he held off his own powerful climax. Waiting for her . . . Her back arched, and her short fingernails dug into his chest until he felt the tightening of her internal muscles around the spar of his cock.

The orgasm swept over him, taking him far out to sea, and deep into the blackness of uncharted waters. His entire body shuddered as he drained himself inside her. Drowning. Willing to remain where he was, as emotion filled him to the very brim. Only his mermaid could save him, and she was as saturated and overwhelmed as Zane was himself.

With Teal tightly wrapped in his arms, his nose buried in the silky fragrance of her hair, he fell off the edge of the world into sleep.

Chapter 12

The storm was heading right for them. After waiting to see if it would veer south or continue on its current path, Zane knew that they were going to take a hit. Normally he wouldn't risk staying on the open sea and getting hammered, but a handful of boats were still hanging around. He didn't like the idea of leaving the *Sea Witch* or the *Good Fortune* or any of the other boats out here alone with the *Vrijheid* while he went into port, his tail between his legs.

Not that anyone would be able to dive during the storm, but it would take time to sail back to the site from the mainland, which gave anyone an open invitation to waltz in and wreak havoc while he was gone.

And he had to admit, the thought of his most irritating rival having the balls to weather a storm that drove him home made him just a little competitive. Not that he'd risk his team's safety to satisfy his own ego, but all indications pointed to the storm being manageable. It didn't even qualify as a category one.

Until now, he'd reasoned that the *Sea Witch* was the only one who knew the extent of the riches that lay beneath them. Now it looked like he had another competitor. Why else would anyone hang out in the middle of the sea during a storm if not to stake their claim to the site? The fact that one of boats was named after an infamous pirate clipper only confirmed his suspicions. But, Jesus! Three little old ladies? It made no fucking sense. The answer was out there. He just couldn't see it. Yet.

They emptied the refrigerator and tossed everything into a huge tub, which they sealed shut, then secured to something immovable. They did the same with all the contents of the cabinets and drawers, sealing the lids with duct tape to ensure things stayed dry. They secured the computers and other electronics with plastic and tape to take with them. In the pilothouse, Zane would be waterproofing everything in the cockpit that he couldn't carry off the boat when they eventually put into port.

Once the storm shutters were secured over the windows in the salon, it was dark inside—not pitch, but dusklike and hot.

Zane waited for the other boats to head in. They didn't. He decided to play chicken and wait them out. Hanging around to see who blinked first grated on his nerves. Now that the ship was fully secured, he decided to slip in a dive before the storm hit. It would clear his head. He asked Teal to be his partner.

"Think they'll leave?" She glared across the chop of the waves as she strapped on her tank.

He strapped on his tank. "Nobody will be able to dive once this storm hits. We have about an hour, then whether they split or not, we'll head in." The sky was gunmetal gray, and there was a tinge of ozone in the air. The sea wasn't too choppy for a dive. But it soon would be.

They suited up, checked tanks, and went down into blue liquid silk. After a long, stressful day, it was a Zen-like moment, and Zane's chest filled with a primal satisfaction. He opened his arms wide, giving her the entire ocean of rippling purples, corals, and golds. After hanging suspended, savoring the pure perfection, he indicated which way he wanted to go.

He was going to use every second of their hour. No work, no salvage, just being one with the pure fathomless beauty of the ocean.

They swam through a school of brightly colored Fairy Basslets, their tiny bicolored bodies mimicking the colors of the sky in swoops of purple and gold. Unafraid, they swam around the two humans in their midst like curious underwater butterflies.

Teal smiled, clearly charmed and delighted as the fish wove and flashed, playing between their rising air bubbles. That smile made Zane's chest ache. Why, he had no idea.

In the frame of her mask, her eyes suddenly narrowed. She grabbed his arm and pointed down. The Basletts scattered in pinpoints of bright color at their sudden tension. Zane drew his knife and spun around to put himself between Teal and—whatever.

Not *what*ever.

*Who*ever.

Silt swirled around three divers as they moved about thirty feet below where Zane and Teal hovered. Oblivious to the divers above them, the men were filling baskets as fast as they could. Helping themselves, Zane thought, furious, to whatever the hell they wanted. Clearly they believed they could steal to their heart's content when he and his team were safely ensconced on the *Decrepit* preparing for the storm.

Well, fuck that for a joke.

Teal's fingers tightened on his arm. She shook her head. *No!*

The smart move would be to slip back to the surface as quietly as they'd arrived. Zane didn't know who these guys were, but greedy men were dangerous, and if they were the bastards who'd tried to disable the *Decrepit,* that made them dangerous *and* potential killers. If the *Decrepit* had sunk, it would've cleared the way to reap what he'd fucking-well worked his ass off to sow.

But while he itched to confront the thieves head-on, he wasn't stupid enough to engage them while Teal was with him. The safest bet was to call in the authorities and have them waiting when the divers surfaced.

The water was becoming darker by the minute as the last of the sun's rays struggled to permeate the water. A strong current pulled them away from the *Decrepit.* Despite the danger—to the dive site and to Teal—Zane hesitated.

Which boat had they dived from? The *Sea Witch*? The *Good Fortune*? One of the others? The figures were all clearly male, and the redhead, as far as he knew, was sailing alone. But again, she could've hired help . . .

Other dark shapes were emerging as the daylight died away. Those thieving bastards weren't the only ones hunting. Out on the far edges of the wreck, sharks emerged to hunt for dinner.

As much as Zane wanted to go down there and whip some ass, the odds were against him. Following these assholes at a safe distance, then letting the authorities do their thing made better sense. This was one situation where he had to curb his impulsiveness. Taking risks could get him killed. Worse, it could get Teal killed.

Not a risk he was willing to take.

He knew Teal well enough to know she wouldn't return to the *Decrepit* without him, although he tried motioning her to go. He scowled when he saw the glint in her eyes and her diving knife in her hand. Being the contrary woman that she was, she shook her head, clearly indicating that if he stayed, so would she.

He motioned that they *both* rise to put some distance between the men and themselves. And keep an eye on the sharks lazily swimming between them and the men on the ocean floor.

With the sun setting, he and Teal would have the cover of darkness soon enough. It was just a case of not being seen. A game of patience.

She nodded, but didn't let go of his forearm as they slowly ascended through tiers of blue.

A swift blur of black swam into Zane's peripheral vision moments before he felt a blow to the side of his head. It was hard enough to make him see spinning starfish for a few seconds, and left him disoriented for a few more. Bubbles obliterated his view of his attacker and he struggled to maintain consciousness as he searched through the gloom for Teal. His heart pounded deafeningly in his ears.

Teal!

Zane righted himself and spun around in a frantic circle. Where the hell . . .

A jerky mess of arms, thrashing legs, and tanks off to his right showed Teal struggling with a man. Zane caught the brief metallic flash of the knife—in Teal's hand or that of her attacker? Jesus—A swift slash was followed by a cloud of red. Zane's heart seized and he propelled himself toward the struggling couple as fast as he could. A shark swiveled into his legs and he kicked hard, hitting it in the side and jettisoning it out of his path.

The man with Teal broke away, streaming red behind him. Thank God. Self-defense—Teal had wisely used her knife.

Zane grabbed the guy's hose, and sliced through it, causing a shower of bubbles to rise with the man as he frantically kicked his way to the surface.

Zane turned back to look for Teal. The other men were still below them. With any fucking luck he could get her the hell out of the water before they realized they'd even been there.

Oh, shit shit shit. Five blacktips were circling her in a slow macabre dance that turned his body to ice.

Reminding himself that blacktips were timid by nature, he kicked off, powerful strokes of his flippers guiding him in a few short bursts of energy. Timid alone, but right here they had an unpredictable fucking mob mentality, and these sharks were known for becoming aggressive in the presence of food. Hard not to anthropomorphize the swirling, swishing fins and tails—but he read hunger gleaming avariciously in those fish-eyed stares. Heart manic, he swam around to face Teal so he didn't frighten her even more.

The largest of the sharks rotated to give him a fuck-off-I'm-about-to-have-dinner glare.

Face pale, eyes terrified behind her mask, Teal jerked in surprise, one hand clamped around her forearm. A mist of red blossomed from between her fingers. Jesus!

Zane's heart went from manic to ballistic. *She had been cut,* no wonder the sharks were circling.

Right now he didn't give a fuck about the bastards who were stealing his treasure, or snarling, circling sharks. Screw his air supply. He had to get Teal the hell out of the water. Now! Go. Go. Go.

Zane pushed her hand away from the slash in her arm, covering the bloody gash with the hard clamp of his own fingers. All that was between them and five hungry sharks were their dive knives. And if the men below them happened to glance up . . .

Show no fear. Zane tugged her along slightly behind him, and pretended the damned sharks weren't there.

For a few moments he thought his bluff was working—

The back of his head exploded with pain. *Nooooo!* He could no longer feel Teal's arm gripped in his hand. Had he let go of her, for fuck sake? His vision wavered and the water started turning black as he struggled to stay conscious.

Stay with it, Ace. A jolt of adrenaline brought him sick-eningly back to his senses. His stomached heaved from the force of the blow, and his vision was seriously impaired, but he had no time to get his shit together. He whipped around to find Teal, but she wasn't there. He couldn't see her. Oh, Jesus. He couldn't see her anywhere.

It was just him and five circling sharks.

He dived down to the sandy bottom, visibility danger-ously lousy with the churned up sand, and the dying natu-ral light. The men were gone. The filled baskets gone with them. And there was no sign of Teal.

Nooooooo.

The pain behind his eyes was nothing compared to the agony of fear in Zane's chest as he rose as quickly as he dared to the surface to get help. What the hell was he thinking, diving in the teeth of a storm? Knowing—fuck it—*knowing* that someone out there was just waiting for the *Decrepit* to pull out so they could swoop in and pirate everything they could get their hands on?

He'd put Teal's life in danger because he was too stub-born, too *stupid* to get the hell out of Dodge when he should have. Asshole.

He felt the brush of a body beside him. Christ. He didn't have time for sharks. He dodged. It swam past him. An-other came straight for him, its black eyes glassy. Zane didn't hesitate. He punched it as hard as he could in the side of the head. It swiveled off in an angry swish of fins. They were going to have to fight with his own self-loathing if they planned to eviscerate him today.

He followed his bubbles to the surface as quickly as he dared.

*   *   *

Ryan and Ben went back down with him. This time with powerful underwater lights. It was insane to dive in this weather. The water was choppy, and almost pitch dark. But he wasn't leaving a stone unturned. The thought of finding Teal—

His brain wouldn't go there. He'd find her if it killed him.

Find her. Alive. That was the only acceptable outcome.

After half an hour of frantic searching, the three of them broke the surface emptyhanded. "They took her," Zane said grimly as they stripped off their tanks on the dive platform. In the blue-gray dusk, the five other boats bobbed on the water a mile away.

"One of those sons of bitches has her." Because the other alternative was that she was dead, and had been dragged off by the sharks. He held to the thought that she'd been taken.

Maggie handed them each a towel. "I've contacted the police. They'll be here within the hour."

Zane's stomach heaved with nausea, and the pain on the back of his head was debilitating. He shook it off. "I'm not waiting an hour."

"Don't do anything rash, honey," Maggie's face creased with worry. "Let the authorities find her."

"Like hell." Zane pulled on a T-shirt and jumped into the speedboat tied on the dive platform. "Anyone want in?"

Several security guys jumped down to join him, as did Ryan and Colson. Maggie had a death grip on Ben's arm. As soon as everyone was in, Zane cranked up the engine with a powerful roar. Thunder rolled in the distance. The rain would start any minute now.

Waves hammered the boat, making it feel as though they were bouncing on cement. He put all his muscle into it, steadily closing the distance between himself and the *Sea Witch,* which was anchored the closest.

The speedboat slewed against the hull of the sleek little boat with a dull thud. The head of his security team wordlessly handed him a Sig 220. Zane didn't like guns. A lot. But he sure as hell wasn't afraid to use it.

He leaped onto the ladder and climbed onto the aft deck as the rain came down. A deathly calm came over him as the others fanned out around the door leading inside.

He kicked the door open. The redhead, curled on the sofa reading, let out a bloodcurdling shriek and jumped to her feet. She grabbed up a nearby a baseball bat in a defensive stance.

The sight of her taking on six heavily armed men with a Louisville Slugger might have been funny if Zane hadn't been so frightened for Teal's safety.

"What the hell do you want, Cutter?" she demanded. Pretty calmly for a lone woman seeing half a dozen armed men show up unexpectedly on her boat. Or had she expected him? She hefted the bat as if she knew how to use it. Her ridiculously vibrant red hair was scraped back in a ponytail, she wore reading glasses, and she was not happy to see him. Too fucking bad.

He strode over and wrapped his large hand around her slender throat, then jammed the barrel of the Sig against her temple. "Where is she, you conniving little bitch?"

"For heaven's sake, Cutter! It was only a little gold bar! Okay, and a few—You're not here about what I took, are . . . you?"

"No. Fuck the gold bars." She'd suddenly noticed his guys behind him, who were now displaying their weapons. An impressive arsenal of machine guns, semiautomatics, and even an Uzi. Zane had to admit, they looked pretty badass.

"What *do* you want, Cutter?"

"You know why I'm here. I want Teal back. *Now.* Where is she?" He indicated that the men should split up and search the boat.

"Who the hell is Teal?" Her expression changed as understanding dawned. "Is she that mousy little brunette you've been spending time with? Because if she is, you should clue her in that her wardrobe is doing nothing for her."

Zane's fingers tightened enough that the redhead's face went pink and she gagged. He ignored her short nails digging into his wrist. "You know exactly who Teal is because you took her. Just like you've been stealing treasure from the *Vrijheid*."

"Treasure?" Her eyes opened wide behind the lenses of her glasses. "Are you telling me there's *treasure* down there?"

He tightened his fingers around her windpipe and she tried to pry his fingers away. "Cut the crap, lady." The walls of the *Sea Witch* were hung with treasures taken from various Cutter salvages over the years like fucking trophies. "If you've hurt her I'll kill you," he told her grimly.

He'd never said that to a living soul in his life, but he was deadly serious. If she'd hurt Teal, he'd—"Stop playing games. Where *is* she?" To punctuate his question he fired a warning shot into the air.

"Are you fucking *insane*?" she demanded as bits of fiberglass and Brazilian hardwood rained down from the hole in her ceiling. "Up yours, Cutter. I don't know what you've gotten yourself into, but you've clearly pissed off some very nasty people. Too bad I don't know anything about it. Not my problem. I'm going to damn well pass out if you keep squeezing my throat like this."

Her face was red. He didn't give a shit. The clock was ticking. Where the fuck had she hidden Teal—had she, God forbid, killed her and tossed her overboard? The very idea chilled Zane to the marrow. He was terrified enough that he didn't give a crap that this treacherous bitch was gasping for air. "Ask me if I give a flying fuck," his voice was hard. He hauled her up another inch on her tiptoes and looked her right in the eye. "Last chance.

Your boat isn't that big. We'll just go ahead and tear it into small pieces while we search."

"Like hell you will." She fumbled for the bat still clenched in her hand and took a swing at him, but he just held her further away, throwing her off balance. She cursed like a sailor and kneed Zane in the balls.

It wasn't a direct strike because he'd been sort of anticipating the move, but it was hard enough for him to grunt in pain. He didn't release her.

Two of his men rushed her, one ripping the bat out of her hand and the other coming up behind her and putting her in a bear hug.

She kicked out in front of her, sending the first man reeling. Then she threw her head back and headbutted the second man. She nearly broke free of his hold, but the other three men pounced on her and managed to pin her arms behind her back.

"Damn if she doesn't fight like a man," said one of his guys, hauling her to the floor and holding her there with his knee. She was bucking and cursing. Zane might have been impressed by her colorful language if he hadn't been so pissed and scared.

A thorough inspection of the ship produced nothing. Teal wasn't aboard. Nor were the divers. The redhead and her fury were alone.

There were fucking *piles* of shit taken from the *Vrijheid*. Just piled in one of the cabins like trophies with familiar pieces from other Cutter salvages over the last few years.

"You have one chance to tell me where Teal is, then we're going to tear this place apart." He had a sinking feeling she wasn't here, but where else was he supposed to look?

"Go to hell." Her enraged shout was muffled by the carpet. Hard to move with a knee in the small of her back. "You and your goons are trespassing. If you don't get the hell off my boat right this fucking second, Zane Cutter, I'm going to disembowel you and your gun-toting thugs with my bare hands." Zane indicated that the guys let her up. Teal wasn't here. They were wasting precious time. He looked at the redhead with hollow eyes and a growing emptiness inside. "I'm disemboweled already, lady."

*   *   *

The lights of the *Good Fortune* emerged through the slashing rain. Between that and the darkness, visibility was almost nil. Odds were the weather and waves would cover any sounds they made so they'd be able to board the ship unseen.

Despite the lights, the ship appeared uninhabited. The three elderly ladies had departed on the launch that morning. That wasn't uncommon. They frequently left to go shopping or whatever they did on shore. Zane had waved back as they passed by, vaguely concerned that they were leaving their very expensive anchored boat to ride out the storm unattended.

It had seemed odd at the time, but he'd had a thousand other things on his mind and promptly forgot them.

The storm was picking up, and the speedboat was being tossed about on enormous waves. In between earth-shaking booms of thunder, bolts of lightning struck the water, sometimes hitting just inches away.

Zane's entire body was shaking with exhaustion as they came alongside the *Good Fortune*. Lights from the main cabin shone on the wet deck, but all was quiet.

The men fanned out, waiting for his signal. Ryan touched his shoulder and pointed. The beautiful bronze urn that had been stolen several days ago stood on the aft deck beside a dive basket. Silent as a cat, Zane crouched down to check out the contents. A two-foot-tall gold cross, a dozen chains, and dozens of coins. A handful of items he couldn't see clearly, lumpy with conglomerate. Fury pulsed behind his eyeballs.

The size and weight of the urn proved that the three thieves who'd taken Teal were indeed on board the *Good Fortune*. Little old ladies be damned. Jesus. What a fucking clever ruse. Who'd suspect a trio of grandmothers of engineering a heist of treasure worth a king's ransom? No one. Certainly not Zane Cutter, that was for sure. Fuckshitdamn.

Clearly the women hadn't done the dirty work themselves. They'd had help for that. They were probably home in Peoria or Poughkeepsie by now with a million dollars' worth of stolen loot, laughing their dentures out. Fuck.

Much more important, and the billion-dollar question, was: Where had their accomplices taken Teal? Was she still on board?

His heart hammered as they skulked below the flybridge enclosure, weapons drawn. One of the men stacked his hands under his cheek, then held up a finger to indicate one man asleep inside. Through the window, Zane saw the guy sacked out on the couch.

He hefted the urn—Jesus, the thing must weigh a hundred pounds—and motioned for Ryan to open the door.

Using the urn to knock out a sleeping man was actually a piece of cake and certainly poetic fucking justice. The hard part was not killing the guy, given the rage boiling inside him.

One down. How many to go?

Zane led the way through the dark first deck using the penlights they'd brought with them. The crew had secured the ship and must be holed up below, waiting for the storm to blow over so they could dive again the second it passed.

The men split up. He quickly searched the captain's cabin, which had been converted into a dorm room with

six bunks. It smelled of sweaty males and beer, proving
his theory.

The next cabin was a storage room, scattered with too-
large-to-transport-on-the-launch artifacts and treasure
pilfered from the *Vrijheid*. He wondered if this was their
primary stash, or if it was just the tip of the iceberg. They
systematically continued their search one deck down. The
next stateroom yielded nothing but a pair of knitting nee-
dles and a half-finished whatever. Shit. Still no Teal.

Damn it to hell, where were the men, and what had the
fuckers done with Teal? Was this yet another dead end?
His chest hurt with the pressure. *Come on, Williams. Show
yourself. Where the hell are you?*

Other than the normal sounds of a ship at sea—creaks
and groans, the slap of waves on the hull—the ship was
eerily quiet. His blood pounded in his ears. Zane didn't
remember ever being this afraid in his life.

He began flinging open doors. The first revealed another room filled with treasure. The next was a filthy food
pantry. The third door was locked. He heard muffled
noises inside.

"Teal?" he demanded, his voice hoarse with strain.
Please God . . .

Thumping. Muffled grunts, the words unintelligible,
but the voice clearly belonged to a woman. A rush of relief
swept through him, and Zane sagged against the wall. She
was alive. Probably pissed as hell, but alive. Thank God.
He saw Ryan and two of the security guys coming out of
the end cabin. "I found Teal—find those sons of bitches,
and secure whoever's topside. The second I get her, we're
outta here."

They turned and ran back to the stairs. Racing back the
way he'd come, Zane swung into the storeroom, grabbed
the ax fixed to the bulkhead, and sprinted back. Two swift
strikes of the sharp blade to the door handle, and the
heavy door blasted open, spilling light into the dark cabin.

Teal's brown eyes shot sparks above the silver duct tape they'd used to gag her. Her muffled cries of fury broke his heart and ratcheted up his anger a couple more notches. He was right there on the incensed scale of livid and he was going to enjoy beating the shit out of the men who'd taken her. As soon as he had her safely away from here.

Three steps took him to her side, Zane ran a hand over her tangled hair. "Ah, sweetheart—"

They'd tied her to a metal chair in the center of the tiny cabin between two bunks. Her ankles were taped to the front legs of the chair, her arms stretched behind her, presumably taped as well. She was spitting mad and started struggling the second she saw him.

Zane pulled his dive knife out as he crouched between her spread knees. "Hang on. Hang on. Don't struggle, you'll just—Let me—okay. Okay, one leg free. Hold on honey, let—There. Move your feet around to get some circulation going until I can cut your hands—What? Oh." He chuckled as she kicked his shin. "Mouth first. Got it. This is gonna hurt, brace your—Good girl."

"About freaking *time* you showed up, Cutter! I've been sitting here, freaking *hog-tied*, in the *dark* for *hours*." Her voice broke from disuse. And relief.

"I'm happy to see you, too, Williams." The understatement of the century. He hated like hell to see her putting a brave face on how damned scared she'd been. Her face was dead white and filthy. He didn't know if the bluish smudge on her temple was dirt or a bruise. But they'd pay either way.

Zane brushed a quick, light kiss to her tender mouth. Her lips clung. Reluctantly he pulled away, touching her dirty cheek with a finger. "Let's get you rescued, then we can do a recap. Okay?"

She nodded, and said in a small voice that about fucking broke his heart, "I wasn't sure—What took you so long?"

He shifted to cut through the duct tape wound around her wrists. The tape had cut deep red marks into the tender skin and the cut on her forearm was crusted with dried blood. He cursed viciously and silently. "Hit the *Sea Bitch* first," he told her, taking a moment to gently chafe some life back into her pale fingers until they pinked up.

She turned her head to see him. "I hope you mean literally."

That's my girl. "Just a little strangulation and the threat of grievous bodily harm," Zane told her dryly. "Can you stand?"

She got to her feet. "Ta da."

He wrapped his arms around her and held her so tightly she squeaked. "You have no idea how fucking happy I am to see you right now." She hugged him as tightly as he was hugging her. But of course they couldn't stay there like that. He gently disentangled their arms.

"I have some idea," she said wryly, rubbing her wrists as he brushed hair out of her eyes because he couldn't not touch her. She covered his hand and brought it to her cheek for a second, before saying briskly, "Is that a gun in your pocket or are you *really* happy to see me?"

He withdrew the Sig. "*And* I'm really happy to see you."

"Did you bring one for me?" she asked hopefully.

He shook his head, taking her hand. "Sorry. No."

"Disappointing, I was looking forward to making Swiss cheese out of the guy who slugged me—Are you thinking about getting us the hell off this boat, or should we ask if we can stay for dinner? I vote for option number one."

"Good plan." His lips twitched. "Can you walk or do you need me to carry you?"

She made a rude noise. "I can walk, Cutter."

Zane wrapped his arm around her waist, and took a second to press his mouth to hers again. The contact was pitifully brief, considering he wanted to do all sorts of things to her just to assure himself that she was alive and in one piece. He reluctantly lifted his head. "You okay? The stab wound—"

"A nick. Don't sweat the small stuff."

"I'll look at it later. Right now we have to haul ass topside. Brought a couple of the guys with me, and the motorboat awaits."

"Yay. What did you do with the bad guys?" Teal whispered as hand in hand they padded down the dimly lit companionway to the stairs leading to the upper deck. They heard scuffling, a bang as if something heavy had been dropped. A dragging sound, and then silence.

He listened for several seconds. "One in the salon," he barely whispered.

"There are five more weasel-assed pirates. Somewhe—" A shot rang out and Teal's fingers squeezed his, hard. He slammed his arm across her body to keep her behind him and two stairs down. "Like *there* for instance," she whispered as a hail of bullets erupted just feet away.

Zane swung her behind him. "Stay put."

"As i—" Her words were cut off by another round of gunfire.

"Keep down," Zane instructed, doubled over as he took the stairs. Crossing the salon was the only way out to the deck and the launch. They had no choice. It was stay pinned in the stairwell, or make a mad, and dangerous, dash across the main cabin for freedom.

Another shot rang out. A scream of pain as the bullet slammed into the TV, shattering it into a shower of glass fragments. Zane squeezed off several shots, and the answering fire had him pressing Teal's head against the stairs. He waited. Waited. Waited. "Okay. Come on."

Shit. What a clusterfuck. He had no idea if it was his

guys doing the shooting or the bad guys, nor did he know who was where. He squeezed off another round blind, All he wanted to do at this point was clear the way. He breached the top step, keeping his body flat and his eyes moving as he tracked the room—the galley. Ryan and three of his security guys had taken cover behind the counter.

He looked toward the door leading onto the aft deck, barely picking out several darker silhouettes against the black sky and driving rain. The bad guys gathered on the deck right outside the shattered windows.

In the next heartbeat, those guys were going to be inside, guns blazing. They'd be sitting ducks. It was going to be a bloodbath.

Teal whispered in his ear—"Let me—"

He didn't want to let her—*anything*. He grabbed her upper arm and yanked her lower beside him, then fired off a shot, still gripping her arm. Afraid as hell to let go.

Click. Out of ammo. *God*—

He yanked the Very flare gun from the waistband of his jeans. A series of bullets, from his crew, sliced through the doorjamb. Chunks of mahogany spewed in the air.

He raised the flare gun over the edge of the granite counter.

One—

The kitchen cabinet over Ryan shattered. Wood, canned peas, and dry pasta exploded across the galley and rained onto the floor.

Men shouted over the noise of more bullets connecting with a horrific screech of metal on metal, peppering into the refrigerator right behind them in an explosion of noise. Cold air pooled around their feet, and the small fucking bulb lit where they were crouched as bright as a spotlight in the semidarkness.

Two.

On a silent three, Zane pulled the Very's trigger, firing

a twelve-gauge flare through the doorframe, directly at the men blocking their exit, weapons raised.

The flash bang lit the room with a brilliant red light that—if they were lucky—would give them seconds to make a mad dash through that door.

Heartbeat louder than the report of wild bullets in his ears, Zane sprinted across the room, slammed through a half-broken door, shoved a guy out of the way, and flew across the deck, dragging Teal in his wake.

He practically threw her down onto the dive platform, and jumped down beside her. The speedboat was nowhere to be seen. Just miles of ink-black water pounding against the hull, "Shit!" He saw *Decrepit's* running lights shimmering in the distance.

A bullet slammed into the deck mere inches away. Teal let out a furious shriek. Without pausing, Zane plunged into the water just as another bullet whizzed so close to his ear he heard it whine.

"Take a breath!" He dived until his ears popped, still gripping Teal's hand for dear life. He only let go when they broke the surface. "Okay?" he shouted.

"You?"

"Save your breath." Someone was firing the Uzi. The sound of rapid gunfire gave him impetus, and he hauled ass. Teal started swimming in strong, powerful strokes that moved her swiftly through the water beside him. He stayed beside her, keeping her in his peripheral vision.

The surrounding black was absolute. Usually he had an excellent sense of direction, but not tonight. The driving rain screwed up his eyesight, his ears were ringing, the waves were enormous, and his fucking heart threatened to leap out of his chest as he tried to put as much distance between them and the enemy ship as physically possible.

If his arms and legs burned from fighting the waves, and his breath was coming in laboring gasps, he was terrified for Teal. Although she was keeping up, they still had almost half a mile to go before they reached safety. He was shit scared that he'd saved her from one fate, only to plunge her into a storm-tossed ocean to drown yards from the *Decrepit*.

Darkness surrounded them. They were midway between the running lights of the *Good Fortune* and the *Decrepit* when he thought he heard the throb of a small engine rapidly approaching. Ryan and the others?

Over the slap crash of the waves he still heard shots from the *Good Fortune*.

The sound of the powerful boat got closer and closer. All he could see was the bulky shape. Black against black. Not the Sea Ray.

Fuckshitdamn. Who was after them now?

Chapter 13

"Geez, you really do have a magic cloak, don't you?" Teal huddled under a pile of blankets in the salon, Zane glued to her side. It was the local police who'd picked them out of the water.

Even though he'd wanted to head for port sooner than later, even though the wind and waves smacked into the hull as if trying to break the *Decrepit* apart, Zane was determined to stay right where they were until his last artifact was safe and sound and headed to port with them.

Maggie had been in her element as she bustled about, administering Band-Aids and coffee. It was a miracle that the list of injuries was so minimal. Teal and Zane sat on the sofa in the salon, while they made their report to some odd little woman who looked like a character in a James Bond movie. The detective proved to be kick-ass and efficient. There'd be miles of paperwork and red tape later. But she got to her feet when she was done writing copious notes.

"Why do you think they took you, Miss Williams?" Detective Simmons asked, putting away her recorder.

"They thought they'd killed Mr. Cutter. They should've just killed you and been free and clear."

"Gee thanks," Teal muttered dryly. The bruises and welts on her wrists burned and throbbed, she had a painful knob on the side of her head, and a headache pulsed behind her eyes. She leaned back against Zane's chest and closed her scratchy eyes, then said a quick thank-you to whoever might be up there listening. "They needed me to guide them into Cutter Cay and open up the Counting House so they could take *all* the treasure."

"The island's impossible to breach unless one knows the lay of the land," Zane told the detective. "Still, they couldn't possibly have known we'd dive before taking off for port," he reasoned, pulling the blanket wrapped around them both up over her shoulder when she shivered.

"They didn't. But they were quick thinking, and seized the opportunity when we presented ourselves. They figured either you were dead, and they'd have time to head in, or, if somehow you made it back here, and found me gone, you'd search for me. In the meantime, I'd lead them straight into Cutter Cay and open the Counting House for them." She snorted. "As if."

"I would've drained the fucking ocean to find you." He brushed a kiss to the top of her head, and his arms tightened around her as if he'd never let her go. "God, you're brave. I was scared witless when I couldn't find you."

"My hero." Teal stroked his chin with the top of her head. It made her dizzy, but since her hands were tucked inside the blanket that was the best she could do. He'd found her, guns blazing. She'd never in her life had anyone rescue her. From *anything*. If anyone had asked, she would've told them she was perfectly capable of rescuing herself.

Her chest hurt from sheer emotion.

Nothing wrong with playing into the fantasy for a few hours. Teal figured she'd earned the right.

For the past hour, they'd watched as the authorities hauled load after load of treasure off the *Good Fortune*. They'd found not only dozens of stolen artifacts, but the tools used to sabotage the hull of Zane's boat, and a log on the onboard computer proving that they'd tracked the *Decrepit*'s every move. Unfortunately, the *Sea Witch* was long gone. But the three elderly women had been arrested as they were leaving St. Maarten on the last flight out before the storm swept in. While they hadn't participated in the thefts, or Teal's kidnapping, they were still under suspicion and were being remanded until they got an attorney. The men, caught red-handed, had been taken to jail. Teal hoped the cops threw away the key to their cell. The police were still gathering evidence. There'd be no shortage of it, she thought, pissed all over again.

Miraculously, none of Zane's security guys had been killed, though one had been grazed by a bullet and had to be taken to the hospital for stitches. The bad guys had taken the brunt of the attack, and two men on board the *Good Fortune* would have longer stays there before they'd join their pals in jail.

The police eventually left to join their boats and head into port ahead of the worst of the storm. The wind was picking up and the rain slashed against the windows like hard pellets. If there was a step beyond exhausted, Teal was right there. Zane, on the other hand, looked bright-eyed and bushytailed, and very pleased with himself. Even after everything. The man was the Energizer Bunny.

All she wanted to do was drag him down to his cabin, curl up against him, and sleep for a week. Too bad there'd be no sleeping for the next several hours.

"I dare you to deny you enjoyed every freaking minute of all the excitement," Teal challenged, eyes closed.

He slid his hand under her hair and caressed the back

of her neck with his thumb. "Bad guys arrested, stolen treasure scheduled to be released back to us in thirty days." She heard the grin in his voice. "Clear sailing ahead, I promise."

"If I stay like this much longer I'm going to be fast asleep. Let me up, I have things to do."

His arms tightened around her, but she unwound them, then fought her way out of the too-hot blanket and got to her feet. She still wore her wet suit and was barefoot. Zane ran his hand up her thigh.

"We're heading to port now." He got up, too, then cupped her cheek. "You can sleep for twenty-four hours when we get there. Don't worry, no more drama, Williams. We have plenty of time to get everything secured and safely into port in St. Maarten. Then we can ride out the rest of the storm on dry land. Get changed. I'll use the PA system to tell everyone to meet back here in five. Move it."

The boat was pitching and so was Teal's stomach.

"I'll be back as soon as I'm done." Getting off the *Decrepit* was looming large in her dizzy brain. *Off. Off. Off.*

He wrapped his arms around her waist and kissed her temple, making Teal's heart stutter with yearning. "I hate letting you out of my sight. Be careful."

She turned her head to brush her lips on his jaw. "No bad guys in my ER, I promise."

"Make it snappy, Williams."

The waves had already risen to five feet and the *Decrepit* was pitching from side to side. Teal ran like hell to her engine room. Sweating, she swiped her hand over her face. Zane's concern was sweet and touched her deeply. His adrenaline had run hot and he was clearly thriving on the high-stakes drama of the last few hours. But for her, the whole episode had been terrifying and exhausting.

She was alive and in one piece. Right now she counted that as good.

* * *

It was hotter than hell, especially belowdecks. The engines had worked their little yellow hearts out to get them safely to port as fast as possible, and she gave them a friendly pat in passing.

She charged around her room, then crashed into the nearest engine as the boat slammed into something. Probably the dock. Good thing she had the wet suit to protect her, but it still hurt like hell.

Teal staggered to her feet, rubbing her hip bone as she set the batteries to take a full charge so the bilge pumps would work. Next, she disconnected the electric and water and shut off her fuel lines, then closed the hull fittings. Water would find its way into even the smallest opening. The bilge would work on aux power until she got back. She used duct tape and plastic to cover vents and plug exhaust pipes.

She rubbed her bandaged arm as she looked around. Satisfied, she went topside to see what else needed doing.

Zane had pulled in to a friend's small marina. The well-constructed concrete slips would provide protection from surging waters to some extent, and the sheltered bay on the leeward side of the island would help deflect the wind a little. They arrived to find only one other moored boat. His friend Phil, who owned the place, had several rental boats, yachts mostly, but they had already been moved inside in anticipation of the storm.

Knowing that Teal was securing the engines, Zane shouted instructions over the rising wind. He turned the *Decrepit* so the bow faced the wind within the mooring. With the men's help, he doubled the mooring and spring lines, distributing the load evenly using the cleats.

"Use *all* the cleats, guys, and use as many lines as each can hold!" Zane reminded them, though he'd given everyone a briefing as they headed into port about running the lines to as many independent points on land as possible.

The other boat was the *Slow Dance,* a party boat. One man was attempting to tie off the lines by himself. Zane ran over and added his muscle to help the guy finish his tie-down, which took a precious fifteen minutes away from his own responsibilities. It wasn't purely altruistic. The party boat was upwind. If she broke free, she could crash into the *Decrepit* and smash her to smithereens, sink her, or leave her hanging in her mooring lines.

"Jesus, thanks man. My guys all left for the day. I just came back to get something, and those lines were already loose." The younger guy was red-faced and clearly stressed as he shook Zane's hand. "It came in fast . . ."

"Yeah," Zane took in the secure lines on the guy's boat as he wiped rain out of his eyes. "It's hard to predict a temperamental tropical storm."

"Need help?" the guy asked, not sounding too enthusiastic; clearly, he wanted to be out of the wind and rain.

"I'm good. Thanks." Zane went back to check each line as his hair blew around his face and stung his cheeks. A quick glance around showed that Teal must still be on board. He hated not having her in sight.

"Be sure to allow enough line to compensate for the tide surges," the guy yelled as sweat and rain ran down his temples. "They're forecasting up to a six-foot tidal surge."

"That big?" Zane nodded as the guy finally left, glad he'd made use of ground anchors as well. The Weather Service had upgraded the tropical storm to a category one. Not huge so far as hurricanes went, but it was better to be safe than sorry. There was no such thing as too many lines, or too many attachments to secure his boat.

Satisfied that the *Decrepit* was as tight as they could make her, he went back on board. He met Ryan coming one way and Ben the other. They'd done a final check of all the tie-downs. Now it was Mother Nature's turn.

"Are you sure you won't come back to our place?" Maggie shouted over the wind howling outside the salon. "We'll squeeze you in somewhere, it'll be like summer camp."

"Thanks, Maggie—" Teal walked in, came straight to his side, and slipped her hand into his without a word. Zane shot her a brief smile before turning back to addressing the other woman.

"Cyd's in New York this week, so I'll take Teal to her place to ride this out. We'll be fine."

Maggie glanced at their entwined fingers and sent Zane a smile, which he returned before adding, "If you can accommodate all the guys, that'd be great." He had to raise his voice to be heard over the howling wind. "Good work, everyone. There's nothing else we can do here. Go with Maggie, and stay safe. We'll reconvene in the morning."

*   *   *

Teal's eyes stung and watered as she leaned into the wind. The raucous storm-warning horns added to the chaos as she and Zane hunched against zinging, sand-spewing rain. "Come on Williams, put your back into it. We'll be inside before you know it."

She hoped so. She tightened her grip on the back of his T-shirt and he pulled her against his side, tucking her under his arm. As they approached the cottage, sand, newspaper, bits of roof tile, and shredded foliage flew by, narrowly missing them as they waded through the flotsam and jetsam of the high winds.

A few people along the way struggled to replace storm shutters that had come loose, but most had done what needed to be done days before and were snugly inside, safe and dry. Clouds boiled dark and thick overhead, and rain blew sideways in dense, stinging sheets.

The hill, coupled with high winds and rain, made it feel as though she was wading through thigh-deep, wet cement. Teal was grateful for the support of Zane's strong arms around her. By the time they reached his friend's small, white cottage, they were both out of breath.

Sky-blue storm shutters were firmly in place covering the windows here, Teal observed, relieved. Zane retrieved a key from a heavy stone flowerpot beside the bright blue front door. Brilliant red geraniums had been chewed by the wind, leaving just a few petals like little flags of defiance. Teal doubted the sunny yellow pot would still be there in the aftermath of the storm. She tried to drag it closer to the front door, but Zane shook his head to leave it.

He unlocked the door, holding it so the wind didn't rip it from his hand. "Make yourself at home," he yelled. "I'm going to do a perimeter check. Be right back."

"I'll—" *Help you.* He disappeared around the corner of the house. Teal grabbed the front door and managed to slam it closed behind her. Her ears vibrated with the relative silence inside the extremely well-insulated bungalow. She slid her palm along the wall, searching for a light switch as her eyes adjusted to the darkness. She found the switch, flipped it, but nothing happened. She would've been surprised if the lights *had* worked.

She looked around, barely able to make out shapes in the semidarkness. One fairly big room, with a galley kitchen on one side, a large white sofa, indicating the sitting area, and a big bed behind a half wall. The rest was nothing more than darker blotches on the pale walls; she presumed the only other interior door was the bathroom.

"Dry clothes, food and water while the going's good," she decided out loud, then jumped, heart racing, as something heavy and metallic—a garbage can?—slammed on the roof. "Hurry, Zane." He'd probably been through dozens of these storms—and worse—living where he did. He could take care of himself.

Seeing a fat candle on a nearby sofa table, Teal opened the small drawer beneath it, found a butane lighter, and flicked it over the wick. Accompanied by the homey scent of vanilla, she went into the small kitchen to forage.

A gas stove and French coffee press meant Zane could come back inside to at least a hot cup of coffee. She made the coffee and rummaged around for something to eat. Finding a couple of wide-necked thermoses in a drawer, she filled one with coffee and started a fresh pot. Then started building sandwiches. She had no idea how long this latest storm would take to blow over.

The front door slammed open against the wall, letting in a cacophony of outside noise until Zane used his weight to shove it shut. Teal's heart skittered in her chest at the sight of him. He looked endearingly wild, with his wet, wind-blown hair, soaking clothes, and his cheeks ruddy from the stinging rain and swirling sand. His intense blue eyes picked up the reflection of the dancing flame in twin pinpoints of light. She loved him so intensely that her heart felt full to bursting. "Everything okay?"

"Cyd and Ron did a good job securing the place before they left."

He took in the sandwiches and thermos, and smiled as he picked up a half and took a quick bite. "Good thinking. Especially if twenty-seven starving teenage boys drop in. We'd better get out of these wet clothes and grab a shower while the water's still hot. I'll find you something dry to put on."

Putting the rest of his sandwich down on the counter, he stepped in front of her and gently brushed her wet, too-long bangs out of the way. "Can't see these pretty eyes. When this is all over, we've got to get you a haircut, Williams," he murmured, his voice husky, his eyes shadowy in the gloomy room. Cupping her chin, he lifted her face. "You took about a quarter century off my age with that kidnapping stunt. No more going off with strange men, hear me?"

Her heart did a little tap dance. "*You're* a strange man."

"I'm *your* strange man." He closed the gap and leaned down to give her a quick, hard kiss on the mouth, then stepped away, picking up the flickering candle. "Take this with you—hang on." He put the candle on the counter again and clasped a compelling hand around her nape, using his thumb to tilt up her chin. "I need one more to hold me."

His lips were cool, but the inside of his mouth, as his tongue swept hers, was furnace hot, and tasted deliciously of peanut butter. Being in Zane's arms was the safest Teal had ever felt in her life. She squeezed her eyes shut and gave herself up to the sweetness of his kiss, feeling as though—for just a little while—she was securely wrapped in Zane's special magic cape.

Outside, the wind howled and the windows rattled and she heard the neighbor's gas-powered generator humming away as several dogs barked. The noise and mayhem outside faded to a sibilant blur as he angled his head, his fingers warm against her scalp.

She murmured her reluctance to break away, but knew she had to be practical. Their wet clothing was dripping on the floor, and they should change and get warm and dry. "I love—" *You.* "—the way you kiss me," she told him, her voice a little thick with emotion. Her lips tingled. She wanted more kisses. More Zane.

He played with her ear. His touch made her insides melt like candle wax. "*Your* mouth is the best thing that ever happened to *my* mouth." His voice was thick, his eyes dark. "Kissing you is a celebration." He brushed another kiss to her lips. "Go shower and get dry."

"That's a contradiction in terms." Teal smiled as she picked up the candle. "What about you?"

She meant changing out of his wet clothes, but Zane being Zane grinned and said, "I'm scared of the dark. Where you and that candle go, so do I."

Teal laughed. "Lead the way, I'll protect you."

They stopped at the closet to find dry clothes for both of them. His friend Cydney's boyfriend lived with her. Teal didn't want even herself to know how relieved she felt at that bit of news. She wouldn't have felt comfortable wearing one of his girlfriends' clothes. Although, wet as she was, she would have done it if push came to shove.

"Cyd, Ryan, Cat, and I went to school together." Zane informed her, nudging her hand up a little so he could see into the closet. "Ryan had a thing for her for a while, but it never worked out. And no, before you ask, Cyd and I never hooked up."

She gave him an innocent look. A little exaggerated maybe. "Did I say anything?"

"I could hear those well-oiled wheels in your brain catching," he told her dryly. "Here, this work?" He handed her T-shirt material shorts and a tank top from a drawer and grabbed Hawaiian swim trunks for himself.

"That water's not going to stay hot long. This way. I think they keep the radio in here."

Here was a miniscule, windowless bathroom, barely big enough for the two of them to stand sideways. Zane placed the candle on the back of the toilet and bent down to check under the sink. The shower stall, she saw, was barely big enough for one, let alone two. But her heart tap-danced, and all her girl parts were doing the happy dance that she was about to be squeezed into the confined space with him.

She had to step sideways to open the door and turn on the water. Zane found the emergency radio in the sink cabinet and placed it beside the candle, then turned it on o listen to the weather report. He yanked his sopping T-shirt over his head, tossing it in the sink with a wet *hwap*. Teal's mouth dried and her heart swelled with emotion as her gaze played over his muscular chest and shoulders. His skin looked as smooth as tawny silk. Good Lord! The man made her wax poetic.

He turned around to look at her. "You have clothes on." He sounded affronted. "Arms up." He slid the wet fabric of her tank top up her chest. Teal obediently raised her arms. He paused to bend his head. His wet hair was cold against her skin, but his open mouth was hot as he closed it, not so gently, around her nipple. He switched sides. "Don't want to play favorites," he murmured as his lips slid into the valley, then up the small hill of her other breast. His teeth worried the tight bud as his hands ran down the curve of her butt.

"Finish one project before you start the next, Cutter," she instructed as her pulses skittered and jumped in response to the sweet tug and pull of his mouth. She tangled her fingers in his hair to ground herself.

"Picky picky," Zane lifted his head, eyes blazing hot. "Up."

She lifted her arms. As soon as the tank was off, she wrapped them around his neck and pressed herself full length against him. "We don't need to shower," she murmured against his strong jaw, then started kissing her way across his face. "That bed out there is nice and wide, and we'll warm up in no time."

Their close proximity, and the fact that she was attempting to have a rational conversation, didn't deter him at all. He used both hands to strip her out of her coveralls and panties, and when they were around her ankles, he instructed, "Step. And step. Thank you.

"We don't need either big or a bed, Williams," he whispered against her mouth as he backed her into the very small, steamy shower, and closed the door. "This will do us nicely." His voice was throaty and sexy as he backed her against the tiles.

The stall wasn't just tiny, it was minuscule. "I really don't think this is possible . . ." Teal said between his drugging kisses. Lukewarm water cascaded down her back, gluing her already wet hair to her cheeks and neck Zane was glued to her front. The hair on his chest tickled her breasts, his erection jumped impatiently against her belly. In spite of the now tepid water, Teal felt feverish and so ready her pulses raced and her skin felt ultra sensitive.

"Ah," he nibbled on the underside of her jaw, skimming his hand down. Over her breast, too briefly brushing feather-light down her side, her hip, and settling on her upper thigh. "Ye of little faith. Lean back—there we go." He hooked his hand under her knee, leaned into her, and slipped his penis inside her sheath to the hilt.

He maneuvered her where he wanted her, his hands sure, his kisses making her drunk with lust, dizzy with love. He knew how to deliver indescribable pleasure with his talented mouth, and marauding fingers. Zane took lovemaking seriously and elevated it to art form. "You've done this before."

"Dress rehearsals, getting ready for you. I want this to be good for you."

The tenderness and sincerity in his voice as he kissed her neck unraveled her. Time warped and and twisted as he filled her senses with mind-bending kisses and touches so intense she couldn't catch her breath.

Making love in the small shower stall wasn't just possible. It was mind-blowingly *spectacular,* Teal thought, her body limp, her mind saturated with love and lust for this man. "I'm a noodle," she told him as he washed her tenderly and managed to get all her parts doing the happy dance. Despite the almost comical contortions. "I'm incapable of rational thought. I can't move a muscle. Show me your manly prowess and carry me to bed," she instructed.

Zane complied and they dropped onto his friend's clean blue cotton sheets, still wet because Zane refused to let her go long enough for either of them to dry off.

*   *   *

"Tell me about your ex-husband," Zane said softly into the darkness. The wind had died down 'round about the fourth time they'd made love. Teal lay half across his body, one arm and her leg draped over him in a boneless sprawl. Their hearts beat in a syncopated rhythm that fascinated him.

She played with the hair on his chest. "Ugh. Do we have to? Why do you want to know about Denny?"

"Because, no matter what he was, he helped shape who you are. And the woman you are today fascinates me."

She brushed her lips to his throat, but her arm tightened across his chest as if holding him in place. Zane rubbed his hand down her slender back in silent encouragement. "When I first met him, he reminded me a little bit of you," she admitted. "Not so much in looks, but he had charm and personality to spare. Everyone adored him. He was easy to love."

"And you loved him." Not a question. He knew her now. Knew that she'd never commit herself unless she was one hundred percent sure.

"I loved . . . the *idea* of him. We met at the marina in Seattle where I'd been working for a couple of years. Big fancy yachts. Lots of work and good money. He was very sweet. Charming. A nice guy. He didn't push me to sleep with him. In fact, he was so smooth that it was me who took the initiative."

Yeah, Zane thought grimly, he'd played that card a time or two with a woman in the past himself.

"My mother had died the year before. I was lonely, rudderless, and like a ripe peach just waiting to fall for the first guy who swept me off my feet. He was the first man who'd ever told me he loved me. And I fell hook, line, and sinker. The ink had barely dried on our marriage license when we moved to San Francisco, and he wanted to change everything about me he'd said he loved so much.

"First, it was my hair. He really dug blondes. I went blond. He liked it long and curly. Ditto. He subtly isolated me from the few friends I'd made at the marina. He didn't like his wife working as a mechanic on his high-society friends' fancy boats. I held out on quitting as long as I could. But a few words with the harbor master and I found myself unemployed.

"He wanted a baby. But I couldn't get pregnant. That pissed him off. I suggested adoption, he went ballistic." She gave a small pained laugh. "Accused me of not trying hard enough. I got an A for effort when he dressed me like a Barbie doll, though. He bought all my clothes, all my makeup, and told the hairdresser exactly what to do with me. I was too fat, so he put me on a strict diet. Then I was unattractively thin, so he watched me eat."

Zane wished it *had* been Denny Ross responsible for all the shit that had gone down. He'd like to have had the opportunity to confront the asswipe face-to-face. Nowhere to put it, Zane kept his revulsion and anger tightly controlled. "That's when you stopped coming to the island."

"We'd been married three years by then. He stripped me of my self-worth and dignity. I was an emotional mess. I didn't want Sam to see me like that. Besides, Denny would never have let me travel without him. I kept Sam a secret from Denny and vice versa."

His throat closed. She'd had fucking *no* support system. How'd she done it? He played with her hair, wanting to comfort her, but infuriatingly helpless to do so. Not that it would ever occur to Teal to *ask* anyone for help. She'd learned early and well that she had only herself to depend on.

More than anything right then, he wished he had the ability to fix what had happened to her. He wished he'd known so that he could've pulled her under his magic cloak and protected her. "What was the straw that broke the camel's back?" he asked softly.

"I started divorce proceedings the day I found myself at a plastic surgeon's office. Denny was telling the doctor how big to blow up my breasts, and how he wanted my nose to look. I suddenly realized that he'd changed almost everything about me, all the while telling me how much he loved me. A lightbulb went on. That wasn't love, that was control. I realized a little freaking late in the day that while Denny never hit me, I was being abused all the same. I got up and walked out of the doctor's office without a word. I stopped at the public phone right there on Clay Street, looked up a lawyer in the yellow pages, and went to the first one who'd see me that day. End of story."

"Not end of story." He stroked the back of her hand, which lay over his heart. "As long as you remember, the fucker still has control. Time to jettison the crap memories and walk into your own version of your life. How about if we make some brand-new, awesome memories to replace them?"

Zane slid over her body, bracing himself on his arms as he looked down at her. "First we have to wipe every single bad memory from your mind."

"Perfect," she smiled, as he eased between her thighs. "A mind-wipe . . . How do we do that?"

He was rock hard and she was wet and ready for him as he thrust into the wet heat of her, burying himself to the hilt. Her legs wrapped tightly around his hips, and she tilted her hips to give him even deeper access. His heart tripped and galloped as her heels dug into his ass.

"It requires dedication," he murmured, then kissed her, a long juicy kiss mimicking the thrust and parry as their hips slapped together. "Persistence," he panted. "Sweat—" He pushed deep and felt her inner contractions as her body welcomed him. He slid out, then slammed back in. "There's a statistical, mathematical equation—

"Not." He speared her on the spar of his dick until she let out a little scream of pleasure. "Just." Pulled out until she clawed his back and cursed. "A good come. I want to give you a mind-blowing, scream until you fly to pieces, high-decibel, carefully calibrated series of . . . orgasms—" The tendons in his neck pulsed as he hung on to his own orgasm with his last thread of control. "—that . . . will wipe every lousy . . . event . . . from your mind—Permanently."

Holding nothing back, Teal was panting, her hair clinging to the sweat on her cheeks, her eyes black with lust as she dug her short nails into his back, speeding up the pace. "Well—if—it's . . . *permanent*—by—all—means . . . let's get calib—" She came apart in his arms.

*   *   *

"That was Ben," Zane flipped his phone closed the next morning and sat down on the bed beside Teal's hip. She lay facedown, nose buried into the pillow. He'd kept her up *calibrating* very late the night before. He grinned like a satisfied cat. The weather had cleared during the night, and he was eager to get back on board and return to the dive site, although he was tempted to blow off for the day.

But her pale, slender bare back and long legs were hard to resist. Zane ran his fingers over her bare ass, loving the softness of her pale skin and the way the muscles contracted on contact. He tried his best to ignore a painfully hard erection. All the inclination in the world, but no time.

"Everyone's fine—Have I mentioned you have a beautiful ass?" He dropped a lingering kiss on one smooth cheek. "And their house didn't have any damage." He ran the sentences together as he kissed his way up the small of her back and felt her shudder.

He nibbled each shoulder blade, then lifted her hair and nibbled her nape, before straightening. He could've pole-vaulted directly to the dive site. "Up and at 'em, Williams. Get dressed, we're hooking up with the Berland brood at Sandy's for breakfast in ten minutes."

She opened one eye. "Another girlfriend?"

"A restaurant on the beach near the marina, and it's doing a brisk business this morning. Ben's already got a table, and they've ordered coffee, so don't dillydally, woman." He gave her bottom a light smack when she buried her face in the pillow again and groaned.

"I'll stay right here and keep your place warm," Teal mumbled, eyes closed.

"Oh no you don't." Zane flipped her over like a rag doll. She curled into his arms, her warm cheek against his chest. He dropped a kiss on her nose. "Rise and shine, gorgeous. Don't you want to eat before you check your precious engines?"

She opened one eye, and he smiled. Other women wanted jewelry; Teal wanted new engines. Hell, she could be motivated by the welfare of the old engines.

"We won't stay long," he told her, standing up with her in his arms. Her head flopped to his chest, and she sleepily wound her arms around his neck as he carried her to the bathroom. "I've already been down to see how *Decrepit* weathered that storm. She's fine. I'd like to get out to the site sooner than later." Zane angled her so she could pull the shower door open in the confined space. "Hopefully, this mess didn't churn up the sand too badly. We'll certainly have to use the blower again. But hopefully we won't lose more than a day or two."

He slid her down his body so her toes touched the floor. She stroked her hand down the front of his tented shorts to close her fingers firmly around his erection. Eyes dancing, she leaned in and whispered against his mouth, "Is *this* the blower, or are you just happy to see me?"

Chapter 14

The day was exquisite, already warm, with not a cloud in the brilliant blue of the sky. Teal put on her sunglasses as they walked along a beachfront path to the restaurant where they were meeting the others. People were joking as they cleaned up the storm damage—business as usual in paradise. A long stretch of debris-strewn, sugary white sand was situated between two outcroppings of rocks. The sun threw diamonds on the surface of clear, tropical, turquoise water, which was already dotted with little white sailboats. The beach was peppered with vacationers swimming, playing volleyball, or stretched out improving their tans; plenty of people were gathering seashells, a bonanza after the storm. Others cleaned up the storm damage from the day before.

Teal's pulse picked up as she heard the foot-tapping sounds of steel drums playing a calypso beat mixed with laughter, plates clinking, and the susurrus of the waves. The outdoor restaurant was packed and Zane seemed to know everyone. As usual. He stopped every half dozen feet or so for a few moments to hug/kiss/shake hands, or chat with people on the way to their table.

"Last stop. I promise," Zane assured her as a man rose from a nearby table, hand outstretched. Zane grinned and shook his hand. "Phil—Thanks, man." He turned to Teal. "Phil owns the marina we tied up in yesterday," he said, then introduced her as simply, "Teal." The two men chatted for a few minutes before shaking hands again. "Another guy I went to school with," Zane told her as they resumed winding their way through tables. He smiled and waved at a few people, but didn't stop. "That table's Phil's office," he told her, then pointed out their group as they got closer.

The Berlands, with Ryan, Colson, and Saul, sat at an umbrella-shaded table right on the beach. "There they are. And perfect timing." A waitress was laying loaded plates out on the table, including at the two empty places.

With them were Cat and her very pregnant partner Liz, another beautiful blonde. Zane kissed all the women, backslapped the guys, and sat down ready to eat. This time, Teal had a much better mental attitude. She found that without her preconceived ideas, she *liked* Zane's friends. Jessie, their little girl, seated between Cat and Liz, was adorable. Teal's chest hurt, looking at the female version of Zane as she jumped up on her chair to give him a sloppy wet kiss and begged to be picked up.

Don't go there, she cautioned herself as Zane picked the child up and swung around with her in his arms.

"Zane, she's just about to eat!" Maggie scolded, but Jessie kept yelling. "Doot gen, Unc! Doot gen!"

Teal smiled with the others as Zane resumed his seat after whispering in the child's ear, making her giggle. He was good with kids. Jessie, like every other female of Zane's acquaintance, was clearly under his magnetic spell. He'd be a great father.

Too permissive, of course, but he'd be so much fun for a child. She suspected he might be a bit of a prude and maybe he *would* be strict with a pretty daughter, but he'd make

sure that child knew how much he or she was loved. He'd
show that every day. His children would always know how
much their father loved them. Lucky, lucky future kids.

The night before had been magical. But Teal knew sex
with Zane didn't mean happily ever after. That way of
thinking would only bring her more heartache. Live for
today was her new motto.

After a great breakfast, the team walked back to the
marina, which was about a mile away. All around them
was evidence of the storm; broken tree limbs, palm fronds,
and other flotsam. The road was covered with a layer of
beach sand and the heavy rains had washed down part of
a hill nearby. But other than the mess, it didn't appear as
if any of the buildings had structural damage.

Teal hoped the same could be said for the *Decrepit*.

"She looks good," Ben observed as they reached Phil's
marina. The shop was open for business, offering rentals
of small sailboats and Jet Skis, as well as small speed
boats and scuba gear. Zane went inside to pay for the night
while the others started untying *Decrepit*.

Teal left them to it and hurried aboard to turn the generator back on and do a safety check of her equipment.
Within an hour, *Decrepit* was on her way back to their
dive site. It never crossed her mind to tell Zane she didn't
want to go.

*   *   *

Scuba diving was a sensual experience for Zane. It never
got old, breathing underwater. Nor did the sensation of
flight. It was sweet listening to the rhythmic song of inha-
lations and exhalations as he and Teal swam through
cloudy water to reach the wreck. Visibility today was
crappy, mere feet. But he hadn't expected any different.
The storm had churned up sand and debris from the

bottom, and the currents shifted and swirled around them. He'd warned Teal to stay close, and she was within touching distance beside him, a sleek black shadow.

The sounds the fish and other underwater life made harmonized with the rhythmic bell-like chimes of the bubbles on the exhale of his regulator. Even though Zane anticipated the glory hole would be covered once again, he felt his usual sense of excitement and anticipation under the water.

And for reasons he didn't want to analyze too deeply, having Teal there beside him enhanced the experience.

Magic.

With any luck, the storm hadn't adversely affected the wreck of the *Vrijheid* and it was just where they'd left it. There was a pretty good chance that they'd have to fan the sand all over again. It would certainly add several days to his schedule, and they were already pressed for time as they entered hurricane season. But the good news was that the *Sea Witch* had moved on, leaving Zane and his crew to excavate the site in peace without any distractions.

He had no idea where she'd gone or how long she'd stay away. Hopefully the police had spooked her and she'd be gone for a good long while. He'd see her again—he was sure of it. But he hoped it was long after he'd claimed every piece of treasure the *Vrijheid* had to offer. He'd left her to the authorities to deal with, but she'd been long gone when they went to haul her ass in for questioning. So be it. He had no doubt he and the redhead would clash again.

Teal touched his arm. She looked as gorgeous and mysterious as a mermaid with her dark hair fanned around her head. He winked at her through his mask. She didn't smile back, and her fingers tightened on his arm. She used her free hand to point behind him and to the left. Jesus. Now what? He reached for his dive knife as he spun around.

What the—

A twin-engine plane was perched like a damned vulture, right smack bang on top of his treasure.

What the fuck?

A Cessna. One wing had been neatly sheared off. *That* could be yards or even miles away. The attached wing had smashed into the few standing ribs of the *Vrijheid* and given them a crew cut. Damn it.

Clearly a casualty of the storm, the small plane had barely made it a hundred miles from St. Maarten or one of the numerous other islands. Someone trying to outrace the storm? How many passengers? Christ—There'd be *bodies*. Man, he didn't want to do this part. Not at all.

Teal grabbed his arm, pointed to her eyes, then the plane. Yeah. He was going to look. He pointed up. As much as the very idea made his scrotum shrink, and his heart sound like a bass drum in his ears, Zane figured he'd do a quick look-see on his own before getting Ben or Ryan and the camera. He'd call it in, but dollars to doughnuts, someone was going to want documentation, and with the water moving around as it was, he needed to hustle.

If someone had flown out of St. Maarten and targeted *Vrijheid* on *purpose*, they couldn't have had better aim. Shitcrapfuck.

He indicated Teal return to the *Decrepit,* but of course, Teal being Teal, she shook her head, no. For several seconds, they had a heated argument in sign language, which neither of them actually knew, ending up with them both laughing and spewing bubbles. The situation wasn't in the least bit funny. But Teal made even a crappy and, frankly, creepy situation manageable.

He ran his hand over her hair, knowing she couldn't feel his touch, but wanting to touch her anyway. Inside her mask her eyes smiled. Good enough to brace him for what was to come.

They searched together. No sign of any bodies. Thank God. There was every chance they'd been thrown clear—possibly somewhere near the missing wing. And while he loved nothing more than salvaging wrecks, he preferred them to be hundreds of years old. Maybe the bastards had gotten lucky and jumped before the plane crashed, complete with parachute and inflatable seat cushions.

They'd be hard to find or possibly shark food by now if they hadn't. Either that, or, no one had been inside when it had hit the water. A damn lucky, quick-thinking save if that were the case. But still, stupid to fly in those high winds. What a dipshit.

Maybe the passengers had been picked up by a boat heading back to one of the islands to out run the weather. Right. In the middle of a major storm. It seemed impossible to him, but stranger things had happened. Whoever had been on the plane must've somehow survived the impact and bailed in time, or the bodies were somewhere out there in the murk.

He just wished it hadn't happened smack bang on top of his treasure.

He'd call it in, then after the authorities had a look at it, he'd offer to move it. He had the crane. Officials could bring a barge . . . Zane's brain went a mile a minute as he cataloged what might be involved. He tried to figure out just how he'd move it, how he'd get it up onto a barge, and what the delay would be while various authorities fought over jurisdiction.

They swam around the plane. Zane knew enough from flight school—one didn't live on a miniscule island without knowing how to fly—that it looked like a wider-span laminar-flow wing, meaning it might be a Cessna Citation. A business jet. Too pricy for a local rental. Pricy. Private. The hair on the back of his neck prickled.

Drugs?

Shit!

He couldn't see any luggage or personal effects, but

that didn't mean anything. Personal shit could be scattered over a mile of ocean. The front windshield was shattered, the body broken in half, tail gone, and one wing sticking up like a middle finger. There was no sign of the second wing.

What a pain in the ass. *Worse, a* hell of a lot worse if this *had* been a drug run. They packed that shit well. They'd want it back.

Feeling atypically grim, Zane pointed up. Time to call it in.

*   *   *

"Hey Barry. Zane Cutter. Listen, just back at my dive site—No, it's not okay. There's what looks like a Cessna CJ Three parked a hundred feet under water and right over my wreck." He paused to listen. "I can tell the difference between a boat and a plane, yeah." He was using his cell phone to call a friend at the airport in St, Maarten. Until he knew who had been on that plane, he wasn't going to use any open channels that anyone could listen in to. He looked out the big windows. The sea was flat calm. The sky a tranquil blue. Considering the shit-storm his salvage operation was about to hit, it didn't seem fair.

He had a bad feeling his life was about to take a detour that he could never have anticipated. "The nose and most of the body," he told his friend. "One wing. Tail's gone. No, we did a thorough search. No one that we could see. Yeah. I hear you. Let me know."

Everyone on board was in the salon as Zane called it in. Their avid glances bored into his back. When he snapped the phone shut and turned, he could see they all looked as worried as he felt.

"Barry over at Princess Juliana International says they didn't get a mayday. Nothing in months, let alone the last twenty-four hours. And no one filed a flight plan for a small aircraft—incoming or outgoing—for twenty-four hours. There was no reason for it to be this far off the beaten track, so it was coming in under the radar. He's going to do a discreet check."

"It's drugs," Colson said with confidence. He was folded over the galley counter like a rag doll, a Coke in one hand, and a slice of Maggie's apple pie in the other.

"Maybe." Zane felt sick to his stomach. Drugs meant an alphabet soup of agencies, not just the DEA, NTSB, and the FAA who'd be investigating if it was an American plane, but Feds, *plus* the local authorities. It also meant ten thousand miles of red tape and strangers all over the *Vrijheid*. He felt as though someone had come and ripped away his magic cape.

He ran both hands through his hair. "I have to stay here. But I want the rest of you to leave. Go back to St. Maarten and wait for me there."

"So that if the drug lords come looking for their drugs you'll be the only one here?" Teal demanded, brown eyes flashing. "Are you insane?"

"Not insane. Cautious. Whatever is going to happen, hopefully it'll be fucking *soon* so we can get back to work while we still have this short window of opportunity."

"Zane, you can't charm a drug . . . salesman, or whatever they're called," Maggie said nervously. "Once they know where their plane is, they'll *kill* you."

"No they won't," Zane said calmly. His insides were coiling around like venomous snakes because he had not a shred of doubt in his mind that Maggie's assessment was accurate. "These are *businessmen*. I tell them the general direction their plane went down, and they go get their product."

"Well, right now they don't know we know where their plane is," Teal said practically. "And we don't know that it *is* a drug plane. Your friend, Barry, will call us back and tell us that some moron got blown off his flight path, and he's drinking a rum drink with an umbrella in it, sitting in the hot tub at some resort hotel as we speak."

Wouldn't that be nice, Zane thought, wrapping his arms around her from behind, and resting his chin on her hair. *Totally fucking unlikely, but nice.* This situation was going to turn from sugar to shit on a dime. The thought of having Teal anywhere dangerous turned him ice cold. He'd already put her in jeopardy once. Once was one too many. "I'll get the security guys with big guns back. Will that make you happy?"

"Knocking you unconscious and dragging you off somewhere *safe* would make me happy."

Maggie exchanged a look with Ben, then shot Zane a sly smile. "At least you two finally figured it out."

They hadn't figured anything out. He was pleased Teal hadn't heard or was ignoring Maggie's comment.

Saul shoved up his sleeves and addressed Zane. "We can try running the fish on the mag, see if we get any hits. Tail and wing are probably aluminum alloy, but there might be something else the mag could pick up."

"Good idea, Saul," Zane told him. "But I don't think they'd be carrying an anchor chain or cannon."

"What other kinds of metals does the magnetometer pick up?" Teal asked, leaning against him as though she did it every day. It felt good having her nestled in his arms. Damn good.

"Just ferrous metals," Saul told her. "As Zane says— anchors, cannon, chain . . ."

"If I could go down and examine the engine, I could see if any of the oil was drained—possibly the cause of the crash. Maybe a broken hose—whatever. If that's the case, ferrous material *would* be present. In the bottom of the sump. Ferrous material could also be in the oil filter canister."

The woman wanted to give him respiratory failure.

"You aren't going anywhere *near* the plane until everything's been cleared." Zane glared at each of them in turn, making himself perfectly clear. "*Nobody* is to go anywhere near it until we hear what Barry has to say first. There's sure to be some 'official' way to do this. Let's not waste our time if they're going to send a swarm of professionals in to do it instead."

Zane reluctantly unwrapped his arms from around Teal and immediately felt . . . alone. Crazy. He stepped away from her. "Maggie, Ben. Cat and Liz are going to need you. You would've been home for the baby next week anyway. I'd feel much better if you two took off. Worry, about all of you, is going to make it that much harder for me to keep focused. I'd like you to take Teal with you."

"I'm not going anywhere!" Teal said stubbornly. "After everything I've been through for this salvage, I'm not letting some mystery plane chase me off. But I do think Maggie and Ben should go. Colson, too." When the younger man tried to protest, Teal pointed a stern finger at him. "You're a minor. Your parents would sue Zane and take everything he owns if you were stupid enough to end up dead."

Zane bit back a smile. She was damn cute when she was bossing someone else around.

"I'll call you the second the coast is clear," Zane assured them.

"There's no need for any of us to stick around," Ryan pointed out, twisting on a bar stool to look at everyone in the room. "What's to stop us from sailing into port, not saying a word, and letting the authorities deal with this mess?"

"That plane is on *my* wreck," Zane pointed out the obvious. "As long as it's there, I'm going to be right here making sure no one helps themselves to our hard work. But you guys need to split."

"I agree," Ben said flatly. "Maggie needs to go back and be with the girls. And, sorry son, Colson has to be away from this mess. But I'm not going anywhere. Maggie and Teal can—"

"I'm not leaving," Teal told the group at large. "End of story. Suck it up. I'm here for the duration. I know a thing or two about drugs and dealers." She shot Maggie a small smile. "*Salesmen* too. I'm going to my engines, call me when things start happening." Ryan watched her go before turning to Zane. "You've lost your touch, Ace. You should've told her she had to *stay*."

Zane smiled. "Yeah. I should've. But then she's so contrary she might have called my bluff."

Maggie put her arms around Zane and rested her cheek on his chest. "I want to stay and see what happens with you two, but I'm going to go because I know you'll worry about me if I stay. I'll take care of our girls and worry about all of you from afar." She gave him a hard squeeze. "None of you do anything stupid, you hear me? We still have a fortune in treasure to find."

*　　*　　*

Teal hadn't done much praying in her life, in fact, only about three times that came to mind, but she bowed her head the second she reached her engine room. "Please God, don't let this plane be trouble. And if it is, don't let Zane be an idiot." That covered a lot of ground. She figured God got it and left it at that.

She got out her tap and die kit to pound some sense into the zincs in the heat exchangers and simultaneously get out some of her frustration.

There was a loud knock on the door. "Can I come in?" Maggie asked. She wore jeans and a bright pink T-shirt that read *eat my bubbles* and carried her straw cowboy hat.

Teal wiped her hands on a rag. "Of course. Are you leaving?"

"Neither Colson nor myself want to go. But Zane's insistent, and Ben's turning Rambo on me." Her smile was rueful. "The girls will be happy to have me home. That helps."

"It was probably a couple of half-soused guys on their way to a party. They'll get a whopping giant fine, and you can get back to *Decrepit* in no time," Teal told the older woman, who was clearly worried as hell.

Maggie walked straight over to Teal and wrapped her arms around her. Teal tensed. "I'm terrified," Maggie whispered into her shoulder. After a brief hesitation, Teal tentatively rubbed Maggie's back. "I'm frightened out of my wits that it *was* a drug deal gone bad and terrible people will show up any second. I'm scared to leave, and honestly, even more scared to *stay*. Give me a barracuda to face any day of the week, and I'm fine. People are a lot less predictable."

"Not our guys, though," Teal told her, hugging Maggie back almost as tightly as Maggie was hugging her. "Zane will kick butts and take names, Ben will bamboozle them with his brilliance, Ryan will help Zane, and Saul will hold coats." Teal smiled, even though her face was being covered by Maggie's blond hair.

Maggie half laughed as Teal had wanted her to. She stepped away, but cupped her palm to Teal's cheek. "I absolutely adore you, you know that, Teal Williams? You've become one of my favorite people. And it's a short list. I'm very selective." Maggie's smile made Teal's chest hurt. She had no idea how to respond. "Even if you weren't a perfect fit for Zane, I'd still count you as one of my faves."

She reached up and kissed Teal on the cheek. "Try to keep the boys out of trouble until I get back, okay?"

"There's not going to *be* any trouble," Teal assured her.

"This is all going to turn into a minor inconvenience, you'll see."

Maggie smiled, then gave her another quick, hard hug. "From your lips to God's ear. Stay safe, honey. I'll see you soon."

As soon as Maggie put on her hat and left, Teal looked up at the ceiling. "Did you hear that, God? If you won't listen to me, listen to her. *Please*."

She stayed in her engine room for as long as she could. She did some unnecessary cleaning, checked all her tools, and read a chapter of her book. There'd be no more diving, and the more alone time Teal had, the more pissed she became at the morons who'd crashed their stupid freaking plane right on top of a wreck filled with yet-undiscovered treasure.

Zane walked in during her one-sided verbal rant. "I can tell you're winning," he said, smiling as she stopped talking abruptly. The smile didn't reach his eyes.

He crossed the room and took her in his arms, burying his face in her hair. "I just need to hold you a minute, do you mind?" Strain laced the amusement in his voice.

Teal tightened her arms around his waist and buried her face against his chest. She inhaled deeply, drawing in the familiar scent of him. His arms were hard and strong around her as she laid her cheek against his chest and heard the steady beat of his heart. "If it'll help, I'll get naked. I've never done it in an engine room before, and that mattress is nice and bouncy."

He laughed softly, lifting her chin on his finger. "We're going to do it in here, and on every flat surface on board, as soon as this mess is resolved. I'll take a nice juicy kiss as a down payment, though."

His mouth was hot and hungry and addictively urgent. He tasted like coming home to her, too. Of safety. And passion. And promises. Teal caught fire from his hunger and wrapped her arms around his neck as he walked her backward. Her spine hit the bulkhead with a small thud. He pushed her back against the wall, holding her there with his weight as his tongue dueled with hers.

Her entire body pulsed and clenched as he made love to her mouth. Her nipples peaked and hardened, but Teal had to be satisfied with the pressure of his chest rubbing against hers, because his hands were fisted in her hair, and his knee pressed between her thighs.

They came apart, both gasping for air, pupils dilated.

Zane rested his forehead on hers, then shifted them both away from the bulkhead. With his arms still around her, he said quietly. "As mind-blowing as that kiss was, I actually came down to get you. We have company."

Despite the strong urge to burrow into him, wrap her arms around him, and just *cling*, Teal accompanied Zane up the spiral stairs to the salon. Pictures of cauliflower-eared men carrying Uzis flashed through her head. Then she realized that was *gangsters* and adjusted it to beefy guys in suits with diamond grills and big ugly handguns. On the other hand, one of her mother's dealers had worn his fast-food manager's uniform. She bit back a nervous laugh. Never good to stereotype. But she'd grown up in a neighborhood chock full of them. All assorted sizes, ethnicities, and sexes.

So when she entered the salon a step behind Zane, Teal was ready for anything.

Except Men in Black.

Chapter 15

The two men both wore black slacks, black T-shirts, black holsters, and black guns. They wore sunglasses—inside—and had Special Forces written all over them.

"Miss Williams," the man on the left said politely, indicating she sit on one of the leather sofas. Zane took her hand and sat down with her. Ben and Saul sat at the counter, and Ryan, looking uncomfortable as hell, was on one of the chairs by the computers. The two men blocked the door leading to the deck as if Zane and the rest of them were going to make a mad dash outside to freedom at any second.

"We believe that the CJ Three that crashed was carrying an Alphachip, stolen from a secure faculty in— Nearby."

Teal had no idea what an Alphachip was. "Couldn't have been a very secure facility if it was stolen," she pointed out dryly. Zane squeezed her hand in warning. The men were not amused.

"You *believe*?" Zane asked, politely enough, but a muscle jumped in his jaw.

"The whereabouts of the Alphachip have been confirmed. It was on board the CJ Three when it crashed.

"We would like you to retrieve said chip immediately. After that, you're free to go."

"Damn good of you," Zane said shortly. "But we aren't going *anywhere*. I'm the custodian and exclusive salvor of the *Vrijheid*. We still have more work to do on our salvage. Your damn stolen chip is right on top of my wreck. So, gentlemen, I suggest you get someone to haul it up and the hell out of my way."

"It's a matter of national security that the Alphachip be retrieved within thirty-nine hours."

Thirty-nine hours seemed strangely precise to Teal.

"Unless this Alphachip is at least the size of a breadbox, it could be anywhere down there," Zane told them, running out of patience. "How do you intend to find and retrieve it within," he glanced at the clock on the wall, "thirty-eight hours and fifty-five minutes? Does it have a homing device on it?"

The two men glanced at one another. "No, it does not."

"Are you claiming the plane *wasn't* carrying drugs?" Teal asked, not sure if these guys were for real. A microchip was smaller than . . . a microchip. Tiny. Made of silicone, impossible to find in a seabed full of sand. Impossible to find underwater in the best of conditions. They didn't *have* good conditions. She and Zane had barely been able to see each other, let alone a little bitty freaking chip, for God's sake.

"No drugs. Just the stolen Alphachip."

"So we're not getting a bunch of drug runners boarding any minute, looking for their drugs?" Ben asked in a tense voice.

"No," Man in Black Left told him before returning to look at Zane with an expression impossible to read behind those damned dark glasses. "But the people who stole the chip will start searching for it themselves very soon. They were headed for Princess Juliana Airport to make the drop. They weren't blown far off their path. As I said. You have thirty-nine hours to find it and deliver it to us."

"If it's that important, then feel free to go down and look for yourselves," Zane told them flatly. "But I have to tell you, it'll be an impossible task. Something that size? In the vastness of the ocean? We couldn't even see one of the plane's *wings*. The storm churned up the seabed, and it's like swimming through a sandstorm as it is down there."

"The Alphachip is sealed inside a red box. About this size." The guy on the right indicated something the size of a loaf of bread. "Nothing must look out of the ordinary when the men who stole it come looking."

The atmosphere in the room was suddenly charged. Teal felt a film of nervous perspiration on her skin. "And you two won't fetch this chip yourselves because . . . ?"

"Neither of us is proficient at deepwater diving."

She could tell by Zane's annoyed expression that he wasn't buying this as he said, "Plenty of experienced divers to be had in St. Maarten."

"Not who know the wreck and location as well as you people do. You've been excavating the area for weeks. Monitoring it even longer. We're certain you have a clear map of the area and its topography. Use it to locate the chip."

Zane leaned forward. "If you want our help, then tell us exactly what's going on." He crossed his arms over his chest.

The men exchanged glances, and the first gave a nearly imperceptible nod.

"Less than ten miles from this site is a top-secret underwater facility. What goes on there is classified, but rest assured, it's of utmost importance to our continued national security that that chip be retrieved in a timely manner."

"A top secret *government* facility?" Zane asked. "These are Dutch waters. Is this facility Dutch?"

Since the men were clearly American, Zane had a valid point.

"Several months ago, we received intelligence that we had a spy in our midst," the guy on the right said without answering Zane's question. "Shortly thereafter, you showed up. We've been monitoring you ever since."

"Then you must know I'm not a threat."

"Anyone lurking around our facility is a threat."

"Is that a threat?" Zane asked with dangerous calm.

"We were simply monitoring you because of your close proximity to an extremely sensitive area."

"Sensitive area, huh?" said Zane. "I suppose that explains why the nav and detection equipment goes haywire whenever we get into these waters. You must have some kind of jamming equipment. Am I right?"

Neither man said a word. They simply stared right through Zane as if he'd never asked the question.

Teal shifted closer to him. These guys made her by turns nervous as hell, and indignant. "What's so important about the chip anyway?"

"We're unable to give specifics, but it contains data vital to national security. The data exists solely on that chip. Anyone in possession of it would have access to top-secret defense systems. Should that happen the ramifications would be catastrophic. This is not a polite request, Mr. Cutter," the first man said. "You are being asked to perform this service by our president. This is a vital matter of national security."

Ryan whistled, Ben and Saul exchanged worried looks. Zane's fingers tightened around Teal's. "And if I refuse this 'service'? Then what?"

"I'd hate to have you removed as custodian from the wreck, and have it revert to the Dutch government, Mr. Cutter. It's vital that the chip be retrieved by friendlies, *before* the bad guys get here to retrieve it themselves," Left Guy said grimly. "It would be a disaster of cataclysmic proportions if they get their hands on it—."

"Again," Teal pointed out. "You didn't do a very good job protecting something *this* important in the first place."

Zane squeezed her hand in warning to take it down a notch. "How do we know you two aren't the guys who stole it in the first place?"

The Right Guy pointed at Zane. "Got your cell phone?"

"Yeah." Zane lifted his butt to get it out of his jeans pocket.

"Get a hold of the White House. He's waiting for your call."

He who? The *president*? Teal shared an incredulous glance with Zane, then he looked back at the men. "What's the number?"

"We could give you a phone number to anyone. Go through the switchboard. Give them your last name followed by the number B Seventeen. We'll wait outside."

B Seventeen was the number on Zane's charts of the *Vrijheid* dive site. How could they have known that? A cold chill permeated Teal's body. *Holy hell.* What had they fallen into?

Teal and the others waited on tenterhooks. Zane rose and started pacing as he obtained the number for the White House. Within minutes, he'd identified himself, then there was a short pause and he said, "Good afternoon, Mr. President. My name is Zane—. Yes, sir. Yes, sir. I understand. People will start gathering again. How can I—? Yes, sir. I'm sure they will."

For several minutes, Zane listened. Slowly the color leached from his face. Seeing his reaction to what he was being told worried the hell out of her. The fact that he was talking to the president of the United States on his cell phone meant this was a very big, scary deal.

"I hate to say this, sir, but there's a good chance *nobody* will be able to find that chip." He paused, stopping midstride in the middle of the room. Outside, the sun shone as if the storm had never been. The two guys dressed in black stood silently waiting for Zane to finish talking to the president.

"Could you please clarify that?" Zane raked his hair back off his face, his cheekbones in stark relief, his eyes shadowed. "Yes, sir. I completely understand. Yes, I agree. Thirty-*eight* hours would be optimal." He disconnected, then stood for a few moments staring out of the window blindly before turning around to address them.

"I'm going to find that fucking chip. I want all of you to pack your things and leave. When I've handed the Alphachip over, I'll call you and you can come back."

"No way," Ryan said flatly. "They said *act normal.* Normal isn't one guy, diving alone for God only knows how many hours at a stretch. Too dangerous. Not going to happen."

Saul rose and came over to clasp Zane on the shoulder. "You'll need all the help you can get. I don't dive well, but I can make sure you're all fed and watered and your tanks are refilled, ready when you are. I'm not leaving."

"Same goes for me," Ben told him firmly. "Four of us have a better chance of finding this thing than you do alone in such a short span of time. Majority rules, son. We all stay."

Zane turned to Teal. "I want you—."

"Two teams," she told him firmly, holding his gaze. "It's already decided. Everyone dives with a buddy. No exceptions. Now, how about you fill us in on the rest of it?"

Zane rubbed his hand across his jaw. "In the event this

chip ever got into the wrong hands, it was programmed to self-detonate. We have thirty-nine hours left."

Ryan was the first to speak. "Wait a minute! Are you telling us if we *don't* find this Alphachip thing, the plane and everything around it will *explode*?"

"Yeah." Zane rubbed his thumb over his phone, still not quite believing who he'd just talked to. "That's the word."

His friend flopped back in the chair he'd just vacated, looking as stunned as Zane felt. "That's asking us to find a specific grain of sand in a sandbox, for crap sake!"

"A bit bigger than a grain of sand," Zane said dryly, walking behind the sofa to go into the galley. As he passed, he brushed his hand lightly over Teal's hair, making her shiver, then kept going.

"You heard what the guy out there said; the chip's in a red box." Like the color would make it easier to see a hundred feet under the water where everything was blue anyway. Jesus. The entire scenario was preposterous. He was still trying to wrap his brain around the fact that he'd just had a conversation with the president. Which about took this situation from bizarre to surreal.

"Oh, no problem finding it then," Teal added her two cents. "It's *huge*. What a relief."

Despite the situation, Teal's predictable pithiness made him smile, as he was sure she intended. She watched him with big, worried, brown eyes. Zane knew unequivocally that her entire concern was for him. For his safety. For the realization of his dream. He felt a swell of emotion tighten his throat and wanted to wrap her in his magical cape and spirit her far away from this mess. But the cape was kind of tattered at the moment, just like his emotions.

"I'm guessing we weren't given the option of refusing?" Ben asked, beads of sweat dotting his forehead.

"I wasn't given that option. No. But that doesn't mean you—*any* of you should stay; in fact—."

"In fact, we've already covered who's staying and who's going," Teal reminded him. "Case closed. Thirty-eight-ish hours doesn't give us much freaking time to argue about it. We'd better make them count."

"Can we use the crane to haul out the wreckage?" Ryan suggested. "Much easier to search it out of the water."

"Yeah. My thoughts as well. That's what we'll have to do. *First*. If that doesn't work . . ." He held up a soda can to the group, then tossed drinks to those who wanted one. He returned to pace, slugging down his Coke as his brain worked a mile a minute.

He'd never used the crane to haul anything so unstable out of the water. The plane could break apart, hell—it probably *would* break apart. But it was their best shot at finding this damned thing.

If they managed the improbable, impossible task of finding the small container, on the bottom of a very large ocean, everything could go back to normal. If not, the plane, and the *Vrijheid*, would blow to smithereens in less than two days. Which was by far the more likely of the two scenarios.

"If *Vrijheid* was blown to hell after she's gone through four hundred years of currents and hurricane action, consider how far bits of her will be flung with a monstrous fucking explosion. And while those two out there want it retrieved, I suspect they'll also be okay with it blowing everything to kingdom come. The end result is they don't want the bad guys to get their hands on that chip again. This is a case of if we don't have it, you don't either."

Ben perched on the arm of the sofa, his face red with an excess of emotion. This wasn't good for his blood pressure, which added another layer of worry on Zane's shoulders. "At least let's bring in more divers."

"You heard," Teal drew her feet up on the sofa and circled her knees with her arms. "That's a big freaking N.O."

"There are five of us," Saul pointed out. "Odds are, we'll find it."

Odds weren't anything of the sort, Zane knew, but he appreciated everyone having a positive attitude. Odds were very much against them. Even as a betting man, Zane didn't like the numbers.

The door opened, and the two men came back into the salon. "All set?" the taller one, who looked like a weight-lifter, asked.

Zane nodded. "As we'll ever be." He wasn't happy about any of this. The very real possibility that the *Vrijheid* would be lost forever sucked, but more important, he wasn't risking the lives of his team. Not for anyone. Up to and including the president. If they told him he had thirty-eight hours, he'd make sure that all of them were far the hell away if the chip wasn't found by hour thirty-*six*. "We'll bring the section of plane onto the deck. Easier to sear—."

"No can do," the agent told him.

"Visibility is down to feet right now," Zane pointed out grimly. "We don't have time for the current to settle. If you don't want this d—."

"You can't have a Citation jet sitting out on your deck for anyone with satellite imagery and the naked eye to see," the agent responded.

Shit. "And what's *your* contribution to this clusterfuck?" Zane demanded, pissed off, and not bothering to hide it.

"We'll stay on board and make sure nobody bothers you while you dive."

Yeah, like that was going to produce the fucking miracle they needed.

*   *   *

Zane and Ryan took the first dive. Teal stayed on deck with Ben and waited. Something she wasn't that good at, she discovered.

It was eleven A.M. on Wednesday. If the explosive device wasn't located and brought to the surface, Zane had told all of them, they'd leave for St. Maarten by eleven P.M. on Thursday—tomorrow night.

Thirty-six hours.

The two men were Davis and Smiley—which he wasn't. They didn't have first names. Davis was short and stocky, with military short, salt-and-pepper hair, and a slight overbite. Smiley was a bit taller and very buff. Weight lifting buff, with bulging biceps and a barrel chest and a don't-fuck-with-me attitude. Teal was glad to know they were the good guys. They were tolerable, and best of all, they were both fully armed.

They returned to their discreet Stingray rental fishing boat tied aft of the *Decrepit* and came back with heavy-looking duffels, which they stowed conveniently nearby in the galley. Teal offered them her old cabin.

"Thank you, ma'am." Smiley took a large—very large—gun out of his duffel, emptied a cutlery drawer into the drawer with the utensils, and slid the gun inside, then snapped the latch closed. "We're working. We don't sleep."

It was much bigger than the one Zane had had when he'd come to rescue her the other day. And intriguing. She was determined to learn how to shoot one. Maybe take the thing apart so she could see it from the inside out. "You have to sleep sometime."

"Not for the next thirty-eight hours."

"Right. Can I hold that?" She indicated his gun in a shoulder holster.

Smiley blanched. "No, ma'am."

Too bad. "Maybe another time?" He gave her a pained look. "I made those sandwiches for you guys as well. Help yourselves."

"Carry on as normal."

"Good idea. Why don't I just go down and take care of my engines?" It was rhetorical and they treated the question as such. "Can I suggest you both change into something that doesn't look quite so . . . You know?"

Davis pulled out a pair of lurid yellow-and-lime-green surf trunks from his duffel. Teal had to chew her smile away. "Perfect."

She went on deck to let Ben know where she was if he needed her, then went down to her engine room to look at the old D398s with fresh eyes. She had some contingency plans of her own, and was happy to have a project to keep her busy. Now all she needed were some parts.

Ben called her when it was their turn to dive. Zane and Ryan had found nothing.

The four of them took turns diving all afternoon and well into dusk, using powerful underwater lamps. Nothing. It was depressing as hell going down and seeing the big freaking plane sitting on top of their wreck.

Bits of gold winked at them in the bright glare of the lights, taunting them from beneath the plane's fuselage and tail. Treasure they couldn't hunt and might lose completely.

Dinner was a somber affair. Everyone was stressed, but Teal was especially aware of Zane's tension. He talked less than usual. She hoped to hell he didn't do anything stupid. Like make them all go to St. Maarten while he hovered over the *Vrijheid* like a demented mother hen. He'd worked his ass off to find her. He shouldn't have to be punished because some criminal stole something and was unlucky enough to crash onto his wreck.

Smiley walked in while they were cleaning the dinner dishes. "We have company."

Teal had noticed the approaching lights out in the darkness a few minutes before. So had Zane, she was sure.

"Everyone knows we're right over a wreck," Zane told him as he handed a plate to Ben to dry. "They'll be curious. We had a crowd here before the storm. I imagine they'll be back. And you guys will, of course, take care of that. Right?" he said grimly. "I won't allow innocent bystanders to be sucked into this mess. Go out there and get rid of them."

"Things have to appear normal," Smiley informed him, his tone even. "If it's the opposition trying to find out if you've seen anything, it would be to our advantage to mislead them into thinking this is a regular dive site."

"Shit." Zane threw the dirty water down the sink and dried his hands. "Well, I guess we can deal with it in the morning. You two will be patrolling all night?"

"Yes, sir."

Zane held his hand out to Teal. "Let's get out of here."

*   *   *

He was on her the second the door to his cabin locked behind them. Grabbing her shoulders Zane spun her around. Her back slammed against the door, and she was held there by two hundred pounds of hard-breathing male. He was shaking, his hands too tight, his lungs labored. He kissed her with bruising force, and Teal gave back as good as she got.

He yanked her T-shirt off, sending it flying, then ripped at his own, flinging it over his shoulder. "Bed," she demanded against his throat.

"Shower." He pulled down her shorts, taking her panties with them, then kicked the bunched fabric at their feet aside all without breaking the kiss. Teal's hands went to his swim trunks, and she wrested them off his narrow hips. "Shower. Later!" Once they were around his knees, she used a foot to drag them to the floor. "Much."

Her nails dug into his biceps as she did a little jump and wrapped her strong legs around his waist and her arms around his neck. She felt his heavy shaft against her backside and shifted to get it where she needed it.

He groaned and bit her earlobe as he walked into the compact head. With blurred vision, she saw her own face reflected in the mirror. Color rode high on her cheekbones, her eyes glittered as though she were feverish. She looked lust crazed. Which she was. She couldn't get enough of him. The feel of his hands on her, the taste of his mouth, the smell of his skin—the sum of him made her wild and greedy for more.

"Look at us." He turned sideways so they could see their reflections in the mirror over the sink. "Look how perfectly you fit my hand." She watched his long fingers tug at her nipple. Saw it. Felt it. Double the eroticism. Zane's hands were a stark contrast against the paleness of her breast.

Her gaze lifted from his hand on her fair skin, to his face.

His expression as he followed the path of his fingers on her breast was feral. Magnificent.

Her heart, beating insanely fast, swelled in her chest as their eyes met in the mirror. Tears blurred her vision as emotion filled her to the brim. *I love you. I love you. I love you.*

His penis, hot and thick, centered at the juncture of her thighs. He swooped in on her mouth again, taking it in a possessive claim. A pirate plundering. Teal was more than okay with that. She matched him stroke for stroke. Her hands reaching, touching, stroking, claiming treasure of her own. The kiss went on and on. With a possessive growl, he lifted her onto the vanity, his fingers digging into her hips.

Dizzy, Teal tightened her arms around his neck and thrust her tongue into his mouth. He tasted of the beer he'd drunk with dinner; his mouth, a hot furnace threatening to engulf her.

The sensations she was feeling were almost too powerful to bear. She whimpered, her entire being focused where they were joined. He thrust forward, and she came hard and fast around the spar of his penis. The climax rolled over her, a tidal wave that never ended. His fingers tightened on her bottom as another climax shuddered through her. Teal's heart was manic, it was impossible to drag in a breath.

She was gratified to realize—in the small reptilian part of her brain that could still think—that some of the heavy breathing came from Zane. He came several times in violent pulses, his fingers biting into her ass cheeks, the tendons in his neck straining as he pumped into her. His head dropped to her shoulder, and his sweat mingled with hers.

After several minutes, their erratic breathing and the pounding of their hearts were the only sounds in the tiny bathroom. Teal opened her mouth over where his neck joined his shoulder. He tasted salty, sexy. Zane shuddered as she touched her tongue to his sweaty skin. Impossibly, her heartbeat reverted to rapid and out of control again.

"I slept with you the night of your father's funeral," she said, her breath heaving hard through her lungs. He was still hard, still deep inside her. Her internal muscles pulsed from the last climax, and she felt another building. The marble counter was cold on her bottom, but Zane's body blazed hot and burned her skin as the climax started rolling toward her like an out of control bullet train.

He paused on the withdrawal. "No . . . What?" He pushed inside her slick sheath. "That's—impossible." He withdrew slowly, showing his remarkable control. Teal tightened her ankles in the small of his back to pull him closer.

"You weren't at—the—Jesus, woman, let me—" He thrust hard and kept pumping until she was on a pinnacle of the highest mountaintop. "I didn't see you at the funeral."

The orgasm pounded over her like surf after high tide. Deaf, dumb, and blind, she held on as Zane rocked her world.

While she lay limply against his chest, he reached out and turned on the shower. Teal started to burble—something. But Zane just laughed and swooped down to kiss her. "Later."

"Good," she muttered against his chin. "I'm an amoeba."

Teal was pretty sure she blanked out as they showered. She suddenly found herself—damp and limp—lying on Zane's crisp white sheets without quite knowing how she'd gotten there.

Eyes closed, she inhaled the unique fragrance of his skin, her fingers tangled in the hair on his chest. "You have super powers," she sounded drugged.

He smiled against her wet hair. Clean and exhausted, Zane drew her against his chest. He couldn't lose this. God, he couldn't lose *her*. "You should sleep. I want to dive at the first hint of daylight."

"Sleep? Are you crazy? And miss a second of this? No way."

He ran his fingers lightly down her back. Her spine of steel. It stunned him how strong she was and yet, how incredibly fragile. "So you took advantage of a man three sheets to the wind?" He ran his fingers up and down the hills and valley of her sweet ass and felt the butterfly kiss of her lashes against his chest.

"My flight was late." Her fingers combed through the hair on his chest, then played with his nipple until he nearly took her again. He couldn't quite manage it again that fast however. He captured her busy fingers and flattened her hand against his chest.

"I got there when it was over. I went to your house . . ."

"Jesus, sweetheart . . ." He'd been a complete and utter fucking mess. The booze hadn't helped his melancholy either. He'd sobbed like a damned baby.

Her lips brushed the underside of his chin. Comfort. Love. Warmth. "I just wanted to comfort you. To *do* something . . . But you were so smashed, you didn't know or care who I was."

"Why didn't you say something sooner?"

"You didn't need someone to give you platitudes. You didn't want to talk. You needed me that night. And I wanted to give you whatever you needed."

He played with the wet strands of her hair clinging around her nape. "Your hair was long."

"I cut it after I left. My divorce was final. That's when I finally managed to elude Denny. I went to Alabama after that. Started fresh."

He brushed a kiss to the top of her head. "Thank you."

"For putting out? It was sex."

"No. It helped me cope with what I was going through. To be honest, I don't remember you, per se. Just a vague memory of silky skin and long hair. What I do remember was warmth, and compassion, and someone giving without the expectation of getting anything back."

She nipped him on his bicep. "Oh, it wasn't *that* altruistic." Her voice was filled with laughter. "Make no mistake. I got back *plenty*."

Zane lazily rolled her warm, pliant body under him and kissed his way from her ear to her mouth. "I feel so used."

"Feel free to pay . . . me back. Hmm . . . a little to the left—ah. Right there . . ."

Chapter 16

The ocean was warm despite the gray, colorless, early morning light. What Zane really wanted was natural sunlight instead of the powerful, yet artificial, aluminum dive lights they were using.

Fortunately, they had flat calm. Visibility would improve as the sun rose. Zane angled his light to see Teal. She gave him a thumbs-up. He gestured toward the blurred white shape of the plane below them.

Maybe if they used their powerful beams together the damn red box would glow or something. The way his luck was going, a shark probably ate it.

This was insane. Mission fucking-well impossible.

He had never felt the vastness of his underwater world as much as he did this morning. It seemed huge. Dangerous. Unfriendly. He resented feeling that way about a place he'd believed magical his whole life.

He nudged the insidious niggle of fear away, concentrating on being pissed off instead. He had everything to lose, not just the *Vrijheid,* but people he cared about—*Teal*—were all in danger unless a fucking miracle occurred and they found this Alphachip by six o'clock that night. He shone the light on his watch. Barely eighteen hours to find a box barely the size of a loaf of rye. The odds on this bet were stacked a mile high against him.

Zane felt sick as they approached the broken plane, its shattered windshield reflecting murky light back at them.

The thing was a fucking abomination, that's what it was. And there wasn't a damn thing he could do to fix the situation. Other than systematically search and pray like hell he found that tiny box in time.

Before the sun had even been a hint on the horizon he'd gathered everyone in his cabin and laid out how he wanted them to search. Slowly, systematically. He had Saul help with mapping out a grid. He'd keep track of the search pattern from his onboard computer. They'd each have their own section, then switch, double-checking each section off the grid. This was how they worked a wreck. The real estate was smaller, but the principle was the same. There was comfort knowing he'd walked this walk before. Still. Zane didn't want Teal with him down there—a lot.

He sucked up the fear and frustration and headed for his section of the cockpit. He'd already searched around the body of the plane, but decided to take a second look in case he'd missed something. Thank God the area around the downed plane was shadowy and still murky. He could barely see in this light that the cannon were once again buried, that his glory hole was gone as if it had never been. And he could avoid seeing the sheared off ribs of his *Vrijheid* buried, once again, beneath the sand and silt.

He drew a mental breath and reminded himself how dangerous it was to get pissed off a hundred feet underwater. Air got used up in the tanks fast when your breathing got beyond a slow, relaxed pace, which meant wasted trips back to the surface. Better to be calm. Deadly calm. And find that fucking box. Teal headed around the nose of the plane to start her search. She was a natural scavenger, searching each grain of sand. Each shell. The doors were both crushed, impossible to open without other tools. But as far as he could see, there was nothing of a personal nature inside the cockpit.

Ninety minutes later, they headed to the surface. Zane read the tension in the line of her back as she climbed the steel ladder into the boat.

"Anything?" Ryan asked before adjusting his mask.

"Not yet." Teal removed her tank. "Maybe we could use the crane and lift it a bit. See if there's anything underneath?"

"Maybe." Zane gritted his teeth. "This is shit. But be thorough." He clapped his hand on Ben's shoulder. "Even when you want to kick sand."

Ben's eyes narrowed as he tossed a glance over his shoulder toward the guards. "I wanna kick something all right, but it isn't sand," he muttered before he jumped into the water, closely followed by Ryan.

Teal didn't want to talk, but for once, neither did Zane. They sat side by side, staring at the water. The sun's bright greeting as it finally woke didn't take away the chill creeping over his bones. He combed his hair back with his fingers, wishing for the impossible.

Ryan and Ben climbed on board, silent as two mourners at a funeral. "Nothing except a crab," Ben told them.

Ryan pointed at the map weighted to the table with a conch shell. "Been there, been there. There. Maybe here?"

Teal's brown eyes grew dark with focus. "We're going to find this, guys. See you in ninety." She went to the edge of the platform and slipped over the side.

Zane jumped after her.

Frustrated and empty-handed, he and Teal returned to the surface ninety minutes later.

Ben and Ryan took their turn. Ninety minutes under, ninety up top.

Zane and Teal went down again.

As he drifted down through the golden shafts of morning sunlight, he opened his mind to the Universe. To God, or Poseidon, or goddamned Zeus. Hey, this mess sucked so bad, why the hell shouldn't he go for the boss of all the gods?

Help me find that box. Just show me where it is.

In response, he heard the blips and knocks of fish, and the Darth Vader sound of Teal's aerator as his ears adjusted to the depth. She was as focused and determined as he was. Undeterred by the enormity of the task. Zane was ridiculously proud of her, and grateful that she'd finally relented. Her agreeing to come on this salvage had literally changed his life.

What a woman. Knowing what she'd done for him after his dad's funeral humbled him. She'd wanted to comfort him and she had. More than she would ever be able to understand. Maybe more than *he* would ever be able to understand. He'd told himself that it was his father's death that had left him feeling so empty after the funeral. Now he could see that that had only been a part of the problem. The other part had been missing that generosity of spirit Teal had shown him. His only regret about the whole situation was that she'd ended up hurt by his lack of recall. Seriously dumbass behavior on his part.

Damn it, he needed time with her. Time without all this fucking tension and danger and distraction. One thing he knew for sure, no matter what the danger to herself, she wasn't going anywhere without him. As long as he was in danger, she'd be stuck like Crazy Glue to his side. And he had no choice in the matter. Zane seriously considered knocking her out when they got back on board. He'd knock her out and have Saul take her to St. Maarten and Maggie . . . Crap. He was losing his mind. He could no sooner hit her, than he could—*Holy shit, what's that?*

He swam closer to the side window and shone the powerful light into the mangled controls on the dash.

Red.

No way. He'd visually searched every square inch of this section.

Red. Small. Square. Shit! Yes, *way*! He tried to angle his body between the crumpled door frame and the seat. He was just too big, bigger with his gear on. The gap was maybe a foot wide. He braced a foot on the bottom edge of the cockpit and used both hands to try and pry the mangled door away from the frame.

The body gave an ominous screech and groan as if it were some beast waking up.

He rapped on his tank, but there was no need, Teal was already zooming over to him, supple as a fish, her eyes wide with fear at the sound. He gave her the okay sign, then shone his light through the shattered side window so she could see the interior. See that corner of red, barely visible behind shattered wood and glass, metal, and strips of leather seat swaying in the current like black seaweed.

She put one hand and flipper into the narrow opening, trying to wedge her knee into the gap. Impossible.

He tapped her on the shoulder. The aluminum frame had sharp, jagged edges that could slice through neoprene or one of her hoses, he didn't want her hurt. No use wasting time. This required the kind of underwater cutting tools *Decrepit* didn't carry.

Zane pointed up, his heart hammering like jungle drums. But at least they now knew where the box was and what they needed to retrieve it. *Yes!*

Sixteen hours to spare. Time to go to St. Maarten, find the tool needed, and be back. Turnaround time, a couple of hours. Three at the most. The relief he felt was staggering.

Almost euphoric, his magic cape firmly back in place, Zane headed up to report the good news to the others.

*   *   *

No one had been on the deck of the sleek luxury yacht earlier, but as he was helping Teal onto the dive platform he noticed several women at the railing. Just what he didn't need. Spectators. Not to mention female spectators, especially when his relationship with Teal was still fragile, and her trust in him shaky at best.

Zane shoved back his mask, then removed his weight belt. He recognized the *Slow Dance* as a rental out of St. Maarten. He'd attended several parties on her over the years. A hundred and forty feet of top-of-the-line luxury, no expenses spared for the people with big bucks who could afford to rent it.

Half a dozen skimpily clad woman leaned over the railing. "Ahoy there! What are you diving for?" an attractive Chinese woman yelled across the space between the two boats. Petite and curvy, she looked like a porcelain doll dressed in a tiny red bikini.

"Nothing yet," Zane smiled with effort as he helped Teal with her tanks. A leggy brunette, wearing just the bottom half of a white bikini, joined the China doll at the rail. "Hi." Her smile was as white as her barely there suit. "Can we watch?"

"Nothing too exciting happening, but sure. Be my guest."

"Cool. Are you all alone over there? Would you like some company?"

He sure as hell wasn't going to tell anyone how many people were on board the *Decrepit*. As innocuous as a boat full of scantily clad woman might be, he had no idea who'd rented that yacht. He might have guessed that Teal wouldn't take their treating her as if she was invisible lightly.

"He's not alone," she told the woman sweetly, sliding her arm around his waist. "*I'm* here, and so are our five *adorable* children. And our Doberman, Hans."

"Maybe later," he told the woman with a laugh, as Teal

preceded him up the ladder to the deck. The invitation in the taller woman's eyes was pretty clear, but it meant nothing compared to what was right in front of him. "We've gotta feed those kids and hungry dog," he said, indicating the upper deck. Smiley leaned back on his chair, holding a fishing pole and shot him a toothy grin.

The two women on the *Slow Dance* were joined by a petite blonde in a cobalt blue one-piece. "Nice," Teal muttered under her breath. "Red, white, and blue. *Very* patriotic."

He stroked her class A ass as she scrambled up ahead of him. "I prefer you in nothing at all."

"Keep that in mind." The second he stood next to her, Teal wrapped her arms around his neck and gave him a French kiss that curled Zane's toes. Wrapping her arms around his neck, she whispered. "Consider me your body-guard, Ace."

He felt an odd tug in his gut at the way she trusted him enough to stake her claim so publicly. "They're over there shaking in their thongs, as we speak," he assured her. With a chuckle, he kissed her nose, then laced his fingers through hers, as he whispered for her ears only. "Let's give everyone the good news."

The brunette leaned over the railing. "Y'all are invited to drinks later if you want. Do y'all have a babysitter?"

"Don't even think about it." Teal nuzzled his cheek, still walking.

"Zane." Saul came to the open doorway of the salon, Zane's cell phone in his hand. He held it out. "Logan."

Shit. A call tomorrow would've been a hell of a lot better. Everything would be over, the story could be exaggerated and built on. Hell, by then it would be the stuff of legends. But for right now, he was nose deep in the shit of it all.

"Wolf, I'm kinda tied up right now," Zane indicated that Smiley come inside and close the door behind him.

The women on the *Slow Dance* were lined up at the railing like magpies, watching them through the large windows of the salon. "Can this wait?" Every second he wasn't prying that box out of the plane was another second closer to the thing detonating.

By accident. By design. By miscalculation.

"No," Logan said shortly. "There's a guy here."

"Here isn't very specific, bro. What guy and where? Somewhere in South America?" Smiley, Davis, and the others weren't that interested in his personal conversation; they were standing around waiting for Zane to give them news. And as much as he loved his brother, Zane didn't want to talk to him right then. "How about if we catch up tonight?" he suggested, about to cut his brother off.

"Cutter Cay," his brother snarled, answering the question as to his location. "Dude is a fancy lawyer from New York. Has a client who *claims* he's our long lost fucking brother."

"What? Christ." His belly cramped. His dad hadn't been called Casanova of the Caribbean for keeping his dick in his pants. "I swear I'll call you later, Logan."

"Are you okay?" Teal frowned as Zane closed his phone, stuffing it into his swim trunks pocket. The call had distracted him when he didn't need any distractions. Now what?

"Later." He wiped a runnel of water from her wet hair off her cheek with his thumb, his blue, blue eyes troubled. Teal shivered at the contact, wanting to slide into his arms so she could feel . . . what? Safe? Loved? Needed? *Get a grip,* she told herself as she stepped away from him.

"We found the box," Zane told everyone as he turned away from her. The relief in the room at his news was as palpable as high pressure being released from a sealed decompression chamber. "Impossible to retrieve without proper equipment," he told them, his voice grim, his shoulders and jaw rigid with tension. "I'm going to St. Maarten to rent what we need."

"Get the Broco cutting system," Teal instructed briskly, shoving her hands in her pockets. "It's hot enough to cut through, or melt, just about anything. It uses a hundred and fifty amps, so it'll run off my generator. And I've used it before, so it'll take less practice time."

"Fine." Zane headed toward his cabin to change, then said over his shoulder, "Will you call around? Find it, then you can tell me where I'm going."

Teal started following him. "I'll go with you—"

"No, stay put. Nothing's going to happen with that party boat anchored out there. Too many witnesses. I can move faster alone."

His logic sucked. But he looked stressed enough without Teal giving him her opinion of his ridiculously alpha idea.

He didn't want her to go with him. Well, instead of pestering him with her own worries, she'd give him space to think. When he came back, he'd remember that they were a team and he needed her. She had time to make one phone call—no Broco cutting system—when Zane entered the room dressed in jeans, deck shoes, and a black T-shirt. He looked somber instead of elated. Teal chewed her now growing thumbnail as her own tension ratcheted up a notch. He hadn't remembered they were a team. She blinked away the threatening wetness at the back of her eyes. Since when did they need to be attached at the hip? If he had to do this alone, then she would support him. "Don't bother with Hampton Wholesale—they don't have the right tool. I'll keep calling and let you know as soon as I find one."

Zane exhaled, as if centering himself, before sending her a grateful smile. "Thanks, sweetheart." He patted his back jeans pocket where he kept his phone. "I'll be listening for you."

Teal blew her bangs out of her eyes and sent him a wink, all while controlling a belly of nerves.

"Don't let anyone on board for the duration," Zane addressed Smiley and Davis, who looked a little affronted that he felt the need to tell them how to do their jobs. "I don't care if it's a blue-haired little old lady. Especially not a blue-haired old lady. Got it? No one." He turned to stare at each of them. "No diving, no heroics. Stay inside. Don't trust *anyone*. I'll be back in a couple of hours."

Davis, who'd walked into the galley and had been talking on his cell phone while Zane had been changing, turned around. "A man named Joseph Young is waiting for you at Bobby's Marina. He's our immediate supervisor. He'll escort you to pick up this piece of equipment, then return here with you."

"I'm going to put in at Phil's," Zane said tightly. His hair was dripping on the collar of his shirt, and he hadn't even run a comb through it. For no reason at all, Teal's heart started to race.

"Too small and intimate," Davis informed him. "We don't want the wrong people following you. Stay in crowded locations and stick with Young. He's a hundred pounds overweight, but he's a professional. You'll recognize him; his face is perpetually red, and he has yellow hair. He's six two, he'll be wearing black pants, blue shirt, open over a white T-shirt." Teal presumed the open shirt observation wasn't a fashion statement. Young would be armed. Good. Knowing Zane would have an armed bodyguard made her feel marginally better about him going off on his own. "You have a gun, right?"

"Won't need it, but yeah." He gave her a quick, hard kiss on the mouth and strode out, closing the salon door firmly behind him. He waved at his fan club still hanging over the rail of the *Slow Dance,* then disappeared as he jumped down to the dive platform and his Sport.

She listened for the well-bred purr of the small engine

starting up. "I've got things to do," Teal told the men. She didn't know *what*, but she didn't want to be watched while she did it.

*   *   *

Young was waiting at the Marina as soon as Zane tied up. "Mr. Cutter," he said by way of greeting, extending a surprisingly small hand for such a corpulent man. His sweat-stained, baggy shirt covered a shoulder holster. Between his weight and the tropical heat, the guy was a heart attack waiting to happen. "I have your Broco torch in my car. Need help carrying the thing. Young lady named Teal found it, paid for it, and had them water seal it by the time I got to the shop."

Of course she had, Zane thought with relief. He'd never doubted her abilities. "I can help," he said, falling into step with the larger man. The guy's slow pace was counterpoint to how fast Zane's heart was racing. He wanted to get what he needed and head back to Teal. To the *Decrepit*. He could practically hear a metronome ticking away in his head.

"How far away are you?"

Young indicated several dozen cars parked in the shade at the tree line which separated the parking lot from a nearby hotel's grounds. "Quarter mile. Lot was full 'cause of the cruise ships."

Crap—papers, branches, the odd soda can—still littered the enormous parking lot; ironic when the sky was a crystalline blue and the sun hot. Smiley and Davis had told them the time restraints. But what if that time line was wrong? Or a lie? Zane shoved his shades up his nose. But why would they lie? Damn. Just because he couldn't think of a logical reason, didn't mean there wasn't one.

"How long have you known Davis and Smiley?" he asked as they walked through the crowded parking lot.

Hundreds of rental cars and dozens of tour buses were parked waiting for the passengers. Although the island was only thirty-seven square miles, it was a popular destination. Several cruise boats were in port and more would come throughout the day. The place was hopping and looked like the crowds at Disneyland.

Young huffed and wheezed but kept going. "Davis, thirty years, Smiley about nine. Good, solid guys. They'll watch your back or die trying."

"Let's hope they have no reason to," Zane said flatly, rubbing the back of his neck as they cut between the rows of look-alike rental cars. The conversation with Logan raised its ugly head, and he ruthlessly shoved it back. A *brother*? He supposed he should be shocked. Surprised. Hell, even *pissed off*, as Logan clearly was. Given their dad had been a womanizing tomcat. Instead, he couldn't imagine another Cutter brother—it had been the three of them forever.

Zane wasn't angry. Not pissed, either; curious, maybe. Intrigued. For sure. He shook his head, clearing his mind of an oddly numbered Cutter family reunion. He had a more immediate problem to deal with.

"What can you tell me about this Alphachip?" he addressed the back of Young's sweat-stained shirt.

Young glanced over his shoulder, his head down as he took rattling breaths. "Classified."

"Yeah," Zane said wryly. "I kinda thought that's what you'd sa—" The other man suddenly crumpled. Zane stumbled into him, and had to grab a nearby rearview mirror to stop them from both going down. He shot out his hand to grab Young's arm to help him up. But Young was too heavy to hold with one hand as he crashed to the ground.

The agent toppled over on his side before Zane could brace him. "Shit."

The guy's eyes were wide open in his sweaty face. He looked shocked.

Shitfuckdamn.

Young *looked* dead.

Heart attack? Even as he crouched down to feel for a pulse at the man's throat, Zane was digging his cell out of his back pocket to call emergency. He didn't feel a heartbeat. Hell. Poor bastard.

As he'd crouched beside him, Zane's knee shifted the man's blue cotton shirt aside. Young's white T-shirt was already saturated in horrifically bright red blood. The smell was metallic, like fresh meat. Gross. Shocking outside under the bright tropical sun. For a nanosecond, Zane's brain didn't compute what he was seeing.

Young had just been shot straight through the heart.

Chapter 17

Something slammed with a shockingly loud metallic *thud screech* into the passenger door of the Volvo behind him, mere inches from Zane's shoulder. Christ Almighty! Someone was shooting at him as well. Fuck this for a joke!

Zane yanked the Sig 220 from under his T-shirt as he looked around for the shooter. As he visually scanned his surroundings, he slid the gun from Young's still secured, underarm holster. He checked the clip, then stuck it under his T-shirt at the small of his back. He hated fucking guns. His father had taught all three of them to shoot. Plenty of long, boring afternoons out at sea. Always good to know how to defend one's treasure from pirates. Not that Zane had ever encountered actual pirates, but thank God, he knew he could actually hit something if necessary. Two loaded weapons gave him better odds.

He hoped it wouldn't become necessary. Being a lover rather than a fighter, he'd always preferred talking his way out of a bad situation. But even he couldn't talk faster than a bullet.

Using the nearest car as cover, he unfolded slowly from his crouch, scanning the surrounding area for the shooter.

He didn't *see* anyone suspicious looking, but he felt as though a giant bull's-eye was painted on his back. He reached up and slid an advertising flyer from under a nearby windshield wiper, tenting it over the Sig. It wasn't going to fool anyone who looked hard enough, but it was all he had.

Every instinct shouted *run.*

No.

Think.

Pause.

Focus.

Decide where the hell I'm going before I'm exposed.

He was in the middle of a car-filled parking lot. If he turned back to the marina, and his boat, he'd be a sitting duck as he untied from the wharf. Not to mention, if he somehow managed all of that alive, he'd lead them straight back to the *Decrepit* and Teal.

Forget it. How about a more public area? Good news, there'd be hundreds of tourists and the shooter might be deterred by that many witnesses. Bad news was the shooter might not give a flying fuck and would shoot into the crowd and possibly hit an innocent bystander. Damned if he did and damned if he didn't.

Straight ahead was a small, touristy shopping area. Duty-free jewelry, booze, and electronics, the street already crowded with people swarming off the cruise boats. If he angled right, he could go through the extensive grounds of the nearby resort. People would be at late breakfast, at the pool, or on the beach by now. Not as many people, and a lot of trees and outbuildings to afford him cover. Also near the crowded beach. Crap! The resort grounds were the best bet for everybody.

Run like hell.

What about the cutting tool? Shit. No idea which car or where. Zane took off toward the tree line on the other side of the narrow strip of beach. Anticipating the slam of a bullet in his back as his legs pumped and his heart beat hard and fast. Now beyond the dubious protection of parked cars, he was out in the open. He ran faster, head ducked down. A smaller target, or a bigger bull's-eye.

He cut across a wide expanse of emerald green lawn, still mushy from an earlier watering. He knew as soon as people started scattering in front of him that someone was hard on his heels. He heard the slam of soles against pavement and dug deeper for more speed. The paper flyer had dropped unnoticed, and the in-plain-sight Sig motivated people in his path to move the hell out of his way. Fast.

Zane veered to the right. There was a small inlet on the leeward side of the island where locals moored their boats at Phil's. The same marina they'd taken shelter in, what seemed a lifetime ago. The same place he'd originally planned to moor while he found the tool they needed—he was glad now that Young had insisted on a different marina. He'd swipe one of Phil's rental boats if he had to.

Run. Run. Run. Reach the *Decrepit*, Teal and the others, warn them that the bad guys were closing in. He wasn't going to be able to warn anyone if he was dead. He hauled ass, groping in his pocket with his free hand for his phone to call them to warn them, to call the cops . . .

Shit. His phone wasn't in his pocket. Dropped somewhere? He felt for Young's gun. Still there.

He zigged and zagged down paths hidden by shrubs, and courtyards being set up for later parties. He heard the running footsteps of his pursuers hot on his heels as they crossed the flagstone path. Several of them? Double shit.

He cut between the tennis courts, passed the tall trees shading one of the swimming pools. Sweat ran down his face and stung his eyes. His manic breathing came more from fear than running for his life. Soon he was going to run out of places to duck. Taking a chance, he dodged down an alleyway, then between two delivery trucks. At the crunch of running steps on the gravel close by, he hopped up and braced his toes in the wheel wells of the trucks, so they wouldn't see his feet as they passed.

Gravel crunched as his pursuers ran by. After several minutes Zane jumped down, then cautiously peered around the back of the truck. He couldn't see the men, but he wanted more time to put some distance between them. Glancing around, he spotted a fenced-in area hiding trash cans at the back of one of the condo buildings. He dashed across the short distance and ducked inside.

Had he managed to elude them? It seemed unlikely, but Zane stayed where he was, straining his ears for the sound of footsteps, breathing, or the chambering of a bullet. *Don't be like the dumb blond chick in the movie who goes into the dark basement to check*, he cautioned himself. *That's always where the psycho killer is lurking.*

He waited for two interminable minutes, scanning his surroundings. Parking area for deliveries. A few trees. A lot of open space between him and the marina. No choice. Zane braced himself and bolted from the protection of the fenced-in cans. The second he was clear, a shot rang out. The bullet passed so close that Zane heard it whiz by.

He squeezed off an answering shot. Then two more. Several people screamed, and half a dozen people scattered and kept on running. Fine by him. Even though getting shot at had been like waiting for the other shoe to drop for the duration, Zane was almost surprised that they'd shoot where anyone could see them.

His legs and arms pumped as he weaved between trees and shrubs and jumped flower beds. Another shot behind him made a muffled thud. *Silencer.* His pursuer was a hell of a lot closer.

Three hundred yards ahead was Sandy's restaurant and cocktail lounge. A few stragglers from the breakfast crowd were still lounging at the outdoor tables. The three-piece group played their steel drums, and all was right with the restaurant patrons' worlds right now. Beyond the shack was the shimmering, twinkling blue of the water. The beach was packed. He shoved the Sig beside Young's gun under his shirt and out of sight.

If he headed inland a bit, he'd bypass the clutter of beachgoers. Zane veered sharply left. He was even more exposed here, but he could also move faster.

A palm trunk a foot to the right exploded in a shower of splinters as a bullet chewed into it. Christ, that was close. His lungs burned as his legs pumped. He heard the whine of the next bullet, braced for it, but it too passed him and hit a decorative lamp post with a loud, sharp *piiing*.

The guys were close, damn close.

Screw being subtle carrying a weapon. He whipped it out again and turned to squeeze off three shots in quick succession. These guys had no fear of the cops showing up, and frankly, Zane would welcome their appearance any time soon. He might have a lot of explaining to do, but it sure as shit would save some time. Without an audience, they were closing in. What the hell did they want? Zane didn't have the Alphachip . . . But did the bad guys know that? Did they think he'd met with Young so he could pass it off? They must've searched the dead guy, found no chip, and presumed Zane still had it on him. Being the confrontational guy that he was, Zane was sorely tempted to stop and hold out his hands and tell them he didn't have the damned thing. Except they'd shoot first and ask questions second.

Zane heard voices before he saw the couple sauntering down the path to the beach. Shit.

He felt the sharp burn as the next bullet creased his arm and had to stagger to prevent falling flat on his face. It didn't hurt, but he instantly felt warm blood pour down his arm. No time to look. Clamping his hand over the wound, he kept running.

The couple coming down the path toward him were

Phil and his girlfriend. Zane thought fast. "Bad guy on my ass. Throw me your keys. I have to get out to the *Decrepit*!" He didn't shout, but Phil got it. Digging into his front pocket, he tossed Zane the keys to his boat without question.

As he passed, Zane slapped the Sig into Phil's hand. Phil had been a Ranger back in the day, and didn't hesitate in the handoff. He got it when Zane yelled, "Cover me! Stay down. Call cops—"

Zane was out of earshot and yanking Young's gun from his waistband as he heard Phil shooting behind him. *Good man.*

Phil's marina was just ahead. Too many damned people for so early in the morning. As he ran, Zane scanned the slips for his friend's yellow-and-white Sea Ray Sport. "Down! Stay down," he yelled. Seeing the boat, Zane jumped over a bunch of fish buckets, waving his arms like a lunatic as he raced down the wharf.

"Bad guys! Guns! Out of my way. Stay down." There wasn't anything else he could do. For now, the guys weren't shooting, but they could open fire any moment. A young guy and a kid, maybe ten years old, sat, legs dangling in the water near Phil's boat, they each held a fishing pole. When the young father looked up and saw Zane, the blood pouring down his arm, a gun drawn, and people scattering, he grabbed his kid and jumped into the water. Smart move.

Zane untied the boat at warp speed and started the engines. The little powerboat tore out of the marina, skimming over the water, bouncing on the waves as if they'd been cast in cement. Each jolt shot a wave of pain up his arm. A glance back showed the curious gathering on the dock. No sign of the gunmen.

Zane knew they wouldn't get their hands on any of the crafts in the cove. The bad guys were going to have to go back the way they'd come, giving Zane at least twenty minutes to reach the *Decrepit* and haul ass out of there.

Fuck the explosive device. People were more important. And if these assholes had chased him through crowds of witnesses, and were willing to shoot in public, they wanted that chip bad.

Fine. They were welcome to it.

He stood at the wheel, the cold spray reviving him, washing the sweat off his face. Adrenaline was starting to leak out of his system, and *now* his arm hurt like hell. Fortunately, it was only a superficial wound and despite the blood that had run down his arm, the bleeding had in fact stopped.

The little boat was going as fast as Zane could make her run. A quick glance behind showed no one had followed him. Yet. He saw the *Decrepit* up ahead with a profound sense of relief. Everything was quiet. Thank God.

Now that he had a moment to *think*, he considered his options. Screw them. He didn't want either of his boats to be blown to hell. He might have time to get *Decrepit* clear. But not his prize wreck. To do that, he'd have to find their damned chip. Without a cutting tool . . . Somehow.

He'd dive from the Sea Ray and insist that Ryan take Teal and the *Decrepit* into port. He could handle this shit better if he knew everyone—Teal—was safe and out of harm's way. He didn't give a flying fuck if she refused to go or not. She'd go. As long as she was somewhere where he didn't have to worry himself insane for her safety.

They'd done as he'd asked and stayed indoors. Teal would be down in the engine room. The *Slow Dancer* was still anchored nearby, music blaring across the water.

The speedboat slewed sideways, almost tipping him out as he did a wheelie, a rooster-tail spray of water shooting up behind him. The gunwale smashed into the side of *Decrepit*'s dive platform with a crunch of fiberglass, making Zane wince as he jumped onto the platform. He didn't bother tying her up; he owed Phil a new boat anyway. He leapt up the ladder and charged across the deck, heading for the salon. His mind raced a mile a minute. They could make faster time in one of the tied-up power-boats, but God—he really, really wanted to get *Decrepit* somewhere safe. He'd have to move fast. Get the hell out of here before those guys tailed him. Head north, Zane decided. Out to sea, away from any of the nearby islands.

"Teal!" He shoved open the door to the salon, then stopped dead in his tracks. A middle-aged man with steel gray hair, horn-rimmed glasses, white slacks, and a collared pink golf shirt, sat in Zane's favorite chair. He was flipping through *Decrepit*'s log book. Zane had a bad feeling. A *really* bad feeling. His day had just gone from bad to worse.

"Who the hell are you?" He reached behind him for Young's gun.

"Uh-uh-ah. I wouldn't do that if I were you, Mr. Cutter." The man spoke in a well-modulated voice with a faint European accent Zane couldn't place. As he lowered the log book, he revealed the large black gun in his left hand. "Place your weapon on the counter if you please."

"I *don't* plea—"

The man pulled the trigger, making a fucking enormous hole in the lovingly restored wood counter a foot from Zane's right knee. He placed the gun on a bar stool, raising his hands to show he was no longer armed.

Every drop of moisture in his body had evaporated as he realized that no one else appeared to be around. *Teal? Ben? Ryan?* Nausea rose to the back of his throat as he suddenly became aware of a god-awful smell. His thoughts raced around his brain like a barracuda chasing a shiny silver lure. There were other possibilities than the gruesome ones flashing through his mind like scenes from a slasher movie. *Teal . . . Please God . . .*

"I repeat, who the fuck are you? And where are my people?"

"My name is not important, Mr. Cutter. You have

something I want. Once you've retrieved it for me, I'll be on my way."

"I had people on board when I left," Zane snarled, not bothering to acknowledge the man's demands. "Where the fuck are they?"

"Behind the counter there. Check for yourself. But please hurry. We have business to conduct that is time sensitive."

Zane barely heard him as he raced down the length of the counter separating the galley from the main room. He rounded the breakfast bar and stopped in his tracks. The first thing he saw was Smiley with his head blown away. Zane gagged. Sprawled facedown beside him was Davis. Obviously dead as well. Zane shifted his attention to the group sprawled against the cabinets under the sink.

Ryan, Ben, and Saul were tied up with the heavy twine from one of the kitchen drawers. All three men looked battered and bloody, their hands and feet securely tied. They were slumped against each other. *Unconscious*, he prayed. Please don't let them be—

He crouched beside Ben, feeling for a pulse. They were all alive. Quickly, before the other man saw what he was doing, he dug his Swiss Army Knife out of his pocket, sliding it between Ryan's limp hands. Slowly, he rose to his feet. "Where's the woman?" The possibilities were too hideous to contemplate.

"Ah, the spitfire. She's enjoying my hospitality on board the *Slow Dance* while you and I have our little chat."

The relief Zane felt was overwhelming. Teal was alive. He glanced out the window at the gleaming white yacht across the water. The *Slow Dance*. Not a party fucking boat at all. "Did you touch her? Harm her in any way?"

"She's sipping a cold drink with all those lovely young ladies I hired straight off the beach. Pretty lures. Too bad your girlfriend was on board to distract you."

"You knew where the plane was all along."

"Indeed. There was supposed to be a handoff just after the storm hit. The flight was delayed. The plane crashed. Very inconvenient."

"Yeah. For me too." Did the guy know that the Alphachip had a freaking shelf life? "Now what?" He'd killed two men, three if you counted Young, and beat the crap out of Ryan, Ben, and Saul. What was to say Teal wasn't lying hurt, or worse, on the yacht? Shit, what a clusterfuck.

"Come and sit down. *Now,* Mr. Cutter."

Zane walked out of the galley, leaving his friends there, tied up and possibly badly hurt, with nothing to defend themselves but a fucking three-inch army knife.

The man rose, oddly elegant. There wasn't a speck of blood on him. Which made Zane think he hadn't done the dirty work himself. So there was at least one other person on board with a meaty fist and a big gun. "Do you have my chip?"

"What do you think the chances are of *that* happening? Finding something the size of a microchip in the Caribbean Ocean, *especially* after that storm? Try slim to none."

"Not for an experienced salvager like you, Cutter. Besides. You *do* know exactly where the container is."

Zane heard someone at his back a second too late. The man behind him wrapped his arm around Zane's throat and squeezed. He felt the hard barrel of a gun being pressed into his kidneys. Black specks danced wildly in his vision. "Wrong."

Pink shirt motioned to the guy squeezing Zane's air pipe. Zane found himself facedown on the floor, a knee pressed hard against his back, a gun to his head.

"You have two choices, Mr. Cutter." All Zane saw from his prone position was the man's white deck shoes. "Either hand it to me now if you've already retrieved it, or go down and get it."

"Or what?" Zane's lungs were severely constricted as the man holding him down applied more pressure.

"Or your uncooperative behavior will be the death of your friends. *And* your pretty girlfriend."

"You're aware that *your* friends on St. Maarten have been apprehended by the police by now?" Zane felt a curious calm come over him and spoke quietly and succinctly. "The authorities are aware of the location of the crash. Aware of what's on board. Aware that it was stolen and prepared to do whatever necessary to ensure *you* don't get it. Not to mention you killed three Federal Agents."

He heard a creak as if the guy had bad knees, then got a closer look at the white hem of his pants. Another gun was pressed to Zane's temple. Hard enough to bruise. The man said tightly, "Then I suggest you retrieve the Alphachip as quickly as possible so that everyone stays alive. Get him up."

Zane was hauled unceremoniously to his feet. The man behind him clamped his fingers over the wound on Zane's upper arm. He almost passed out from the sharp pain. Hot blood seeped between the guy's fingers to run in rivulets down Zane's forearm. A flurry of black snow danced in front of his eyes.

"How the hell am I supposed to do that when you've knocked the crap out of my team? I don't have anyone to help me."

"Four of my men will dive with you. You have thirty minutes to locate the chip and bring it to me, or you will secure the Cessna in the crane's harness, and we will search for it here, on your deck."

"That's not enough time or enough people. And I wouldn't give you great odds of the wreckage staying intact long enough to haul it to the surface."

"Then you have only two choices, Mr. Cutter. Find my Alphachip where it lies, or make sure the Cessna remains viable so we can bring it on deck and search for the chip here. If the chip is not found—by you—in the next two hours, I will dedicate the remaining time it takes you to locate it to inflicting unspeakable pain on your lady friend. It behooves you to hurry."

He glanced at Zane's bloody arm with obvious distaste. "Can't have the sharks coming after you because of all that blood. Slap a Band-Aid on that, Mr. Cutter, then suit up."

*   *   *

"Would you all please shut up so I can hear myself *think*!" Teal demanded of the whining, whimpering bikini babes. Six of them had been locked in a fancy stateroom with her. They had bitched and complained and told her this wasn't worth any hundred bucks, for the last freaking *hour.*

She rubbed her bruised jaw as she paced, impatiently waving aside anyone who accidently moved into her path. She'd been taken by surprise on the *Decrepit*. Heard the sound of what she later realized was a couple of gunshots. She'd raced out of the engine room to find out what the hell was happening when she'd slammed into some strange man. He'd slugged her before she could get away.

She'd come to with six high-pitched female voices weeping and wailing and slapping wet washcloths in her face. As if being punched in the freaking face wasn't enough to give her a headache.

The stateroom was fairly large; two queen-sized beds, a private head. A porthole facing the wrong damned way and four out of six women who didn't have half a brain between them. Teal figured she could jimmy the lock. She searched the head first. Bottles of expensive shampoo and conditioner, assorted bottles of bubble bath, a half empty tampon box in the drawer, a melted down candle, a book of matches with two matches in it, and a small bag of M&Ms.

She took the candy and gave it to one of the girls to share. They fell on it as if they hadn't eaten in a month. Teal shook her head and went back to pacing around like a tiger, opening and closing drawers, shooing her idiotic roommates out of her way as she went. There wasn't a nail file in sight.

"I don't suppose any of you have a credit card on you?"

Several of them said no, but a woman with champagne-colored hair and enhanced . . . *everything*, gave Teal a puzzled look. "I don't think there's a gift shop on board."

Teal gave her a sour look. She bet when the girl was born her parents were sure she was going to be the first female president of the United States. Good thing she was pretty. Teal kept searching. And while she looked for something to use on the door, she tried to figure out what to do with the six women.

She was going to steal the *Slow Dance*'s tender and hotfoot it into St. Maarten to warn Zane. She sighed. She supposed she'd have to somehow load them all on board, without anyone seeing or hearing them. This was going to be like herding freaking cats.

"Would this work?" the brunette in the patriotic bikini asked. There wasn't a hint of breathiness in her voice now. She handed Teal a glossy, laminated diving brochure. Teal took it absently as she strained to identify the sound of a powerful engine approaching. *Fast.* Zane. Damn it, she had to warn him!

The only view she had through the porthole was open water.

That was *not* the sound of Zane's 205 Sport. Teal didn't know whether to be relieved or more freaking worried than she was already.

She used the brochure to jimmy the lock. It took just

under a minute. Not that anyone was timing her, but it *was* her personal best. "Janelle and Maria, right?"

Teal motioned for the two women who had brains in addition to their killer bodies and wide-eyed flirtatious looks. They nodded. "Are either of you familiar with driving a powerboat?" There was no point running through the *Slow Dance* like chickens with their heads cut off. She needed a plan.

"I can," the brunette, Maria, said calmly.

"Me too," the other woman said.

"Okay." Teal spoke quietly so her voice didn't carry across the room to the others. "We have to get all of you to the back of the boat and down onto the dive platform. *Without* anyone seeing you."

"They have guns," Janelle, a voluptuous blonde in a miniscule green bikini, told her nervously.

Of course they did. "Know how many men there are?" Teal asked, chewing her pinkie nail down to the quick.

"There were nine or ten when they invited us on board at St. Maarten," Maria offered. "But then Mr. Werner took five guys on the smaller boat over to your boat a couple of hours ago."

Yeah. She knew about that. One of them had a fist like a sledgehammer, and her jaw was still aching.

"Let's pretend that not everyone on board have shown their faces," Teal said, practically. "Let's go with at least a dozen armed men lounging around waiting for some action. How do we distract them and get them looking somewhere we're not?"

Teal was talking, but her brain was already sorting through and discarding various scenarios.

"They've seen practically all of us already," Janelle said dryly. "So flashing them wouldn't get any kind of rise out of them whatsoever." She smiled, before sobering. "What we need is a big . . . *something.*"

"Yeah," Maria chimed in, "Something they'd all

respond to that would get them to the front of the boat while we get into the motorboat and get away, but what?"

"A big explosion," Teal said, practically rubbing her hands together. It was her favorite idea.

"Weeeell, yes," Janelle said dubiously. "But I haven't a clue how to make something explode, do you?"

Oh, yeah. "Let me put it this way," Teal told her, grinning. "I'd kill for a little ammonium-nitrate and a can of gasoline. But since fertilizer isn't going to be lying around on a boat, alcohol will work in a pinch. Ladies, we're going to make a couple of Molotov cocktails. Where can I find the booze?"

This was something they knew. "Two doors down on the right," Maria told her. "Mr. Werner's stateroom. I saw a tray of liquor in there when I passed earlier."

"Janelle, there are three giant bottles of bubble bath in the head. Empty them until there's only about a third left in the bottom. Maria, grab the box of tampons and the matches. When that's all set, start drawing anything you can remember about this boat. I'm thinking stairs, companionways, cabins . . . any escape routes or hiding places between here and the back of the boat. *Everyone* contribute to that drawing. Our lives are going to depend on it."

"Be really careful," Maria whispered.

"Sure. Be right back." Teal opened the door a crack and looked right, left, and right again. Then she stepped into the empty companionway and darted two doors down to the owner's stateroom as the door clicked softly behind her.

*   *   *

Zane's hopes that the four muscle-bound men diving with him didn't know how to dive were dashed as soon as he saw them with their own equipment. Sabotaging their tanks was out of the question; he couldn't get close enough without one of the guards pushing him back.

He held his mask in place and jumped into the water feet first, his four watchdogs hot on his heels. He looked at his dive watch. Five minutes after three. On his own timetable, he had three hours before all hell broke loose. On Smiley's—five.

Sunlight streamed through the clear water. A decent dive day despite visibility only being about thirty feet, but it would have been a pleasure to work over the *Vrijheid*. Zane turned off the fear, the yearning, and the anger. *Focus.*

Somehow, he had to get rid of these guys. Get rid of them long enough to swim to the *Slow Dance* and find Teal. *Slow Dance* had a small motorboat tied in back. The other boat's faster speedboat was tied to the *Decrepit*.

His goal was to find Teal, send her to St. Maarten to safety, and have her send help. Zane knew he couldn't leave Ryan, Ben, and Saul unprotected, neither was he going to abandon his boat. Or his wreck.

The plan was simple, the execution problematic.

One against four was sucky odds at best. He figured he had about thirty minutes to come up with a game plan. If they didn't surface with the chip by then, Pink Shirt expected him to secure the Cessna to the rigging of the crane. That gave them at least ninety minutes of air before the man on the *Decrepit* would expect to see them again.

These men didn't know that he knew exactly where that damned Alphachip was. Nor did they know that the only way to reach it was with the use of an underwater cutting tool.

So that meant hauling the highly explosive plane onto his boat, which he had no intention of doing for several reasons. One, he wasn't going to aid and abet them in blowing his boat to hell, and two, once they had the plane, they wouldn't need him or his crew or his boat.

He'd be dead before the Cessna hit the deck. He led the men to the plane and swam backward, extending his arms wide in a gesture that encompassed the whole ocean. *Have at it, assholes.*

Chapter 18

Teal quietly closed and locked the door behind her. This stateroom was larger than the one they'd stuck all the women in. It smelled strongly of Kenzo, the same expensive men's cologne Denny used to favor. The smell of cardamom and grapefruit still made her eyes water or maybe it was just the freaking memory of Denny. Whatever it was, the familiar scent made her even more jumpy.

She ran over to the large porthole and got a view of the *Decrepit*. A yellow-and-white Sea Ray was tied up. She'd barely been able to hear the engine of the speedboat approaching over the whine of the women and had hoped it was the cavalry coming to the rescue. Had Maggie and Colson decided to come back? But no, she saw that this was a newer model. Not Maggie, thank God. Maggie and Colson were safely on St. Maarten. Waiting for news.

There was no sign of Zane's red Sport. Shouldn't he be back by now with the cutting tool? She glanced at the bedside clock. He should've returned a good half hour ago, if not before. Worry ate at her. She wanted him back so she'd know where he was. She wanted him to stay the hell away because all the bad stuff was on the *Decrepit*, lying in wait for him.

Had something terrible happened while he was on the island? He'd met with another government type. All those guys were trained professionals with fully loaded guns. She pressed her fingers to her pounding temples. No. She had to believe that Zane was okay and on his way back with the Broco.

"Don't buy trouble," she whispered, taking another searching look at the *Decrepit* for any signs of life. There were none. The women had told her that Werner and his men had taken the launch over to the *Decrepit*. What had they done to the guys? *Her* guys? Ryan, Ben, and Saul?

Someone had knocked her out and brought her over to the *Slow Dance*. Did that mean her guys had been brought here as well? Really. This freaking kidnapping crap was getting old.

Staring out a window wasn't going to get everyone to safety. Reluctantly, Teal turned away.

She saw the tray of booze, but took a few moments to search the head for anything useful. Same bottles of shampoo and bubble bath. Another couple of romantic candles, and a fresh book of matches. She stuck the matches in her front pocket and emptied most of the liquid out of the large glass bottles, tucking them under her arms.

Back in the stateroom, she ran her gaze over the selection of alcohol. Most of the bottles were unopened. *Thank you very much*.

She checked labels, looking for the highest amount of alcohol. *Ethanol* as far as she was concerned. There were several large bottles of something called Austrian Stroh 80. She whistled when she read the alcohol by volume number on the label of the rum bottles. Eighty percent. That was one hundred and sixty proof. Her heartbeat went into overdrive. *Perfect!*

After a thorough but fast look around, she found a

plastic garbage bag lining the trash container by the desk. "Very thoughtful of you to provide shopping bags to your thieves, Mr. Werner, sir." Teal grinned as she loaded her booty very carefully into the bag.

Arranging washcloths between the bottles so that they didn't clink, she opened the door, slipped down the companionway, and used her elbow to open the door to the other stateroom.

"Lock that," she told Maria, who quickly complied.

Teal unloaded her supplies, lining the big bottles up beside the three the others had retrieved and prepared while she was gone. The small amount of palm oil in the bubble bath would do nicely to thicken the alcohol so it stuck to whatever it was thrown on.

With four pale-faced women watching, Teal and her two accomplices, Maria and Janelle, filled the six two-liter bottles with the Stroh rum and added a few bottles of cognac with high proof alcohol to top them off. "Shake these," she told whoever was closest. "Get me a glass, please." She sent one of the quiet women scurrying into the head, as she took each well-shaken bottle and started stuffing a tampon into the top, leaving the string hanging out.

When the woman returned, Teal filled the glass with the Stroh rum she'd saved.

"Oh, my God," Janelle whispered as Teal carefully poured the rum onto each tampon to saturate it. The white fiber swelled, sealing in the contents of the bottles. "That's incredibly clever. But is it going to *work*?"

"We're about to find out. Let me look at that drawing you ladies made of the boat."

*   *   *

With the sheet of *Slow Dance*'s stationery in hand, Teal ordered Maria to bring up the rear and Janelle to be in the middle. The other four women were already terrorized by everything that had happened. This escape plan was a tricky proposition, and she'd warned them that it might not work. The men had locked them up to keep them out of the way and in the dark. They were not going to take kindly to having the women escape and run back to St. Maarten and the authorities.

She'd gone over the plan several times, made a couple of them repeat the instructions. Warned them that once on the launch they had to stay lying flat on the floor, keep their mouths shut, and let Janelle drive. As fast as she could. She told Janelle to put on as many flotation devices as she could get around her body.

It was the only protection she could suggest. They both knew that if any of the men spotted their departure, he'd shoot first and ask questions later.

They got it.

She hoped.

The first thing Teal had to do was get six bikini-clad, extremely spooked women up two decks, *unseen*. From there, it was up to Maria and Janelle to wait until exactly the right moment to herd them aft to where the motor launch was tied up.

Teal told them they'd better run for their lives when the time was right.

It wasn't a lie.

*   *   *

Zane had intentionally not suggested lights. They had none. And although visibility was thirty to forty feet, without the lights to illuminate the deeply shadowed crevices and crannies, they weren't likely to spot the box, hidden as it was beneath crumpled dash equipment. And even if they did manage to see it, they didn't have any tools other than their dive knives to try and get at it. Been there, tried that. He could've saved them time trying to pry the jammed doors free. Even with their brute strength that wasn't going to work. He let them go for it, though.

He swam around, pretending to help them search for the box, but since he knew where it was, he was just doing busywork. Mostly checking on the condition of his wreck, but they didn't need to know that. He pointed out a couple of possible locations, separating the men as they searched. He also made sure he churned up silt, clouding the water to make visibility difficult.

Looking up, he saw the dark shadows of the hulls of *Decrepit* and the *Slow Dance* almost directly above them. His boat was closest. The smaller shadow of Phil's Sea Ray and the other dinghies were tethered to *Decrepit*. The *Slow Dance* had one small shadow aft.

Teal, where the hell are you? He'd rip the *Slow Dance* apart from stem to stern to find her. Zane refused to believe that she wasn't alive and well—and pissed off as hell right about now. He kept the image of Teal, furious but competent, in his head.

He rapped on his tank to indicate he'd found more of the plane a few hundred feet from the fuselage. A dozen, two-foot-long yellow grubs, their gray bodies pinstriped in yellow, shot out from under a small outcropping of coral inches in front of him.

Two men swam over, while the other two tried to pry the doors off the Cessna. They were far enough away to only be seen through the opaque veil of sand and sediment that they were churning up as they put their weight into pulling at the doors. They were exerting themselves dangerously as air bubbles frothed over their heads unnoticed.

They had ten minutes before the lift on the crane was lowered. Ten, fifteen minutes to attach all the cables . . . Once the plane was secured, he'd be redundant.

He swam parallel to the bottom, saw a straight, not from nature, line in the sand. Another about twelve feet away. The two cannon, lost, then found, then lost again, now lay just under the sediment kicked up by the storm. He eyeballed the length and distances, while a single, tiny, brilliant-hued blue chromis darted past, its color only slightly muted at this depth.

The crane on deck made a peculiar groaning cry when it was activated and Zane heard it now. *Hell.* Pink Shirt had activated the mechanism early. Zane heard that almost human moan under the water and knew his time was up. Worse, Teal's time had just taken a drastic spiral turn.

He waited for the men to swim closer, then pointed to the pieces of white aluminum, and chunks of metal scattered across the sand with the combined strength of the storm, and the force of the Cessna's crash landing.

They dived down to get a closer look. Both men wore weapons strapped to their biceps. A gun worked just fine underwater. There were four men to one. Zane's only advantage was he was familiar with what was on the seabed. He had to make use of the element of surprise. He couldn't second-guess himself. It was them or him who had to die. He chose them.

He reminded himself that he'd only have one chance at this. He went in low, swimming fast, grabbed the first guy around the throat, yanked his gun from his holster, then pulled off his mask and knocked out his regulator in a shockingly quick move that stunned the guy before he knew what hit him.

The man tumbled backward, arms and legs flailing, churning up silt in a smoky cloud around him. His leg lashed out, and the gun sailed out of Zane's grip to land in the soft sand.

Zane flipped over, went in again, this time with his diving knife in hand. He made a grab for the other man's hose, but the guy rolled out of Zane's way, presenting his back. Zane grabbed him by the tank strap to hold him. The man struggled like a maniac, bubbles rising like steam over his head. Zane put his entire body weight and strength into stabbing his dive knife into the guy's aluminum tank. It barely made a dent, and the man turned on him faster than a snake. Zane lashed out, grabbed the guy's hose, and severed it, releasing his oxygen into the sediment-filled water. The guy's eyes went wide before he ditched the tank with the quick release latch on the front of his BC. The whole tank, hoses and BC, fell to the ocean floor as he shot upward. He jettisoned his weight belt, too, to get up faster.

The guy flexed his body as his air disappeared. Survival instinct was a powerful motivation for the guy to get to the surface fast, and even then, he was going to have to deal with his too-rapid ascent to the surface. He'd be out of commission for a while.

The heavy chains from the crane hit the water with a small *boom*, then started snaking almost musically through the water with muted chinks and rattles. Small schools of fish scattered in flashes of silver and blue.

The second man turned at the noise and the sight of the churned up sediment. He came for Zane as fast and powerfully as a shark. Zane dove and grabbed the dropped gun. His knee struck the cannon, and he fanned a quick hole for himself behind its length. Shallow, but better than nothing.

A bullet whined its way through the water, passing his left shoulder, close enough for Zane to feel its passage through the water. He saw the guy's pale face, his murderous expression through his mask a second before he aimed his gun. But Zane was quicker. He fired. Once. Twice. The man did a slow-mo cartwheel, bubbles and blood combining in a reddish mist over his body as he slowly rose through his death.

The other two men, alerted by the obvious sounds of gunshots, were already on their way toward him.

Zane fired. Fuckshitcrap. *Missed*.

A bullet came spiraling through the water directly for

him, fine bubbles delineated its rapid trajectory. Zane flattened himself in the sand behind the ten-foot-long saker. Inches of ancient bronze saved his ass and made his ears ring as the bullet hit the cannon instead of his body. Zane fired blindly. They fired back. The bullets went wild over his head.

He squeezed the trigger again. Thought he hit the goon on the left, by the rapid exhalation of bubbles, but the man kept coming, a dangerous black shadow, moving fast.

They had only minutes of air left.

Zane raised his head over the barrel of the saker and fired another shot. It went wild as an enormous explosion above made the water ripple and bend in a surreal amber-colored glow.

Overhead, the bow of the *Slow Dance* erupted into flames.

* * *

Teal's arms shook and burned from lugging twelve liters of liquid explosive all over the *Slow Dance*. While *skulking*. That was almost five pounds per bottle, and she'd carried six of them for a good twenty minutes.

The women's map had been pretty good. She'd found the head on deck two when she'd heard voices, and stayed in there for several minutes as two men passed in the companionway, just feet away. Thankfully, neither of the men had needed to make a pit stop. She ducked out of sight at even the smallest sound, terrified she'd be caught at any second.

The loud retort of a gunshot traveled across the water, and she froze, then reminded herself there was no time to dillydally. The girls were waiting to get the hell off this boat. Waiting for *her*.

Still, that sound spooked her. She was a freakin' mechanic, making use of tampons and liquor to save those girls, making things up as she went along, not some high-tech super spy who actually had a clue what in the hell she was doing. Sweat beaded on her forehead, and her heart beat even faster than before. Sweet Jesus, she wished Zane was here. But he wasn't. She ducked into a small library to look out a window, praying that Zane hadn't been the target. She saw several men working around the *Decrepit*'s crane. Obviously they were going to try and bring the Cessna up on deck to facilitate their search.

Did they know they only had—she glanced at the fancy boat's brass clock on the wall—less than two hours, if that, before that Alphachip exploded?

Not seeing Zane or his Sport overwhelmed Teal with a deep sense of relief. For all she knew, Zane was on his way back with the authorities. They'd show up with guns blazing and arrest all these sorry-ass bad guys. Until then, she would do her part.

Lugging the plastic bag of homemade explosives, she climbed the sweeping stairs to the upper observation lounge. She blinked against the bright glare, noting the nautical theme and cluttered furniture she'd have to navigate as if she were a ghost. The air conditioner gave her overheated skin goose bumps. No bad guys.

Her breath came out in a shaky sigh. So far, so good. Large, angled windows overlooked the calm, deep blue ocean and the bow of the boat. Teal kept to the highly-polished teak walls, bypassing the groupings of sofas and chairs.

Standing to one side of the large bank of windows, she saw, with satisfaction, that directly outside the windows was a cantilevered rooftop. Gleaming white, shiny, which meant slippery, but right over the prow. She couldn't get further away from the back of the boat where the women were gathered, waiting for her signal.

She had a nice view of the *Decrepit*'s praying mantis yellow crane as its arm swung over the water, and someone lowered the lifting mechanism. The chains dropped into the water in a frothy white splash. *Good luck with that.*

She'd inspected the crane thoroughly, along with every other mechanical inch of the *Decrepit,* when she'd first come on board. It was serviceable, but not reliable. It needed work. But that wasn't her problem at the moment.

One-handed, she carefully shoved the heavy window casing aside. Hot, salty air blew against her sweat-dampened skin. The open window also allowed her to overhear men's voices from below and out of sight. They were apparently watching the progress of the crane as the chains sank beneath the water.

Teal tried to separate how many voices she heard, but quickly realized it was impossible. The good news was the bunch of muscle-bound guys was gathered on the prow watching the *Decrepit.* All together. In one space. And neatly confined to the front wedge of the *Slow Dance* like cornered rats. The bad news? If any of them glanced up, they'd see her slithering on her belly along the level above them.

Very carefully, clutching the plastic bag and bottles in one arm, she crawled out of the window, onto the roof of what was probably the salon below. It wasn't meant to be walked on, and the shiny white paintwork was slick and slightly sloped. As the men talked, their voices covered the crinkling of the plastic bag and the chink of glass on glass as she moved cautiously into position, flat on her stomach.

Carefully withdrawing her Molotov cocktails, she lined them up under the window she'd just come through.

Maria and Janelle were to wait for the second explosion before they crossed the open back deck, then they had to run like hell for the dive platform and the launch. They'd be waiting back there now, scared and eager to go.

She lifted her hip and, two-fingered, withdrew a book of matches. Lighting the tampon in the first bottle, Teal kept her head down, and lobbed it over the edge of the roof. One. Two—It shattered on the narrow deck walkway below with a gratifying *boom*! She felt the heat of the flames and the rush of air from the explosion, but didn't waste time looking as she belly-crawled to the other side and lit and dropped the next one as black smoke billowed among the leaping flames. *Boom!* Pause . . . *Whoosh!*

The men went ballistic, and she heard the clicks and snaps of guns as they yelled at one another to "Go there, go over there. Get—"

Suppressing a cough as the smoke tickled her throat, she lit the fuse of the third, let it roll down the slope of the roof toward them. *Boom!* Pause . . . *Whoosh!* Several men jumped overboard to avoid the ensuing explosion. There was nowhere to run because both narrow decks leading to the front of the boat were engulfed in super cool looking, ten-foot-high flames.

With relief, Teal heard the faint sound of the launch's engine's starting up. *Go. Go. Go.* She lit another match, held it to the fuse. The match blew out. She struck another. Shit. The wind got that one too. Four matches later, she managed to touch it to the tampon fuse. This time, it flared, then caught the alcohol-saturated cotton. She let that bottle roll off to one side of the roof, lit another, and sent that one down the opposite side. The sound of the rolling glass was lost in all the other noise of shooting flames, men yelling, and a couple of sharp retorts of gunfire. Nobody was going to hear her stomping around up there.

The entire front wedge of the *Slow Dance*'s bow was engulfed in leaping flames. And leaping *men* as more of them went into the water, screaming like little girls.

Teal grinned as she crawled backward, staying low.

Not that any of them had time to look up; they probably thought the bombs had come from across the water. Taking the last cocktail with her, she climbed back inside the window, then paused to admire her handiwork before she used some muscle to throw the last bottle far and wide.

She dusted off her hands, pleased with her work. Smiling, she turned around and slammed smack into the man standing directly behind her.

Uh-oh.

"You appear to have a death wish, young lady."

The flames shooting up behind her reflected in the mirrored surface of the man's black-rimmed glasses. Salt-and-pepper hair, pink shirt. Big scowl. Throbbing forehead vein. Angry as hell. Which meant his tight control, as he jammed his fists into the front pockets of his pristine white dress slacks, was scarier.

She was already beyond scared. Being this close to evil brought her right back to her childhood and the various "uncles" her mother had entertained. She angled her chin, as if she didn't have a care in the world. "Wanna back up, big guy?" She narrowed her eyes. "I don't like being hit by some goon or imprisoned against my will," Teal told the man she presumed was Werner.

He was too in control and too well dressed to not be the boss. He wasn't alone. Two burly guys flanked him. Teal kept her attention on him, knowing he was the most dangerous of the three. She tried to see his eyes. Tried to gauge what was coming next. But all she could see were leaping orange flames and black smoke reflected in the lenses covering his expression. She coughed as some of the smoke blew in through the open window behind her.

Please, let the girls have escaped.

"My men said you were a spitfire." He reached out his finger to caress her cheek and it was all Teal could do not to cringe. "You, my dear, are my bargaining chip," he said with a faint German accent. "Unfortunately, you will have to accept my hospitality for a little longer while we wait for Mr. Cutter to return my property."

The three men had her backed against the bank of windows with the most excellent view of the incinerated prow. She got some satisfaction watching the flames dance in the man's lenses.

"You picked the wrong bargaining chip. He doesn't give a rat's ass about me," she said flatly. "Where is he?"

"Who? Your Mr. Cutter?"

"Not mine, but yeah. Where is he?" Teal couldn't even feel her heart, it was beating so fast. Or hell, maybe it had stopped.

"He's attaching the lift to bring the Cessna up on deck."

So Zane had come back. Alone? "Then what?"

"Then he must retrieve the chip from the wreckage and give it to me."

"And then you'll kill him."

His lips curved with unpleasant satisfaction. "And before we do *that, Schatzie,* we have promised your lover that we will do everything in our power to encourage his speed and compliance. With you."

Okay. There was her heart. Throbbing loud enough to hear it as dizziness made her skin heat, then freeze. She didn't want to know how or what. The threat was sufficient to terrify her.

She struggled to find moisture to lubricate her tongue. She was damned if she'd go down whimpering. "The girls are gone. They're coming back with the cops."

"Too bad. But you did save us time. We were going to have to dispose of them anyway. Did you help them escape?" When Teal nodded, he showed large, too white teeth, and absolutely no humor behind that toothy smile. "What an enterprising young woman you are. We'll have to find a more secure location for the rest of your visit. Which, if your lover doesn't hurry, will be woefully short." He snapped his fingers at the man on his right, then turned to leave.

The man grabbed her upper arm in a fist the size of a Thanksgiving turkey. "Wait! Oh, please," Teal put every ounce of her seventh-grade drama skills into her voice as the older man glanced back. "Please, please don't put me anywhere there are big engines. The noise . . ." She let her voice break and tried to look girly and very frightened and completely unthreatening. The first two she was. "*Machines* of *any* kind. I'm claustrophobic and the vibrations and the smell make me deathly sick. I'll—" She managed a full body shudder. "*Anywhere* else, okay? I promise I won't even *try* to get away again. A guest cabin . . . ?"

"Shut her up."

Shit. She'd overplayed her hand.

The man gripping her arm pulled back his fist. Teal glared at him as her spit dried up again, and her heart went manic. She struggled to get out of the way, her neck arching painfully. "Don't you *da*—"

Everything went black.

*   *   *

Pink Shirt was going to expect the plane to start surfacing within ten, fifteen minutes, tops.

The two men split up, flanking Zane's position and coming at him fast, darting through the water like fucking barracudas. Zane squeezed off a shot. A dead click. Out of bullets. Shit. He dropped the gun, tightening his fingers around his dive knife. Inside his suit, he was bathed in a cold sweat, and his heartbeat was hard and fast. He warned himself to control his breathing and stay focused.

This wasn't a fight. This was combat. They were experienced, he wasn't. Which meant he had to stay cool, and calm, and two steps ahead of them at all times.

A blur of black, a white face behind the mask, filled with cold intent. Zane threw himself backward as the first guy hit his shoulder with a powerful fist. Bubbles shot through the water from their regulators. A moray eel shot out of hiding, teeth bared, but quickly became a shadow of movement as it darted away. All Zane saw was an arching blur of steel catch the light where his heart had been a moment before.

He rolled and twisted out of reach, then came back into the guy. There was no doubt the other man wanted blood. His expression was set, his eyes, behind his mask, telegraphed death. He was also shocked that he hadn't done what he planned with the attack.

Him or me. Him or me. Zane chanted in his head, as he tightened his grip on his knife. These men weren't just tough guys. They were battle ready, professional killers. They'd been *ordered* to get the Alphachip and kill *him.*

They had orders. Zane had Teal. It was as simple and complicated as that. The second man came in fast, hovering somewhere near Zane's left shoulder. Zane used his flippers to angle out of reach as fast as possible, but they came at him in perfect unison, knives flashing. Zane pushed the inflation button on his buoyancy vest, causing him to rapidly shoot upward, out of reach, with seconds to spare.

Their surprise didn't last long; with arms and feet churning, they came after him. Zane dived down. Fast. He'd spotted something that might come in useful on the sand. But he had to get there in one piece to grab it.

Anything he could use to his advantage, against their experience and training, was a plus.

As the first man came at him, his knife held like a fist, Zane picked up the gold bar and rammed it into the man's mask, putting his body behind the blow. The mask cracked and slid off the man's shocked face. His mouthpiece floated free and bubbles shot upward in a rapid silver stream.

Zane grabbed him from behind, his elbow around the guy's throat. He used his struggling body as a shield as the second guy came in for the kill.

The man was swimming in fast, coming at Zane from above. *Wait for it. Wait for it.* Zane shot out his arm, the gold bar clutched tightly in his fist. He hit the guy in the balls with all his might. He rolled up like a centipede. Screaming into his air bubbles as he gripped his dick with both hands, and rolled around and around, suspended in agony.

Zane released the guy he was holding onto and let him float up slowly. He swam to his doubled-over friend and cut his regulator hose, releasing a frantic ribbon of bubbles as the man's eyes went wide and terrified with the knowledge. He hung in the water, then slowly started rising.

Zane glanced at his dive watch, angling it to catch more light. Heartbeat fast, but fairly steady, he knew he was now well beyond the thirty-minute mark.

And while there was fuck-all Pink Shirt could do to him down here, there was Teal stuck on board the *Slow Dance* to consider.

Zane put on speed and swam to the Cessna. The chains from the crane hung down like a delicate cage around the broken fuselage. Time. It ticked in his brain as though a fucking clock was right by his ear. *Go. Go. Go!*

He grabbed the lead chain and started dragging it away from the plane. It was hard going, sweat filmed his skin, the wet suit itched, his slashed arm burned, his right hand, the one he'd used to strike the men, throbbed. A glance up showed four divers still suspended in the water. They hadn't reached the surface. Yet.

Zane didn't want to think about whether they were alive or not. He pulled and tugged that fucking chain, using one arm to hold it over his shoulder as he swam, dragged it through water that felt as thick and viscous as honey. *Hurry-hurry-hurry.*

When he reached the first cannon, he swam the chain around it several times, fixing the lifts to the heavy, ten-foot length of solid bronze. Then took a length and swam the twelve feet to the other saker, wrapping and securing the chain around that one as well.

It would take a while to raise the weight. They'd take their time, mindful that the Cessna could break apart further, and drop back to the ocean floor in smaller pieces. The cannon would delay them, but not for long. Let them suck on that.

Zane started swimming toward the *Slow Dance*. And Teal.

Chapter 19

Holding her hot face where the second guy had punched her, Teal shifted her jaw to see if he'd broken it. Nothing appeared busted, but it ached like hell. The bastard. She was lying on a cold vinyl floor. The familiar, comforting throb of a generator soothed her frazzled, indignant nerves. The lights were very bright overhead. She closed her eyes again and waited for the dizziness and nausea to abate before she sat up.

The double pain in her jaw was nothing compared to her elation when she realized where they'd put her.

Ah, man. "This is what I'm talking about!" The *Slow Dance*'s engine room. She took a moment to have severe engine envy. The 3516s were stark white, and someone had splurged on the chrome package for the luxury pleasure craft's beautiful engines. The place gleamed like a gangster's dental work.

Teal coveted those engines for the *Decrepit* like a druggie craved crack. She would've given anything to spend a couple of hours there. Instead, she got up and looked around for tools. She had no idea how much time she had, but she wasn't going to waste a second. Even to stroke and

ondle a sweet pair of 3516s. The *Slow Dance* might have
pristine and beautiful engines, but whoever worked in the
ER was a slob. His tools were stuffed along with dirty rags
n a nearby tool drawer. "Tsk tsk. *Shame* on you. You're a
disgrace to our profession."

A curled sandwich, still wrapped in plastic, and two
cookies sat on top of the desk beside an unplugged laptop.
Woo hoo. Someone's untouched lunch. Her stomach grumbled loudly. Unwrapping the slightly wilted cheese sandwich, Teal took a bite as she looked over the slob's tools.

"Thank you, engine gods." Helping herself to a ratchet,
a socket set, and two screwdrivers, she went to locate the
ECMs, the engine's brains. *Bingo.* The Engine Control
Modules, little black boxes about ten inches by eight inches
high, and just a couple of inches thick, were held in place
by 2-20 pin connectors and four easily removed bolts.

Done and done. Without the ECMs, the engines
couldn't start.

She took another bite of sandwich. The bilges were
next. Just pull the drain plug and the oil pan would drain.
Done. A slight twinge of guilt hit her in the gut. She hated
ruining such beautiful engines. Sacrilege. But when it
came to helping Zane, no sacrifice was too big. She yanked
the plug to drain the coolant as well, while she was at it. A
messy business, as everything was now puddling onto the
once pristine white floor.

"My bad." Teal grinned, moving out of the way as
various liquids started spreading across the floor. She felt
sorry for whoever had rented the *Slow Dance* out. But
they shouldn't rent their pretty boat to bad guys.

She used a handy-dandy slim-jim from the tool drawer
to pop the door lock.

Now to go and see what trouble Zane was about to
walk into.

Teal figured the prow would still be in flames, black
smoke billowing. Unless the bad guys planned to go down

with the ship, most of them would be busy trying to pu
out her handiwork. That still left Werner, who she already
knew got other people to do his dirty work. He'd probably
stay safely on deck sucking on a fat Cuban stogie as the
men loaded the plane onto the *Decrepit.*

Bottom line, the guys were all accounted for, and she
was home free, since they assumed she was still out for
the count and locked in the engine room until they needed
to pull off her wings to freak out Zane.

Quickly, but cautiously, she paused at every companionway intersection, making sure the coast was clear before
she raced across. She heard a strange noise and froze,
pressing her back against the bulkhead. Quiet. She took
another step, same noise. It took her a few still-life moments to realize her shoes, covered with assorted engine
goop, were squishing. Her poor manic heart didn't care
that it was shoes giving her palpitations. *Sheesh.* She took
off her sneakers, carrying them until she found a utility
closet, then tossed them inside. Barefoot, she started to run
flat out, heading for the back of the boat. She found the
stairs leading to the kitchen, and from there, she was able
to take the companionways and bypass the public rooms.

There'd be no launch from the aft deck to get her off
the *Slow Dance,* but maybe there'd be dive gear or, hell,
the distance between the boats was only about quarter of
a mile. She could swim that. No problem.

Wrong, she thought as she ran down the hall. Big
problem—she'd be seen as soon as she started swimming
between the two boats. The guys who'd jumped into the
water must be out now, but they would all be facing the
Decrepit to watch the goings-on. And even though
she could hold her breath for quite a while, she couldn't
hold it that long.

The *Slow Dance,* as a rental, probably came stocked
with diving gear. That gear would be right where it was

supposed to be. On the dive platform. *Superb*. She could stop picturing her head exploding like a freaking watermelon from a gunshot to the back of the head as she swam the distance.

Yes! The last set of stairs were right where Janelle and the others had drawn them. Give or take a deck, and a couple of companionways. Teal took the steps three at a time, her bare feet soundless. A glance at a nearby clock told her that the explosion had passed Zane's get-out-earlier-than-later deadline of six P.M. She hoped Smiley's original time of eight was correct. It was already six fifty.

They were rapidly running out of wiggle room.

The tick-tock-tick-tock countdown in her head was as precise as an engine timer, but louder and not nearly as satisfying. She was slightly out of breath as she reached the top of the stairs and saw the door leading out onto the back deck. Sweet. Through the glass door she could see a happy little block of clear blue sky and a few wispy clouds. Beyond that door was the dive platform. Fifteen feet. Tops.

She sucked in a deep breath. Okay. This was it.

Hand on the door handle, she cautiously peered through the window to make sure the coast was clear. It was. Nary a soul in sight. Nor was there a launch—she hadn't expected one—or any dive equipment on the platform. Well, crap. She was going to have to swim.

Easing the heavy door open, inch by inch, she squeezed through the opening, sucking in a deep breath as she did so. She was going to have to get in the water, *fast*. Go under quickly, and *stay* under until she absolutely, positively had to come up to breathe.

One.

Two.

Thr—

A hard hand clamped across her face, surprising the

hell out of her. She kicked back, wiggling and squirming
in the man's hold, digging her short nails into the arm he
had clamped across her body. His chest was a brick wall,
his arms as tight as clamps. Teal put some muscle into her
struggles and bit down on the hand across her mouth.

"Ouch! Shh," he hissed against her cheek. "It's me."

Zane. Teal went limp with relief.

He was alive. *Here*.

He pulled her to the side of the door and under the over-
hang so they couldn't be seen. She turned around and flung
her arms around his neck, burying her face against his
throat. His strong arms came around her hard, and he almost squeezed the life out of her, his hold was so tight. "I've
got you, sweetheart. I've got you. Thank God," he whispered hoarsely. Random kisses landed wherever he could
reach without letting her go.

"Shit," he muttered against the frantic pulse at her
temple as he pulled away a little. "We've gotta go. *Now*."

"Excellent idea," Teal said dryly, lifting her hand to
touch his face. He was alive, in one piece. He was wearing his wetsuit, and tanks, and his mask was pushed up
into his dripping wet hair. There was a gash in the sleeve
of his suit.

"What—" Suddenly his fingers clasped painfully on
her shoulders. Intense blue eyes searched her face. His
lips thinned. Alarmed, Teal grabbed his arm. "Oh, hell.
Now what?"

Zane felt an overwhelming and completely foreign
emotion surge through him as he looked at Teal's bruised
face. Sheer, unadulterated fury. Fear for her. Love—
God—*love* for her knocked his breath out and left him
shaken with the deluge of unfamiliar emotions coursing
through his body. He lifted his hand and gently touched
her bruised, slightly swollen jaw. "Who hit you?" he demanded, his voice cold, his gaze hot.

"Don't freak me out like that!" Teal sagged with obvious relief. "Werner. Don't worry about it—"

Rage boiled inside him. He wanted go find the son of a bitch and rip him limb from limb. "Sadist asshole."

Teal's slender, infinitely capable, hands held him in place. "Who's on our boat?" she asked, ever the pragmatist.

Our boat. *Yeah*. He brought her sweet, bruised face back into focus and drowned in the chocolaty depth of her eyes. Zane was shocked to realize how much he'd come to depend on her to center him. He'd thought himself completely self-sufficient, but Teal had taught him that there was more than just scratching the surface of life. He tended to be a little frenetic. Teal steadied him and gave him a place to rest. Jesus, what an insane time to have this kind of revelation. "Ryan. Ben. Saul. Pink Shirt and at least one other guy."

"Pink Shirt is Werner. He's *here*. At least one of his men must be with him. Let's say two left over there, so we aren't surprised. We can take them," she said with so much confidence Zane had to grin. She reached up and pressed a quick kiss to his mouth. "Okay. What's the plan?"

"Get back to our boat and deal with whoever's there."

She saw there was only one tank and came to the right conclusion immediately. "Buddy breathing?"

"No choice. Ready?"

She nodded. They'd be sharing the regulator after every breath, but right now, as badly as he knew they needed to get the hell off of this boat, he wanted to plant his mouth on hers, exchanging every breath with her, as part of him, not just sharing his damn regulator.

"Let's get this party started then. Hold on to my equipment straps and do not, under *any* circumstances, let go. Oh, one more thing?" She turned to give him a frowning look of impatience.

Zane smiled. "I love you, Williams." Not giving her time to answer, he hustled Teal to the edge of the dive platform, hand on her ass, and dropped into the water with her wrapped in his arms.

They went down ten feet. Deep enough, he hoped to escape immediate detection. Problem was, the water was as clear as glass, so anyone *looking* would see them and the bubbles. Teal was hanging on to his buoyancy compensator vest. He angled his body to swim over her, so that they presented only one target, and he got whatever was coming first. Other than hauling ass as far and fast as he could, that was the best he could do to protect her.

They shared his regulator as if they'd practiced the technique a hundred times. Damn. She was amazing.

The sound of an engine churning up water made them swim faster. A projectile hit the water about three feet to their right with a low *thwump* on impact. Another arrowed through the water in a spiral of tiny white bubbles that Zane felt against his cheek. He motioned for Teal to dive.

She arched her back and went down immediately, Zane right with her. She wasn't letting go of him. As soon as they got to twenty-five feet, she spit out the regulator. He took a few breaths, then handed it back.

A man suddenly dropped into the water in front of them. He'd appeared out of nowhere, and Zane automatically drew Teal hard against his body, positioning her behind him. The man pointed upward.

One guy . . . Zane thought about it, but the man was joined by another, then a third who dropped into view out of nowhere. It was fucking raining bad guys.

A black shadow suddenly appeared overhead from behind them, and the muffled roar of a small engine vibrated in his ears through the water.

Shitcrapdamn!

From this close, he and Teal were literally like fish in a

barrel as far as shooting went. He motioned for her to rise to the surface. She shook her head. Zane clamped his hand over hers on his vest and hauled her up with him.

". . . area," a man bellowed into a bullhorn. There were two men dressed in wet suits on a sleek black powerboat, which rode low in the water. Zane didn't recognize the make or model.

One of the men leaned over the gunwale. "Cutter?" he shouted over the *whop whop whop* sound of helicopters flying low overhead.

"Yeah."

"Targets acquired!" the guy yelled to someone else, then reached out and yanked Teal on board with one arm in a swift, impressive show of strength. He reached out to hand Zane on board behind her. "Stay low, we haven't apprehended all of them yet."

Saved by the cavalry. Or out of the frying pan and into the fire? Shit if he knew. Zane flattened himself over Teal as the fast boat did a wild turn, sending up a wave of spray as it headed toward the *Decrepit.*

"Evacuate the area!" The slight echo of the amplified voice joined the cacophony of sound. "Evacuate the area immediately!"

The beating of a helicopter's blades, the shouts over the bullhorns, plus the intermittent sound of gunshots, kept Zane's body pressed to Teal's back. Only when he felt the bump, signaling their arrival at the *Decrepit's* platform, did he lift his head and leverage himself off of her.

The helicopter hovered directly overhead and several men were rappelling down to the deck. "Your boat's secure, Mr. Cutter." The man indicated he and Teal were to board and to keep low. "Get her out of the area. *Now.*"

Zane pulled off his flippers and, with Teal's help, armed his way out of the vest holding his tanks. "What about—"

"We dropped the chain from the crane and your crew's inside. Go."

He went. With his arm around Teal's waist, Zane hauled her along with him. They passed the salon, and she stopped so abruptly he almost stepped on her feet. "Go," she yelled. "I'll be right there."

He didn't have time to argue. "Come through my cabin," he shouted, then ran toward the wheelhouse. Someone had already started the engines, he felt the vibrations beneath his feet. Despite all the men boarding the *Slow Dance,* shots were still being fired, and he kept his profile low as he moved.

He arrived inside the wheelhouse as the *Decrepit* started moving. Ben, Ryan, and Saul were there waiting for him. "Everyone okay?" he demanded, giving each man a quick once-over.

"We're all good," Ben assured him. "That chip is about to blow everything within a five-mile radius to hell and gone."

A tall guy in a strange-looking black wet suit rose from the pilot seat. "Cutter? Michael Wright. You're aware of the self-destruct mechanism programmed into the Alphachip?" They didn't shake hands, but Wright stepped aside for Zane to take his seat at the controls. Zane sat down, automatically setting dials. "How much time do we have?"

"Twelve minutes." Wright touched a finger to an earpiece. "Why isn't that boat moving?" he demanded into a lip mic. He paused to listen, then gave Zane an inquiring glance. "That so? By—?"

Teal slipped into the crowded wheelhouse. "Are you talking about the *Slow Dance*?" she asked Wright.

"Hold—Yes, ma'am. You know something about the engines being disabled?"

Zane laughed without turning. "I'm sure she does."

"That boat won't be moving anytime soon," Teal told the man, a smile coloring her words. "I took out the engines. For good."

"Engines permanently out of commission. Get everyone off," Wright instructed through his mic. "ASAP." He paused to listen. "Seven minutes. What's the problem?" His lips twitched as he disconnected. "Can this boat go any faster?"

Zane glanced at him. Didn't the guy think he had the *Decrepit* going as fast as he could without busting apart? "She's at full capac—"

"No," Teal told him, edging closer. "We can go a *lot* faster. Excuse me. Sorry Ryan." She wedged herself beside Zane and started flipping switches that hadn't been there yesterday. He shook his head with admiration as the *Decrepit* leapt into high gear and skimmed across the water, leaving the *Slow Dance* in her wake.

Teal perched on the arm of his chair, resting her hip against his arm. Her clothing was still wet, but he felt the heat of her skin through the cool material. "Did you think I was in my engine room all that time eating bon-bons and reading *Playgirl*?"

"Ah . . . Ma'am?" Wright said quietly. "Can I take that from you?"

Zane glanced at Wright to see what was putting the dry amusement in his voice. Although the man wasn't smiling, there was a distinct twinkle in his eye.

Zane glanced to his right as Teal. The large handgun looked obscene in her slender hand.

"Shit." He smiled, despite the tension permeating the wheelhouse. "Where the hell did *that* come from?"

Teal hefted the large handgun in one slender hand. "One of the Men in Black stuck it in the cutlery drawer. I'm going to shoot back." Her voice was filled to the brim with enthusiasm. "The bastards!"

"I don't think you'll be needing it now." Wright held out his hand.

"Ahh, man! I was hoping I'd have a chance to shoot at something."

Wright accepted the weapon with a small smile. "Not today."

Ryan, Saul, and Ben laughed. Zane just shook his head. "Have you ever used a gun?" he asked, his concentration on getting his boat as far away from the impending explosion as possible. *Seven minutes? Shit!*

Teal put her hand on the back of his neck, in a show of solidarity he suspected was unconscious. "No, but I figured this was a perfect opportunity to learn."

The *Decrepit* flew over the water, causing her to bounce in her own chop, the thump, thump, bone-jarring in its rhythm. "Whatever you did to the engines was damn-well brilliant!" Zane told her with admiration. Just the thought of her handling a loaded weapon in the confined space made him shudder. "Jesus, I've never seen her move like this."

"She still needs the new engines," Teal said proprietarily.

"Anything you want." The throbbing whop-whop of the helicopters directly above made talking further impossible.

Even though Zane had been anticipating the explosion, the loud percussion caused his body to tense as he braced for whatever would come next. The boat rocked violently, and he made a grab for Teal, wrapping an arm around her waist. Everyone staggered, holding on to whatever they could reach as the boat bounced and gimbaled on the shocks of surging waves.

"Everyone okay?" Zane shouted, but he doubted they heard him as they held on for their lives. Teal's cold fingers tightened on his nape as they heaved and bucked. It took all Zane's concentration to steady his boat and continue to haul ass. It was like riding a bucking bronco. Part of him was fucking scared that the *Decrepit* couldn't take the torque, that her old body would snap in two.

The other half of him was stoked by the adrenaline rush and the sheer excitement of the challenge. The Alphachip was betting, in no uncertain terms, that he wouldn't make it.

Game on.

Chapter 20

Since the epicenter of the explosion was a hundred miles offshore, there was nothing much to show for Zane losing four years' worth of work, other than a debris field from the *Slow Dance* and wave surges. Considering the excitement and drama of the past few hours, their return trip to St. Maarten was proving unexceptional. Under the blue bowl of the cloudless sky, the *Decrepit* cruised at normal speed. All Zane's people were shaken but unharmed. His boat, which had been crawling with special ops guys, was now quiet. Several helicopters had swooped overhead, and men had disappeared as suddenly as they'd appeared, leaving only Michael Wright behind.

Still sitting on the arm of his chair, Teal remained glued to Zane's side for the entire trip. He liked having her butt pressed against his arm. Loved that she wanted to give him whatever support she could, and all without a lot of platitudes and chitchat. Every now and then, her fingers would tighten on his nape, or she'd run her hand over his hair. He wondered if she was even aware of how much he craved the physical contact with her right then.

Almost high on the adrenaline still surging through his body, Zane could smell Teal's skin and her heat. Lust and the residue of excitement from the last few hours was a powerful aphrodisiac. He wanted to throw her over his shoulder, carry her down to his cabin, and sink into her softness. He made do by brushing a kiss to her upper arm, which was in line with his lips. Her hand tightened on his neck, her strong fingers kneading the taut tendons there.

The surges from the explosion were flattening, the closer they got to land. Zane had no idea how they were going to explain the news of the explosion that must've been passed along over marine radios from boaters who were close enough to hear it. He'd leave those explanations to Wright and his people.

Wright entered the wheelhouse, wearing a pair of Zane's jeans and a ratty gray T-shirt. Without being told, Zane realized that Wright would blend in with the crowds waiting for them at the marina. There'd be no sign of the black-garbed special ops guys or Werner and his men at all. It was going to be business as usual. Who were these guys? Zane would bet what was left of the *Decrepit* that they didn't come from the same group as Davis and Smiley. Maybe vaguely from the same side of the law, but Wright's team had a decidedly more intense focus and worked together like a well-oiled machine. "What happened to the *Slow Dance*?" Zane asked Wright.

"In pieces and sunk somewhere near your wreck, I suspect," Wright answered easily. "We apprehended Werner and his people. Got them evaced before she blew. Nice job on the fire and disabling those engines," he smiled at Teal. "If you ever want a job, give me a call."

"I don't think so," she told him.

Zane coughed back a laugh and rested his arm across her thighs in a subtle show of possession Wright couldn't miss. A quirk of the other man's lips told Zane he hadn't.

320   Cherry Adair

"I think my wife, Tally, would enjoy you, Teal. She has a thing for explosions, too."

Teal smiled. "Good to know you have someone watching your back. I thought you secret hero types didn't get married."

"Guys like me never think so either," his tone was wry. "Then *wham*! In walks the right woman at the wrong time and we're goners."

God, wasn't that the truth!

"Are we ever going to be told what that Alphachip was all about?" Zane asked as Phil's marina came into view, and he saw the crowds waiting on the wharf.

"No," Wright replied without elaboration. "But I'm sure someone will be appreciative that you attempted to retrieve it."

"It blew Zane's treasure ship to hell," Teal told him indignantly. "A ship that took him four freaking *years* to find! What can compensate him for *that*?"

Wright looked over Teal's head to meet Zane's eyes. "I suspect he found something of even greater value. We always like to see the good guys win a few." He stepped up and held out his hand to Zane. "It's been interesting, Cutter." He shook Zane's hand, then Teal's.

"Where are you going?" Teal asked, puzzled. "Don't you have to do—*something* when we get in?"

Wright slung a small, black bag over his shoulder. "The authorities will meet you as soon as you dock. My job here is done." He shook hands with the other three men, then went down on deck.

He'd already informed Zane and his team that they would be taken for "debriefing" as soon as they were ashore, and not to discuss the "incident" with anyone else.

"Cool guy," Ryan said, watching Wright disappear into the salon.

"Special ops," Saul told them. "I read an article about

them a while back. Think he'll want to grab a beer and tell us some war stories?"

"He didn't leave a number or any contact info, so I'm guessing no," Teal said practically. "So much for the job offer," she added with a laugh. "Oh, my God! Look at all those people waiting for us. I want to go with that other guy."

"You're with me, Teal," Zane said with a kiss that had Ryan and Ben whistling. "From now until forever, there'll be no other guys." Teal snagged him by the shirt to hold him there. She gave him a flinty look as she warned, "Or *women*, Ace." The small marina was crowded with the press and curious onlookers, all being held back by a police cordon.

"We have nothing to hide," Zane reminded them as he brought the *Decrepit* alongside the dock where several men waited to assist with tying his boat. "Wright said to answer what we can noncommittally and not talk to anyone but the authorities about what actually happened out there." He took Teal's hand and got to his feet. "Let's get this over with, people."

*   *   *

Teal and the others had been picked up the moment they'd stepped foot on the dock at St. Maarten, and immediately taken by unmarked vehicles to a local hotel. There they'd been separated for questioning. It was all very cloak and dagger, but anticlimactic after the day's events. After an hour of telling her story, and with no sign of Zane, she'd been flown by helicopter, alone, back to Cutter Cay. The pilot hadn't said more than a handful of words to her the entire flight.

Teal was okay with that. She'd had more than enough interaction in the last few weeks to last a freaking lifetime.

By the time she was dropped off, it was late afternoon. There were no cars on Cutter Cay, but a golf cart was parked at the small landing strip for convenience. With the sun hot on her head, Teal opted to walk, and trudged down the hill, almost dizzy with fatigue and adrenaline overload even now, hours later. Unlike Zane, who'd been juiced and energized by the time *Decrepit* had put into port, she felt as though she'd been through a war. She probably looked like she'd been in one, too. Not that she cared.

Should she stay and wait for Zane? Or just cut her losses and leave before there were any embarrassing good-byes? Because there was no doubt in her mind that there *would* be good-byes in her very near future.

Her footsteps lagged as she passed the marina and the Counting House. Curious to see the *Decrepit*'s treasure laid out in all its glory and collected in one place, she was tempted to go inside and say hi to Brian and his team. She'd love to see more of the cleaned and identified artifacts. But instead of stopping, Teal picked up her pace.

Seeing Zane's dream spread out, without him there to enjoy it with her, wouldn't be the same. His exuberance, his sheer joy at each discovery—no matter how small or insignificant—had made the entire experience . . . magical.

Even though he'd retrieved a considerable fortune in treasure, the rest of it was now scattered all over hell and gone on the ocean floor by the explosion. It would be hard, if not impossible to recover it now. "But not for Ace Cutter." Teal smiled as she headed up the dirt road to her cabin. She knew he'd go back as soon as possible to *try*.

Zane of the magic cape would pull it off, too.

But she wouldn't be there to share his excitement. When she found somewhere she wanted to put down roots, she'd let Logan know. He could mail her a check for her share.

Her future was more uncertain now than it had been when she'd gotten the job offer from Logan. The phone call from Sam asking her to come "fill in for a while." She didn't want to start missing Zane before she absolutely *had* to and put some speed in her steps. He'd said he loved her in the heat of the moment. But of course she wasn't stupid enough to believe it.

He hadn't invited her forever, and she wasn't going to be the one to overstay her welcome. Despite Logan's generous offer of employment, she was going to enjoy what little time she had left with Zane, then . . . who knew?

That pain of being brokenhearted was delayed for the moment as Zane made arrangements to take the *Decrepit* to the dry dock in Ft. Lauderdale, later in the week. At this point, as a ship's mechanic without a ship, she was redundant.

No, she decided, she wouldn't think of it that way. She'd contributed to Zane's treasure hunting, and she'd helped save the *Decrepit* from getting blown up at the same time as the *Slow Dance*. If she could have saved the treasure, she would've, but it had been out of her hands. Her future wasn't bleak, she realized. Not only was she going to get her share of the treasure already secured in the Counting House, there was an entire world out there just waiting to be discovered. She'd go and discover something.

The thought, instead of cheering her, was somehow incredibly depressing.

She walked faster, her breath catching with this different kind of exercise. Not wanting to think further than the upcoming confrontation, Teal broke into a jog, the sun hot on her head. The air smelled of green things, but it was the salty tang of the sea that made her eyes mist.

"Get over yourself!" she told herself firmly, her steps slowing the closer she got to Sam's bungalow. This was something she should've done years ago. Just because she didn't want to do it, didn't mean it had been okay to let it go. Heart manic, she banged on the door. Too quickly, it was opened by Cookie. "Teal." She smiled a wide, genuine smile. She was a plump, motherly woman in her late sixties, with Marilyn Monroe blond hair. Deeply tanned, she favored bright colored muumuus—today's was purple with orange parrots—and flip-flops. "Come in, honey. Sam just woke up from his nap. He's having a real good day! He'll be happy to see you. We were sitting out back. Want cold tea or a Coke?"

"Nei—"

"I know you like Coke. I'll bring it out, go see your father."

Teal was directed past the kitchen and went through the living room, which was crowded with white wicker furniture, a tropical garden of cushions, and knickknacks *everywhere*. Cookie's touch. Sam favored minimalist furnishings and no tchotchkes. Teal pushed open the screened door at the back of the small house. She didn't look out over the spectacular, panoramic view of the bay. Her eyes focused on the man in the chair.

God, he looked small. He was fading away, and Teal's heart wrenched painfully, seeing him like this. He was a shadow of the robust man he'd once been. His blond crew cut was shorter and much grayer, and he'd aged about fifteen years with his illness.

He sat on a lounger in the shade of a giant-sized, red canvas umbrella; his expression, one of a man deep in thought. "Hi." Her voice stuck in her dry throat, but Sam turned his head. His face changed dramatically when he saw her.

"You're back. How was the d—"

"What can I do to make you like me?" Teal blurted out as she stepped onto the grassy patio. Shit! She should have rehearsed something. *Anything.* Asked him how he felt. Said anything. Told him how glad she was he'd changed his mind about getting treatment. But now that she'd slammed open the door, she couldn't stop. She sank down beside him on the wrought iron lounger when he didn't say anything. "Would you like me if I dyed my hair blond again? Or wore girlie clothes? Makeup? Please. Tell me what I can do." Oh, God. She was *crying*. She swiped her palm across her eyes.

Sam looked even more drawn than he had when she'd first come outside. "Do? I don't want you to *do* anything."

"You must! *Please*. I'll be anyone you want. I can't bear not having some kind of relationship when you're going to be gone. Sorry, not diplomatic. But we have no more time to make this right. Meet me halfway. Please." Once Sam died, she'd be alone. She'd be, she thought with just a glimmer of her usual self-deprecating humor, an *orphan*. Her heart felt as if it was breaking. And this was just part one of a two-parter as far as good-byes and heartbreak went. The knot in her chest reached critical mass.

Sam took her hand, startling her. They'd rarely touched, and then by accident. His hand was frail and papery, but he held on tightly. Her chest hurt and she saw him through a blur of tears she refused to let fall.

"Teal, you're talking crazy. I wasn't taken by the blond hair, I didn't much like your citified clothes. I liked you with brown hair and grease under your fingernails. That's my girl. But I don't care how you fix yourself up, or not."

Her heart slowed and she breathed in small hiccups. Of course, it wouldn't have been anything so superficial. "Do I have some sort of character flaw you can't stand? Tell me what I can do to make you love me!"

"Baby, I loved you the second your mother phoned and told me you existed! Why'd you think I begged her to let you come live with me for all those years?"

"What? No—You wanted me to *live* here on Cutter Cay with you?"

"Spent a brick-load of money trying to make it happen." Sam's eyes, so much like her own, snapped with anger. "She didn't tell you."

Teal shook her head. "She said you were doing your duty. Child support, the money for school—"

"A drop in the bucket to what I offered to pay her to give me sole custody. She wouldn't hear it."

"She would have spent a lump sum in a weekend," Teal said bitterly. Sam had been her mother's cash cow for all those years. "Why didn't you ever say anything when I came?"

"Said she'd turn you against me if I breathed a word. Sometimes thought she already had. I saw how much you did for her. Made me madder than hell, but you were determined and devoted. How could I break that bond? To offer you what? A life on a seven-square-mile island? No kids your own age? I would've had to send you away to school anyway . . ." He trailed off, his fingers tightening around hers.

"I never knew." Her past, so filled with anger toward this man for not loving her enough to save her, didn't matter as much anymore. Her mother's story was over. As Zane said, this was a new chapter.

"Being around you was frequently like tiptoeing through a minefield as it was. We're too much alike, baby. And that's no lie. Keep it all deep inside where no one knows how bad we're hurting. But make no mistake, Teal. I've *always* loved you." He tugged at her hand until she leaned closer, then wrapped his arms around her, drawing her head onto his chest. Teal folded like a creampuff as her father's arms tightened around her. She buried her face against his chest and held on as tightly as she dared, then cried until she was limp and drained.

The sun sank into the calm turquoise waters in a spectacular display of gold and fuchsia, and at some point,

Cookie brought out sodas and sandwiches, then left them alone to talk.

"I wanted one of the Cutter boys for you," Sam told her quietly. "Logan at first—but he was much too serious for you. Nick's a good man. But too cold. He'd kill your spirit without meaning to. Zane—Zane balances the darkness in you with his light. And you'll stabilize his wild fancies with your levelheadedness."

Teal let the sound of the night fill her stunned silence better than she could. How could he know? "Your call to ask me to come here for you was a trick."

"Not that. I wanted you to have a chance at happiness."

At eleven that night, when Teal and her father sat in companionable silence, looking at the velvety night sky sprinkled with brilliant stars, there was a knock at the front door. A few minutes later, Zane emerged onto the patio. "Sam, how're you doing?"

"Best night of my life," her father told him. He'd looked ready for bed hours ago, but wouldn't hear of her leaving. She'd watched him doze for a couple of hours earlier. Teal had sat there in the companionable silence, wondering how different her life might have been if she'd had Sam as her custodial parent for all those years.

Zane smiled, his teeth white in the lights from inside the bungalow. "Somehow thought it would be." He turned to Teal and said gently, "Ready to go?"

No. But she couldn't sit here savoring her newfound closeness with her father all night. He was a sick man. He needed to go to bed. She nodded.

Zane held out his hand, and she took it so he could pull her to her feet. She leaned over to kiss her father's cheek, and then, because it felt so damn good, leaned down and kissed him again.

He brought his hand up and touched her face. "I love you, Teal. I don't want you to ever forget that."

"I love you, too." She'd never thought to hear those words from her father, and she'd never thought to be able to say them while he was alive and willing to hear her. Her heart brimmed to overflowing.

The fact that Zane had come to find her meant a lot, but she tried not to attach too much emotion to what was probably just a friendly gesture. He'd said things in the heat of the moment that she shouldn't take at face value. That's what guys said. Especially guys like Zane who had the world at their feet, and any woman they wanted in their arms. His magic cloak, she reminded herself firmly, was for *one*.

They strolled down toward the marina, the path lit by moonlight. "Where are we going?" Not that she cared. She was emotionally exhausted and exhilarated at the same time. They'd passed the bungalow she'd had temporary use of, and he didn't head toward his house up the hill, either.

He wrapped his arm around her shoulders, tucking her tightly against his side. His skin felt warm, and smelled of soap. "This is an official kidnapping."

Teal rested her head on his shoulder. "Again?"

"Don't you want to know where or why?" She heard the suppressed laughter in his voice.

"Nope. It worked out okay before." She'd go anywhere with him. Should she tell him? Confronting her father with her feelings had revealed a truth worth fighting for.

"Not even curious?"

She managed a small shake of her head. "Nope."

They arrived at the dock. *Decrepit* looked beautiful in the moonlight, but Zane led Teal past the boat and over to the Sea Ray cruiser.

Teal groaned, her hand over her belly, which didn't even rumble. "Out to sea?"

"Untie that line—yeah. You know three's a charm as far as kidnappings go." He handed her on board. "I brought you a change of clothes, and the water's hot for a shower."

"You have a very nice shower at your house," she suggested as he started the engine. The boat moved through the dark water, steered by a very sexy captain. "On land."

"Later."

"Are you going to join me?" she asked hopefully. Was he planning on saying good-bye when they were out in the middle of the ocean? Did he think she'd make a scene? Not likely, conceited oaf. She loved him so much her heart swelled and her body leaned toward him, filled with yearning.

"Sweetheart, I like nothing better than making love to you in the shower, but unfortunately, not one *this* size."

"There's actually a shower smaller than the ones we've been in?"

Caught by a moonbeam, his earring glinted. "Come up on deck when you're ready."

*   *   *

Zane was nervous as hell. He'd never done this before. And God help him, with Teal his plans could all be shot to hell in a heartbeat. He pushed the boat to its maximum speed.

He'd been working on this project all evening. He didn't want her anywhere where she could hide. Either physically or emotionally. The engine room was too damn small for even her to want to stay in for any length of time. Zane grinned. For a man who loved a challenge, he'd picked the perfect woman.

"Where are we?" Teal came onto the bridge wearing a towel and a scowl. His smile widened. "Perfect timing. And I must say, Williams, you chose my second favorite outfit to wear tonight."

"I live to serve," she said dryly, padding over to take

the glass of wine he handed her. "You aren't thinking of plying me with alcohol and tossing me overboard are you? Because, buddy, I've spent all day kicking bad guys' butts. I'm not afraid of y—"

Zane pulled her into his arms and crushed her sassy, scared mouth under his. She tasted of toothpaste, and her lips clung to his. It was a good thing he'd already dropped anchor.

He lifted his head, gratified to see that her big brown eyes were glazed with passion, and her mouth swollen. The damp towel was a puddle around her feet on the teak deck. Holy Mother of God. She did nothing in half measures. Changing his mind, his hand made a U-turn to return to the prize he'd just uncovered.

"Well, well," he managed to unglue his tongue from the roof of his mouth. "What do we have here? Did you forget to put on your underwear, Miss Williams?"

"I was too hot."

"A hazard in the tropics," he concurred soberly. "It's extremely unhealthy to get overheated. As an incentive, I'm going to give *you* your heart's desire, Williams."

"Hmm?" She tightened her arms around his neck to nibble at his earlobe.

"I brought the Caterpillar catalogue. You can have any damned engines you want."

She lifted her head, her eyes gleaming avariciously. "Even 3516s *and* the chrome package?"

Zane laughed as he stroked his hands down her tight, gorgeous ass. "You can chrome the *Decrepit* from prow to stern if you like."

"Now see? That's just plain extravagant. I'd be happy with a nice new paint job."

"Done."

"Are you going to get naked too?" she asked politely, rubbing her breasts across his chest. Her skin looked like pearl in the moonlight, making him dizzy with lust.

"I want to look at stars."

She gave him an incredulous look. "Did you hit your head sometime today?"

He wanted her to know, without a doubt, how he felt. And as much as he wanted to rush to get to the good part of the evening's program, this was all for her.

He pulled the long cushion off the bench seat onto the deck. The thick, canvas-covered cushion was soft, but too narrow. It was only wide enough for one of them to stretch out comfortably. Holding her hand, he sat down, then tugged her onto his lap. As soon as she snuggled close, he maneuvered her onto his prone body. Her back to his chest. Wrapping his arms around her waist, he nuzzled the side of her neck. She smelled intoxicatingly of coconut soap and warm woman. Zane wanted her more than his next breath.

"Very gallant." She wiggled to get comfortable, nestling her butt against his groin in a calculated move guaranteed to inflame him to madness.

Moving a strand of her dark hair out of his face, he nibbled her ear and whispered, "Isn't that better?"

She turned her head to whisper back, "You're not much softer than the deck. You don't make a very comfortable mattress. Why don't we go down to the cabin . . ."

"We're the only two people in the world. How cool is that?"

"Very," she murmured dryly, wiggling on top of him. "The last two people in the world have a lovely soft bed not ten feet away. And while this position is intriguing and I'm sure with a little ingenuity, *possible*, why don't we go for straight missionary and save ourselves from dislocating something important?"

"Cooperate, woman." The slap of the waves against the hull served much better than music. Zane slid his hand down her thigh. Her skin was silky smooth and warmed to his light touch. The moonlight leached the color from her skin, making her look ethereal and other-worldly. A mermaid risen from the sea. A fantasy come true. *His* fantasy come true.

He brushed his lips up the side of her throat, and she turned her head to give him better access. She started to roll over, but Zane clamped a hand on her bare hip, then lingered in the hollow his questing fingers discovered. "No. Stay."

"I want to touch you, too."

"You're touching me in every way that counts right now. Let me pleasure you." He cupped both breasts in his palms and stroked his thumb over the hard tips until she moaned low in her throat, her head shifting restively on his chest, her fragrant hair tickling beneath his chin. "I love you, Teal Williams." He said softly.

Both her hands came up to cover his, pressing his palms to her breasts. "You make me ache," she said brokenly, not acknowledging the words. Ah. So she didn't need to hide in an engine room to avoid the truth. Zane smiled. His prickly Teal.

Her skin was as smooth as warm satin and incredibly sensitive to his touch as her beaded nipples showed. "Here?"

"Hmmm . . ." Her hands pressed his palms more firmly where she wanted them. "Too light."

He opened his mouth on her bared shoulder and bit down lightly. Teal lifted her hips, then pressed them back into the unforgiving, rock-hard erection pressed urgently against her. "Zane, please . . ." Her voice rose pleadingly.

Sound carried and was amplified on the water, and she wasn't whispering. Zane nibbled her ear. He explored the shell of her ear with his tongue while rubbing the hard buds of her nipples in the center of his palms.

"You're torturing me!" Her breathing was ragged and goose bumps rose all over her skin. Her short nails dug into the backs of his hands, which moved slowly over her breasts in a caress intended to drive her mad.

He trailed one hand down the middle of her body, teased a circle around her navel, smoothed his hand down her belly, until he came to the downy triangle between her thighs. He felt her sigh travel through her body in a head-to-toe shudder.

He slowly slid his palm up her thigh as he inhaled the fragrance of her skin. Inexplicably, his throat closed. Everything about Teal turned him on.

"Zane—"

"Patience. Trust me. Look at the stars. Have you ever seen them so clear?" This was for her, but his own brain was fogged with lust as he strung out her impending climax. He knew her body. Knew what made her hot and how to cool her. He built each peak, let it simmer, turned up the heat, let her come to a rolling boil . . .

"Beautiful," Teal said breathlessly, trailing her fingers lazily down the back of his hand as he teased her. As eager as he was, every inch of bared skin distracted him, and he had to stroke and caress before going to the next favorite place.

"The poets are right," she whispered. "The stars do look like diamonds twinkling on black velvet."

Every atom of his body was suddenly filled with a powerful adrenaline rush, and the stars turned into a kaleidoscope above him.

She laughed softly. "That's just making me hotter."

"Look at the stars," Zane told her, his voice stern but softer than a whisper against her ear. "See Albireo over there?"

"Don't give a flying flip! Let's go to the cabin." Her voice was ragged.

"There's no one to see or hear us."

"And a bright, moonlit night," she whispered unevenly.

"It's hot, there might be boats out there somewhere with their windows open."

He brushed the soft cleft between her thighs, then slid a finger into her wet heat. "Then we need to be very, very, very quiet." Her hips lifted, but he used his palm to press her against his straining erection. This was all for Teal, but he tortured himself with the clenching of her butt cheeks against his dick.

She was so wet his fingers were saturated, and he could feel the small, internal convulsions, impossible to control.

Suddenly, she was fighting him. "Stop. Sto-p." It took a second, but he finally realized what she'd said. He immediately stopped, but God, it wasn't easy. "What's the matte . . ."

She rolled onto the deck on her hands and knees, head bowed, bare skin glistening with sweat. She was panting, gasping for air. "C-can't take any more." Before he could reach for her, Teal's mouth came down over his jutting penis. The shock of her warm mouth over his sensitized flesh rendered him deaf, dumb, and blind. While his life flashed before his eyes, Teal sat up, then slid one long leg across Zane's hips to straddle him.

Moonlight glinted in her eyes as she placed her hands on his chest to balance herself. Back arched, nails digging into his pecs, she sheathed him to the hilt.

She said his name on a taut, uneven breath as they climaxed together. Their bodies bucked and heaved, clenching as wave after wave of intense pleasure split their atoms apart, then reconfigured them to make a strong new whole.

After what felt like an eternity, or a nanosecond, Zane rolled over, onto the hard deck, taking her with him, their bodies still joined. He tightened his arms around her, nestling her head into the curve of his shoulder.

"Marry me, Teal. Marry me and drive me crazy every

day for the rest of our lives. I want to grow old with you. Even," he laughed unevenly as her internal muscles milked him. "Even if I age before my time. I love you more than I ever imagined loving a woman. You're funny, and infuriating, and the woman of my wildest dreams."

"You do realize we're right in the middle of having wild sex, right here in front of anyone looking, right?"

"I'd noticed. Just say yes so we can get back to where we were." The tendons in his neck were about to snap with the tension of holding off the powerful orgasm that was building to an agonizing peak. His hands, gripping her hips, shook with the anticipation of relief at any second.

He fumbled for his swim trunks somewhere beside him.

Teal groaned. "Can't we just complete one project at a time?"

"Hand!" Zane instructed.

She lifted her hand weakly from his chest. Zane grabbed it and slid on the emerald ring he'd salvaged what felt like a lifetime ago. It fit her perfectly. "Where did—" The orgasm hit them both at the same time, and Zane gritted his teeth as Teal pumped her body faster and faster to take him in.

When it was all over, except for their uneven breathing, he cradled her against his chest again. Their skin was slick with sweat, they were both out of breath, and he'd never been happier. "Don't you have anything to say to me?" he demanded, his voice uneven.

"Thanks for a pleasant evening?" Teal teased, laughter in her voice, she kissed his chest. "I love you, Zane," she said soberly, taking his face in her palm and looking deeply into his eyes. "I love you more than I ever thought possible to love another human being. I love that you wear your magic cloak and surround everyone you love in that magic. I love your boat—with the new engines—and I love your island. But most of all, I love your humor, and your passion for what you do. I've loved you since the first time I saw you, and even though that love has changed and grown over the last twenty something years, I've *always* loved you. And always will."

"Ah, woman. You're going to lead me a merry chase for the next eighty-eight years, aren't you?"

She kissed his jaw. "Even if I have to chase you in my walker."

"Good thing I won't be any more than an arm's length away from you, then." He kissed her tenderly, his entire body suffused with love. "You are, Teal Williams, absolutely perfect for me in every way."

She held out her hand and the ring shot off sparks of green and white fire in the moonlight. "I love my ring, thank you. It couldn't be more fitting."

Zane got to his feet, hauling her up with him. His knees were weak, his heart steady as he looked down at her kiss-swollen mouth, and her love-drenched big brown eyes. "Let's get some sleep. I want to dive tomorrow. See how the *Vrijheid* is doing first thing in the morning."

"Is that where we are?" Teal turned to stare out at the moonlit water. She leaned back against him, and Zane wrapped her in his arms, resting his chin on her silky hair.

"I got us close as I could in the dark."

"With your magic cloak, she's going to be right where we left her, just waiting for us. You'll see."

*　　*　　*

Teal and Zane dove at dawn. The sparkling colors of the fish rainbowed in the water as the morning sun's buttery rays filtered through the crystal clear, turquoise water.

They'd agreed not to be disappointed if they couldn't find the wreck. Between the storm, the explosion, and the debris field left by the *Slow Dance*, it might take years to recover her again.

Despite her pragmatism, Teal wasn't all that surprised, really, to see that Zane's coordinates had been right on. And that the *Vrijheid*, unsettled by the explosion, had spilled all her treasures in a flashy display, just waiting to be brought to the surface.

When they broke the surface, Zane kissed Teal until she had to break away to drag in a shaky breath. "What was that for?"

"All of this is great," Zane's Cutter-blue eyes were dark and filled with tender emotion as he cupped her face in both hands and held her gaze. "The *Vrijheid* and her smorgasbord of priceless treasures are the frosting on the cake. But you, Teal Williams, are better than gold bars or coin, better than any emerald. Hell, better than my magic cloak. I'll be grateful every day for the next eighty-eight years with you, my most priceless treasure of all."

Don't miss Nick Cutter's story!

More treasure, adventure,
and romance awaits...

RIPTIDE

ISBN: 978-0-312-37198-2

The next book in the Cutter Key series from
New York Times bestselling author

CHERRY ADAIR

Coming Summer 2011